William Black

Judith Shakespeare

Her Love Affairs and Other Adventures

William Black

Judith Shakespeare
Her Love Affairs and Other Adventures

ISBN/EAN: 9783337063382

Printed in Europe, USA, Canada, Australia, Japan

Cover: Foto ©Andreas Hilbeck / pixelio.de

More available books at **www.hansebooks.com**

JUDITH SHAKESPEARE

Her Love Affairs and Other Adventures

BY

WILLIAM BLACK

AUTHOR OF " A PRINCESS OF THULE " " STRANGE ADVENTURES OF A PHAETON "
" THAT BEAUTIFUL WRETCH " " SUNRISE " ETC., ETC.

.

ILLUSTRATED BY E. A. ABBEY

NEW YORK

HARPER & BROTHERS, FRANKLIN SQUARE

1884

CONTENTS.

ILLUSTRATIONS.

JUDITH SHAKESPEARE:

HER LOVE AFFAIRS AND OTHER ADVENTURES.

CHAPTER I.

AN ASSIGNATION.

It was a fair, clear, and shining morning, in the sweet May-time of the year, when a young English damsel went forth from the town of Stratford-upon-Avon to walk in the fields. As she passed along by the Guild Chapel and the Grammar School, this one and the other that met her gave her a kindly greeting; for nearly every one knew her, and she was a favorite; and she returned those salutations with a frankness which betokened rather the self-possession of a young woman than the timidity of a girl. Indeed, she was no longer in the first sensitive dawn of maidenhood—having, in fact, but recently passed her five-and-twentieth birthday—but nevertheless there was the radiance of youth in the rose-leaf tint of her cheeks, and in the bright cheerfulness of her eyes. Those eyes were large, clear, and gray, with dark pupils and dark lashes; and these are a dangerous kind; for they can look demure, and art-less, and innocent, when there is nothing in the mind of the owner of them but a secret mirth; and also—and alas!—they can effect another kind of concealment, and when the heart within is inclined to soft pity and yielding, they can refuse to confess to any such surrender, and can maintain, at the bid-ding of a willful coquetry, an outward and obstinate coldness and indifference. For the rest, her hair, which was somewhat short and curly, was of a light and glossy brown, with a touch of sunshine in it; she had a good figure, for she came of a

1

quite notedly handsome family; she walked with a light step and a gracious carriage; and there were certain touches of style and color about her costume which showed that she did not in the least undervalue her appearance. And so it was "Good-morrow to you, sweet Mistress Judith," from this one and the other; and "Good-morrow, friend So-and-so," she would answer; and always she had the brightest of smiles for them as they passed.

Well, she went along by the church, and over the footbridge spanning the Avon, and so into the meadows lying adjacent to the stream. To all appearance she was bent on nothing but deliberate idleness, for she strayed this way and that, stooping to pick up a few wild flowers, and humming to herself as she went. On this fresh and clear morning the air seemed to be filled with sweet perfumes after the close atmosphere of the town; and if it was merely to gather daisies, and cuckoo-flowers, and buttercups, that she had come, she was obviously in no hurry about it. The sun was warm on the rich green grass; the swallows were dipping and flashing over the river; great humble-bees went booming by; and far away somewhere in the silver-clear sky a lark was singing. And she also was singing, as she strayed along by the side of the stream, picking here and there a speedwell, and here and there a bit of self-heal or white dead-nettle; if, indeed, that could be termed singing that was but a careless and unconscious recalling of snatches of old songs and madrigals. At one moment it was:

> *Why, say you so? Oh no, no, no;*
> *Young maids must never a-wooing go.*

And again it was:

> *Come, blow thy horn, hunter!*
> *Come, blow thy horn, hunter!*
> *Come, blow thy horn, jolly hunter!*

And again it was:

> *For a morn in spring is the sweetest thing*
> *Cometh in all the year!*

And in truth she could not have lit upon a sweeter morning than this was; just as a chance passer-by might have said to himself that he had never seen a pleasanter sight than this

young English maiden presented as she went idly along the
river-side, gathering wild flowers the while.

But in course of time, when she came to a part of the Avon
from which the bank ascended sharp and steep, and when she
began to make her way along a narrow and winding foot-path
that ascended through the wilderness of trees and bushes hanging on this steep bank, she became more circumspect. There
was no more humming of songs; the gathering of flowers was
abandoned, though here she might have added a wild hyacinth
or two to her nosegay; she advanced cautiously, and yet with
an affectation of carelessness; and she was examining, while
pretending not to examine, the various avenues and open
spaces in the dense mass of foliage before her. Apparently,
however, this world of sunlight and green leaves and cool
shadow was quite untenanted; there was no sound but that
of the blackbird and the thrush; she wandered on without
meeting any one. And then, as she had now arrived at a little dell or chasm in the wood, she left the foot-path, climbed
up the bank, gained the summit, and finally, passing from
among the bushes, she found herself in the open, at the corner
of a field of young corn.

Now if any one had noticed the quick and searching look
that she flashed all around on the moment of her emerging
from the brush-wood—the swiftness of lightning was in that
rapid scrutiny—he might have had some suspicion as to the
errand that had brought her hither; but in an instant her eyes
had recovered their ordinary look of calm and indifferent observation. She turned to regard the wide landscape spread out
below her; and the stranger, if he had missed that quick and
eager glance, would have naturally supposed that she had
climbed up through the wood to this open space merely to
have a better view. And indeed this stretch of English-looking country was well worth the trouble, especially at this particular time of the year, when it was clothed in the fresh and
tender colors of the spring-time; and it was with much seeming content that this young English maiden stood there and
looked abroad over the prospect—at the placid river winding
through the lush meadows; at the wooden spire of the church
rising above the young foliage of the elms; at here and there
in the town a red-tiled house visible among the thatched roofs

and gray walls and orchards—these being all pale and ethereal
and dream-like in the still sunshine of this quiet morning. It
was a peaceful English-looking picture that ought to have interested her, however familiar it may have been; and perhaps
it was only to look at it once more that she had made her way
up hither; and also to breathe the cool sweet air of the open, and
to listen to the singing of the birds, that seemed to fill the
white wide spaces of the sky as far as ever she could hear.

Suddenly she became aware that some one was behind her
and near her, and instantly turning, she found before her an
elderly man with a voluminous gray beard, who appeared to
affect some kind of concealment by the way he wore his hat
and his long cloak.

"God save you, sweet lady!" he had said, almost before she
turned.

But if this stranger imagined that by his unlooked-for approach and sudden address he was likely to startle the young
damsel out of her self-possession, he knew very little with
whom he had to deal.

"Good-morrow to you, good Master Wizard," said she, with
perfect calmness, and she regarded him from head to foot with
nothing beyond a mild curiosity. Indeed, it was rather he
who was embarrassed. He looked at her with a kind of wonder—and admiration also; and if she had been sufficiently
heedful and watchful she might have observed that his eyes,
which were singularly dark, had a good deal of animation in
them for one of his years. It was only after a second or so
of this bewildered and admiring contemplation of her that he
managed to say, in a grave and formal voice, something in
praise of her courage in thus keeping the appointment he had
sought.

"Nay, good sir," said she, with much complacency, "trouble not yourself about me. There is no harm in going out to
gather a few flowers in the field, surely. If there be any danger, it is rather you that have to fear it, for there is the pil-
lory for them that go about the country divining for gold and
silver.",

"It is for no such vain and idle purposes that I use my
art," said he; and he regarded her with such an intensity of
interest that sometimes he stumbled forgetfully in his speech,

"GOD SAVE YOU, SWEET LADY!"

as if he were repeating a lesson but ill prepared. "It is for the revelation of the future to them that are born under fortunate planets. And you are one of these, sweet lady, or I would not have summoned you to a meeting that might have seemed perilous to one of less courage and good heart. If it please you to listen, I can forecast that that will befall you—"

"Nay, good sir," said she, with a smile, "I have heard it frequently, though perhaps never from one so skilled. 'Tis but a question between dark and fair, with plenty of money and lands thrown in. For that matter, I might set up in the trade myself. But if you could tell me, now—"

"If I were to tell you—if by my art I could show you," said he, with a solemnity that was at least meant to be impressive (though this young maid, with her lips inclining to a smile, and her inscrutable eyes, did not seem much awe-stricken)—"if I could convince you, sweet lady, that you shall marry neither dark nor fair among any of those that would now fain win you—and rumor says there be several of those—what then?"

"Rumor?" she repeated, with the color swiftly mantling in her face. But she was startled, and she said, quickly, "What do you say, good wizard? · Not any one that I know? What surety have you of that? Is it true? Can you show it to me? Can you assure me of it? Is your skill so great that you can prove to me that your prophecy is aught but idle guessing? No one that I have seen as yet, say you? Why," she added, half to herself, "but that were good news for my gossip Prue."

"My daughter," said this elderly person, in slow and measured tones, "it is not to all that the stars have been so propitious at their birth."

"Good sir," said she, with some eagerness, "I beseech you forgive me if I attend you not; but—but this is the truth, now, as to how I came in answer to your message to me. I will speak plain. Perchance rumor hath not quite belied herself. There may be one or two who think too well of me, and would have me choose him or him to be my lover; and—and—do you see now?—if there were one of those that I would fain have turn aside from idle thoughts of me and show more favor to my dear cousin and gossip Prudence Shawe—nay, but to tell the truth, good wizard, I came here to seek of your skill whether it could afford some charm and magic that would direct his heart to her. I have heard of such things—"

And here she stopped abruptly, in some confusion, for she had in her eagerness admitted a half-belief in the possible power of his witchcraft which she had been careful to conceal before. She had professed incredulity by her very manner; she had almost laughed at his pretensions; she had intimated that she had come only out of curiosity; but now she had blundered into the confession that she had cherished some vague hope of obtaining a love-philtre, or some such thing, to transfer away from herself to her friend the affections of one of those suitors whose existence seemed to be so well known to the wizard. However, he soon relieved her from her embarrassment by assuring her that this that she demanded was far away beyond the scope of his art, which was strictly limited to the discovery and revelation of such secrets as still lay within the future.

"And if so, good sir," said she, after a moment's reflection, "that were enough, or nearly enough, so that you can convince us of it."

"To you yourself alone, gracious lady," said he, "can I reveal that which will happen to you. Nay, more, so fortunate is the conjunction of the planets that reigned at your birth— the *ultimum supplicium auri* might almost have been declared to you—that I can summon from the ends of the earth, be he where he may, the man that you shall hereafter marry, or soon or late I know not: if you will, you can behold him at such and such a time, at such and such a place, as the stars shall appoint."

She looked puzzled, half-incredulous and perplexed, inclined to smile, blushing somewhat, and all uncertain.

"It is a temptation—I were no woman else," said she, with a laugh. "Nay, but if I can see him, why may not others? And if I can show them him who is to be my worshipful lord and master, why, then, my gossip Prue may have the better chance of reaching the goal where I doubt not her heart is fixed. Come, then, to prove your skill, good sir. Where shall I see him, and when? Must I use charms? Will he speak, think you, or pass as a ghost? But if he be not a proper man, good wizard, by my life I will have none of him, nor of your magic either."

She was laughing now, and rather counterfeiting a kind of scorn; but she was curious; and she watched him with a lively interest as he took forth from a small leather bag a little folded piece of paper, which he carefully opened.

"I can not answer all your questions, my daughter," said he; "I can but proceed according to my art. Whether the person you will see may be visible to others I know not, nor can I tell you aught of his name or condition. Pray Heaven he be worthy of such beauty and gentleness; for I had heard of you, gracious lady, but rumor had but poor words to describe such a rarity and a prize."

"Nay," said she, in tones of reproof (but the color had mounted to a face that certainly showed no sign of displeasure), "you speak like one of the courtiers now."

"This charm," said he, dropping his eyes, and returning to his grave and formal tones, "is worth naught without a sprig of rosemary; that must you get, and you must place it within the paper in a threefold manner—thus; and then, when Sol and Luna are both in the descendant— But I forget me, the terms of my art are unknown to you; I must speak in the vulgar tongue; and meanwhile you shall see the charm, that there is nothing wicked or dangerous in it, but only the wherewithal to bring about a true lovers' meeting."

He handed her the open piece of paper; but she, having glanced at the writing, gave it him back again.

"I pray you read it to me," she said.

He regarded her for a second with some slight surprise; but he took the paper, and read aloud, slowly, the lines written thereon:

"Dare you haunt our hallowed green?
None but fairies here are seen.
Down and sleep,
Wake and weep,
Pinch him black, and pinch him blue,
That seeks to steal a lover true.
When you come to hear us sing,
Or to tread our fairy ring,
Pinch him black, and pinch him blue—
Oh, thus our nails shall handle you!"

"Why, 'tis like what my father wrote about Herne the Hunter," said she, with a touch of indifference; perhaps she had expected to hear something more weird and unholy.

"Please you, forget not the rosemary; nothing will come of it else," he continued. "Then this you must take in your hand secretly, and when no one has knowledge of your outgoing; and when Luna—nay, but I mean when the moon has risen to-night so that, standing in the church-yard, you shall see it over the roof of the church, then must you go to the yew-tree that is in the middle of the church-yard, and there you shall scrape away a little of the earth from near the foot of the tree, and bury this paper, and put the earth firmly down on it again, saying thrice, *Hieronymo! Hieronymo! Hieronymo!* You follow me, sweet lady ?"

"'Tis simple enough," said she, "but that on these fine evenings the people are everywhere about; and if one were to be seen conjuring in the church-yard—"

"You must watch your opportunity, my daughter," said he, speaking with an increased assumption of authority. "One minute will serve you; and this is all that needs be done."

"Truly? Is this all?" said she, and she laughed lightly. "Then will my gallant, my pride o' the world, my lord and master, forthwith spring out of the solid ground? God mend me, but that were a fearful meeting—in a church-yard! Gentle wizard, I pray you—"

"Not so," he answered, interrupting her. "The charm will work there; you must let it rest; the night dews shall nourish it; the slow hours shall pass over it; and the spirits that haunt these precincts must know of it, that they may prepare the meeting. To-night, then, sweet lady, you shall place this charm in the church-yard at the foot of the yew-tree, and to-morrow at twelve of the clock—"

"By your leave, not to-morrow," said she, peremptorily. "Not to-morrow, good wizard; for my father comes home to-morrow; and, by my life, I would not miss the going forth to meet him for all the lovers between here and London town!"

"Your father comes home to-morrow, Mistress Judith ?" said he, in somewhat startled accents.

"In truth he does; and Master Tyler also, and Julius Shawe —there will be a goodly company, I warrant you, come riding to-morrow through Shipston and Tredington and Alderminster; and by your leave, reverend sir, the magic must wait."

"That were easily done," he answered, after a moment's

thought, "by the alteration of a sign, if the day following might find you at liberty. Will it so, gracious lady?"

"The day after? At what time of the day?" she asked.

"The alteration of the sign will make it but an hour earlier, if I mistake not; that is to say, at eleven of the forenoon you must be at the appointed place—"

"Where, good wizard?" said she—"where am I to see the wraith, the ghost, the phantom husband that is to own me?"

"That know I not myself as yet; but my aids and familiars will try to discover it for me," he answered, taking a small sun-dial out of his pocket and adjusting it as he spoke.

"And with haste, so please you, good sir," said she, "for I would not that any chance comer had a tale of this meeting to carry back to the gossips."

He stooped down and placed the sun-dial carefully on the ground, at a spot where the young corn was but scant enough on the dry red soil, and then with his forefinger he traced two or three lines and a semicircle on the crumbling earth.

"South by west," said he, and he muttered some words to himself. Then he looked up. "Know you the road to Bidford, sweet lady?"

"As well as I know my own ten fingers," she answered.

"For myself, I know it not, but if my art is not misleading, there should be about a mile or more along that road, another road at right angles with it, bearing to the right, and there at the junction should stand a cross of stone. Is it so?"

"'Tis the lane that leads to Shottery; well I know it," she said.

"So it has been appointed, then," said he, "if the stars continue their protection over you. The day after to-morrow, at eleven of the forenoon, if you be within stone's-throw of the cross at the junction of the roads, there shall you see, or my art is strangely mistaken, the man or gentleman—nay, I know not whether he be parson or layman, soldier or merchant, knight of the shire or plain goodman Dick—I say there shall you see him that is to win you and wear you; but at what time you shall become his wife, and where, and in what circumstances, I can not reveal to you. I have done my last endeavor."

"Nay, do not hold me ungrateful," she said, though there was a smile on her lips, "but surely, good sir, what your skill

1*

has done, that it can also undo. If it have power to raise a
ghost, surely it has power to lay him. And truly, if he be a
ghost, I will not have him. And if he be a man, and have a red
beard, I will not have him. And if he be a slape-face, I will
have none of him. And if he have thin legs, he may walk his
ways for me. Good wizard, if I like him not, you must undo
the charm."

"My daughter, you have a light heart," said he, gravely.
"May the favoring planets grant it lead you not into mischief; there be unseen powers that are revengeful. And now
I must take my leave, gracious lady. I have given you the
result of much study and labor, of much solitary communion
with the heavenly bodies; take it, and use it with heed, and so
fare you well."

He was going, but she detained him.

"Good sir, I am your debtor," said she, with the red blood
mantling in her forehead, for all through this interview she
had clearly recognized that she was not dealing with any ordinary mendicant fortune-teller. "So much labor and skill I
can not accept from you without becoming a beggar. I pray
you—"

He put up his hand.

"Not so," said he, with a certain grave dignity. "To have
set eyes on the fairest maid in Warwickshire—as I have heard
you named—were surely sufficient recompense for any trouble;
and to have had speech of you, sweet lady, is what many a
one would venture much for. But I would humbly kiss your
hand; and so again fare you well."

"God shield you, most courteous wizard, and good-day,"
said she, as he left; and for a second she stood looking after
him in a kind of wonder, for this extraordinary courtesy and
dignity of manner were certainly not what she had expected
to find in a vagabond purveyor of magic. But now he was
gone, and she held the charm in her hand, and so without further ado she set out for home again, getting down through
the brush-wood to the winding path.

She walked quickly, for she had heard that Master Bushell's
daughter, who was to be married that day, meant to beg a
general holiday for the school-boys; and she knew that if this
were granted these sharp-eyed young imps would soon be here,

"THERE, NOW, IS MY SWEETHEART OF SWEETHEARTS."

there, and everywhere, and certain to spy out the wizard if he were in the neighborhood. But when she had got clear of this hanging copse, that is known as the Wier Brake, and had reached the open meadows, so that from any part around she could be seen to be alone, she had nothing further to fear, and she returned to her leisurely straying in quest of flowers. The sun was hotter on the grass now; but the swallows were busy as ever over the stream; and the great bees hummed loud as they went past; and here and there a white butterfly fluttered from petal to petal; and, far away, she could hear the sound of children's voices in the stillness. She was in a gay mood. The interview she had just had with one in league with the occult powers of magic and witchery did not seem in the least to have overawed her. Perhaps, indeed, she had not yet made up her mind to try the potent charm that she had obtained; at all events the question did not weigh heavily on her. For now it was,

> *Oh, mistress mine, where are you roaming?*

and again it was,

> *For a morn in spring is the sweetest thing*
> *Cometh in all the year!*

and always another touch of color added to the daintily arranged bouquet in her hand. And then, of a sudden, as she chanced to look ahead, she observed a number of the school-boys come swarming down to the foot-bridge; and she knew right well that one of them—to wit, young Willie Hart—would think a holiday quite thrown away and wasted if he did not manage to seek out and secure the company of his pretty cousin Judith.

"Ah! there, now," she was saying to herself, as she watched the school-boys come over the bridge one by one and two by two, "there, now, is my sweetheart of sweethearts; there is my prince of lovers! If ever I have lover as faithful and kind as he, it will go well. 'Nay, Susan,' says he, 'I love you not; you kiss me hard, and speak to me as if I were a child; I still love Judith better.' And how cruel of my father to put him in the play, and to slay him so soon; but perchance he will call him to life again—nay, it is a favorite way with him to do that; and pray Heaven he brings home with him to-morrow the rest of the story, that Prue may read it to me. And so are you

there, among the unruly imps, you young Prince Mamillius?
Have you caught sight of me yet, sweetheart blue-eyes? Why,
come, then; you will outstrip them all, I know, when you get
sight of Cousin Judith, for as far off as you are, you will
reach me first, that I am sure of; and then, by my life, sweetheart Willie, you shall have a kiss as soft as a dove's breast!"

And so she went on to meet them, arranging the colors of
her straggling blossoms the while, with now and again a snatch
of careless song:

> *Come, blow thy horn, hunter!*
> *Come, blow thy horn, hunter!*
> *Come, blow thy horn—jolly hunter!*

CHAPTER II.

SIGNIOR CRAB-APPLE.

THERE was much ado in the house all that day, in view of
the home-coming on the morrow, and it was not till pretty late
in the evening that Judith was free to steal out for a gossip
with her friend and chief companion, Prudence Shawe. She
had not far to go—but a couple of doors off, in fact; and her
coming was observed by Prudence herself, who happened to be
sitting at the casemented window for the better prosecution of
her needle-work, there being still a clear glow of twilight in
the sky. A minute or so thereafter the two friends were in
Prudence's own chamber, which was on the first floor, and
looking out to the back over barns and orchards; and they
had gone to the window, to the bench there, to have their
secrets together. ~ This Prudence Shawe was some two years
Judith's junior—though she really played the part of elder sister to her; she was of a pale complexion, with light straw-col-
ored hair; not very pretty, perhaps, but she had a restful kind
of face that invited friendliness and sympathy, of which she
had a large abundance to give in return. Her costume was of
a Puritanical plainness and primness, both in the fashion of it
and in its severe avoidance of color; and that was not the only
point on which she formed a marked contrast to this dear cousin and willful gossip of hers, who had a way of pleasing herself
(more especially if she thought she might thereby catch her fa-

ther's eye) in apparel as in most other things. And on this occasion—at the outset at all events—Judith would not have a word said about the assignation of the morning. The wizard was dismissed from her mind altogether. It was about the home-coming of the next day that she was all eagerness and excitement; and her chief prayer and entreaty was that her friend Prudence should go with her to welcome the travellers home.

"Nay, but you must and shall, dear Prue; sweet mouse, I beg it of you!" she was urging. "Every one at New Place is so busy that they have fixed upon Signior Crab-apple to ride with me; and you know I can not suffer him; and I shall not have a word of my father all the way back, not a word; there will be nothing but a discourse about fools, and idle jests, and wiseman Matthew the hero of the day—"

"Dear Judith, I can not understand how you dislike the old man so," her companion said, in that smooth voice of hers. "I see no garden that is better tended than yours."

"I would I could let slip the mastiff at his unmannerly throat!" was the quick reply—and indeed for a second she looked as if she would fain have seen that wish fulfilled. "The vanity of him!—the puffed-up pride of him!—he thinks there be none in Warwickshire but himself wise enough to talk to my father; and the way he dogs his steps if he be walking in the garden—no one else may have a word with him!—sure my father is sufficiently driven forth by the preachers and the psalm-singing within-doors that out-of-doors, in his own garden, he might have some freedom of speech with his own daughter—"

"Judith, Judith," her friend said, and she put her hand on her arm, "you have such willful thoughts, and wild words too. I am sure your father is free of speech with every one—gentle and simple, old and young, it matters not who it is that approaches him."

"This Signior Crab-apple truly!" the other exclaimed, in the impetuosity of her scorn. "If his heart be as big as a crab-apple, I greatly doubt; but that it is of like quality I'll be sworn. And the bitterness of his railing tongue! All women are fools —vools he calls them, rather—first and foremost; and most men are fools; but of all fools there be none like the fools of Warwickshire—that is because my worshipful goodman gardener comes all the way from Bewdley. 'Tis meat and drink

to him, he says, to discover a fool, though how he should have
any difficulty in the discovering, seeing that we are all of us
fools, passes my understanding. Nay, but I know what set
him after that quarry; 'twas one day in the garden, and my
father was just come home from London, and he was talking
to my uncle Gilbert, and was laughing at what his friend Benjamin Jonson had said, or had written, I know not which.
'Of all beasts in the world,' says he, 'I love most the serious
ass.' Then up steps goodman Matthew. 'There be plenty of
'em about 'ere, zur,' says he, with a grin on his face like that
on a cat when a dog has her by the tail. And my father, who
will talk to any one, as you say truly, and about anything, and
always with the same attention, must needs begin to challenge
goodman Crab-apple to declare the greatest fools that ever he
had met with; and from that day to this the ancient sour-face
hath been on the watch—and it suits well with his opinion of
other people and his opinion of himself as the only wise man
in the world—I say ever since he hath been on the watch for
fools; and the greater the fool the greater his wisdom, I reckon,
that can find him out. A purveyor of fools!—a goodly trade!
I doubt not but that it likes him better than the tending of ap-
ricots when he has the free range of the ale-houses to work on.
He will bring a couple of them into the garden when my father
is in the summer-house. ''Ere, zur, please you come out and
look 'ere, zur; 'ere be a brace of rare vools.' And the poor
clowns are proud of it; they stand and look at each other and
laugh. 'We be, zur—we be.' And then my father will say
no, and will talk with them, and cheer them with assurance of
their wisdom; then must they have spiced bread and ale ere
they depart; and this is a triumph for Master Matthew—the
withered, shrivelled, dried-up, cankered nutshell that he is!"

"Dear Judith, pray have patience—indeed you are merely
jealous."

"Jealous!" she exclaimed, as if her scorn of this ill-con-
ditioned old man put that well out of the question.

"You think he has too much of your father's company, and
you like it not; but consider of it, Judith, he being in the garden, and your father in the summer-house, and when your father is tired for the moment of his occupation, whatever that
may be, then can he step out and speak to this goodman Mat-

thew, that amuses him with his biting tongue, and with the
self-sufficiency of his wisdom—nay, I suspect your father holds
him to be a greater fool than any that he makes sport of, and
that he loves to lead him on."

"And why should my father have to be in the summer-
house but that in-doors the wool-spinning is hardly more constant than the lecturing and the singing of psalms and hymns?"

"Judith! Judith!" said her gentle friend, with real trouble
on her face, "you grieve me when you talk like that—indeed
you do, sweetheart! There is not a morning nor a night
passes that I do not pray the Lord that your heart may be softened and led to our ways—nay, far from that, but to the Lord's
own ways—and the answer will come; I have faith; I know
it; and God send it speedily, for you are like an own sister to
me, and my heart yearns over you!"

The other sat silent for a second. She could not fail to be
touched by the obvious sincerity, the longing kindness of her
friend, but she would not confess as much in words.

"As yet, sweet Prue," said she, lightly, "I suppose I am of
the unregenerate, and if it is wicked to cherish evil thoughts
of your neighbor, then am I not of the elect, for I heartily wish
that Tom Quiney and some of the youths would give Matthew
gardener a sound ducking in a horse-pond, to tame his arro-
gance withal. But no matter. What say you, dear Prue?
Will you go with me to-morrow, so that we may have the lad
Tookey in charge of us, and Signior Crab-apple be left to his
weeding and graffing and railing at human kind? Do, sweet
mouse—"

"The maids are busy now, Judith," said she, doubtfully.

"But a single day, dear mouse!" she urged. "And if we
go early we may get as far as Shipston, and await them there.
Have you no desire to meet your brother, Prudence—to be the
first of all to welcome him home? Nay, that is because you can
have him in your company as often as you wish; there is no
goodman-wiseman-fool to come between you."

"Dear heart," said Prudence Shawe, with a smile, "I know
not what is the witchery of you, but there is none I wot of
that can say you nay."

"You will, then?" said the other, joyfully. "Ah, look,
now, the long ride home we shall have with my father, and

all the news I shall have to tell him! And all good news,
Prue; scarcely a whit or bit that is not good news: the roan
that he bought at Evesham is well of her lameness—good; and
the King's mulberry is thriving bravely (I wonder that wiseman Matthew has not done it a mischief in the night-time, for
the King, being above him in station, must needs have nothing
from him but sour and envious words); and then the twenty
acres that my father so set his heart upon he is to have—I hear
that the Combes have said as much—and my father will be
right well pleased; and the vicar is talking no longer of building the new piggery over against the garden—at least for the
present there is nothing to be done: all good news; but there is
better still, as you know; for what will he say when he discovers that I have taught Bess Hall to ride the mastiff?"

"Pray you have a care, dear Judith," said her friend, with
some apprehension on her face. "'Tis a dangerous-looking
beast."

"A lamb, a very lamb!" was the confident answer. "Well,
now, and as we are riding home he will tell me of all the
things he has brought from London; and you know he has always something pretty for you, sweet Puritan, though you regard such adornments as snares and pitfalls. And this time
I hope it will be a silver brooch for you, dear mouse, that so
you must needs wear it and show it, or he will mark its absence; and for the others let us guess; let us see. There may
be some more of that strange-fashioned Murano glass for Susan,
for as difficult as it is to carry; and some silk hangings or the
like for my mother, or store of napery, perchance, which she
prizeth more; and be sure there is the newest book of sermons
from Paul's Church-yard for the Doctor; a greyhound, should
he hear of a famous one on the way, for Thomas Combe; toys
for the little Harts, that is certain; for my aunt Joan—what?—
a silver-topped jug, or some perfumes of musk and civet?—
and what else—and for whom else—well—"

"But what for yourself, dear Judith?" her friend said, with
a smile. "Will he forget you? Has Matthew gardener driv-
en you out even from his recollection? Will he not have for
you a pretty pair of rose shoe-strings, or one of the new tas-
selled French hoods they are speaking of, or something of the
kind, that will turn the heads of all the lads in Stratford twice

further round? You are a temptress surely, sweetheart; I half forget that such vanities should displease me when I see the way you wear them; and that I think you must take from your father, Judith; for no matter how plain his apparel is—and it is plain indeed for one that owns the New Place—he wears it with such an ease, and with such a grace and simplicity, that you would say a prince should wear it even so."

"You put me off, Prue," her friend said, with a sort of good-natured impatience. "Why, I was showing you what nice-lings and delicates my father was bringing, and what I had thought to say was this: that he may have this for one, and that for the other, and many a one proud to be remembered (as I shall be if he thinks of me), but this that I know he is bringing for little Bess Hall is something worth all of these, for it is nothing less than the whole love of his heart. Nay, but I swear it; there is not a human creature in the world to compare with her in his eyes; she is the pearl that he wears in his heart of hearts. If it were London town she wanted, and he could give it to her, that is what he would bring for her."

"What! are you jealous of her too?" said Prudence, with her placid smile.

"By yea and nay, sweet Puritan, if that will content you, I declare it is not so," was the quick answer. "Why, Bess is my ally! We are in league, I tell you; we will have a tussle with the enemy ere long; and, by my life, I think I know that that will put goodman-wiseman's nose awry!"

At this moment the secret confabulation of these two friends was suddenly and unexpectedly broken in upon by a message from without. Something white came fluttering through the open casement, and fell, not quite into Judith's lap, which was probably its intended destination, but down toward her feet. She stooped and picked it up; it was a letter, addressed to her, and tied round with a bit of rose-red silk ribbon that was neat-ly formed into a true-lover's knot.

CHAPTER III.

THE PLANTING OF THE CHARM.

THE embarrassment that ensued—on her part only, for the pale and gentle face of her friend betrayed not even so much as surprise—was due to several causes. Judith could neither read nor write. In her earlier years she had been a somewhat delicate child, and had consequently been excused from the ordinary tuition, slight as that usually was in the case of girls; but when, later on, she grew into quite firm and robust health, in her willfulness and pride and petulance she refused to retransform herself into a child and submit to be taught children's lessons. Moreover, she had an acute and alert brain; and she had a hundred reasons ready to show that what was in reality a mere waywardness on her part was the most wise and natural thing in the world; while her father, who had a habitual and great tolerance for everything and everybody that came within his reach, laughed with her rather than at her, and said she should do very well without book-learning so long as those pink roses shone in her cheeks. But she had one reason that was not merely an excuse. Most of the printed matter that reached the house was brought thither by this or that curate, or by this or that famous preacher, who, in going through the country, was sure of an eager and respectful welcome at New Place; and perhaps it was not kindly nor civilly done of them —though it may have been regarded as a matter of conscience —that they should carry thither and read aloud, amongst other things, the fierce denunciations of stage-plays and stage-players which were common in the polemical and puritanical literature of the day. Right or wrong, Judith resented this with a vehement indignation; and she put a ban upon all books, judging by what she had heard read out of some; nay, one day she had come into the house and found her elder sister, who was not then married, greatly distressed, and even in the bitterness of tears; and when she discovered that the cause of this was a pamphlet that had been given to Susanna, in which not only were the heinous wickednesses of plays and players denounced, but also her own father named by his proper name, Judith, with hot cheeks and flashing eyes, snatched the pamphlet from her sister's hand and forthwith sent it flying through the open window into the mud without, notwithstanding that books and pamphlets were scarce and valuable things, and that this one had been lent. And when she discovered that this piece of writing had been brought to the house by the pious and learned Walter Blaise—a youthful divine he was who had a small living some few miles from Stratford, but who lived in the town, and was one of the most eager and disputatious of the Puritanical preachers there—it in no way mitigated her wrath that this worthy Master Blaise was regarded by many, and even openly spoken of, as a suitor for her own hand.

"God mend me," said she, in her anger (and greatly to the distress of the mild-spoken Prudence), "but 'tis a strange way of paying court to a young woman to bring into the house abuse of her own father! Sir Parson may go hang, for me!" And for many a day she would have nothing to say to him; and steeled and hardened her heart not only against him, but against the doctrines and ways of conduct that he so zealously advocated; and she would not come in to evening prayers when he happened to be present; and wild horses would not have dragged her to the parish church on the Sunday afternoon that it was his turn to deliver the fortnightly lecture there. However, these things abated in time. Master Walter Blaise was a civil-spoken and an earnest and sincere young man, and Prudence Shawe was the gentle intermediary. Judith suffered his presence, and that was about all as yet; but she would not look the way of printed books. And when Prudence tried to entice her into a study of the mere rudiments of reading and writing, she would refuse peremptorily, and say, with a laugh, that, could she read, the first thing she should read would be plays, which, as sweet cousin Prue was aware, were full of tribulation and anguish, and fit only for the foolish Galatians of the world, the children of darkness and the devil. But this obstinacy did not prevent her overcoming her dear cousin Prue's scruples, and getting her to read aloud to her in the privacy of their secret haunts this or the other fragment of a play, when that she had adroitly purloined a manuscript from the summer-house in New Place; and in this surreptitious manner she had acquired a knowledge of what was going on at the Globe and the Blackfriars theatres in London, which, had they but guessed of it, would have considerably astounded her mother, her sister, and good Parson Blaise as well.

In more delicate matters still, Prudence was her confidante, her intermediary, and amanuensis; and ordinarily this caused her no embarrassment, for she wished for no secrets with any of human kind. But in one direction she had formed certain suspicions; and so it was that on this occasion, when she stooped down and picked up the letter that had been so deftly thrown in at the casement, her face flushed somewhat.

"I know from whom it comes," said she, and she seemed inclined to put it into the little wallet of blue satin that hung at her side.

Then she glanced at Prudence's eyes. There was nothing there in the least approaching displeasure or pique, only a quiet amusement.

"It was cleverly done," said Prudence, and she raised her head cautiously and peeped through one of the small panes of pale green glass. But the twilight had sunk into dusk, and any one outside could easily have made his escape unperceived through the labyrinth of barns and out-houses.

Judith glanced at the handwriting again, and said, with an affectation of carelessness:

"There be those who have plenty of time, surely, for showing the wonders of their skill. Look at the twisting and turning and lattice-work of it—truly he is a most notable clerk; I would he spent the daylight to better purpose. Read it for me, sweet Prue."

She would have handed the letter—with much studied indifference of look and manner—to her friend, but that Prudence gently refused it.

"'Tis you must undo the string; you know not what may be inside."

So Judith herself opened the letter, which contained merely a sprig of rosemary, along with some lines written in a most ornate caligraphy.

"What does he say?" she asked, but without any apparent interest, as she gave the open letter to her companion.

Prudence took the letter and read aloud:

> *Rosemary is for remembrance*
> *Between us day and night ;*
> *Wishing that I might always have*
> *You present in my sight.*

This from your true well-wisher, and one that would be your loving servant unto death. T. Q."

"The idle boy!" she said, and again she directed a quick and penetrating look of inquiry to her friend's face. But Prudence was merely regarding the elaborate handwriting. There was no trace of wounded pride or anything of the kind in her eyes. Nay, she looked up and said, with a smile,

"For one that can wrestle so well, and play at foot-ball, and throw the sledge as they say he can, he is master of a most delicate handwriting."

"But the rosemary, Prue!" Judith exclaimed, suddenly, and she groped about at her feet until she had found it. "Why, now, look there, was ever anything so fortunate? Truly I had forgotten all about rosemary, and my reverend wizard, and the charm that is to be buried to-night; and you know not a word of the story. Shall I tell you, sweet mouse? Is there time before the moon appears over the roof of the church ?—for there I am summoned to fearful deeds. Why, Prue, you look as frightened as if a ghost had come into the room—you yourself are like a ghost now in the dusk—or is it the coming moonlight that is making you so pale ?"

"I had thought that better counsels would have prevailed with you, Judith," she said, anxiously. "I knew not you had gone to see the man, and I reproach myself that I have been an agent in the matter."

"A mouth-piece only, sweet Prue!—a mere harmless, innocent whistle that had nothing to do with the tune. And the business was not so dreadful either; there was no caldron, nor playing with snakes and newts, no, nor whining for money, which I expected most; but a most civil and courteous wizard, a most town-bred wizard as ever the sun set eye on, that called me 'gracious lady' every other moment, and would not take a penny for his pains. Marry, if all the powers of evil be as well-behaved, I shall have less fear of them; for a more civil-spoken gentleman I have never encountered; and 'sweet lady' it was, and 'gracious lady,' and a voice like the voice of my lord bishop; and the assurance that the planets and the stars were holding me in their kindest protection; and a promise of a ghost husband that is to appear that I may judge whether I like him or like him not; and all this and more—and he would kiss my hand, and so farewell, and the reverend magician makes his obeisance and vanishes, and I am not a penny the poorer, but only the richer because of my charm! There, I will show it to you, dear mouse."

After a little search she found the tiny document; and Prudence Shawe glanced over it.

"Judith! Judith!" said she, almost in despair, "I know not whither your willfulness will carry you. But tell me what happened. How came you by this paper? And what ghost husband do you speak of?"

Then Judith related, with much circumstantiality, what had occurred that morning; not toning it down in the least, but rather exaggerating here and there; for she was merry-hearted, and she liked to see the sweet Puritan face grow more and more concerned. Moreover, the dull gray light outside, instead of deepening into dark, appeared to be becoming a trifle clearer, so that doubtless the moon was declaring itself somewhere; and she was looking forward, when the time came, to securing Prudence's company as far as the church-yard, if her powers of persuasion were equal to that.

"But you will not go, darling Judith," said Prudence, in accents of pathetic entreaty. "You know the sin of dealing with such ungodly practices—nay, and the danger too, for you would of your own free-will seek a meeting with unholy things, whereas I have been told that not so long ago they used in places to carry a pan of frankincense round the house each night to keep away witchcraft from them as they slept. I beseech you, dearest Judith, give me the paper, and I will burn it!"

"Nay, nay, it is but an idle tale, a jest; I trust it not," said her friend to re-assure her. "Be not afraid, sweet Prue. Those people who go about compelling the planets and summoning spirits and the like have lesser power than the village folk imagine, else would their own affairs thrive better than they seem to do."

"Then give me the paper; let me burn it, Judith!"

"Nay, nay, mouse," said she, withholding it; and then she added, with a sort of grave merriment or mischief in her face: "Whether the thing be aught or naught, sure I can not treat so ill my courteous wizard. He was no goose-herd, I tell you, but a most proper and learned man; and he must have the chance of working the wonders he foretold. Come, now, think of it with reason, dear Prue. If there be no power in the charm, if I go to Shottery for my morning walk and find no one in the lane, who is harmed? Why, no one; and Grandmother Hathaway is pleased, and will show me how her garden is growing. Then, on the other hand, should the charm work, should there be some one there, what evil if I regard him as I pass from the other side of the way? Is it such a wonder that one should meet a stranger on the Bidford road? And what more? Man or ghost, he can not make me marry him if I will not. He can not make me speak to him if I will not. And if he would put a hand on me, I reckon Roderigo would speedily have him by the throat, as I hope he may some day have goodman Matthew."

"But, Judith, such things are unlawful and forbidden—"

"To you, sweet saint—to you," said the other, with much good-humor. "But I have not learned to put aside childish things as yet; and this is only a jest, good Prue; and you, that are so faithful to your word, even in the smallest trifle, would not have me break my promise to my gentle wizard? 'Gracious lady,' he says, and 'sweet lady,' as if I were a dame of the court; it were unmannerly of me not to grant him this small demand—"

"I wish I had misread the letter," said Prudence, so occupied with her own fears that she scarcely knew what to do.

"What!" exclaimed her friend, in tones of raillery; "you would have deceived me? Is this your honesty, your singleness of heart, sweet Puritan? You would have sent me on some fool's errand, would you?"

"And if it were to be known you had gone out to meet this conjurer, Judith, what would your mother and sister say?— and your father?"

"My mother and sister—hum!" was the demure reply. "If he had but come in the garb of a preacher, with a Bible under one arm and a prayer-book under the other, I doubt not that he would have been welcome enough at New Place—ay, and everything in the house set before him, and a Flanders jug full of Quiney's best claret withal to cheer the good man. But when you speak of my father, dear Prue, there you are wide of the mark—wide, wide of the mark; for the wizard is just such an one as he would be anxious to know and see for himself. Indeed, if my mother and Susan would have the house filled with preachers, my father would rather seek his company from any strange kind of vagrant cattle you could find on the road—ballad-singers, strolling players, peddlers, and the like; and you should see him when some ancient harper in his coat of green comes near the town—nay, the constable shall not interfere with him, license or no license—my father must needs entertain him in the garden; and he will sit and talk to the old man; and the best in the house must be brought out for him; and whether he try his palsied fingers on the strings, or perchance attempt a verse of 'Pastime with good company' with his quavering old voice, that is according to his own good will and pleasure; nothing is demanded of him but that he have good cheer, and plenty of it, and go on his way the merrier, with a groat or two in his pouch. Nay, I mind me, when Susan was remonstrating with my father about such things, and bidding him have some regard for the family name— 'What?' says he, laughing; 'set you up, Madam Pride! Know you not, then, whence comes our name? And yet 'tis plain enough. *Shacks*, these are but vagrant, idle, useless fellows; and then we come to *pere*, that is, an equal and companion. There you have it complete—*Shackspere*, the companion of strollers and vagabonds, of worthless and idle fellows. What say you, Madam Pride?' And, indeed, poor Susan was sorely displeased, insomuch that I said, 'But the spear in the coat of arms, father—how came we by that?' 'Why, there, now,' says he, 'you see how regardless the heralds are of the King's English. I warrant me they would give a ship to Shipston and a hen to Enstone.' Indeed, he will jest you out of anything. When your brother would have left the Town Council, Prue—"

But here she seemed suddenly to recollect herself. She rose quickly, thrust open the casement still wider, and put out her head to discover whereabouts the moon was; and when she

withdrew her head again there was mischief and a spice of excitement in her face.

"No more talking and gossip now, Prue; the time has
arrived for fearful deeds."

Prudence put her small white hand on her friend's arm.

"Stay, Judith. Be guided—for the love of me be guided,
sweetheart! You know not what you do. The profaning of
sacred places will bring a punishment."

"Profaning, say you, sweet mouse? Is it anything worse
than the children playing tick round the grave-stones; or even,
when no one is looking, having a game of King-by-your-leave?"

"It is late, Judith. It must be nine o'clock. It is not
seemly that a young maiden should be out-of-doors alone at
such an hour of the night."

"Marry, that say I," was the light answer. "And the better reason that you should come with me, Prue."

"I?" said Prudence, in affright.

"Wherefore not, then? Nay, but you shall suffer no harm
through the witchery, sweet mouse; I ask your company no
further than the little swing-gate. One minute there, and I
shall be back with you. Come, now, for your friend's sake;
get your hood and your muffler, dear Prue, and no one shall
know either of us from the witch of Endor, so quickly shall
we be there and back."

Still she hesitated.

"If your mother were to know, Judith—"

"To know what, sweetheart? That you walked with me as
far as the church and back again? Why, on such a fine and
summer-like night I dare be sworn, now, that half the good
folk of Stratford are abroad; and it is no such journey into
a far country that we should take one of the maids with us.
Nay, come, sweet Prue! We shall have a merry ride to-morrow; to-night for your friendship's sake you must do me this
small service."

Prudence did not answer, but somewhat thoughtfully, and
even reluctantly, she went to a small cupboard of boxes that
stood in the corner of the apartment, and brought forth some
articles of attire which (although she might not have confessed
it) were for the better disguising of herself, seeing that the night
was fine and warm. And then Judith, having also drawn a

2

muffler loosely round her neck and the lower half of her face,
was ready to go, and was gone, in fact, as far as the door,
when she suddenly said:

"Why, now, I had nearly forgot the rosemary, and without
that the charm is naught.   Did I leave it on the window-shelf ?"

She went back and found it, and this time she took the pre-
caution of folding it within the piece of paper that she was to
bury in the church-yard.

"Is it fair, dear Judith ?" Prudence said, reproachfully, before she opened the door.   "Is it right that you should take
the bit of rosemary sent you by one lover, and use it as a charm
to bring another ?"

"Nay, why should you concern yourself, sweet mouse ?"
said Judith, with a quick glance, but indeed at this end of the
room it was too dark for her to see anything.   "My lover,
say you ?   Let that be as the future may show.   In the mean
time I am pledged to no one, nor anxious that I should be so.
And a scrap of rosemary, now, what is it ?   But listen to this,
dear Prue: if it help to show me the man I shall marry—if
there be aught in this magic—will it not be better for him that
sent the rosemary that we should be aware of what is in store
for us ?"

"I know not—I scarcely ever know—whether you are in
jest or in earnest, Judith," her friend said.

"Why, then, I am partly in starched cambric, good mouse,
if you must know, and partly in damask, and partly in taffeta
of popinjay blue.   But come, now, let us be going.   The awful hour approaches, Prue.   Do you not tremble, like Faustus
in the cell ?   What was't he said ?

It strikes ; it strikes.   Now, body, turn to air !

Come along, sweet Prue."

But she was silent as they left.   Indeed, they went down the
dark little staircase and out at the front door with as little
noise as might be.   Judith had not been mistaken: the fine,
clear, warm evening had brought out many people; and they
were either quietly walking home or standing in dusky little
groups at the street corners talking to each other; whilst here
and there came a laugh from a ruddy-windowed ale-house; and
here and there a hushed sound of singing, where a casement

had been left a bit open, told that the family within were at
their devotional exercises for the night. The half-moon was
now clear and silvery in the heavens. As they passed under
the massive structure of the Guild Chapel the upper portions of
the tall windows had a pale greenish glow shining through
them that made the surrounding shadows look all the more
solemn. Whether it was that their mufflers effectually prevented their being recognized, or whether it was that none of
their friends happened to be abroad, they passed along without
attracting notice from any one, nor was a word spoken between
themselves for some time.

But when they drew near to the church, the vast bulk of
which, towering above the trees around, seemed almost black
against the palely clear sky, the faithful Prudence made bold
to put in a final word of remonstrance and dissuasion.

"It is wickedness and folly, Judith. Naught can come of
such work," she said.

"Then let naught come of it, and what harm is done?" her
companion said, gayly. "Dear mouse, are you so timorous?
Nay, but you shall not come within the little gate; you shall
remain without. And if the spirits come and snatch me, as
they snatched off Doctor Faustus, you shall see all the pageant,
and not a penny to pay. What was it in the paper?

'*Pinch him black, and pinch him blue,
That seeks to steal a lover true.*'

Did it not run so? But they can not pinch you, dear heart; so
stand here now, and hush!—pray you do not scream if you see
them whip me off in a cloud of fire—and I shall be with you
again in a minute."

She passed through the little swinging gate and entered the
church-yard, casting therewith a quick glance around. Apparently no one was within sight of her, either among the gray
stones or under the black-stemmed elms by the river; but there
were people not far off, for she could hear their voices—doubtless they were going home through the meadows on the other
side of the stream. She looked but once in that direction. The
open country was lying pale and clear in the white light; and
under the wide branches of the elms one or two bats were silently darting to and fro; but she could not see the people, and
she took it for granted that no one could now observe what

she was about.   So she left the path, made her way through the
noiseless grass, and reached the small yew-tree standing there
among the grave-stones.   The light was clear enough to allow
her to open the package and make sure that the sprig of rosemary was within; then she rapidly, with her bare hand, stooped down and scooped a little of the earth away; she imbedded
the packet there, repeating meanwhile the magic words; she replaced the earth, and brushed the long grass over it, so that,
indeed, as well as she could make out, the spot looked as if it
had not been disturbed in any manner.   And then, with a
quick look toward the roof of the church to satisfy herself that
all the conditions had been fulfilled, she got swiftly back to
the path again, and so to the little gate, passing through the
church-yard like a ghost.

"The deed is done, good Prue," said she, gayly, but in a
tragic whisper, as she linked her arm within the arm of her
friend and set out homeward.   "Now are the dark powers of
the earth at league to raise me up—what think you, sweetheart?—such a gallant as the world ne'er saw!   Ah! now
when you see him come riding in from Shottery, will not the
town stare?   None of your logget-playing, tavern-jesting,
come-kiss-me-Moll lovers, but a true-sworn knight on his white
war steed, in shining mail, with a golden casque on his head
and ostrich feathers, and on his silver shield 'St. George and
England!'"

"You are light-hearted, Judith," said the timid and gentle-
voiced Puritan by her side; "and in truth there is nothing
that you fear.   Well, I know not, but it will be in my prayers
that no harm come of this night."

CHAPTER IV.

A PAGEANT.

ON the morning after the arrival of Judith's father he was out and abroad with his bailiff at an early hour, so that she had no chance of speaking to him; and when he returned to New Place he went into the summer-house in the orchard, where it was the general habit and custom to leave him undisturbed. And yet she only wished to ask permission to take the mastiff with her as far as Shottery; and so, when she had performed her share of the domestic duties, and got herself ready, she went out and through the back court and into the garden, thinking that he would not mind so brief an interruption.

It was a fresh and pleasant morning, for there had been some rain in the night, and now there was a slight breeze blowing from the south, and the air was sweet with the scent of the lilac bushes. The sun lay warm on the pink and white blossoms of the apple-trees and on the creamy masses of the cherry; martins were skimming and shooting this way and that, with now and again a rapid flight to the eaves of the barn; the bees hummed from flower to flower, and everywhere there was a chirping, and twittering, and clear singing of birds. The world seemed full of light and color, of youth, and sweet things, and gladness: on such a morning she had no fear of a refusal, nor was she much afraid to go near the summer-house that the family were accustomed to hold sacred from intrusion.

But when she passed into the orchard, and came in sight of it, there was a sudden flash of anger in her eyes. She might have guessed—she might have known. There, blocking up the doorway of the latticed and green-painted tenement, was the figure of goodman Matthew; and the little bandy-legged pippin-faced gardener was coolly resting on his spade while he addressed his master within. Was there ever (she asked herself) such hardihood, such audacity and impertinence? And then she rapidly bethought her that now was a rare opportunity for, putting in practice a scheme of revenge that she had

carefully planned. It is true that she might have gone forward
and laid her finger on Matthew's arm (he was rather deaf),
and so have motioned him away. But she was too proud to
do that. She would dispossess and rout him in another fashion. So she turned and went quickly again into the house.

Now at this time Dr. Hall was making a round of professional visits at some distance away in the country; and on such
occasions Susanna Hall and her little daughter generally came
to lodge at New Place, where Judith was found to be an eager
and assiduous, if somewhat impatient and unreasoning, nurse,
playmate, and music-mistress. In fact, the young mother had
to remonstrate with her sister, and to point out that, although
baby Elizabeth was a wonder of intelligence and cleverness—
indeed, such a wonder as had never hitherto been beheld in the
world—still, a child of two years and three months or so could
not be expected to learn everything all at once; and that it was
just as reasonable to ask her to play on the lute as to imagine
that she could sit on the back of Don the mastiff without being
held. However, Judith was fond of the child, and that in-
comparable and astute small person had a great liking for her
aunt (in consequence of benefits received), and a trust in her
which the wisdom of maturer years might have modified; and
so, whenever she chose, Judith found no difficulty in obtaining
possession of this precious charge, even the young mother
showing no anxiety when she saw the two go away together.

So it was on this particular morning that Judith went and
got hold of little Bess Hall, and quickly smartened up her
costume, and carried her out into the garden. Then she went
to the barn, outside of which was the dog's kennel; she un-
clasped the chain and set free the huge, slow-stepping, dun-colored beast, that seemed to know as well as any one what was
going forward; she affixed to his collar two pieces of silk ribbon that did very well for reins; and then she sat little Bess
Hall on Don Roderigo's back, and gave her the reins to hold,
and so they set out for the summer-house.

On that May morning the wide and gracious realm of England—which to some minds, and especially at that particular
season of the year, seems the most beautiful country of any in
the world—this rich and variegated England lay basking in the
sunlight, with all its lush meadows and woods and hedges in

the full and fresh luxuriance of the spring; and the small
quiet hamlets were busy in a drowsy and easy-going kind of
fashion; and far away around the white coasts the blue sea
was idly murmuring in; but it may be doubted whether in all
the length and breadth of that fair land there was any fairer
sight than this that the wit of a young woman had devised.
She herself was pleasant enough to look on (and she was always
particularly attentive about her attire when her father was at
home), and now she was half laughing as she thought of her
forthcoming revenge; she had dressed her little niece in her
prettiest costume of pink and white, and pink was the color of
the silken reins; while the great slow-footed Don bore his part in
the pageant with a noble majesty, sometimes looking up at
Judith as if to ask whether he were going in the right direction.
And so the procession passed on between the white-laden cherry-
trees and the redder masses of the apple-blossom; and the
miniature Ariadne, sitting sideways on the back of the great
beast, betrayed no fear whatsoever; while her aunt Judith held
her, walking by her, and scolding her for that she would not
sing.

"Tant sing, Aunt Judith," said she.

"You can sing well enough, you little goose, if you try,"
said her aunt, with the unreasoning impatience of an unmarried young woman. "What is the use of your going hunting
without a hunting song? Come along, now:

> ' The hunt is up, the hunt is up,
> And it is well-nigh day ;'—

try it, Bess!"

"Hunt is up, hunt is up," said the small rider; but she
was occupied with the reins, and clearly did not want to be
bothered.

"No, no, that is not singing, little goose. Why, sing it like
this, now:

> ' The hunt is up, the hunt is up,
> And it is well-nigh day ;
> And Harry our king is gone hunting
> To bring his deer to bay !' "

However, the music lesson came to an abrupt end. They had
by this time almost reached the summer-house. Saturnine
Matthew gardener, who still stood there, blocking up the door-

way, had not heard them approach, but his master within had.
The next instant goodman Matthew suddenly found himself
discarded, dismissed, and treated, indeed, as if he were simply
non-existent in the world; for Judith's father, having paused
for a moment to regard from the doorway the pretty pageant
that had been arranged for him (and his face lit up, as it were,
with pleasure at the sight), was the next minute down beside
his little granddaughter, with one knee on the ground, so that
he was just on a level with her outstretched hands.

"What, Bess?" he said, as he caught her by both hands and
feet. "You imp, you inch, you elfin queen, you!—would you
go a-hunting, then?"

"Send away Don—me want to ride the high horse," said the
small Bess, who had her own ideas as to what was most comfortable, and also secure.

"And so you shall, you sprite, you Ariel, you moonlight
wonder!" he exclaimed, as he perched her on his shoulder
and rose to his feet again. "The high horse, truly; indeed,
you shall ride the high horse! Come, now, we will go see
how the King's mulberry thrives; that is the only tree we have
that is younger than yourself, you ancient, you beldame, you
witch of Endor, you!"

"Father," said Judith, seeing that he was going away perfectly regardless of anybody or anything except his granddaughter, "may I take the Don with me for an hour or so?"

"Whither away, wench—whither?" he asked, turning for a
moment.

"To Shottery, father."

"Well, well," said he, and he turned again and went off.

"Come, Bess, you world's jewel, you, you shall ride with
me to London some day, and tell the King how his mulberry
thrives; that shall you, you fairy, you princess, you velvet-
footed maidiekin! To London, Bess—to London!"

Judith did not stay to regard them further; but she could
not help casting a look before she left at goodman Matthew,
who stood there discomfited, dispossessed, unheeded, annihila-
ted, as it were. And then, calling the dog after her, she went
in by the back court and through the house again (for Chapel
Lane was in a sad condition after the rain of the night, and was
not a pleasant pathway even in the best of times). And she

was laughing to herself at Matthew's discomfiture, and she was singing to herself as she went out by the front door,

There's never a maid in all the town,
But well she knows that malt's come down.

And in the street it was "Good-morrow to you, Master Jelleyman; the rain will do good, will it not?" and, again, "Goodmorrow, Neighbor Pike; do you know that my father is come home?" and again, "Get you within the doorway, little Parsons, else the wagon-wheels will be over thee." And then, when she was in the freedom of the fields, she would talk blithely to Don Roderigo, or snatch a buttercup here or there from among the long, lush, warm grass, or return to her careless singing:

For malt's come down, and malt's come down—
Oh, well she knows that malt's come down!

CHAPTER V.

IN A WOODED LANE.

Now it would be extremely difficult to say with what measure of faith or skepticism, of expectation or mere curiosity, she was now proceeding through these meadows to the spot indicated to her by the wizard. Probably she could not have told herself, for what was really uppermost in her mind was a kind of malicious desire to frighten her timid Puritan friend with the wildness of such an adventure. And then she was pretty safe. Ostensibly she was going to Shottery to pay a visit to her grandmother; to look at the pansies, the wall-flowers, the forget-me-nots in the little garden, and see how the currants and raspberries were getting on. She could hardly expect a ghost to rise from the ground in broad daylight. And if any mere strangers happened to be coming along the lane leading in from the Bidford road, Don Roderigo was a sufficient guardian. On the other hand, if there was anything real and of verity in this witchcraft—which had sought her, and not she it —was it not possible that the wizard might on one point have been mistaken? If her future husband were indeed to appear,

2*

would it not be much more likely to be Parson Blaise or Tom
Quiney, or young Jelleyman, or one or other of them that she
knew in everyday life ? But yet she said to herself—and there
was no doubt about her absolute conviction and certainty on
this point—that, even if she were to meet one of those coming
in from Evesham, not all the magic and mystery and wizardry
in the world would drive her to marry him but of her own
free good-will and choice.

When she had passed through the meadows and got near to
the scattered cottages and barns and orchards of the little hamlet, instead of going forward to these, she bore away to the left,
and eventually found herself in a wide and wooded lane. She
was less light of heart now; she wished the place were not so
still and lonely. It was a pretty lane, this; the ruddy-gray.
road that wound between luxuriant hedges and tall elms was
barred across by alternate sunlight and shadow, and every now
and again she had glimpses of the rich and fertile country lying around, with distant hills showing an outline serrated by
trees along the pale, summer-like sky. But there was not a
human being visible anywhere, nor a sound to be heard but
the soft repeated note of the cuckoo. She wished that there
were some farm people near at hand, or a shepherd lad, or anybody. She spoke to Roderigo, and her voice sounded strange
—it sounded as if she were afraid that some one was listening.
Nay, she began, quite unreasonably, to be angry with the wizard. What business had he to interfere with her affairs, and
to drive her on to such foolish enterprises ? What right had
he to challenge her to show that she was not afraid ? She was
not afraid, she assured herself. She had as good a title to walk
along this lane as any one in Warwickshire. Only she thought
that as soon as she had got as far as the cross at the meeting
of the roads (this was all that had been demanded of her) she
would go back to Stratford by the public highway rather than
return by this solitary lane, for on the public highway there
would be farm servants and laden wains and carriers, and
such-like comfortable and companionable objects.

The next minute—she had almost reached the cross—her
heart bounded with an unreasoning tremor of fear: she had
suddenly become aware that a stranger was entering the lane
from the wide highway beyond. She had only one glimpse of

him,·for instantly and resolutely she bent her eyes on Don Roderigo, and was determined to keep them there until this person should have passed; and yet that one lightning-like glimpse had told her somewhat. The stranger was young, and of a distinguished bearing and presence; and it certainly was a singular and unusual thing that a gentleman (as he seemed to be, although his travelling cloak concealed most of his attire) should be going afoot and unattended. But her only concern was to let him pass. Ghost or man as he might be, she kept her eyes on Roderigo. And then, to her increased alarm, she found that the stranger was approaching her.

"I beseech your pardon, lady," said he, in a most respectful voice, "but know you one in this town of the name of Master Shakespeare ?"

She certainly was startled, and even inwardly aghast; but she had a brave will. She was determined that nothing would drive her either to scream or to run away. And indeed when she looked up and said, rather breathlessly, "There be several of the name, sir," she was quickly assured that this was no ghost at all, but a substantial and living and breathing young man, tall and dark, of a pleasant expression of face, though in truth there was nothing in those singularly black eyes of his but the most ordinary and matter-of-fact inquiry.

"One Master William Shakespeare," said he, in answer to her, "that is widely known."

"It is my father, sir, you speak of," said she, hastily, and, in fact, somewhat ashamed of her fright.

At this news he removed his hat and made her a gracious obeisance, yet simply, and with not too elaborate a courtesy.

"Since I am so fortunate," said he, "may I beg you to direct me how I shall find the house when I get to the town ? I have a letter for him, as you may see."

He took out a letter, and held it so that, if she liked, she might read the superscription—"*To my loving good friend Master William Shakespeare: Deliver these.*" But Judith merely glanced at the writing.

"'Tis from Master Ben Jonson—that you know of, doubtless, madam—commending me to your father. But perhaps," he added, directing toward her a curious timid look of inquiry, "it were as well that I did not deliver it ?"

"How so, sir?" she asked.

"I am one that is in misfortune," said he, simply; "nay, in peril."

"Truly I am sorry for that, sir," said she, regarding him with frank eyes of sympathy, for indeed there was a kind of sadness in his air, that otherwise was distinguished enough, and even noble. And then she added: "But surely that is the greater reason you should seek my father."

"If I dared—if I knew," he said, apparently to himself. And then he addressed her: "If I make so bold, sweet lady, as to ask you if your father be of the ancient faith—or well disposed toward that, even if he do not openly profess it—I pray you set it down to my need and hard circumstances."

She did not seem to understand.

"I would ask if he be not at heart with the Catholic gentlemen that are looking for better times—for indeed I have heard it stated of him."

"Oh no, sir—surely not," said Judith, in some alarm, for she knew quite enough about the penal laws against priests and recusants, and would not have her father associated in any way with these, especially as she was talking with a stranger.

"Nay, then, it were better I did not deliver the letter," said the young man, with just a touch of hopelessness in his tone. "Under the protection of your father I might have had somewhat more of liberty, perchance; but I am content to remain as I am until I can get proofs that will convince them in authority of my innocence; or mayhap I may get away from the country altogether, and to my friends in Flanders. If they would but set my good friend Walter Raleigh free from the Tower, that also were well, for he and I might make a home for ourselves in another land. I crave your pardon for detaining you, madam, and so bid you farewell."

He raised his hat and made her a most respectful obeisance, and was about to withdraw.

"Stay, sir," said she, scarcely knowing what she said, but with trouble and anxiety in her gentle eyes.

Indeed, she was somewhat bewildered. So sudden had been the shock of surprise that she had forgotten, or very nearly forgotten, all about ghosts and wizards, about possible lovers or husbands, and only knew that here, in actual fact, was a stranger—and a modest young stranger, too—that was in great trouble, and yet was afraid to seek shelter and aid from her father. That he had no reason to be thus afraid she was certain enough; and yet she dared not assume—she had no reason for believing—that her father was secretly inclined to favor those that were still hoping for the re-establishment of the Catholic faith. The fact was that her father scarcely ever spoke of such matters. Hê would listen, if he happened to be in the house, to any theological discussion that might be going on, and he would regard this or that minister or preacher calmly, as if trying to understand the man and his opinions; but he would take no part in the talk; and when the discussion became disputatious, as sometimes happened, and the combatants grew warm and took to making hot assertions, he would rise and go out idly into the garden, and look at the young apple-trees or talk to Don Roderigo. Indeed, at this precise moment, Judith was quite incapable of deciding for herself which party her father would most likely be in sympathy with—the Puritans, who were sore at heart because of the failure of the Hampton Court Conference, or the Catholics, who were no less bitter on account of the severity of the penal laws—and a kind of vague wish arose in her heart that she could ask Prudence Shawe (who paid more attention to such matters, and was, in fact, wrapped up in them) before sending this young man away with his letter of commendation unopened.

"Your brother-in-law, madam, Dr. Hall," said he, seeing that she did not wish him to leave on the instant, "is well esteemed by the Catholic gentry, as I hear."

Judith did not answer that; she had been rapidly considering what she could do for one in distress.

"By your leave, sir, I would not have you go away without making further inquiry," said she. "I will myself get to know how my father is inclined, for indeed he never speaks of such matters to us; and sure I am that, whatever be his opinion, no harm could come to you through seeking his friendship. That I am sure of. If you are in distress, that is enough; he will not ask you whence you come; nor has he censure for any one; and that is a marvel in one that is so good a man himself, that he hath never a word of blame for

any one, neither for the highwayman that was taken red-hand·
ed, as it were, last Sunday near to Oxford—'Why,' says my father, 'if he take not life, and be a civil gentleman, I grudge
him not a purse or two'—nor for a lesser criminal, my cousin
Willie Hart, that but yesterday let the Portuguese singing-
bird escape from its cage. 'Well, well,' says my father, 'so
much the better, if only it can find food for itself.' Indeed,
you need fear naught but kindness and gentleness; and sure
I am that he would be but ill pleased to know that one coming
from his friend Benjamin Jonson had been in the neighborhood and gone away without having speech of him."

"But this is no matter of courtesy, sweet lady," said he.
"It is of a more dangerous cast; and I must be wary. If,
now, you were inclined to do as you say—to make some discreet
inquiry as to your good father's sentiments—"

"Not from himself," said she, quickly, and with some color
mounting to her cheeks—"for he would but laugh at my speaking of such things—but from my gossip and neighbor I think
I could gain sufficient assurance that would set your fears at
rest."

"And how should I come to know?" he said, with some hesitation—for this looked much like asking for another meeting.

But Judith was frank enough. If she meant to confer a
kindness, she did not stay to be too scrupulous about the manner of doing it.

"If it were convenient that you could be here this evening,"
said she, after a moment's thought, "Willie Hart and myself
often walk over to Shottery after supper. Then could I let
you know."

"But how am I to thank you for such a favor?" said he.

"Nay, it is but little," she answered, "to do for one that
comes from my father's friend."

"Rare Ben, as they call him," said he, more brightly. "And
now I bethink me, kind lady, that it ill becomes me to have
spoken of nothing but my own poor affairs on my first having
the honor of meeting with you. Perchance you would like
to hear something of Master Jonson, and how he does? May
I accompany you on your homeward way for a space, if you
are returning to the town? The road here is quiet enough
for one that is in hiding, as well as for pleasant walking;

and you are well escorted, too," he added, looking at the grave and indifferent Don. "With such a master as your father, and such a sweet mistress, I should not wonder if he became as famous as Sir John Harrington's Bungey that the Prince asked about. You have not heard of him?—the marvellous dog that Sir John would intrust with messages all the way to the court at Greenwich; and he would bring back the answer without more ado. I wonder not that Prince Henry should have asked for an account of all his feats and doings."

Now insensibly she had turned and begun to walk toward Shottery (for she would not ask this unhappy young man to court the light of the open highway), and as he respectfully accompanied her his talk became more and more cheerful, so that one would scarcely have remembered that he was in hiding, and in peril of his life mayhap. And he quickly found that she was most interested in Jonson as being her father's friend and intimate.

"Indeed, I should not much marvel to hear of his being soon in this very town of Stratford," said he, "for he has been talking of late—nay, he has been talking this many a day of it, but who knows when the adventure will take place?—of travelling all the way to Scotland on foot, and writing an account of his discoveries on the road. And then he has a mind to get to the lake of Lomond, to make it the scene of a fisher and pastoral play, he says; and his friend Drummond will go with him; and they speak of getting still further to the north, and being the guests of the new Scotch lord, Mackenzie of Kintail, that was made a peer last winter. Nay, friend Ben, though at times he gibes at the Scots, at other times he will boast of his Scotch blood—for his grandfather, as I have heard, came from Annandale—and you will often hear him say that whereas the late Queen was a niggard and close-fisted, this Scotch King is lavish and a generous patron. If he go to Scotland, as is his purpose, surely he will come by way of Stratford."

"It were ill done of him else," said Judith. But truly this young gentleman was so bent on entertaining her with tales of his acquaintance in London, and with descriptions of the court shows and pageants, that she had not to trouble herself much to join in the conversation.

"A lavish patron the King has been to him truly," he continued, stooping to pat the Don's head, as if he would make friends with him too, "what with the masks, and revels, and so forth. Their last tiltings at Prince Henry's barriers exceeded everything that had gone before, as I think—and I marvel not that Ben was found at his best, seeing how the King had been instructing him. Nay, but it was a happy conceit to have our young Lord of the Isles addressed by the Lady of the Lake, and have King Arthur hand him his armor out of the clouds—"

"But where was it, good sir?" said she (to show that she was interested). And now he seemed so cheerful and friendly that she ventured to steal a look at him. In truth, there was nothing very doleful or tragic in his appearance. He was a handsomely made young man, of about eight-and-twenty or so, with fine features, a somewhat pale and sallow complexion (that distinguished him markedly from the rustic red and white and sun-brown she was familiar with), and eyes of a singular blackness and fire that were exceedingly respectful, but that could, as any one might see, easily break into mirth. He was well habited too, for now he had partly thrown his travelling cloak aside, and his slashed doublet and hose and shoes were smart and clearly of a town fashion. He wore no sword; in his belt there was only a small dagger, of Venetian silver-work on the handle, and with a sheath of stamped crimson velvet.

"Dear lady, you must have heard of them," he continued, lightly—"I mean of the great doings in the banqueting-house at Whitehall, when Prince Henry challenged so many noble lords. 'Twas a brave sight, I assure you; the King and Queen were there, and the ambassadors from Spain and Venice, and a great and splendid assemblage. And then, when Ben's speeches came to be spoken, there was Cyril Davy, that is said to have the best woman's voice in London, as the Lady of the Lake, and he came forward and said,

> *'Lest any yet should doubt, or might mistake*
> *What Nymph I am, behold the ample Lake*
> *Of which I'm styled; and near it Merlin's tomb';*

and then King Arthur appeared, and our young Lord of the

Isles had a magic shield handed to him. Oh, 'twas a noble sight, I warrant you! And I heard that the Duke of Lennox and the Earls of Arundel and Southampton and all of them were but of one mind, that friend Ben had never done better."

Indeed, the young man, as they loitered along the pretty wooded lane in the hush of the warm still noon (there was scarce enough wind to make a rustle in the great branching elms), and as he talked of all manner of things for the entertainment of this charming companion whom a happy chance had thrown in his way, seemed to be well acquainted with the court and its doings, and all the busy life of London. If she gathered rightly, he had himself been present when the King and the nobles went in the December of the previous year to Deptford to witness the launching of the great ship of the East India Company—the *Trade's Encrease*, it was called—for he described the magnificent banquet in the chief cabin, and how the King gave to Sir Thomas Smith, the Governor, a fine chain of gold, with his portrait set in a jewel, and how angry his Majesty became when they found that the ship could not be launched on account of the state of the tide. But when he again brought in the name of Jonson, and said how highly the King thought of his writings, and what his Majesty had said of this or the other device or masque that had been commanded of him, Judith grew at length to be not so pleased; and she said, with some asperity, "But the King holds my father in honor also, for he wrote him a letter with his own hand."

"I heard not of that," said he, but of course without appearing to doubt her word.

"Nay, but I saw it," said she—"I saw the letter; and I did not think it well that my father should give it to Julius Shawe, for there are some others that would have valued it as much as he—yes, and been more proud of it, too."

"His own daughter, perchance ?" he said, gently.

Judith did not speak. It was a sore subject with her; indeed, she had cried in secret, and bitterly, when she learned that the letter had been casually given away, for her father seemed to put no great store by it. However, that had nothing to do with this unhappy young gentleman that was in hiding. And soon she had dismissed it from her mind, and was engaged in fixing the exact time at which, as she hoped, she would be able to bring him that assurance, or that caution, in the evening.

"I think it must be the province of women to be kind to the unfortunate," said he, as they came in sight of the cottages; and he seemed to linger and hesitate in his walk, as if he were afraid of going further.

"It is but a small kindness," said she; "and I hope it will bring you and my father together. He has but just returned from London, and you will not have much news to give him from his friend; but you will be none the less welcome, for all are welcome to him, but especially those whom he can aid."

"If I were to judge of the father by the daughter, I should indeed expect a friendly treatment," said he, with much courtesy.

"Nay, but it is so simple a matter," said she.

"Then fare you well, Mistress Judith," said he, "if I may make so bold as to guess at a name that I have heard named in London."

"Oh, no, sir ?" said she, glancing up with some inquiry.

"But indeed, indeed," said he, gallantly. "And who can wonder ? 'Twas friend Ben that I heard speak of you; I marvel not that he carried your praises so far. But now, sweet lady, that I see you would go—and I wish not to venture nearer the village there—may I beseech of you at parting a further grace and favor ? It is that you would not reveal to any one, no matter what trust you may put in them, that you have seen me or spoken with me. You know not my name, it is true, though I would willingly confide it to you—indeed, it is Leofric Hope, madam; but if it were merely known that you had met with a stranger, curious eyes might be on the alert."

"Fear not, sir," said she, looking at him in her frank way —and there was a kind of friendliness, too, and sympathy in her regard. "Your secret is surely safe in my keeping. I can promise you that none shall know through me that you are in the neighborhood. Farewell, good sir. I hope your fortunes will mend speedily."

"God keep you, sweet Mistress Judith," said he, raising his hat and bowing low, and not even asking to be allowed to take her hand. "If my ill fortune should carry it so that I see you not again, at least I will treasure in my memory a vision of kindness and beauty that I trust will remain forever there. Farewell, gentle lady; I am your debtor."

And so they parted; and he stood looking after her and the great dog as they passed through the meadows; and she was making all the haste she might, for although, when Judith's father was at home, the dinner hour was at twelve instead of at eleven, still it would take her all the time to be punctual, and she was scrupulous not to offend. He stood looking after her as long as she was in sight, and then he turned away, saying to himself:

"Why, our Ben did not tell us a tithe of the truth!—for why?—because it was with his tongue, and not with his pen, that he described her. By heaven, she is a marvel!—and I dare be sworn, now, that half the clowns in Stratford imagine themselves in love with her."

CHAPTER VI.

WITHIN-DOORS.

WHEN in the afternoon Judith sought out her gentle gossip, and with much cautious tact and discretion began to unfold her perplexities to her, Prudence was not only glad enough to hear nothing further of the wizard—who seemed to have been driven out of Judith's mind altogether by the actual occurrences of the morning—but also she became possessed with a secret wonder and joy; for she thought that at last her dearest and closest friend was awaking to a sense of the importance of spiritual things, and that henceforth there would be a bond of confidence between them far more true and abiding than any that had been before. But soon she discovered that politics had a good deal to do with these hesitating inquiries; and at length the bewildered Prudence found the conversation narrowing and narrowing itself to this definite question: Whether, supposing there were a young man charged with complicity in a Catholic plot, or perhaps having been compromised in some former affair of the kind, and supposing him to appeal to her father, would he, Judith's father, probably be inclined to shelter him and conceal him, and give him what aid was possible until he might get away from the country?

"But what do you mean, Judith?" said Prudence, in dismay. "Have you seen any one? What is't you mean? Have you seen one of the desperate men that were concerned with Catesby?"

Indeed, it was not likely that either of these two Warwickshire maidens had already forgotten the terrible tidings that rang through the land but a few years before, when the Gunpowder Treason was discovered; nor how the conspirators fled into this very county; nor yet how in the following January, on a bitterly cold and snowy day, there was brought into the town the news of the executions in St. Paul's church-yard and at Westminster. And, in truth, when Prudence Shawe mentioned Catesby's name, Judith's cheek turned pale. It was but for an instant. She banished the ungenerous thought the moment that it occurred to her. No, she was sure that the unhappy young man who had appealed to her compassion could not have been concerned in any such bloody enterprise. His speech was too gentle for that. Had he not declared that he only wanted time to prove his innocence? It is true he had said something about his friends in Flanders, and often enough had she heard the Puritan divines denouncing Flanders as the very hot-bed of the machinations of the Jesuits; but that this young man might have friends amongst the Jesuits did not appear to her as being in itself a criminal thing, any more than the possibility of his being a Catholic was sufficient of itself to deprive him of her frank and generous sympathy.

"I may not answer you yea nor nay, sweet mouse," said she; "but assure yourself that I am not in league with any desperate villain.' I but put a case. We live in quiet times now, do we not, good Prue? and I take it that those who like not the country are free to leave it. But tell me, if my father were to speak openly, which of the parties would he most affect? And how stands he with the King? Nay, the King himself, of what religion is he at heart, think you?"

"These be questions!" said Prudence, staring aghast at such ignorance.

"I but use my ears," said Judith, indifferently, "and the winds are not more variable than the opinions that one listens to. Well you know it, Prue. Here is one that says the King is in conscience a papist, as his mother was; and that he gave a guarantee to the Catholic gentry ere he came to the throne; and that soon or late we shall have mass again; and then comes another with the story that the Pope is hot and angry because the King misuseth him in his speech, calling him Antichrist and the like; and that he has complained to the French King on the matter, and that there is even talk of excommunication. What can one believe? How is one to know? Indeed, good mouse, you would have me more anxious about such things; but why should one add to one's difficulties? I am content to be like my father, and stand aside from the quarrel."

"Your wit is too great for me, dear Judith," her friend said, rather sadly; "and I will not argue with you. But well I know there may be a calmness that is of ignorance and indifference, and that is slothful and sinful; and there may be a calmness that is of assured wisdom and knowledge of the truth, and that I trust your father has attained to. That he should keep aside from disputes, I can well understand."

"But touching the King, dear cousin," said Judith, who had her own ends in view. "How stands my father with the King and his religion? Nay, but I know, and every one knows, that in all other matters they are friends; for your brother has the King's letter—"

"That I wish you had yourself, Judith, since your heart is set upon it," said her companion, gently.

Judith did not answer that.

"But as regards religion, sweet Prue, what think you my father would most favor, were there a movement any way?—a change to the ancient faith, perchance?"

She threw out the question with a kind of studied carelessness, as if it were a mere matter of speculation; but there was a touch of warmth in Prudence's answer:

"What, then, Judith? You think he would disturb the peace of the land, and give us over again to the priests and their idol-worship? I trow not." Then something seemed to occur to her suddenly. "But if you have any doubt, Judith, I can set your mind at rest—of a surety I can."

"How, then, dear mouse?"

"I will tell you the manner of it. No longer ago than yesterday evening I was seated at the window reading—it was the volume that Dr. Hall brought me from Worcester, and that I value more and more the longer I read it—and your father came into the house asking for Julius. So I put the book on the table, with the face downward, and away I went to seek for my brother. Well, then, sweet cousin, when I came back to the room, there was your father standing at the window reading the book that I had left, and I would not disturb him; and when he had finished the page, he turned, saying, 'Good bishop! good bishop!' and putting down the book on the table just as he had found it. Dear Judith, I hope you will think it no harm and no idle curiosity that made me take up the book as soon as my brother was come in, and examine the passage, and mark it—"

"Harm!—bless thee, sweetheart!" Judith exclaimed. And she added, eagerly: "But have you the book? Will you read it to me? Is it about the King? Do, dear cousin, read to me what it was that my father approved. Beshrew me! but I shall have to take to school lessons, after all, lest I outlive even your gentle patience."

Straightway Prudence had gone to a small cupboard of boxes in which she kept all her most valued possessions, and from thence she brought a stout little volume, which, as Judith perceived, had a tiny book-mark of satin projecting from the red-edged leaves.

"Much comfort indeed have I found in these Comfortable Notes," said she. "I wish, Judith, you, that can think of everything, would tell me how I am to show to Dr. Hall that I am more and more grateful to him for his goodness. What can I do?—words are such poor things!"

"But the passage, good Prue—what was't he read? I pray you let me hear," said Judith, eagerly; for here, indeed, might be a key to many mysteries.

"Listen, then," said her companion, opening the book. "The Bishop, you understand, Judith, is speaking of the sacrifices the Jews made to the Lord, and he goes on to say:

"'Thus had this people their peace-offerings; that is, duties of thankfulness to their God for the peace and prosperity vouchsafed unto them. And most fit it was that He should often be thanked for such favors. The like mercies and goodness remain to us at this day: are we either freed from the duty or left without means to perform it? No, no; but as they had oxen and kine, and sheep and goats, then appointed and allowed, so have we the calves of our lips and the sacrifice of thanksgiving still remaining for us, and as strictly required of us as these (in those days) were of them. Offer them up, then, with a free heart and with a feeling soul. Our peace is great; our prosperity comfortable; our God most sweet and kind; and shall we not offer? The public is sweet, the private is sweet, and forget you to offer? We lay us down and take our rest, and this our God maketh us dwell in safety. Oh, where is your offering? We rise again and go to our labor, and a dog is not heard to move his tongue among us: Owe no offering? O Lord, O Lord, make us thankful to Thee for these mercies: the whole state we live in, for the common and our several souls, for several mercies now many years enjoyed! O touch us; O turn us from our fearful dullness, and abusing of this so sweet, so long, and so happy peace! Continue thy sacred servant'—surely you know, Judith, whom he means—'the chiefest means under Thee of this our comfort, and ever still furnish him with wise helps, truly fearing Thee, and truly loving him. Let our heads go to the grave in this peace, if it may be Thy blessed pleasure, and our eyes never see the change of so happy an estate. Make us thankful and full of peace-offerings; be Thou still ours, and ever merciful. Amen! Amen!'"

"And what said he, sweet Prue—what said my father?" Judith asked, though her eyes were distant and thoughtful.

"'Good bishop! good bishop!' said he, as if he were right well pleased, and he put down the book on the table. Nay, you may be certain, Judith, that your father would have naught to do with the desperate men that would fain upset the country, and bring wars among us, and hand us over to the Pope again. I have heard of such; I have heard that many of the great families have but a lip loyalty, and have malice at their heart, and would willingly plunge the land in blood if they could put the priests in power over us again. Be sure your father is not of that mind."

"But if one were in distress, Prudence," said the other, ab-

sently, "perchance with a false charge hanging over him
that could be disproved—say that one were in hiding, and
only anxious to prove his innocence, or to get away from the
country, is my father likely to look coldly on such a one in
misfortune ?   No, no, surely, sweet mouse !"

"But of whom do you speak, Judith ?" exclaimed her friend,
regarding her with renewed alarm.   "It can not be that you
know of such a one ?   Judith, I beseech you speak plainly!
You have met with some stranger that is unknown to your
own people ?   You said you had but put a case, but now you
speak as if you knew the man.   I beseech you, for the love
between us, speak plainly to me, Judith !"

"I may not," said the other, rising.   And then she added,
more lightly, "Nay, have no fear, sweet Prue; if there be any
danger, it is not I that run it, and soon there will be no occasion for my withholding the secret from you, if secret there be."

"I can not understand you, Judith," said her friend, with
the pale, gentle face full of a tender wistfulness and anxiety.

"Such timid eyes!" said Judith, laughing good-naturedly.
"Indeed, Prudence, I have seen no ghost, and goodman Wizard has failed me utterly; nor sprite nor phantom has been
near me.   In sooth I have buried poor Tom's bit of rosemary
to little purpose.   And now I must get me home, for Master
Parson comes this afternoon, and I will but wait the preaching
to hear Susan sing: 'tis worth the penance.   Farewell, sweet
mouse; get you rid of your alarm.   The sky will clear all in
good time."

So they kissed each other, and she left; still in much perplexity, it is true, but nevertheless resolved to tell the young
man honestly and plainly the result of her inquiries.

As it turned out, she was to hear something more about the
King and politics and religion that afternoon; for when she
got home to New Place, Master Blaise was already there, and
he was eagerly discussing with Judith's mother and her sister
the last news that had been brought from London; or rather
he was expounding it, with emphatic assertions and denunciations that the women-folk received for the most part with a
mute but quite apparent sympathy.   He was a young man of
about six-and-twenty, rather inclined to be stout, but with
strongly lined features, fair complexion and hair, an intellect-

ual forehead, and sharp and keen gray eyes. The one point that recommended him to Judith's favor—which he openly and frankly, but with perfect independence, sought—was the uncompromising manner in which he professed his opinions. These frequently angered her, and even at times roused her to passionate indignation; and yet, oddly enough, she had a kind of lurking admiration for the very honesty that scorned to curry favor with her by means of any suppression or evasion. It may be that there was a trace of the wisdom of the serpent in this attitude of the young parson, who was shrewd-headed as well as clear-eyed, and was as quick as any to read the fear- less quality of Judith's character. At all events, he would not yield to any of her prejudices; he would not stoop to flatter her; he would not abate one jot of his protests against the vanity and pride, the heathenish show and extravagance, of women; the heinousness and peril of indifferentism in matters of doctrine; and the sinfulness of the life of them that countenanced stage plays and such like devilish iniquities. It was this last that was the real stumbling-block and conten- tion between them. Sometimes Judith's eyes burned. Once she rose and got out of the room. "If I were a man, Master Parson," she was saying to herself, with shut teeth, "by the life of me I would whip you from Stratford town to Warwick!" And indeed there was ordinarily a kind of armed truce be- tween these two, so that no stranger or acquaintance could very easily decide what their precise relations were, although every one knew that Judith's mother and sister held the young divine in great favor, and would fain have had him of the family.

At this moment of Judith's entrance he was much exercised, as has been said, on account of the news that was but just come from London—how that the King was driving at still further impositions because of the Commons begrudging him supplies; and naturally Master Blaise warmly approved of the Commons, that had been for granting the liberties to the Puritans which the King had refused. And not only was this the expression of a general opinion on the subject, but he maintained as an individual—and as a very emphatic individ- ual too—that the prerogatives of the crown, the wardships and purveyances and what not, were monstrous and abominable, and a way of escape from the just restraint of Parliament, and he declared with a sudden vehemence that he would rather perish at the stake than contribute a single benevolence to the royal purse. Judith's mother, a tall, slight, silver-haired woman, with eyes that had once been of extraordinary beauty, but now were grown somewhat sad and worn, and her daughter Susanna Hall, who was darker than her sister Judith as regarded hair and eyebrows, but who had blue-gray eyes of a singular clearness and quickness and intelligence, listened and acquiesced; but perhaps they were better pleased when they found the young parson come out of that vehement mood; though still he was sharp of tongue and sarcastic, saying as an excuse for the King that now he was revenging himself on the English Puritans for the treatment he had received at the hands of the Scotch Presbyterians, who had harried him not a little. He had not a word for Judith; he addressed his discourse entirely to the other two. And she was content to sit aside, for indeed this discontent with the crown on the part of the Puritans was nothing strange or novel to her, and did not in the least help to solve her present perplexity.

And now the maids (for Judith's father would have no serving-men, nor stablemen, nor husbandmen of any grade whatever, come within-doors; the work of the house was done entirely by women-folk) entered to prepare the long oaken table for supper, seeing which Master Blaise suggested that before that meal it might be as well to devote a space to divine worship. So the maids were bidden to stay their preparations, and to remain, seating themselves dutifully on a bench brought crosswise, and the others sat at the table in their usual chairs, while the preacher opened the large Bible that had been fetched for him, and proceeded to read the second chapter of the Book of Jeremiah, expounding as he went along. This running commentary was, in fact, a sermon applied to all the evils of the day, as the various verses happened to offer texts; and the ungodliness and the vanity and the turning away from the Lord that Jeremiah lamented were attributed in no unsparing fashion to the town of Stratford and the inhabitants thereof: "Hear ye the word of the Lord, O house of Jacob, and all the families of the house of Israel: thus saith the Lord, What iniquity have your fathers found in me, that they are gone far from me, and have walked after vanity, and are become vain?" Nor did he spare himself and his own calling: "The priests said not, Where is the Lord? and they that should minister the law knew me not: the pastors also offended against me, and the prophets prophesied in Baal, and went after things that did not profit." And there were bold paraphrases and inductions, too: "What hast thou now to do in the way of Egypt, to drink the waters of Nilus? or what makest thou in the way of Asshur, to drink the waters of the river?" Was not that the seeking of strange objects—of baubles, and jewels, and silks, and other instruments of vanity—from abroad, from the papist land of France, to lure the eye and deceive the senses, and turn away the mind from the dwelling on holy things? "Can a maid forget her ornament, or a bride her attire? yet my people have forgotten me days without number." This was, indeed, a fruitful text, and there is no doubt that Judith was indirectly admonished to regard the extreme simplicity of her mother's and sister's attire; so that there can be no excuse whatever for her having in her mind at this very moment some vague fancy that as soon as supper was over she would go to her own chamber and take out a certain beaver hat. She did not often wear it, for it was a present that her father had once brought her from London, and it was ranked among her most precious treasures; but surely on this evening (she was saying to herself) it was fitting that she should wear it, not from any personal vanity, but to the end that this young gentleman, who seemed to know several of her father's acquaintances in London, should understand that the daughter of the owner of New Place was no mere country wench, ignorant of what was in the fashion. It is grievous that she should have been concerned with such frivolous thoughts. However, the chapter came to an end in due time.

Then good Master Blaise said that they would sing the One-hundred-and-thirty-seventh Psalm; and this was truly what Judith had been waiting for. She herself was but an indifferent singer. She could do little more than hum such snatches of old songs as occurred to her during her careless rambles, and that only for her private ear; but her sister Susanna had a most noble, pure, and clear contralto voice, that could at any

time bring tears to Judith's eyes, and that, when she joined
in the choral parts of the service in church, made many a
young man's heart to tremble strangely.   In former days she
used to sing to the accompaniment of her lute; but that was
given over now.   Once or twice Judith had brought the discarded instrument to her, and said,

"Susan, sweet Susan, for once, for once only, sing to me ' *The
rose is from my garden gone.*' "

"Why, then—to make you cry, silly one ?" the elder sister
would answer.   "What profit those idle tears, child, that are
but a luxury and a sinful indulgence ?"

"Susan, but once !" Judith would plead (with the tears almost already in her eyes)—"once only, ' *The rose is from my
garden gone.*'   There is none can sing it like you."

But the elder sister was obdurate, as she considered was
right; and Judith, as she walked through the meadows in the
evening, would sometimes try the song for herself, thinking, or
endeavoring to think, that she could hear in it the pathetic
vibration of her sister's voice.   Indeed, at this moment the
small congregation assembled around the table would doubtless have been deeply shocked had they known with what a
purely secular delight Judith was now listening to the words
of the psalm.   There was but one Bible in the house, so that
Master Blaise read out the first two lines (lest any of the maids
might have a lax memory):

> " *When as we sat in Babylon,*
>   *The rivers round about*";

and that they sang; then they proceeded in like manner:

> "*And in remembrance of Sion,*
>   *The tears for grief burst out ;*
> *We hanged our harps and instruments*
>   *The willow-trees upon ;*
> *For in that place men for their use*
>   *Had planted many a one.*"

It is probable, indeed, that Judith was so wrapped up in her
sister's singing that it did not occur to her to ask herself
whether this psalm, too, had not been chosen with some regard to the good preacher's discontent with those in power.
At all events, he read out, and they sang, no further than
these two verses:

THE BIBLE READING.

" Then they to whom we prisoners were,
Said to us tauntingly :
Now let us hear your Hebrew songs
And pleasant melody.
Alas ! (said we) who can once frame
His sorrowful heart to sing
The praises of our loving God
Thus under a strange king ?

" But yet if I Jerusalem
Out of my heart let slide,
Then let my fingers quite forget
The warbling harp to guide ;
And let my tongue within my mouth
Be tied forever fast,
If that I joy before I see
Thy full deliverance past."

Then there was a short and earnest prayer; and, that over,
the maids set to work to get forward the supper; and young
Willie Hart was called in from the garden—Judith's father being away at Wilmcote on some important business there.   In
due course of time, supper being finished, and a devout thanksgiving said, Judith was free; and instantly she fled away to
her own chamber to don her bravery.   It was not vanity (she
again said to herself), it was that her father's daughter should
show that she knew what was due to him and his standing in
the town; and, indeed, as she now regarded herself in the little
mirror—she wore a half-circle farthingale, and had on one of
her smartest ruffs—and when she set on her head of short
brown curls this exceedingly pretty hat (it was of gray beaver
above, and underneath it was lined with black satin, and all
around the rim was a row of hollow brass beads that tinkled
like small bells), she was quite well satisfied with her appearance, and that she was fairly entitled to be.   Then she went
down and summoned her sweetheart Willie, to act as her companion and protector and ally; and together these two passed
forth from the house—into the golden clear evening.

CHAPTER VII.

A FAREWELL.

ALWAYS, when she got out into the open air, her spirits rose into a pure content; and now, as they were walking westward through the peaceful meadows, the light of the sunset was on her face; and there was a kind of radiance there, and careless happiness, that little Willie Hart scarce dared look upon, so abject and wistful was the worship that the small lad laid at his pretty cousin's feet. He was a sensitive and imaginative boy; and the joy and crown of his life was to be allowed to walk out with his cousin Judith, her hand holding his; and it did not matter to him whether she spoke to him, or whether she was busy with her private thinking, and left him to his own pleasure and fancies. He had many of these; for he had heard of all kinds of great and noble persons—princesses, and empresses, and queens; but to him his cousin Judith was the Queen of queens; he could not believe that any one ever was more beautiful—or more gentle and lovable, in a magical and mystical way—than she was; and in church, on the quiet Sunday mornings, when the choir was singing, and all else silence, and dreams were busy in certain small brains, if there were any far-away pictures of angels in white and shining robes, coming toward one through rose-red celestial gardens, be sure they had Judith's eyes and the light and witchery of these; and that, when they spoke (if such wonderful creatures vouchsafed to speak), it was with the softness of Judith's voice. So it is not to be conceived that Judith, who knew something of this mute and secret adoration, had any malice in her heart when, on this particular evening, she began to question the boy as to the kind of sweetheart he would choose when he was grown up: the fact being that she spoke from idleness, and a wish to be friendly and companionable, her thoughts being really occupied elsewhere.

"Come, now, Willie, tell me," said she, "what sort of one you will choose, some fifteen or twenty years hence, when you

arc grown up to be a man, and will be going abroad from place
to place. In Coventry, perchance, you may find her, or over
at Evesham, or in Warwick, or Worcester, or as far away as
Oxford: in all of them are plenty of pretty maidens to be had
for the asking, so you be civil-spoken enough, and bear yourself well. Now tell me your fancy, sweetheart: what shall her
height be?"

"Why, you know, Judith," said he, rather shamefacedly.
"Just your height."

"My height?" she said, carelessly. "Why, that is neither
the one way nor the other. My father says I am just as high
as his heart; and with that I am content. Well, now, her hair
—what color of hair shall she have?"

"Like yours, Judith; and it must come round about her
ears like yours," said he, glancing up for a moment.

"Eyes: must they be black, or gray, or brown, or blue?
Nay, you shall have your choice, sweetheart Willie: there be
all sorts, if you go far enough afield and look around you.
What eyes do you like, now?"

"You know well, Judith, there is no one has such pretty
eyes as you; these are the ones I like, and no others."

"Bless the boy!—would you have her to be like me?"

"Just like you, Judith — altogether," said he, promptly;
and he added, more shyly, "For you know there is none as
pretty, and they all of them say that."

"Marry, now!" said she, with a laugh. "Here be news.
What? When you go choosing your sweetheart, would you
pick out one that had as large hands as these?"

She held forth her hands, and regarded them ; and yet with
some complacency, for she had put on a pair of scented gloves
which her father had brought her from London, and these
were beautifully embroidered with silver, for he knew her
tastes, and that she was not afraid to wear finery, whatever the
preachers might say.

"Why, you know, Judith," said he, "that there is none
has such pretty hands as you, nor so white, nor so soft."

"Heaven save us! am I perfection, then?" she cried (but
she was pleased). "Must she be altogether like me?"

"Just so, Cousin Judith; altogether like you; and she must
wear pretty things like you, and walk as you walk, and speak

like you, else I shall not love her nor go near her, though she
were the Queen herself."

"Well said, sweetheart Willie!—you shall to the court some
day, if you can speak so fair. And shall I tell you, now, how
you must woo and win such a one?" she continued, lightly.
"It may be you shall find her here or there—in a farm-house,
perchance; or she may be a great lady with her coach; or a
wench in an ale-house; but if she be as you figure her, this is
how you shall do : you must not grow up to be too nice and
fine and delicate-handed; you must not bend too low for her
favor; but be her lord and governor; and you must be ready
to fight for her, if need there be—yes, you shall not suffer a
word to be said in dispraise of her; and for slanderers you must
have a cudgel and a stout arm withal; and yet you must be
gentle with her, because she is a woman; and yet not too gentle,
for you are a man; and you must be no slape-face, with whining through the nose that we are all devilish and wicked and
the children of sin; and you must be no tavern-seeker, with
oaths and drunken jests and the like; and when you find her
you must be the master of her—and yet a gentle master: marry, I can not tell you more; but, as I hope for heaven, sweet
Willie, you will do well and fairly if she love thee half as much
as I do."

And she patted the boy's head. What sudden pang was it
that went through his heart?

"They say you are going to marry Parson Blaise, Judith,"
said he, looking up at her.

"Do they, now?" said she, with a touch of color in her face.
"They are too kind that would take from me the business of
choosing for myself."

"Is it true, Judith?"

"It is but idle talk; heed it not, sweetheart," said she, rather
sharply. "I would they were as busy with their fingers as with
their tongues; there would be more wool spun in Warwickshire!"

But here she remembered that she had no quarrel with the
lad, who had but innocently repeated the gossip he had heard;
and so she spoke to him in a more gentle fashion; and, as they
were now come to a parting of the ways, she said that she had
a message to deliver, and bade him go on by himself to the cot-

tage, and have some flowers gathered for her from out of the
garden by the time she should arrive. He was a biddable boy,
and went on without further question. Then she turned off
to the left, and in a few minutes was in the wide and wooded
lane where she was to meet the young gentleman that had appealed to her friendliness.

And there, sure enough, he was; and as he came forward,
hat in hand, to greet her, those eloquent black eyes of his expressed so much pleasure (and admiration of a respectful kind)
that Judith became for a moment a trifle self-conscious, and
remembered that she was in unusually brave attire. There
may have been something else: some quick remembrance of
the surprise and alarm of the morning; and also—in spite
of her determination to banish such unworthy fancies—some
frightened doubt as to whether, after all, there might not be a
subtle connection between her meeting with this young gentleman and the forecasts of the wizard. This was but for a moment, but it confused her in what she had intended to say
(for, in crossing the meadows, she had been planning out certain speeches as well as talking idly to Willie Hart), and she
was about to make some stumbling confession to the effect that
she had obtained no clear intelligence from her gossip Prudence Shawe, when the young gentleman himself absolved her
from all further difficulty.

"I beseech your pardon, sweet lady," said he, "that I have
caused you so much trouble, and that to no end; for I am of
a mind now not to carry the letter to your father, whatever
hopes there might be of his sympathy and friendship."

She stared in surprise.

"Nay, but, good sir," said she, "since you have the letter,
and are so near to Stratford, that is so great a distance from
London, surely it were a world of pities you did not see my
father. Not that I can honestly gather that he would have
any favor for a desperate enterprise upsetting the peace of the
land—"

"I am in none such, Mistress Judith, believe me," said he,
quickly. "But it behooves me to be cautious; and I have
heard that within the last few hours which summons me away.
If I were inclined to run the risk, there is no time at this
present; and what I can do now is to try to thank you for the

3*

kindness you have shown to one that has no habit of forgetting."

"You are going away forthwith?" said she.

There was no particular reason why she should be sorry at his departure from the neighborhood, except that he was an extraordinarily gentle-spoken young man, and of a courteous breeding, whom her father, as she thought, would have been pleased to welcome as being commended from his friend Ben Jonson. Few visitors came to New Place; the faces to be met with there were grown familiar year after year. It seemed a pity that this stranger—and so fair-spoken a stranger, moreover—should be close at hand, without making her father's acquaintance.

"Yes, sweet lady," said he, in the same respectful way, "it is true that I must quit my present lodging for a time; but I doubt whether I could find anywhere a quieter or securer place—nay, I have no reason to fear you; I will tell you freely that it is Bassfield Farm, that is on the left before you go down the hill to Bidford; and it is like enough I may come back thither, when that I see how matters stand with me in London."

And then he glanced at her with a certain diffidence.

"Perchance I am too daring," said he; "and yet your courtesy makes me bold. Were I to communicate with you when I return—"

He paused, and his hesitation well became him: it was more eloquent in its modesty than many words.

"That were easily done," said Judith at once, and with her usual frankness; "but I must tell you, good sir, that any written message you might send me I should have to show to my friend and gossip Prudence Shawe, that reads and writes for me, being so skilled in that; and when you said that to no one was the knowledge to be given that you were in this neighborhood—"

"Sweet lady," said he, instantly, with much gratitude visible in those handsome dark eyes, "if I may so far trespass on your goodness, I would leave that also within your discretion. One that you have chosen to be your friend must needs be trustworthy—nay, I am sure of that."

"But my father too, good sir—"

"Nay, not so," said he, with some touch of entreaty in his

voice. . "Take it not ill of me, but one that is in peril must use precautions for his safety, even though they savor of ill manners and suspicion."

"As you will, sir—as you will; I know little of such matters," Judith said. "But yet I know that you do wrong to mistrust my father."

"Nay, dearest lady," he said, quickly, "it is you that do me wrong to use such words. I mistrust him not; but, indeed, I dare not disclose to him the charge that is brought against me until I have clearer proofs of my innocence, and these I hope to have in time, when I may present myself to your father without fear. Meanwhile, sweet Mistress Judith, I can but ill express my thanks to you that you have vouchsafed to lighten the tedium of my hiding through these few words that have passed between us. Did you know the dullness of the days at the farm—for sad thoughts are but sorry companions —you would understand my gratitude toward you—"

"Nay, nothing, good sir, nothing," said she; and then she paused, in some difficulty. She did not like to bid him farewell without any reference whatsoever to the future; for in truth she wished to hear more of him, and how his fortunes prospered. And yet she hesitated about betraying so much interest—of however distant and ordinary a kind—in the affairs of a stranger. Her usual frank sympathy conquered: besides, was not this unhappy young man the friend of her father's friend?

"Is it to the farm that you return when you have been to London?" she asked.

"I trust so: better security I could not easily find elsewhere; and my well-wishers have means of communication with me, so that I can get the news there. Pray Heaven I may soon be quit of this skulking in corners! I like it not: it is not the life of a free man."

"I hope your fortunes will mend, sir, and speedily," said she, and there was an obvious sincerity in her voice.

"Why," said he, with a laugh—for, indeed, this young man, to be one in peril of his life, bore himself with a singularly free and undaunted demeanor; and he was not looking around him in a furtive manner, as if he feared to be observed, but was allowing his eyes to rest on Judith's eyes, and on the details of

her costume (which he seemed to approve), in a quite easy and
unconcerned manner—"the birds and beasts we hunt are allowed to rest at times, but a man in hiding has no peace nor
freedom from week's end to week's end—no, nor at any moment of the day or night. And if the good people that shelter
him are not entirely of his own station, and if he cares to have
but little speech with them, and if the only book in the house
be the family Bible, then the days are like to pass slowly with
him. Can you wonder, sweet Mistress Judith," he continued,
turning his eyes to the ground in a modest manner, "that I
shall carry away the memory of this meeting with you as a
treasure, and dwell on it, and recall the kindness of each word
you have spoken ?"

"In truth, no, good sir," said she, with a touch of color in
her cheeks, that caught the warm golden light shining over
from the west. "I would not have you think them of any
importance, except the hope that matters may go well with
you."

"And if they should," said he, "or if they should go ill,
and if I were to presume to think that you cared to know
them, when I return to Bassfield I might make so bold as to
send you some brief tidings, through your friend Mistress Prudence Shawe, that I am sure must be discreet, since she has
won your confidence. But why should I do so?" he added, after a second. "Why should I trouble you with news of one
whose good or evil fortune can not concern you ?"

"Nay, sir, I wish you well," said she, simply, "and would
fain hear better tidings of your condition. If you may not
come at present to New Place, where you would have better
counsel than I can give you, at least you may remember that
there is one in the household there that will be glad when
she hears of your welfare, and better pleased still when she
learns that you are free to make her father's friendship."

This was clearly a dismissal; and after a few more words of
gratitude on his part (he seemed almost unable to take away
his eyes from her face, or to say all that he would fain say of
thanks for her gracious intervention and sympathy) they parted; and forthwith Judith—now with a much lighter heart, for
this interview had cost her not a little embarrassment and
anxiety—hastened away back through the lane in the direction

of the barns and gardens of Shottery. All these occurrences of the day had happened so rapidly that she had had but little time to reflect over them; but now she was clearly glad that she should be able to talk over the whole affair with Prudence Shawe. There would be comfort in that, and also safety; for, if the truth must be told, that wild and bewildering fancy that perchance the wizard had prophesied truly would force itself on her mind in a disquieting manner. But she strove to reason herself and laugh herself out of such imaginings. She had plenty of courage and a strong will. From the first she had made light of the wizard's pretensions ; she was not going to alarm herself about the possible future consequences of this accidental meeting. And, indeed, when she recalled the particulars of that meeting, she came to think that the circumstances of the young man could not be so very desperate. He did not speak nor look like one in imminent peril; his gay description of the masques and entertainments of the court was not the talk of a man seriously and really in danger of his life. Perhaps he had been in some thoughtless escapade, and was waiting for the bruit of it to blow over; perhaps he was unused to confinement, and may have exaggerated (for this also occurred to her) somewhat in order to win her sympathy. But, anyhow, he was in some kind of misfortune or trouble, and she was sorry for him; and she thought that if Prudence Shawe could see him, and observe how well-bred and civil-spoken and courteous a young gentleman he seemed to be, she, too, would pity the dullness of the life he must be leading at the farm, and be glad to do anything to relieve such a tedium. In truth, by the time Judith was drawing near her grandmother's cottage, she had convinced herself that there was no dark mystery connected with this young man; that she had not been holding converse with any dangerous villain or conspirator; and that soon everything would be cleared up, and perhaps he himself present himself at New Place, with Ben Jonson's letter in his hand. So she was in a cheerful enough frame of mind when she arrived at the cottage.

This was a picturesque little building of brick and timber, with a substantial roof of thatch, and irregularly placed small windows; and it was prettily set in front of a wild and variegated garden, and of course all the golden glow of the west

was now flooding the place with its beautiful light, and causing the little rectangular panes in the open casements to gleam
like jewels. And here, at the wooden gate of the garden, was
Willie Hart, who seemed to have been using the time profitably, for he had a most diverse and sweet-scented gathering of
flowers and herbs of a humble and familiar kind—forget-me-
nots, and pansies, and wall-flower, and mint, and sweet-brier,
and the like—to present to his pretty cousin.

"Well done, sweetheart! and are all these for me?" said
she, as she passed within the little gate, and stood for a moment
arranging and regarding them.   "What, then, what is this?—
what mean you by it, Cousin Willie?"

"By what, Cousin Judith?" said the small boy, looking up
with his wondering and wistful eyes.

"Why," said she, gayly, "this pansy that you have put
fair in the front.   Know you not the name of it?"

"Indeed I know it not, Cousin Judith."

"Ah, you cunning one! well you know it, I'll be sworn!
Why, 'tis one of the chiefest favorites everywhere.   Did you
never hear it called 'kiss-me-at-the-gate'?   Marry, 'tis an excellent name; and if I take you at your word, little sweetheart?"

And so they went into the cottage together; and she had
her arm lying lightly round his neck.

CHAPTER VIII.

A QUARREL.

BUT instantly her manner changed.   Just within the doorway of the passage that cut the rambling cottage into two
halves, and attached to a string that was tied to the handle of
the door, lay a small spaniel-gentle, peacefully snoozing; and
well Judith knew that the owner of the dog (which she had
heard, indeed, was meant to be presented to herself) was inside.   However, there was no retreat possible, if retreat she
would have preferred; for here was the aged grandmother—a
little old woman, with fresh pink cheeks, silver-white hair,
and keen eyes—come out to see if it were Judith's footsteps

"'HERE BE FINERY!' SHE SAID."

she had heard; and she was kindly in her welcome of the girl, though usually she grumbled a good deal about her, and would maintain that it was pure pride and willfulness that kept her from getting married.

"Here be finery!" said she, stepping back as if to gain a fairer view. "God's mercy, wench, have you come to your senses at last?—be you seeking a husband?—would you win one of them? They have waited a goodly time for the bating of your pride; but you must after them at last—ay, ay, I thought 'twould come to that."

"Good grandmother, you give me no friendly welcome," said Judith. "And Willie here; have you no word for him, that he is come to see how you do?"

"Nay, come in, then, sweetings both; come in and sit ye down: little Willie has been in the garden long enough, though you know I grudge you not the flowers, wench. Ay, ay, there is one within, Judith, that would fain be a nearer neighbor, as I hear, if you would but say yea; and bethink ye, wench, an apple may hang too long on the bough—your bravery may be put on to catch the eye when it is overlate—"

"I pray you, good grandmother, forbear," said Judith, with some asperity. "I have my own mind about such things."

"All's well, wench, all's well," said the old dame, as she led the way into the main room of the cottage. It was a wide and spacious apartment, with heavy black beams overhead, a mighty fire-place, here or there a window in the walls just as it seemed to have been wanted, and in the middle of the floor a plain old table, on which were placed a jug and two or three horn tumblers.

Of course Judith knew whom she had to expect: the presence of the little spaniel-gentle at the door had told her that. This young fellow that now quickly rose from his chair and came forward to meet her—"Good-even to you, Judith," said he, in a humble way, and his eyes seemed to beseech her favor —was as yet but in his two-and-twentieth year, but his tall and lithe and muscular figure had already the firm set of manhood on it. He was spare of form and square-shouldered; his head smallish, his brown hair short; his features were regular, and the forehead, if not high, was square and firm; the general look of him was suggestive of a sculptured Greek or Roman wrestler, but that this deprecating glance of the eyes was not quite consistent. And, to tell the truth, wrestling and his firm-sinewed figure had something to do with his extreme humility on this occasion. He was afraid that Judith had heard something. To have broken the head of a tapster was not a noble performance, no matter how the quarrel was forced on him; and this was but the most recent of several squabbles; for the championship in the athletic sports of a country neighborhood is productive of rivals, who may take many ways of provoking anger. "Good-even to you, Judith," said he, as if he really would have said, "Pray you believe not all the ill you hear of me!" Judith, however, did not betray anything by her manner, which was friendly enough in a kind of formal way, and distinctly reserved. She sat down, and asked her grandmother what news she had of the various members of the family, that now were widely scattered throughout Warwickshire. She declined the cup of merry-go-down that the young man civilly offered to her. She had a store of things to tell about her father; and about the presents he had brought; and about the two pieces of song-music that Master Robert Johnson had sent, that her father would have Susan try over on the lute; and the other twenty acres that were to be added; and about the talk there had been of turning the house opposite New Place, at the corner of Chapel Street and Scholars Lane, into a tavern, and how that had happily been abandoned—for her father wanted no tavern-revelry within hearing; and so forth; but all this was addressed to the grandmother. The young man got scarce a word, though now and again he would interpose gently, and, as it were, begging her to look his way. She was far kinder to Willie Hart, who was standing by her side; for sometimes she would put her hand on his shoulder, or stroke his long yellow-brown hair.

"Willie says he will have just such another as I, grandmother," said she, when these topics were exhausted, "to be his sweetheart when he grows up; so you see there be some that value me."

"Look to it that you be not yourself unmarried then, Judith," said the old dame, who was never done grumbling on this account. "I should not marvel; they that refuse when they are sought come in time to wonder that there are none to seek—nay, 'tis so, I warrant you. You are hanging late on the bough, wench; see you be not forgotten."

"But, good grandmother," said Judith, with some color in her cheeks (for this was an awkward topic in the presence of this youth), "would you have me break from the rule of the family? My mother was six-and-twenty when she married, and Susan four-and-twenty; and indeed there might come one of us who did not perceive the necessity of marrying at all."

"In God's name, if that be your mind, wench, hold to it. Hold to it, I say!" And then the old dame glanced with her sharp eyes at the pretty costume of her visitor. "But I had other thoughts when I saw such a fine young madam at the door; in truth, they befit you well, these braveries; indeed they do; though 'tis a pity to have them bedecking out one that is above the marrying trade. But take heed, wench, take heed lest you change your mind when it is too late: the young men may hold you to your word, and you find yourself forsaken when you least expected it."

"Give ye thanks for your good comfort, grandmother," said Judith, indifferently. And then she rose. "Come, Willie, 'tis about time we were going through the fields to the town. What message have you, grandmother, for my father? He is busy from morning till night since his coming home; but I know he will be over to visit you soon. The flowers, Willie—did you leave them on the bench outside?"

But she was not allowed to depart in this fashion. The old dame's discontents with her pretty granddaughter—that was now grown into so fair and blithe a young woman—were never of a lasting nature; and now she would have both Judith and little Willie taste of some gingerbread of her own baking, and then Judith had again to refuse a sup of the ale that stood on the table, preferring a little water instead. Moreover, when they had got out into the garden, behold! this young man would come also, to convoy them home on their way across the fields. It was a gracious evening, sweet and cool; there was a clear twilight shining over the land; the elms were dark against the palely luminous sky. And then, as the three of them went across the meadows toward Stratford town, little Willie Hart was intrusted with the care of the spaniel-gentle—that was young and wayward, and possessed with a mad purpose of hunting sparrows—and as the dog kept him running this way and that, he was mostly at some distance from these other two, and Judith's companion, young Quiney, had every opportunity of speaking with her.

"I sent you a message, Judith," said he, rather timidly, but anxiously watching the expression of her face all the time, "a token of remembrance: I trust it did not displease you?"

"You should have considered through whose hands it would come," said she, but without regarding him.

"How so?" he asked, in some surprise.

"Why, you knew that Prudence would have to read it."

"And why not, Judith? Why should she not? She is your friend; and I care not who is made aware that—that—well, you know what I mean, dear Judith, but I fear to anger you by saying it. You were not always so hard to please."

There was a touch of reproach in this that she did not like. Besides, was it fair? Of course she had been kinder to him when he was a mere stripling—when they were boy and girl together; but now he had put forth other pretensions; and they stood on a quite different footing; and in his pertinacity he would not understand why she was always speaking to him of Prudence Shawe, and extolling her gentleness and sweet calm wisdom and goodness. "The idle boy!" she would say to herself; "why did God give him such a foolish head that he must needs come fancying me?" And sometimes she was angry because of his dullness and that he would not see; though, indeed, she could not speak quite plainly.

"You should think," said she, on this occasion, with some sharpness, "that these idle verses that you send me are read by Prudence. Well, doubtless, she may not heed that—"

"Why should she heed, Judith?" said he. "'Tis but an innocent part she takes in the matter—a kindness, merely."

She dared not say more, and she was vexed with him for putting this restraint upon her. She turned upon him with a glance of sudden and rather unfriendly scrutiny.

"What is this now that I hear of you?" said she. "Another brawl! A tavern brawl! I marvel you have escaped so long with a whole skin."

"I know not who carries tales of me to you, Judith," said he, quite warmly, "but if you yourself were more friendly you would take care to choose a more friendly messenger. It is always the worst that you hear. If there was a brawl, it was none of my seeking. And if my skin is whole, I thank God I can look after that for myself; I am not one that will be smitten on one cheek and turn the other—like your parson friend."

This did not mend matters much.

"My parson friend?" said she, with some swift color in her cheeks. "My parson friend is one that has respect for his office, and has a care for his reputation, and lives a peaceable, holy life. Would you have him frequent ale-houses, and fight with drawers and tapsters? Marry and amen! but I find no fault with the parson's life."

"Nay, that is true, indeed," said he, bitterly: "you can find no fault in the parson—as every one says. But there are others who see with other eyes, and would tell you in what he might amend—"

"I care not to know," said she.

"It were not amiss," said he, for he was determined to speak—"it were not amiss if Sir Parson showed a little more honesty in his daily walk—that were not amiss, for one thing."

"In what is he dishonest, then?" said she, instantly, and she turned and faced him with indignant eyes.

Well, he did not quail. His blood was up. This championship of the parson, that he had scarce expected of her, only fired anew certain secret suspicions of his; and he had no mind to spare his rival, whether he were absent or no.

"Why, then, does he miscall the King, and eat the King's bread?" said he, somewhat hotly. "Is it honest to conform in public, and revile in private? I say, let him go forth, as others have been driven forth, if the state of affairs content him not. I say that they who speak against the King—marry, it were well done to chop the rogues' ears off!—I say they should be ashamed to eat the King's bread."

"He eats no King's bread!" said Judith—and alas! her eyes had a look in them that pierced him to the heart: it was not the glance he would fain have met with there. "He eats the bread of the Church, that has been despoiled of its possessions again and again by the Crown and the lords; and why should he go forth? He is a minister: is there harm that he should

wish to see the services reformed? He is at his post; would
you have him desert it, or else keep silent? No, he is no such
coward, I warrant you. He will speak his mind; it were ill
done of him else!"

"Nay, he can do no harm at all—in your judgment," said
he, somewhat sullenly, "if all be true that they say."

"And who is it, then, that should speak of idle tales and the
believing of them?" said she, with indignant reproach. "You
say I welcome evil stories about you? And you? Are you so
quick to put away the idle gossip they bring you about me?
Would you not rather believe it? I trow you would as lief believe it as not. That it is to have friends! That it is to have
those who should defend you in your absence; but would rather listen to slander against you! But when they speak about
women's idle tongues, they know little; it is men who are the
readiest to listen, and to carry evil report and lying!"

"I meant not to anger you, Judith," said he, more humbly.

"Yes, but you have angered me," said she (with her lips becoming tremulous, but only for a second). "What concern
have I with Parson Blaise? I would they that speak against
him were as good men and honest as he—"

"Indeed, they speak no ill of him, Judith," said he (for he
was grieved that they were fallen out so, and there was nothing he would not have retracted that so he might win back
to her favor again, in however small a degree), "except that
he is disputatious, and would lead matters no one knows whither. 'Tis but a few minutes ago that your grandmother there
was saying that we should never have peace and quiet in
Church affairs till the old faith was restored—"

Here, indeed, she pricked up her ears; but she would say no
more. She had not forgiven him yet; and she was proud and
silent.

"And though I do not hold with that—for there would be a
bloody struggle before the Pope could be master in England
again—nevertheless, I would have the ministers men of peace,
as they profess to be, and loyal to the King, who is at the
head of the Church as well as of the realm. However, let it
pass. I wish to have no quarrel with you, Judith."

"How does your business?" said she, abruptly changing the
subject.

"Well—excellently well; it is not in that direction that I have any anxiety about the future."

"Do you give it your time? You were best take heed, for else it is like to slip away from you," she said; and he thought she spoke rather coldly, and as if her warning were meant to convey something more than appeared.

And then she added:

"You were at Wilmecote on Tuesday?"

"You must have heard why, Judith," he said. "Old Pike was married again that day, and they would have me over to his wedding."

"And on the Wednesday, what was there at Bidford, then, that you must needs be gone when my mother sent to you?"

"At Bidford?" said he (and he was sorely puzzled as to whether he should rejoice at these questions as betraying a friendly interest in his affairs, or rather regard them as conveying covert reproof, and expressing her dissatisfaction with him, and distrust of him). "At Bidford, Judith—well, there was business as well as pleasure there. For you must know that Daniel Hutt is come home for a space from the new settlements in Virginia, and is for taking back with him a number of laborers that are all in due time to make their fortunes there. Marry, 'tis a good chance for some of them, for broken men are as welcome as any, and there are no questions asked as to their having been intimate with the constable and the justice. So there was a kind of merry-meeting of Daniel's old friends, that was held at the Falcon at Bidford—and the host is a good customer of mine, so it was prudent of me to go thither —and right pleasant was it to hear Daniel Hutt tell of his adventures by sea and shore. And he gave us some of the tobacco that he had brought with him. And to any that will go back with him to Jamestown he promises allotments of land, though at first there will be tough labor, as he says, honestly. Oh, a worthy man is this Daniel Hutt, though as yet his own fortune seems not so secure."

"With such junketings," said she, with ever so slight a touch of coldness, "'tis no wonder you could not spare the time to come and see my father on the evening of his getting home."

"There, now, Judith!" he exclaimed. "Would you have me break in upon him at such a busy season, when even you yourselves are careful to refrain? It had been ill-mannered of me to do such a thing; but 'twas no heedlessness that led to my keeping away, as you may well imagine."

"It is difficult to know the reasons when friends hold aloof," said she. "You have not been near the house for two or three weeks, as I reckon."

And here again he would have given much to know whether her speech—which was curiously reserved in tone—meant that she had marked these things out of regard for him, or that she wished to reprove him.

"I can give you the reasons for that, Judith," said this tall and straight young fellow, who from time to time regarded his companion's face with some solicitude, as if he fain would have found some greater measure of friendliness there. "I have not been often to New Place of late because of one I thought I might meet there who would be no better pleased to see me than I him; and—and perhaps because of another— that I did not know whether she might be the better pleased to have me there or find me stay away—"

"Your reasons are too fine," said she. "I scarce understand them."

"That is because you won't understand; I think I have spoken plain enough ere now, Judith, I make bold to say."

She flushed somewhat at this; but it was no longer in anger. She seemed willing to be on good terms with him, but always in that measured and distant way.

"Willie!" she called. "Come hither, sweetheart!"

With some difficulty her small cousin made his way back to her, dragging the reluctant spaniel so that its head seemed to be in jeopardy.

"He *will* go after the birds, Cousin Judith; you will never teach him to follow you."

"I?" she said.

"Willie knows I want you to have the dog, Judith," her companion said, quickly. "I got him for you when I was at Gloucester. 'Tis a good breed—true Maltese, I can warrant him; and the fashionable ladies will scarce stir abroad without one to follow them, or to carry with them in their coaches when they ride. Will you take him, Judith?"

She was a little embarrassed.

"'Tis a pretty present," said she, "but you have not chosen the right one to give it to."

"What mean you?" said he.

"Nay, now, have not I the Don?" she said, with greater courage. "He is a sufficient companion if I wish to walk abroad. Why should you not give this little spaniel to one that has no such companion—I mean to Prudence Shawe?"

"To Prudence!" said he, regarding her; for this second introduction of Judith's friend seemed strange, as well as the notion that he should transfer this prized gift to her.

"There, now, is one so gentle and kind to every one and everything that she would tend the little creature with care," she continued. "It would be more fitting for her than for me."

"You could be kind enough, Judith—if you chose," said he, under his breath, for Willie Hart was standing by.

"Nay, I have the Don," said she, "that is large, and worldly, and serious, and clumsy withal. Give this little playfellow to Prudence, who is small and neat and gentle like itself; surely that were fitter."

"I had hoped you would have accepted the little spaniel from me, Judith," said he, with very obvious disappointment.

"Moreover," said she, lightly, "two of a trade would never agree: we should have this one and the Don continually quarrelling, and sooner or later the small one would lose its head in the Don's great jaws."

"Why, the mastiff is always chained, and at the barn gate, Judith," said he. "This one would be within-doors, as your playfellow. But I care not to press a gift."

"Nay, now, be not displeased," said she, gently enough. "I am not unthankful; I think well of your kindness; but it were still better done if you were to change your intention and give the spaniel to one that would have a gentler charge over it, and think none the less of it, as I can vouch for. Pray you give it to Prudence."

"A discarded gift is not worth the passing on," said he; and as they were now come quite near to the town, where there was a dividing of ways, he stopped as though he would shake hands and depart.

"Will you not go on to the house? You have not seen my father since his coming home," she said.

"No, not to-night, Judith," he said. "Doubtless he is still busy, and I have affairs elsewhere."

She glanced at him with one of those swift keen glances of hers.

"Where go you to spend the evening, if I may make so bold?" she said.

"Not at the ale-house, as you seem to suspect," he answered, with just a trifle of bitterness; and then he took the string to lead away the spaniel, and bade her farewell—in a kind of half-hearted and disappointed and downcast way—and left.

She looked after him for a second or so, as she fastened a glove-button that had got loose. And then she sighed as she turned away.

"Sweetheart Willie," said she, putting her hand softly on the boy's shoulder, as he walked beside her, "I think you said you loved me?"

"Why, you know I do, Cousin Judith," said he.

"What a pity it is, then," said she, absently, "that you can not remain always as you are, and keep your ten years forever and a day, so that we should always be friends as we are now!"

He did not quite know what she meant, but he was sufficiently well pleased and contented when he was thus close by her side; and when her hand was on his shoulder or on his neck it was to him no burden, but a delight. And so walking together, and with some gay and careless prattle between them, they went on and into the town.

CHAPTER IX.

THROUGH THE MEADOWS.

SOME two or three days after that, and toward the evening, Prudence Shawe was in the church-yard, and she was alone, save that now and again some one might pass along the gravelled pathway, and these did not stay to interrupt her. She had with her a basket, partly filled with flowers, also a small rake and a pair of gardener's shears, and she was engaged in going from grave to grave, here putting a few fresh blossoms to replace the withered ones, and there removing weeds, or cutting the grass smooth, and generally tending those last resting-places with a patient and loving care. It was a favorite employment with her when she had a spare afternoon; nor did she limit her attention to the graves of those whom she had known in life; her charge was a general one, and when they who had friends or relatives buried there came to the church of a Sunday morning, and perhaps from some distance, and when they saw that some gentle hand had been employed there in the interval, they knew right well that that hand was the hand of Prudence Shawe. It was a strange fancy on the part of one who was so averse from all ornament or decoration in ordinary life that nothing was too beautiful for a grave. She herself would not wear a flower, but her best, and the best she could beg or borrow anywhere, she freely gave to those that were gone away; she seemed to have some vague imagination that our poor human nature was not worthy of this beautifying care until it had become sanctified by the sad mystery of death.

It was a calm, golden-white evening, peaceful and silent; the rooks were cawing in the dark elms above her; the swallows dipping and darting under the boughs; the smooth-flowing yellow river was like glass, save that now and again the perfect surface was broken by the rising of a fish. Over there in the wide meadows beyond the stream a number of boys were playing at rounders, or prisoner's-base, or some such noisy game; but the sound of their shouting was softened by the dis-

4

tance; so quiet was it here, as she continued at her pious task, that she might almost have heard herself breathing. And once or twice she looked up, and glanced toward the little gate as if expecting some one.

It was Judith, of course, that she was expecting; and at this moment Judith was coming along to the church-yard to seek her out. What a contrast there was between these two—this one pale and gentle and sad-eyed, stooping over the mute graves in the shadow of the elms; that other coming along through the warm evening light with all her usual audacity of gait, the peach-bloom of health on her cheek, carelessness and content in her clear-shining eyes, and the tune of "Green Sleeves" ringing through a perfectly idle brain. Indeed, what part of her brain may not have been perfectly idle was bent solely on mischief. Prudence had been away for two or three days, staying with an ailing sister. All that story of the adventure with the unfortunate young gentleman had still to be related to her. And again and again Judith had pictured to herself Prudence's alarm and the look of her timid eyes when she should hear of such doings, and had resolved that the tale would lose nothing in the telling. Here, indeed, was something for two country maidens to talk about. The even current of their lives was broken but by few surprises; but here was something more than a surprise—something with suggestions of mystery and even danger behind it. This was no mere going out to meet a wizard. Any farm wench might have an experience of that kind; any plough-boy, deluded by the hope of digging up silver in one of his master's fields. But a gentleman in hiding—one that had been at court—one that had seen the King sitting in his chair of state, while Ben Jonson's masque was opened out before the great and noble assemblage—this was one to speak about, truly, one whose fortunes and circumstances were like to prove a matter of endless speculation and curiosity.

But when Judith drew near to the little gate of the church-yard, and saw how Prudence was occupied, her heart smote her.

> *Green sleeves was all my joy,*
> *Green sleeves was my delight,*

went clean out of her head. There was a kind of shame on

her face; and when she went along to her friend she could not help exclaiming, "How good you are, Prue!"

"I?" said the other, with some touch of wonder in the upturned face. "I fear that can not be said of any of us, Judith."

"I would I were like you, sweetheart," was the answer, with a bit of a sigh.

"Like me, Judith?" said Prudence, returning to her task (which was nearly ended now, for she had but few more flowers left). "Nay, what makes you think that? I wish I were far other than I am."

"Look, now," Judith said, "how you are occupied at this moment. Is there another in Stratford that has such a general kindness? How many would think of employing their time so?—how many would come away from their own affairs—"

"It may be I have more idle time than many," said Prudence, with a slight flush. "But I commend not myself for this work; in truth, no; 'tis but a pastime; 'tis for my own pleasure."

"Indeed, then, good Prue, you are mistaken, and that I know well," said the other, peremptorily. "Your own pleasure? Is it no pleasure, then, think you, for them that come from time to time, and are right glad to see that some one has been tending the graves of their friends or kinsmen? And do you think, now, it is no pleasure to the poor people themselves—I mean them that are gone—to look at you as you are engaged so, and to think that they are not quite forgotten? Surely it must be a pleasure to them. Surely they can not have lost all their interest in what happens here—in Stratford—where they lived; and surely they must be grateful to you for thinking of them, and doing them this kindness? I say it were ill done of them else. I say they ought to be thankful to you. And no doubt they are, could we but learn."

"Judith! Judith! you have such a bold way of regarding what is all a mystery to us," said her gentle-eyed friend. "Sometimes you frighten me."

"I would I knew, now," said the other, looking absently across the river to the boys that were playing there, "whether my little brother Hamnet—had you known him you would have loved him as I did, Prudence—I say I wish I knew whether he is quite happy and content where he is, or whether he would not rather be over there now with the other boys. If he looks down and sees them, may it not make him sad sometimes—to be so far away from us? I always think of him as being alone there, and he was never alone here. I suppose he thinks of us sometimes. Whenever I hear the boys shouting like that at their play I think of him; but indeed he was never noisy and unruly. My father used to call him the girl-boy; but he was fonder of him than of all us others; he once came all the way from London when he heard that Hamnet was lying sick of a fever."

She turned to see how Prudence was getting on with her work; but she was in no hurry; and Prudence was patient and scrupulously careful; and the dead, had they been able to speak, would not have bade her cease and go away, for a gentler hand never touched a grave.

"I suppose it is Grandmother Hathaway who will go next," Judith continued, in the same absent kind of way; "but indeed she says she is right well content either to go or to stay; for now, as she says, she has about as many kinsfolk there as here, and she will not be going among strangers. And well I know she will make for Hamnet as soon as she is there, for like my father's love for Bess Hall was her love for the boy while he was with us. Tell me, Prudence, has he grown up to be of my age? You know we were twins. Is he a man now, so that we should see him as some one different? Or is he still our little Hamnet, just as we used to know him?"

"How can I tell you, Judith?" the other said, almost in pain. "You ask such bold questions; and all these things are hidden from us and behind a veil."

"But these are what one would like to know," said Judith, with a sigh. "Nay, if you could but tell me of such things, then you might persuade me to have a greater regard for the preachers; but when you come and ask about such real things, they say it is all a mystery; they can not tell; and would have you be anxious about schemes of doctrine, which are but strings of words. My father, too: when I go to him—nay, but it is many a day since I tried—he would look at me and say, 'What is in your brain now? To your needle, wench, to your needle!'"

"But naturally, Judith! Such things are mercifully hidden from us now, but they will be revealed when it is fitting for us to know them. How could our ordinary life be possible if we knew what was going on in the other world? We should have no interest in the things around us, the greater interest would be so great."

"Well, well, well," said Judith, coming with more practical eyes to the present moment, "are you finished, sweet mouse, and will you come away? What, not satisfied yet? I wonder if they know the care you take? I wonder if one will say to the other: 'Come and see. She is there again. We are not quite forgotten.' And will you do that for me, too, sweet Prue? Will you put some pansies on my grave, too?—and I know you will say out of your charity, 'Well, she was not good and pious, as I would have had her to be; she had plenty of faults; but at least she often wished to be better than she was.' Nay, I forgot," she added, glancing carelessly over to the church; "they say we shall lie among the great people, since my father bought the tithes—that we have the right to be buried in the chancel; but indeed I know I would a hundred times liefer have my grave in the open here, among the grass and the trees."

"You are too young to have such thoughts as these, Judith," said her companion, as she rose and shut down the lid of the now empty basket. "Come; shall we go?"

"Let us cross the foot-bridge, sweet Prue," Judith said, "and go through the meadows, and round by Clopton's bridge, and so home; for I have that to tell you will take some time: pray Heaven it startle you not out of your senses withal!"

It was not, however, until they had got away from the church-yard, and were out in the clear golden light of the open, that she began to tell her story. She had linked her arm within that of her friend. Her manner was grave; and if there was any mischief in her eyes, it was of a demure kind, not easily detected. She confessed that it was out of mere wanton folly that she had gone to the spot indicated by the wizard, and without any very definite hope or belief. But as chance would have it, she did encounter a stranger—one, indeed, that was coming to her father's house. Then followed a complete and minute narrative of what the young man had said—the glimpses he had given her of his present condition, both on the occasion of that meeting and on the subsequent one, and how she had obtained his permission to state these things to this gentle gossip of hers. Prudence listened in silence, her eyes cast down; Judith could not see the gathering concern on her face. Nay, the latter spoke rather in a tone of raillery; for, having had time to look back over the young gentleman's confessions, and his manner, and so forth, she had arrived at a kind of assurance that he was in no such desperate case. There were many reasons why a young man might wish to lie perdu for a time; but this one had not talked as if any very imminent danger threatened him; at least, if he had intimated as much, the impression produced upon her was not permanent. And if Judith now told the story with a sort of careless bravado—as if going forth in secret to meet this stranger was a thing of risk and hazard—it was with no private conviction that there was any particular peril in the matter, but rather with the vague fancy that the adventure looked daring and romantic, and would appear as something terrible in the eyes of her timid friend.

But what now happened startled her. They were going up the steps of the foot-bridge, Prudence first, and Judith, following her, had just got to the end of her story. Prudence suddenly turned round, and her face, now opposed to the westering light, was, as Judith instantly saw, quite aghast.

"But, Judith, you do not seem to understand!" she exclaimed. "Was not that the very stranger the wizard said you would meet?—the very hour, the very place? In good truth, it must have been so! Judith, what manner of man have you been in company with?"

For an instant a flush of color overspread Judith's face, and she said, with a sort of embarrassed laugh:

"Well, and if it were so, sweet mouse? If that were the appointed one, what then?"

She was on the bridge now. Prudence caught her by both hands, and there was an anxious and piteous appeal in the loving eyes.

"Dear Judith, I beseech you, be warned! Have nothing to do with the man! Did I not say that mischief would come of planting the charm in the church-yard, and shaming a sacred place with such heathenish magic? And now look already—

"THERE WAS AN ANXIOUS AND PITYING APPEAL IN THE LOVING EYES."

here is one that you dare not speak of to your own people; he is in secret correspondence with you. Heaven alone knows what dark deeds he may be bent upon, or what ruin he may bring upon you and yours. Judith, you are light-hearted and daring, and you love to be venturesome; but I know you better than you know yourself, sweetheart. You would not willingly do wrong, or bring harm on those that love you; and for the sake of all of us, Judith, have nothing to do with this man."

Judith was embarrassed, and perhaps a trifle remorseful; she had not expected her friend to take this adventure so very seriously.

"Dear Prue, you alarm yourself without reason," she said (but there was still some tell-tale color in her face). "Indeed, there is no magic or witchery about the young man. Had I seen a ghost, I should have been frightened, no doubt, for all that Don Roderigo was with me; and had I met one of the Stratford youths at the appointed place, I should have said that perhaps the good wizard had guessed well; but this was merely a stranger coming to see my father; and the chance that brought us together—well, what magic was in that?—it would have happened to you had you been walking in the lane: do you see that, dear mouse?—it would have happened to yourself had you been walking in the lane, and he would have asked of you the question that he asked of me. Nay, banish that fancy, sweet Prue, else I should be ashamed to do anything further for the young man that is unfortunate, and very grateful withal for a few words of friendliness. And so fairly spoken a young man, too; and so courtly in his bearing; and of such a handsome presence—"

"But, dear Judith, listen to me!—do not be led into such peril! Know you not that evil spirits can assume goodly shapes—the Prince of Darkness himself—"

She could not finish what she had to say, her imagination was so filled with terror.

"Sweet Puritan," said Judith, with a smile, "I know well that he goeth about like a raging lion, seeking whom he may devour; I know it well; but believe me it would not be worth his travail to haunt such a lonely and useless place as the lane that goes from Shottery to the Bidford road. Nay, but I will convince you, good mouse, by the best of all evidence, that there is nothing ghostly or evil about the young man; you shall see him, Prue—indeed you must and shall. When that he comes back to his hiding, I will contrive that you shall see him and have speech with him, and sure you will pity him as much as I do. Poor young gentleman, that he should be suspected of being Satan! Nay, how could he be Satan, Prue, and be admitted to the King's court? Hath not our good King a powerful insight into the doings of witches and wizards and the like? and think you he would allow Satan in person to come into the very Banqueting-hall to see a masque?"

"Judith! Judith!" said the other, piteously, "when you strive against me with your wit, I can not answer you; but my heart tells me that you are in exceeding danger. I would warn you, dear cousin; I were no true friend to you else."

"But you are the best and truest of friends, you dearest Prue," said Judith, lightly, as she released her hands from her companion's earnest grasp. "Come, let us on, or we shall go supperless for the evening."

She passed along and over the narrow bridge, and down the steps on the other side. She did not seem much impressed by Prudence's entreaties; indeed, she was singing aloud:

> *Hey, good fellow, I drink to thee,*
> *Pardonnez moi, je vous en prie;*
> *To all good fellows, where'er they be,*
> *With never a penny of money!*

Prudence overtook her.

"Judith," said she, "even if he be not of that fearful kind —even if he be a real man, and such as he represents himself, bethink you what you are doing! There may be another such gathering as that at Dunchurch; and would you be in correspondence with a plotter and murderer? Nay, what was't you asked of me the other day?" she added, suddenly; and she stood still to confront her friend, with a new alarm in her eyes. "Did you not ask whether your father was well affected toward the Papists? Is there another plot?—another treason against the King?—and you would harbor one connected with such a wicked, godless, and blood-thirsty plan?"

"Nay, nay, sweet mouse! Have I not told you? He declares he has naught to do with any such enterprise; and if

you would but see him, Prudence, you would believe him.
Sure I am that you would believe him instantly. Why, now,
there be many reasons why a young gentleman might wish to
remain concealed—"

"None, Judith, none!" the other said, with decision.
"Why should an honest man fear the daylight?"

"Oh, as for that," was the careless answer, "there be many
an honest man that has got into the clutches of the twelve-in-
the-hundred rogues; and when the writs are out against such
a one, I hold it no shame that he would rather be out of the
way than be thrown among the wretches in Bocardo. I know
well what I speak of; many a time have I heard my father
and your brother talk of it; how the rogues of usurers will
keep a man in prison for twelve years for a matter of sixteen
shillings—what is it they call it?—making dice of his bones?
And if the young gentleman fear such treatment and the horrible company of the prisons, I marvel not that he should prefer
the fresh air of Bidford, howsoever dull the life at the farm
may be."

"And if that were all, why should he fear to bring the letter
to your father?" the other said, with a quick glance of suspicion: she did not like the way in which Judith's ready brain
could furnish forth such plausible conjectures and excuses.
"Answer me that, Judith. Is your father one likely to call
aloud and have the man taken, if that be all that is against
him? Why should he be afraid to bring the letter from your
father's friend? Nay, why should he be on the way to. the
house with it, and thereafter stop short and change his mind?
There is many a mile betwixt London and Stratford; 'tis a
marvellous thing he should travel all that way, and change
his mind within a few minutes of being in the town. I love
not such dark ways, Judith; no good thing can come of them,
but evil; and it were ill done of you—even if you be careless of
danger to yourself, as I trow you mostly are—I say it is ill
done of you to risk the peace of your family by holding such
dangerous converse with a stranger, and one that may bring
harm to us all."

Judith was not well pleased; her mouth became rather proud.

"Marry, if this be your Christian charity, I would not give
a penny ballad for it!" said she, with some bitterness of tone.

4*

"I had thought the story had another teaching—I mean the story of him that fell among thieves and was beaten and robbed and left for dead—and that we were to give a helping hand to such, like the Samaritan. But now I mind me 'twas the Priest that passed by on the other side—yes, the Priest and the Levite—the godly ones who would preserve a whole skin for themselves, and let the other die of his wounds, for aught they cared! And here is a young man in distress—alone and friendless—and when he would have a few words of cheerfulness, or a message, or a scrap of news as to what is going on in the world—no, no, say the Priest and the Levite—go not near him—because he is in misfortune he is dangerous—because he is alone he is a thief and a murderer—perchance a pirate, like Captain Ward and Dansekar, or even Catesby himself come alive again. I say, God keep us all from such Christian charity!"

"You use me ill, Judith," said the other, and then was silent.

They walked on through the meadows, and Judith was watching the play of the boys. As she did so, a leather ball, struck a surprising distance, came rolling almost to her feet, and forthwith one of the lads came running after it. She picked it up and threw it to him—threw it awkwardly and clumsily, as a girl throws, but nevertheless she saved him some distance and time, and she was rewarded with many a loud "Thank you! thank you!" from the side who were out. But when they got past the players and their noise, Prudence could no longer keep silent; she had a forgiving disposition, and nothing distressed her so much as being on unfriendly terms with Judith.

"You know I meant not that, dear Judith," said she. "I only meant to shield you from harm."

As for Judith, all such trivial and temporary clouds of misunderstanding were instantly swallowed up in the warm and radiant sunniness of her nature. She broke into a laugh.

"And so you shall, dear mouse," said she, gayly; "you shall shield me from the reproach of not having a common and ordinary share of humanity; that shall you, dear Prue, should the unfortunate young gentleman come into the neighborhood again; for you will read to me the message that he sends me, and together we will devise somewhat on his behalf. No? Are you afraid to go forth and meet the pirate Dansekar? Do you expect to find the ghost of Gamaliel Ratsey walking on the Evesham road? Such silly fears, dear Prue, do not become you: you are no longer a child."

"You are laying too heavy a burden on me, Judith," the other said, rather sadly. "I know not what to do; and you say I may not ask counsel of any one. And if I do nothing, I am still taking a part."

"What part, then, but to read a few words and hold your peace?" said her companion, lightly. "What is that? But I know you will not stay there, sweet mouse. No, no; your heart is too tender. I know you would not willingly do any one an injury, or harbor suspicion and slander. You shall come and see the young gentleman, good Prue, as I say; and then you will repent in sackcloth and ashes for all that you have urged against him. And perchance it may be in New Place that you shall see him—"

"Ah, Judith, that were well!" exclaimed the other, with a brighter light on her face.

"What? Would you desire to see him, if he were to pay us a visit?" Judith said, regarding her with a smile.

"Surely, surely, after what you have told me: why not, Judith?" was the placid answer.

"There would be nothing ghostly about him then?"

"There would be no secret, Judith," said Prudence, gravely, "that you have to keep back from your own people."

"Well, well, we will see what the future holds for us," said Judith, in the same careless fashion. "And if the young gentleman come not back to Stratford, why, then, good fortune attend him, wherever he may be! for one that speaks so fair and is so modest sure deserves it. And if he come not back, then shall your heart be all the lighter, dear Prue; and as for mine, mine will not be troubled—only, that I wish him well, as I say, and would fain hear of his better estate. So all is so far happily settled, sweet mouse; and you may go in to supper with me with untroubled eyes and a free conscience: marry, there is need for that, as I bethink me; for Master Parson comes this evening, and you know you must have a pure and joyful heart with you, good Prudence, when you enter into the congregation of the saints."

" Judith, for my sake !"

"Nay, I meant not to offend, truly; it was my wicked, idle tongue, that I must clap a bridle on now—for, listen!—"

They were come to New Place. There was singing going forward within; and one or two of the casements were open; but perhaps it was the glad and confident nature of the psalm that led to the words being so clearly heard without:

> *The man is blest that hath not bent*
> *To wicked rede his ear ;*
> *Nor led his life as sinners do,*
> *Nor sat in scorner's chair.*
> *But in the law of God the Lord*
> *Doth set his whole delight,*
> *And in that law doth exercise*
> *Himself both day and night.*
>
> *He shall be like the tree that groweth*
> *Fast by the river's side ;*
> *Which bringeth forth most pleasant fruit*
> *In her due time and tide ;*
> *Whose leaf shall never fade nor fall,*
> *But flourish still and stand :*
> *Even so all things shall prosper well*
> *That this man takes in hand.*

And so, having waited until the singing ceased, they entered into the house, and found two or three neighbors assembled there, and Master Walter was just about to begin his discourse on the godly life, and the substantial comfort and sweet peace of mind pertaining thereto.

Some few days after this, and toward the hour of noon, the mail-bearer came riding post-haste into the town; and in due course the contents of his saddle-bags were distributed among the folk entitled to them. But before the news-letters had been carefully spelled out to the end, a strange rumor got abroad. The French king was slain, and by the hand of an assassin. Some, as the tidings passed quickly from mouth to mouth, said the murderer was named Ravelok, others Havelok; but as to the main fact of the fearful crime having been committed, there was no manner of doubt. Naturally the bruit of this affair presently reached Julius Shawe's house; and when the timid Prudence heard of it—and when she thought of the man who had been in hiding, and who had talked with Judith, and had been so suddenly and secretly summoned away—her face grew even paler than its wont, and there was a sickly dread at her heart. She would go to see Judith at once; and yet she scarcely dared to breathe even to herself the terrible forebodings that were crowding in on her mind.

CHAPTER X.
A PLAY-HOUSE.

But Judith laughed aside these foolish fears; as it happened, far more important matters were just at this moment occupying her mind.

She was in the garden. She had brought out some after-dinner fragments for the Don; and while the great dun-colored beast devoured these, she had turned from him to regard Matthew gardener; and there was a sullen resentment on her face; for it seemed to her imagination that he kept doggedly and persistently near the summer-house, on which she had certain dark designs. However, the instant she caught sight of Prudence, her eyes brightened up; and, indeed, became full of an eager animation.

"Hither, hither, good Prue!" she exclaimed, hurriedly. "Quick! quick! I have news for you."

"Yes, indeed, Judith," said the other; and at the same moment Judith came to see there was something wrong—the startled pale face and frightened eyes had a story to tell.

"Why, what is to do?" said she.

"Know you not, Judith? Have you not heard? The French king is slain—is murdered by an assassin!"

To her astonishment the news seemed to produce no effect whatever.

"Well, I am sorry for the poor man," Judith said, with perfect self-possession. "They that climb high must sometimes have a sudden fall. But why should that alarm you, good Prue? Or have you other news that comes more nearly home?"

And then, when Prudence almost breathlessly revealed the

apprehensions that had so suddenly filled her mind, Judith
would not even stay to discuss such a monstrous possibility.
She laughed it aside altogether. That the courteous young
gentleman who had come with a letter from Ben Jonson should
be concerned in the assassination of the King of France was
entirely absurd and out of the question.

"Nay, nay, good Prue," said she, lightly, "you shall make
him amends for these unjust suspicions; that you shall, dear
mouse, all in good time. But listen now: I have weightier
matters; I have eggs on the spit, beshrew me else! Can you
read me this riddle, sweet Prue? Know you by these tokens
what has happened? My father comes in to dinner to-day in
the gayest of humors; there is no absent staring at the window,
and forgetting of all of us; it is all merriment this time; and
he must needs have Bess Hall to sit beside him; and he would
charge her with being a witch; and reproach her for our simple meal, when that she might have given us a banquet like
that of a London Company, with French dishes and silver
flagons of Theologicum, and a memorial to tell each of us
what was coming. And then he would miscall your brother—
which you know, dear Prudence, he never would do were he in
earnest—and said he was chamberlain now, and was conspiring
to be made alderman, only that he might sell building materi-
als to the Corporation and so make money out of his office.
And I know not what else of jests and laughing; but at length
he sent to have the Evesham roan saddled; and he said that
when once he had gone along to the sheep-wash to see that the
hurdles were rightly up for the shearing, he would give all the
rest of the day to idleness—to idleness wholly; and perchance
he might ride over to Broadway to see the shooting-match going forward there. Now, you wise one, can you guess what
has happened? Know you what is in store for us? Can you
read me the riddle?"

"I see no riddle, Judith," said the other, with puzzled eyes.
"I met your father as I came through the house; and he asked
if Julius were at home: doubtless he would have him ride
to Broadway with him."

"Dear mouse, is that your skill at guessing? But listen
now"—and here she dropped her voice as she regarded goodman Matthew, though that personage seemed busily enough oc-

cupied with his watering-can. "This is what has happened: I know the signs of the weather. Be sure he has finished the play—the play that the young prince Mamillius was in: you remember, good Prue?—and the large fair copy is made out and locked away in the little cupboard, against my father's next going to London; and the loose sheets are thrown into the oak chest, along with the others. And now, good Prue, sweet Prue, do you know what you must manage? Indeed, I dare not go near the summer-house while that ancient wiseman is loitering about; and you must coax him, Prue; you must get him away; sometimes I see his villain eyes watching me, as if he had suspicion in his mind—"

"'Tis your own guilty conscience, Judith," said Prudence, but with a smile; for she had herself connived at this offense ere now.

"By fair means or foul, sweet mouse, you must get him away to the other end of the garden," said she, eagerly; "for now the Don has nearly finished his dinner, and goodman-wiseman-fool will wonder if we stay longer here. Nay, I have it, sweet Prue: you must get him along to the corner where my mother grows her simples; and you must keep him there for a space, that I may get out the right papers; and this is what you must do: you will ask him for something that sounds like Latin—no matter what nonsense it may be; and he will answer you that he knows it right well, but has none of it at the present time; and you will say that you have surely seen it among my mother's simples, and thus you will lead him away to find it, and the longer you seek the better. Do you understand, good Prue?—and quick! quick!"

Prudence's pale face flushed.

"You ask too much, Judith. I can not deceive the poor man so."

"Nay, nay, you are too scrupulous, dear mouse. A trifle—a mere trifle."

And then Prudence happened to look up, and she met Judith's eyes; and there was such frank self-confidence and audacity in them, and also such a singular and clear-shining beauty, that the simple Puritan was in a manner bedazzled. She said, with a quiet smile, as she turned away her head again:

"Well, I marvel not, Judith, that you can bewitch the

young men, and bewilder their understanding. 'Tis easy to
see—if they have eyes and regard you, they are lost; but how
you have your own way with all of us, and how you override
our judgment, and do with us what you please, that passes me.
Even Dr. Hall: for whom else would he have brought from
Coventry the green silk stockings and green velvet shoes?—you
know such vanities find little favor in his own home—"

"Quick, quick, sweetheart, muzzle me that gaping ancient!"
said Judith, interrupting her. "The Don has finished; and I
will dart into the summer-house as I carry back the dish. Detain him, sweet Prue; speak a word or two of Latin to him; he
will swear he understands you right well, though you yourself
understand not a word of it—"

"I may not do all you ask, Judith," said the other, after
a moment's reflection (and still with an uneasy feeling that she
was yielding to the wiles of a temptress), "but I will ask the
goodman to show me your mother's simples, and how they
thrive."

A minute or two thereafter Judith had swiftly stolen into
the summer-house—which was spacious and substantial of its
kind, and contained a small black cupboard fixed up in a corner of the walls, a table and chair, and a long oak chest on
the floor. It was this last that held the treasure she was in
search of; and now, the lid having been raised, she was down
on one knee, carefully selecting from a mass of strewn papers
(indeed, there were a riding-whip, a sword and sword-belt, and
several other articles mixed up in this common receptacle) such
sheets as were without a minute mark which she had invented
for her own private purposes. These secured and hastily hidden in her sleeve, she closed the lid, and went out into the
open again, calling upon Prudence to come to her, for that she
was going into the house.

They did not, however, remain within-doors at New Place,
for that might have been dangerous; they knew of a far safer
resort. Just behind Julius Shawe's house, and between that
and the garden, there was a recess formed by the gable of a
large barn not quite reaching the adjacent wall. It was a
three-sided retreat; overlooked by no window whatsoever;
there was a frail wooden bench on two sides of it, and the entrance to it was partly blocked up by an empty cask that had

been put there to be out of the way. For outlook there was nothing but a glimpse of the path going into the garden, a bit of greensward, and two apple-trees between them and the sky. It was not a noble theatre, this little den behind the barn; but it had produced for these two many a wonderful pageant; for the empty barrel and the bare barn wall and the two trees would at one time be transformed into the forest of Arden, and Rosalind would be walking there in her pretty page costume, and laughing at the love-sick Orlando; and again they would form the secret haunts of Queen Titania and her court, with the jealous Oberon chiding her for her refusal; and again they would become the hall of a great northern castle, with trumpets and cannon sounding without as the King drank to Hamlet. Indeed, the elder of these two young women had an extraordinarily vivid imagination; she saw the things and people as if they were actually there before her; she realized their existence so intensely that even Prudence was brought to sympathize with them, and to follow their actions now with hot indignation, and now with triumphant delight over good fortune come at last. There was no stage-carpenter there to distract them with his dismal expedients; no actor to thrust his physical peculiarities between them and the poet's ethereal visions; the dream-world was before them, clear and filled with light; and Prudence's voice was gentle and of a musical kind. Nay, sometimes Judith would leap to her feet. "You shall not!—you shall not!" she would exclaim, as if addressing some strange visitant that was showing the villainy of his mind; and tears came quickly to her eyes if there was a tale of pity; and the joy and laughter over lovers reconciled brought warm color to her face. They forgot that these walls that inclosed them were of gray mud; they forgot that the prevailing odor in the air was that of the malt in the barn; for now they were regarding Romeo in the moonlight, with the dusk of the garden around, and Juliet uttering her secrets to the honeyed night; and again they were listening to the awful voices of the witches on the heath, and guessing at the sombre thoughts passing through the mind of Macbeth; and then again they were crying bitterly when they saw before them an old man, gray-haired, discrowned, and witless, that looked from one to the other of those standing by, and would ask who the sweet lady was that sought with tears for his benediction. They could hear the frail and shaken voice:

> *"Methinks I should know you, and know this man;*
> *Yet I am doubtful: for I am mainly ignorant*
> *What place this is: and all the skill I have*
> *Remembers not these garments ; nor I know not*
> *Where I did lodge last night. Do not laugh at me;*
> *For, as I am a man, I think this lady*
> *To be my child Cordelia."*

And now, as they had retired into this sheltered nook, and Prudence was carefully placing in order the scattered sheets that had been given her, Judith was looking on with some compunction.

"Indeed I grieve to give you so much trouble, sweetheart," said she. "I would I could get at the copy that my father has locked away—"

"Judith!" her friend said, reproachfully. "You would not take that? Why, your father will scarce show it even to Julius, and sure I am that none in the house would put a hand upon it—"

"If it were a book of psalms and paraphrases, they might be of another mind," Judith said ; but Prudence would not hear.

"Nay," said she, as she continued to search for the connecting pages. "I have heard your father say to Julius that there is but little difference; and that 'tis only when he has leisure here in Stratford that he makes this copy writ out fair and large; in London he takes no such pains. Truly I would not that either Julius or any of his acquaintance knew of my fingering in such a matter: what would they say, Judith ? And sometimes, indeed, my mind is ill at ease with regard to it—that I should be reading to you things that so many godly people denounce as wicked and dangerous—"

"You are too full of fears, good mouse," said Judith, coolly, "and too apt to take the good people at their word. Nay, I have heard; they will make you out everything to be wicked and sinful that is not to their own minds; and they are zealous among the saints ; but I have heard, I have heard."

"What, then ?" said the other, with some faint color in her face.

"No matter," said Judith, carelessly. "Well, I have heard that when they make a journey to London they are as fond of claret wine and oysters as any; but no matter: in truth the winds carry many a thing not worth the listening to. But as regards this special wickedness, sweet mouse, indeed you are innocent of it; 'tis all laid to my charge; I am the sinner and temptress; be sure you shall not suffer one jot through my iniquity. And now have you got them all together? Are you ready to begin?"

"But you must tell me where the story ceased, dear Judith, when last we had it; for indeed you have a marvellous memory, even to the word and the letter. The poor babe that was abandoned on the sea-shore had just been found by the old shepherd—went it not so?—and he was wondering at the rich bearing-cloth it was wrapped in. Why, here is the name— Perdita," she continued, as she rapidly scanned one or two of the papers—"who is now grown up, it appears, and in much grace; and this is a kind of introduction, I take it, to tell you all that has happened since your father last went to London— I mean since the story was broken off. And Florizel—I remember not the name—but here he is so named as the son of the King of Bohemia—"

A quick laugh of intelligence rose to Judith's eyes; she had an alert brain.

"Prince Florizel?" she exclaimed. "And Princess Perdita! That were a fair match, in good sooth, and a way to heal old differences. But to the beginning, sweetheart, I beseech you; let us hear how the story is to be; and pray Heaven he gives me back my little Mamillius, that was so petted and teased by the court ladies."

However, as speedily appeared, she had anticipated too easy a continuation and conclusion. The young Prince Florizel proved to be enamored, not of one of his own station, but of a simple shepherdess; and although she instantly guessed that this shepherdess might turn out to be the forsaken Perdita, the conversation between King Polixenes and the good Camillo still left her in doubt. As for the next scene—the encounter between Autolycus and the country clown—Judith wholly and somewhat sulkily disapproved of that. She laughed, it is true; but it was sorely against her will. For she suspected that goodman Matthew's influence was too apparent here; and that, were he ever to hear of the story, he would in his vanity claim this part as his own; moreover, there was a kind of familiarity and every-day feeling in the atmosphere—why, she herself had been rapidly questioned by her father about the necessary purchases for a sheep-shearing feast, and Susan, laughing, had struck in with the information as to the saffron for coloring the warden-pies. But when the sweet-voiced Prudence came to the scene between Prince Florizel and the pretty shepherdess, then Judith was right well content.

"Oh, do you see, now, how her gentle birth shines through her lowly condition!" she said, quickly. "And when the old shepherd finds that he has been ordering a king's daughter to be the mistress of the feast—ay, and soundly rating her, too, for her bashful ways—what a fright will seize the good old man! And what says she in answer?—again, good Prue—let me hear it again—marry, now, I'll be sworn she had just such another voice as yours!"

"To the King Polixenes," Prudence continued, regarding the manuscript, "who is in disguise, you know, Judith, she says:

> ' Welcome, sir !
> It is my father's will I should take on me
> The hostess-ship o' the day :—you're welcome, sir.'

And then to both the gentlemen:

> ' Give me those flowers there, Dorcas.—Reverend sirs,
> For you there's rosemary and rue ; these keep
> Seeming and savor all the winter long :
> Grace and remembrance be to you both,
> And welcome to our shearing !' "

"Ah, there, now, will they not be won by her gentleness?" she cried, eagerly. "Will they not suspect and discover the truth? It were a new thing for a prince to wed a shepherdess, but this is no shepherdess, as an owl might see! What say they then, Prue? Have they no suspicion?"

So Prudence continued her patient reading—in the intense silence that was broken only by the twittering of the birds in the orchard, or the crowing of a cock in some neighboring yard; and Judith listened keenly, drinking in every varying phrase. But when Florizel had addressed his speech to the

pretty hostess of the day, Judith could no longer forbear: she
clapped her hands in delight.

"There, now, that is a true lover; that is spoken like a true
lover," she cried, with her face radiant and proud. "Again,
good Prue—let us hear what he says—ay, and before them all,
too, I warrant me he is not ashamed of her."

So Prudence had to read once more Florizel's praise of his
gentle mistress:

> "'*What you do
> Still betters what is done. When you speak, sweet,
> I'd have you do it ever: when you sing,
> I'd have you buy and sell so; so give alms;
> Pray so; and, for the ordering your affairs,
> To sing them too. When you do dance, I wish you
> A wave o' the sea, that you might ever do
> Nothing but that; move still, still so, and own
> No other function. Each your doing,
> So singular in each particular,
> Crowns what you are doing in the present deeds,
> That all your acts are queens!*'"

"In good sooth, it is spoken like a true lover," Judith said,
with a light on her face as if the speech had been addressed
to herself. "Like one that is well content with his sweetheart, and is proud of her, and approves! Marry, there be few
of such in these days; for this one is jealous and unreason-
able, and would have the mastery too soon; and that one would
frighten you to his will by declaring you are on the highway
to perdition; and another would have you more civil to his
tribe of kinsfolk. But there is a true lover, now; there is one
that is courteous and gentle; one that is not afraid to approve:
there may be such in Stratford, but, God wot, they would seem
to be a scarce commodity! Nay, I pray your pardon, good
Prue: to the story, if it please you—and is there aught of the
little Mamillius forth-coming?"

And so the reading proceeded; and Judith was in much delight that the old King seemed to perceive something unusual
in the grace and carriage of the pretty Perdita.

"What is't he says? What are the very words?"

> "'*This is the prettiest low-born lass that ever
> Ran on the greensward: nothing she does or seems
> But smacks of something greater than herself;
> Too noble for this place.*'"

"Yes! yes! yes!" she exclaimed, quickly. "And sees he not
some likeness to the Queen Hermione? Surely he must remember the poor injured Queen, and see that this is her daughter? Happy daughter, that has a lover that thinks so well of
her! And now, Prue?"

But when in the course of the hushed reading all these fair
hopes came to be cruelly shattered; when the pastoral romance
was brought to a sudden end; when the King, disclosing himself, declared a divorce between the unhappy lovers, and was
for hanging the ancient shepherd, and would have Perdita's
beauty scratched with briers; and when Prudence had to repeat the farewell words addressed to the prince by his hapless
sweetheart—

> *"' Will't please you, sir, be gone?*
> *I told you what would come of this. Beseech you,*
> *Of your own state take care: this dream of mine—*
> *Being now awake, I'll queen it no inch further,*
> *But milk my ewes, and weep—' "*

—there was something very like tears in the gentle reader's
eyes; but that was not Judith's mood; she was in a tempest
of indignation.

"God's my life!" she cried, "was there ever such a fool as
this old King? He a king! He to sit on a throne! Better
if he sate in a barn and helped madge-howlet to catch mice!
And what says the prince? Nay, I'll be sworn he proves himself a true man, and no summer playfellow; he will stand by
her; he will hold to her, let the ancient dotard wag his beard
as he please!"

And so, in the end, the story was told, and all happily settled; and Prudence rose from the rude wooden bench with a
kind of wistful look on her face, as if she had been far away,
and seen strange things. Then Judith—pausing for a minute
or so as if she would fix the whole thing in her memory, to be
thought over afterward—proceeded to tie the pages together for
the better concealment of them on her way home.

"And the wickedness of it?" said she, lightly. "Wherein
lies the wickedness of such a reading, sweet mouse?"

Prudence was somewhat shamefaced on such occasions; she
could not honestly say that she regretted as she ought to have
done giving way to Judith's importunities.

"Some would answer you, Judith," she said, "that we had but ill used time that was given us for more serious purposes." "And for what more serious purposes, good gossip? For the repeating of idle tales about our neighbors? Or the spending of the afternoon in sleep, as is the custom with many? Are we all so busy, then, that we may not pass a few minutes in amusement? But, indeed, sweet Prue," said she, as she gave a little touch to her pretty cap and snow-white ruff, to put them right before she went out into the street, "I mean to make amends this afternoon. I shall be busy enough to make up for whatever loss of time there has been over this dangerous and godless idleness. For, do you know, I have everything ready now for the new Portugal receipts that you read to me; and two of them I am to try as soon as I get home; and my father is to know nothing of the matter—till the dishes be on the table. So fare you well, sweet mouse; and give ye good thanks, too: this has been but an evil preparation for the church-going of the morrow, but remember, the sin was mine—you are quit of that."

And then her glance fell on the roll of papers that she held in her hand.

"The pretty Perdita!" said she. "Her beauty was not scratched with briers, after all. And I doubt not she was in brave attire at the court; though methinks I better like to remember her as the mistress of the feast, giving the flowers to this one and that. And happy Perdita, also, to have the young prince come to the sheep-shearing, and say so many sweet things to her! Is't possible, think you, Prue, there might come such another handsome stranger to our sheep-shearing that is now at hand?"

"I know not what you mean, Judith."

"Why, now, should such things happen only in Bohemia?" she said, gayly, to the gentle and puzzled Prudence. "Soon our shearing will begin, for the weather has been warm, and I hear the hurdles are already fixed. And there will be somewhat of a merry-making, no doubt; and—and the road from Evesham hither is a fair and goodly road, that a handsome young stranger might well come riding along. What then, good mouse? If one were to meet him in the lane that crosses to Shottery—and to bid him to the feast—what then?"

"Oh, Judith, surely you are not still thinking of that dangerous man!" the other exclaimed.

But Judith merely regarded her for a second, with the clear-shining eyes now become quite demure and inscrutable.

CHAPTER XI.

A REMONSTRANCE.

NEXT morning was Sunday; and Judith, having got through her few domestic duties at an early hour, and being dressed in an especially pretty costume in honor of the holy day, thought she need no longer remain within-doors, but would walk along to the church-yard, where she expected to find Prudence. The latter very often went thither on a Sunday morning, partly for quiet reverie and recalling of this one and the other of her departed but not forgotten friends whose names were carven on the tombstones, and partly—if this may be forgiven her—to see how the generous mother earth had responded to her week-day labors in the planting and tending of the graves. But when Judith, idly and carelessly as was her wont, reached the church-yard, she found the wide, silent space quite empty; so she concluded that Prudence had probably been detained by a visit to some one fallen sick; and she thought she might as well wait for her; and with that view—or perhaps out of mere thoughtlessness—she went along to the river-side, and sat down on the low wall there, having before her the slowly moving yellow stream and the fair, far-stretching landscape beyond.

There had been some rain during the night; the roads she had come along were miry; and here the grass in the church-yard was dripping with the wet; but there was a kind of suffused rich light abroad that bespoke the gradual breaking through of the sun; and there was a warmth in the moist atmosphere that seemed to call forth all kinds of sweet odors from the surrounding plants and flowers. Not that she needed these, for she had fixed in her bosom a little nosegay of yellow-leaved mint, that was quite sufficient to sweeten the scarcely moving air. And as she sat there in the silence it seemed to her as if all the world were awake—and had been awake for hours—but that all the human beings were gone out of it. The rooks were cawing in the elms above her; the bees hummed as they flew by into the open light over the stream; and far away she could hear the lowing of the cattle on the farms; but there was no sound of any human voice, nor any glimpse of any human creature in the wide landscape. And she grew to wonder what it would be like if she were left alone in the world, all the people gone from it, her own relatives and friends no longer here and around her, but away in the strange region where Hamnet was, and perhaps, on such a morning as this, regarding her not without pity, and even, it might be, with some touch of half-recalled affection. Which of them all should she regret the most? Which of them all would this solitary creature—left alone in Stratford, in an empty town—most crave for, and feel the want of? Well, she went over these friends and neighbors and companions and would-be lovers; and she tried to imagine what, in such circumstances, she might think of this one and that; and which of them she would most desire to have back on the earth and living with her. But right well she knew in her heart that all this balancing and choosing was but a pretense. There was but the one; the one whose briefest approval was a kind of heaven to her, and the object of her secret and constant desire; the one who turned aside her affection with a jest; who brought her silks and scents from London as if her mind were set on no other things than these. And she was beginning to wonder whether, in those imagined circumstances, he might come to think differently of her and to understand her somewhat; and indeed she was already picturing to herself the life they might lead—these two, father and daughter, together in the empty and silent but sun-lit and sufficiently cheerful town—when her idle reverie was interrupted. There was a sound of talking behind her; doubtless the first of the people were now coming to church; for the doors were already open.

She looked round, and saw that this was Master Walter Blaise who had just come through the little swinging gate, and that he was accompanied by two little girls, one at each side of him, and holding his hand. Instantly she turned her head away, pretending not to have seen him.

"Bless the man!" she said to herself, "what does he here of

a Sunday morning? Why is so diligent a pastor not in charge of his own flock?"

But she felt secure enough. Not only was he accompanied by the two children, but there was this other safeguard that he would not dare to profane the holy day by attempting anything in the way of wooing. And it must be said that the young parson had had but few opportunities for that, the other members of the household eagerly seeking his society when he came to New Place, and Judith sharp to watch her chances of escape.

The next moment she was startled by hearing a quick footstep behind her. She did not move.

"Give you good-morrow, Judith," said he, presenting himself, and regarding her with his keen and confident gray eyes. "I would crave a word with you; and I trust it may be a word in season, and acceptable to you."

He spoke with an air of cool authority, which she resented. There was nothing of the clownish bashfulness of young Jelleyman about him; nor yet of the half timid, half sulky jealousy of Tom Quiney; but a kind of mastery, as if his office gave him the right to speak, and commanded that she should hear. And she did not think this fair, and she distinctly wished to be alone; so that her face had but little welcome in it, and none of the shining radiance of kindness that Willy Hart so worshipped.

"I know you like not hearing of serious things, Judith," said he (while she wondered whither he had sent the two little girls: perhaps into the church?), "but I were no true friend to you, as I desire to be, if I feared to displease you when there is need."

"What have I done, then? In what have I offended? I know we are all miserable sinners, if that be what you mean," said she, coldly.

"I would not have you take it that way, Judith," said he; and there really was much friendliness in his voice. "I meant to speak kindly to you. Nay, I have tried to understand you; and perchance I do in a measure. You are in the enjoyment of such health and spirits as fall to the lot of few; you are well content with your life and the passing moment; you do not like to be disturbed, or to think of the future. But

"HE SPOKE WITH AN AIR OF COOL AUTHORITY, WHICH SHE RESENTED."

the future will come, nevertheless, and it may be with altered
circumstances; your light-heartedness may cease, sorrow and
sickness may fall upon you, and then you may wish you had
learned earlier to seek for help and consolation where these
alone are to be found. It were well that you should think
of such things now, surely; you can not live always as you
live now—I had almost said a godless life, but I do not wish
to offend; in truth, I would rather lead you in all kindliness
to what I know is the true pathway to the happiness and peace
of the soul. I would speak to you, Judith, if in no other way,
as a brother in Christ; I were no true friend to you else; nay,
I have the command of the Master whom I serve to speak and
fear not."

She did not answer, but she was better content now. So
long as he only preached at her, he was within his province,
and within his right.

"And bethink you, Judith," said he, with a touch of reproach in his voice, "how and why it is you enjoy such health
and cheerfulness of spirits: surely through the Lord in His
loving-kindness answering the prayers of your pious mother.
Your life, one might say, was vouchsafed in answer to her sup-
plications; and do you owe nothing of duty and gratitude to
God, and to God's Church, and to God's people ? Why should
you hold aloof from them ? Why should you favor worldly
things, and walk apart from the congregation, and live as if to-
morrow were always to be as to-day, and as if there were to be
no end to life, no calling to account as to how we have spent
our time here upon earth? Dear Judith, I speak not unkindly;
I wish not to offend; but often my heart is grieved for you;
and I would have you think how trifling our present life is in
view of the great eternity whither we are all journeying; and
I would ask you, for your soul's sake, and for your peace of
mind here and hereafter, to join with us, and come closer with
us, and partake of our exercises. Indeed you will find a truer
happiness. Do you not owe it to us ? Have you no gratitude
for the answering of your mother's prayers ?"

"Doubtless, doubtless," said she (though she would rather
have been listening in silence to the singing of the birds, that
were all rejoicing now, for the sun had at length cleared away
the morning vapors, and the woods and the meadows and the

far uplands were all shining in the brilliant new light). "I go to church as the others do, and there we give thanks for all the mercies that have been granted."

"And is it enough, think you?" said he—and as he stood, while she sat, she did not care to meet those clear, keen, authoritative eyes that were bent on her. "Does your conscience tell you that you give sufficient thanks for what God in His great mercy has vouchsafed to you? Lip-service every seventh day!—a form of words gone through before you take your afternoon walk! Why, if a neighbor were kind to you, you would show him as much gratitude as that; and this is all you offer to the Lord of heaven and earth for having in His compassion listened to your mother's prayers, and bestowed on you life and health and a cheerful mind?"

"What would you have me do? I can not profess to be a saint while at heart I am none," said she, somewhat sullenly.

It was an unlucky question. Moreover, at this moment the bells in the tower sent forth their first throbbing peals into the startled air; and these doubtless recalled him to the passing of time, and the fact that presently the people would be coming into the church-yard.

"I will speak plainly to you, Judith; I take no shame to mention such a matter on the Lord's day; perchance the very holiness of the hour and of the spot where I have chanced to meet you will the better incline your heart. You know what I have wished; what your family wish; and indeed you can not be so blind as not to have seen. It is true, I am but a humble laborer in the Lord's vineyard; but I magnify my office; it is an honorable work; the saving of souls, the calling to repentance, the carrying of the Gospel to the poor and stricken ones of the earth—I say that is an honorable calling, and one that blesses them that partake in it, and gives a peace of mind far beyond what the worldlings dream of. And if I have wished that you might be able and willing—through God's merciful inclining of your heart—to aid me in this work, to become my helpmeet, was it only of my own domestic state I was thinking? Surely not. I have seen you from day to day—careless and content with the trifles and idle things of this vain and profitless world; but I have looked forward to what might befall in the future, and I have desired with all my heart—yea, and with prayers to God for the same—that you should be taught to seek the true haven in time of need. Do you understand me, Judith?"

He spoke with little tenderness, and certainly with no show of lover-like anxiety; but he was in earnest; and she had a terrible conviction pressing upon her that her wit might not be able to save her. The others she could easily elude when she was in the mind; this one spoke close and clear; she was afraid to look up and face his keen, acquisitive eyes.

"And if I do understand you, good Master Blaise," said she, desperately; "if I do understand you—as I' confess I have gathered something of this before—but—but surely—one such as I—such as you say I am—might she not become pious— and seek to have her soul saved—without also having to marry a parson?—if such be your meaning, good Master Blaise."

It was she who was in distress and in embarrassment; not he.

"You are not situated as many others are," said he. "You owe your life, as one may say, to the prayers of God's people; I but put before you one way in which you could repay the debt—by laboring in the Lord's vineyard, and giving the health and cheerfulness that have been bestowed on you to the comfort of those less fortunate—"

"I? Such a one as I? Nay, nay, you have shown me how all unfit I were for that," she exclaimed, glad of this one loophole.

"I will not commend you, Judith, to your face," said he, calmly, "nor praise such worldly gifts as others, it may be, overvalue; but in truth I may say you have a way of winning people toward you; your presence is welcome to the sick; your cheerfulness gladdens the troubled in heart; and you have youth and strength and an intelligence beyond that of many. Are all these to be thrown away?—to wither and perish as the years go by? Nay, I seek not to urge my suit to you by idle words of wooing, as they call it, or by allurements of flattery; these are the foolish devices of the ballad-mongers and the players, and are well fitted, I doubt not, for the purposes of the master of these, the father of lies himself; rather would I speak to you words of sober truth and reason; I would show you how you can make yourself useful in the garden of the Lord, and so offer some thanksgiving for the bounties bestowed on you. Pray consider it, Judith; I ask not for yea or nay at this moment; I would have your heart meditate over it in your own privacy, when you can bethink you of what has happened to you and what may happen to you in the future. Life has been glad for you so far; but trouble might come; your relatives are older than you; you might be left so that you would be thankful to have one beside you whose arm you could lean on in time of distress. Think over it, Judith, and may God incline your heart to what is right and best for you."

But at this moment the first of the early comers began to make their appearance—strolling along toward the church-yard, and chatting to each other as they came—and all at once it occurred to her that if he and she separated thus, he might consider that she had given some silent acquiescence to his reasons and arguments; and this possibility alarmed her.

"Good Master Blaise," said she, hurriedly, "pray mistake me not. Surely, if you are choosing a helpmeet for such high and holy reasons, it were well that you looked further afield. I am all unworthy for such a place—indeed I know it; there is not a maid in Stratford that would not better become it; nay, for my own part, I know several that I could point out to you, though your own judgment were best in such a matter. I pray you think no more of me in regard to such a position; God help me, I should make a parson's wife such as all the neighbors would stare at; indeed I know there be many you could choose from—if their heart were set in that direction— that are far better than I."

And with this protest she would fain have got away; and she was all anxiety to catch a glimpse of Prudence, whose appearance would afford her a fair excuse. How delightful would be the silence of the great building and the security of the oaken pew! with what a peace of mind would she regard the soft-colored beams of light streaming into the chancel, and listen to the solemn organ music, and wait for the silver-clear tones of Susan's voice! But good Master Walter would have another word with her ere allowing her to depart.

"In truth you misjudge yourself, Judith," said he, with a firm assurance, as if he could read her heart far better than she herself. "I know more of the duties pertaining to such a station than you; I can foresee that you would fulfill them

worthily, and in a manner pleasing to the Lord. Your parents,
too: will you not consider their wishes before saying a final
nay ?"

"My parents ?" she said, and she looked up with a quick surprise. "My mother, it may be—"

"And if your father were to approve also ?"

For an instant her heart felt like lead; but before this sudden fright had had time to tell its tale in her eyes she had re-
assured herself. This was not possible.

"Has my father expressed any such wish ?" said she; but
well she knew what the reply would be.

"No, he has not, Judith," he said, distinctly; "for I have
not spoken to him. But if I were to obtain his approval, would
that influence you ?"

She did not answer.

"I should not despair of gaining that," said he, with a calm
confidence that caused her to lift her eyes and regard him for
a second, with a kind of wonder, as it were, for she knew not
what this assurance meant. "Your father," he continued,
"must naturally desire to see your future made secure, Judith.
Think what would happen to you all if an accident befell him
on his journeyings to London. There would be no man to pro-
tect you and your mother. Dr. Hall has his own household
and its charges, and two women left by themselves would surely feel the want of guidance and help. If I put these worldly
considerations before you, it is with no wish that you should
forget the higher duty you owe to God and His Church, and
the care you should have of your own soul. Do I speak for
myself alone ? I think not. I trust it is not merely selfish
hopes that have bidden me appeal to you. And you will reflect, Judith; you will commune with yourself before saying
the final yea or nay; and if your father should approve—"

"Good Master Blaise," said she, interrupting him—and she
rose and glanced toward the straggling groups now approaching the church—"I can not forbid you to speak to my father,
if it is your wish to do that; but I would have him understand
that it is through no desire of mine; and—and, in truth, he
must know that I am all unfit to take the charge you would
put upon me. I pray you hold it in kindness that I say so:—
and there, now," she quickly added, "is little Willie Hart, that

I have a message for, lest he escape me when we come out again."

He could not further detain her; but he accompanied her as she walked along the path toward the little swinging gate, for she could see that her small cousin, though he had caught sight of her, was shyly uncertain as to whether he should come to her, and she wished to have his hand as far as the church door. And then—alas! that such things should befall—at the very same moment a number of the young men and maidens also entered the church-yard; and foremost among them was Tom Quiney. One rapid glance that he directed toward her and the parson was all that passed; but instantly in her heart of hearts she knew the suspicion that he had formed. An assignation?—and on a Sunday morning, too! Nay, her guess was quickly confirmed. He did not stay to pay her even the ordinary courtesy of a greeting. He went on with the others; he was walking with two of the girls; his laughter and talk were louder than any. Indeed, this unseemly mirth was continued to within a yard or two of the church door—perhaps it was meant for her to hear?

Little Willie Hart, as he and his cousin Judith went hand in hand through the porch, happened to look up at her.

"Judith," said he, "why are you crying?"

"I am not!" she said, angrily. And with her hand she dashed aside those quick tears of vexation.

The boy did not pay close heed to what now went on within the hushed building. He was wondering over what had occurred—for these mysteries were beyond his years. But at least he knew that his cousin Judith was no longer angry with him; for she had taken him into the pew with her, and her arm, that was interlinked with his, was soft and warm and gentle to the touch; and once or twice, when the service bade them to stand up, she had put her hand kindly on his hair. And not only that, but she had at the outset taken from her bosom the little nosegay of mint and given it to him; and the perfume of it (for it was Judith's gift, and she had worn it near her heart, and she had given it him with a velvet touch of her fingers) seemed to him a strange and sweet and mystical thing—something almost as strange and sweet and inexplicable as the beauty and shining tenderness of her eyes.

CHAPTER XII.

DIVIDED WAYS.

SOME few weeks passed quite uneventfully, bringing them to the end of June; and then it was that Mistress Hathaway chanced to send a message into the town that she would have her granddaughter Judith come over to see her roses, of which there was a great show in the garden. Judith was nothing loath; she felt she had somewhat neglected the old dame of late; and so, one morning—or rather one mid-day it was, for the family had but finished dinner—found her in her own room, before her mirror, busy with an out-of-door toilet, with Prudence sitting patiently by. Judith seemed well content with herself and with affairs in general on this warm summer day; now she spoke to Prudence, again she idly sang a scrap of some familiar song, while the work of adornment went on apace.

"But why such bravery, Judith?" her friend said, with a quiet smile. "Why should you take such heed about a walk through the fields to Shottery?"

"Truly I know not," said Judith, carelessly; "but well I wot my grandmother will grumble. If I am soberly dressed, she says I am a sloven, and will never win me a husband; and if I am pranked out, she says I am vain, and will frighten away the young men with my pride. In Heaven's name, let them go, say I; I can do excellent well without them. What think you of the cap, good Prue? 'Twas but last night I finished it, and the beads I had from Warwick."

She took it up and regarded it, humming the while:

> " O say, my Joan, say, my Joan, will not that do?
> I can not come every day to woo."

"Is't not a pretty cap, good gossip?"

Prudence knew that she ought to despise such frivolities, which truly were a snare to her, for she liked to look at Judith when she was dressed as she was now, and she forgot to condemn these pretty colors. On this occasion Judith was

5*

clad in a gown of light gray, or rather buff, with a petticoat of
pale blue taffeta, elaborately quilted with her own handiwork;
the small ruff she wore, which was open in front, and partly
showed her neck, was snow-white and stiffly starched; and she
was now engaged in putting on her soft brown hair this cap
of gray velvet, adorned with two rows of brass beads, and with
a bit of curling feather at the side of it.   Prudence's eyes were
pleased, if her conscience bade her disapprove; nay, sometimes
she had to confess that at heart she was proud to see her dear
gossip wear such pretty things, for that she became them so well.

"Judith," said she, "shall I tell you what I heard your
father say of you last night?   He was talking to Julius, and
they were speaking of this one and that, and how they did;
and when you were mentioned, ' Oh yes,' says your father, ' the
wench looks bravely well; 'tis a pity she can not sell the painting of her cheeks: there may be many a dame at the court would
buy it of her for a goodly sum.' "

Judith gave a quick, short laugh: this was music in her ears
—coming from whence it did.

"But, Judith," said her friend, with a grave inquiry in her
face, "what is't that you have done to Tom Quiney that he
comes no longer near the house ?—nay, he will avoid you when
he happens to see you abroad, for that I have observed myself,
and more than once.   What is the matter ?   How have you
offended him ?"

"What have I done ?" she said; and there was a swift and
angry color in her face.   "Let him ask what his own evil imaginings have done.   Not that I care, in good sooth!"

"But what is it, Judith ?   There must be a reason."

"Why," said Judith, turning indignantly to her, " you remember, sweetheart, the Sunday morning that Mrs. Pike's little boy was taken ill, and you were sent for, and did not come
to church ?   Well, I had gone along to the church-yard to
seek you, and was waiting for you, when who must needs
make his appearance but the worthy Master Blaise—nay, but
I told you, good Prue, the honor he would put upon me; and
thank Heaven, he hath not returned to it, nor spoken to my father yet, as far as I can learn.   Then, when the good parson's
sermon was over—body o' me, he let me know right sharply
I was no saint, though a saint I might become, no doubt, were

I to take him for my master—as I say, the lecture he gave me
was over, and we were walking to the church door, when who
should come by but Master Quiney and some of the others.
Oh, well I know my gentleman! The instant he clapped eyes
on me he suspected there had been a planned meeting—I could
see it well—and off he goes in high dudgeon, and not a word
nor a look—before the others, mind you, before the others,
good Prue; that was the slight he put upon me. Marry, I care
not! Whither he has gone, there he may stay!"

She spoke rapidly and with warmth: despite the scorn that
was in her voice, it was clear that that public slight had touched her deeply.

"Nay, Judith," said her gentle companion, "'twere surely a
world of pity you should let an old friend go away like that—
through a mischance merely—"

"An old friend?" said she. "I want none of such friends,
that have ill thoughts of you ere you can speak. Let him
choose his friends elsewhere, say I; let him keep to his tapsters, and his ale-house wenches; there he will have enough
of pleasure, I doubt not, till his head be broke in a brawl
some night!"

Then something seemed to occur to her. All at once she
threw aside the bit of ribbon she had in her fingers, and
dropped on her knee before her friend, and seized hold of Prudence's hands.

"I beseech your pardon, sweet Prue!—indeed, indeed, I
knew not what I said; they were but idle words; good mouse,
I pray you heed them not. He may have reasons for distrust-
ing me; and in truth I complain not; 'tis a small matter; but
I would not have you think ill of him through these idle words
of mine. Nay, nay, they tell me he is sober and diligent, that
his business prospers, that he makes many friends, and that the
young men regard him as the chief of them, whether it be at
merriment or aught else."

"I am right glad to hear you speak so of the young man, Judith," Prudence said, in her gentle way, and yet mildly wondering at this sudden change of tone. "If he has displeased
you, be sure he will be sorry for it, when he knows the truth."

"Nay, nay, sweet mouse," Judith said, rising and resuming
her careless manner, as she picked up the ribbon she had thrown

aside. "'Tis of no moment. I wish the young man well. I pray you speak to none of that I have told you; perchance 'twas but an accident, and he meant no slight at all; and then —and then," she added, with a kind of laugh, "as the good parson seems determined that willy-nilly I must wed him and help him in his charge of souls, that were a good ending, sweet Prue?"

She was now all equipped for setting forth, even to the feather fan that hung from her girdle by a small silver cord.

"But I know he hath not spoken to my father yet, else I should have heard of it, in jest or otherwise. Come, mouse, shall we go? or the good dame will have a scolding for us."

Indeed, this chance reference to the slight put upon her in the church-yard seemed to have left no sting behind it. She was laughing as she went down the stair, at some odd saying of Bess Hall's that her father had got hold of. When they went outside she linked her arm within that of her friend, and nodded to this or the other passer-by, and had a merry or a pleasant word for them, accordingly as they greeted her. And

> *Green sleeves was all my joy,*
> *Green sleeves was my delight,*

came naturally into her idle brain; for the day seemed a fit one for holiday-making: the skies were clear, with large white clouds moving slowly across the blue; and there was a fair west wind to stir the leaves of the trees and the bushes, and to touch warmly and softly her pink-hued cheek and pearly neck.

"Ah, me," said she, in mock desolation, "why should one go nowadays to Shottery? What use is in't, sweet Prue, when all the magic and enticement is gone from it? Aforetime I had the chance of meeting with so gracious a young gentleman, that brought news of the King's court, and spoke so soft you would think the cuckoo in the woods was still to listen. That were something to expect when one had walked so far—the apparition—a trembling interview—and then so civil and sweet a farewell! But now he is gone away, I know not whither; and he has forgotten that ever he lodged in a farm-house, like a king consorting with shepherds; and doubtless he will not seek to return. Well—"

"You have never heard of him since, Judith?" her friend said, with a rapid look.

"Alas, no!" she said, in the same simulated vein. "And sometimes I ask myself whether there ever was such a youth —whether the world ever did produce such a courtly gentleman, such a paragon, such a marvel of courtesy—or was it not but a trick of the villain wizard? Think of it, good Prue—to have been walking and talking with a ghost, with a thing of air, and that twice, too! Is't not enough to chill the marrow in your bones? Well, I would that all ghosts were as gentle and mannerly; there would be less fear of them among the War-wickshire wenches. But do you know, good Prue," she said, suddenly altering her tone into something of eagerness, "there is a matter of more moment than ghosts that concerns us now. By this time, or I am mistaken quite, there must be a goodly bulk of the new play lying in the oaken chest; and again and again have I tried to see whether I might dare to carry away some of the sheets, but always there was some one to hinder. My father, you know, has been much in the summer-house since the business of the new twenty acres was settled; and then again, when by chance he has gone away with the bailiff some-where, and I have had my eye on the place, there was good-man Matthew on the watch, or else a maid would come by to gather a dish of green gooseberries for the baking, or Susan would have me seek out a ripe raspberry or two for the child, or my mother would call to me from the brew-house. But 'tis there, Prue, be sure; and there will come a chance, I warrant; I will outwit the ancient Matthew—"

"Do you never bethink you, Judith, what your father would say were he to discover?" her friend said, glancing at her, as they walked along the highway.

Judith laughed, but with some heightened color.

"My father?" said she. "Truly, if he alone were to discov-er, I should have easy penance. Were it between himself and me, methinks there were no great harm done. A daughter may fairly seek to know the means that has gained for her fa-ther the commendation of so many of the great people, and placed him in such good estate in his own town. Marry, I fear not my father's knowing, were I to confess to himself; but as for the others, were they to learn of it—my mother, and

Susan, and Dr. Hall, and the pious Master Walter—I trow there might be some stormy weather aboard. At all events, good Prue, in any such mischance, you shall not suffer; 'tis I that will bear the blame, and all the blame; for indeed I forced you to it, sweet mouse, and you are as innocent of the wickedness as though you had ne'er been born."

And now they were just about to leave the main road for the foot-path leading to Shottery, when they heard the sound of some one coming along on horseback; and turning for a second, they found it was young Tom Quiney, who was on a smart galloway nag, and coming at a goodly pace. As he passed them he took off his cap, and lowered it with formal courtesy.

"Give ye good-day," said he; but he scarcely looked at them, nor did he pull up for further talk or greeting.

"We are in such haste to be rich nowadays," said Judith, with a touch of scorn in her voice, as the two maidens set forth to walk through the meadows, "that we have scarce time to be civil to our friends."

But she bore away no ill-will; the day was too fine for that. The soft west wind was tempering the heat and stirring the leaves of the elms; red and white wild roses were sprinkled among the dark green of the hedges; there was a perfume of elder blossom in the air; and perhaps also a faint scent of hay, for in the distance they could see the mowers at work among the clover, and could see the long sweep of the scythe. The sun lay warm on the grass and the wild flowers around them; there was a perfect silence but for the singing of the birds; and now and again they could see one of the mowers cease from his work, and a soft clinking sound told them that he was sharpening the long, curving blade. They did not walk quickly; it was an idle day.

Presently some one came up behind them and overtook them. It was young Master Quiney, who seemed to have changed his mind, and was now on foot.

"You are going over to Shottery, Prudence?" said he.

Prudence flushed uneasily. Why should he address her, and have no word for Judith?

"Yes," said she; "Mistress Hathaway would have us see her roses; she is right proud of them this year."

"'Tis a good year for roses," said he, in a matter-of-fact way, and as if there were no restraint at all on any of the party.

And then it seemed to occur to him that he ought to account for his presence.

"I guessed you were going to Shottery," said he, indifferently, and still addressing himself exclusively to Prudence; "and I got a lad to take on the nag and meet me at the cross-road; the short-cut through the meadows is pleasant walking. To Mistress Hathaway's, said you? I dare promise you will be pleased with the show; there never was such a year for roses; and not a touch of blight anywhere, as I have heard. And a fine season for the crops, too; just such weather as the farmers might pray for; Look at that field of rye over there, now—is't not a goodly sight?"

He was talking with much appearance of self-possession; it was Prudence who was embarrassed. As for Judith, she paid no heed; she was looking before her at the hedges and the elms, at the wild flowers around, and at the field of bearded rye that bent in rustling gray-green undulations before the westerly breeze.

"And how does your brother, Prudence?" he continued. "'Tis well for him his business goes on from year to year without respect of the seasons; he can sleep o' nights without thinking of the weather. It is the common report that the others of the Town Council hold him in great regard, and will have him become alderman ere long: is it not so?"

"I have heard some talk of it," Prudence said, with her eyes cast down.

At this moment they happened to be passing some patches of the common mallow that were growing by the side of the path; and the tall and handsome youth who was walking with the two girls (but who never once let his eyes stray in the direction of Judith) stooped down and pulled one of the brightest clusters of the pale lilac blossoms.

"You have no flower in your dress, Prudence," said he, offering them to her.

"Nay, I care not to wear them," said she; and she would rather have declined them; but as he still offered them to her, how could she help accepting them and carrying them in her hand? And then, in desperation, she turned and addressed the perfectly silent and impassive Judith.

"Judith," said she, "you might have brought the mastiff with you for a run."

"Truly I might, sweetheart," said Judith, cheerfully, "but that my grandmother likes him not in the garden; his ways are overrough."

"Now that reminds me," said he, quickly (but always addressing Prudence), "of the little spaniel-gentle that I have. Do you know the dog, Prudence? 'Tis accounted a great beauty, and of the true Maltese breed. Will you accept him from me? In truth I will hold it a favor if you will take the little creature."

"I?" said Prudence, with much amazement; for she had somehow vaguely heard that the dog had been purchased and brought to Stratford for the very purpose of being presented to Judith.

"I assure you 'tis just such an one as would make a pleasant companion for you," said he; "a gentle creature as ever was, and affectionate too—a most pleasant and frolicsome playfellow. Will you take it, Prudence?—for what can I do with the little beast? I have no one to look after it."

"I had thought you meant Judith to have the spaniel," said she, simply.

"Nay, how would that do, sweetheart?" said Judith, calmly. "Do you think the Don would brook such invasion of his domain? Would you have the little thing killed? You should take it, good cousin; 'twill be company for you should you be alone in the house."

She had spoken quite as if she had been engaged in the conversation all the way through; there was no appearance of anger or resentment at his ostentatious ignoring of her presence: whatever she felt she was too proud to show.

"Then you will take the dog, Prudence," said he. "I know I could not give it into gentler hands, for you could not but show it kindness, as you show to all."

"Give ye good thanks," said Prudence, with her pale face flushing with renewed embarrassment, "for the offer of the gift; but in truth I doubt if it be right and seemly to waste such care on a dumb animal when there be so many of our fellow-

creatures that have more pressing claims on us. And there
are enough of temptations to idleness without our willfully adding to them. But I thank you for the intention of your kindness—indeed I do."

"Nay, now, you shall have it, good Prudence, whether you
will or no," said he, with a laugh. "You shall bear with the
little dog but for a week, that I beg of you; and then if it
please you not, if you find no amusement in its tricks and an-
tics, I will take it back again. 'Tis a bargain; but as to your
sending of it back, I have no fears; I warrant you 'twill overcome your scruples, for 'tis a most cunning and crafty playfellow, and merry withal; nor will it hinder you from being as
kind and helpful to those around you as you have ever been.
I envy the dog that is to have so gentle a guardian."

They were now come to a parting of the ways; and he said
he would turn off to the left, so as to reach the lane at the end
of which his nag was awaiting him.

"And with your leave, Prudence," said he, "I will bring the
little spaniel to your house this evening, for I am only going
now as far as Bidford; and if your brother be at home he may
have half an hour to spare, that we may have a chat about the
Corporation, and the new ordinances they propose to make.
And so fare you well, and good wishes go with you!"

And with that he departed, and was soon out of sight.

"Oh, Judith," Prudence exclaimed, almost melting into
tears, "my heart is heavy to see it!"

"What, then, good cousin?" said Judith, lightly.

"The quarrel."

"The quarrel, dear heart! Think of no such thing. In sober
truth, dear Prudence, I would not have matters other than they
are; I would not; I am well content; and as for Master Quiney,
is not he improved? Did ever mortal hear him speak so fair
before? Marry, he hath been learning good manners, and pro-
fited well. But there it is: you are so gentle, sweetheart, that
every one, no matter who, must find you good company;
while I am fractious, and ill to bear with; and do I marvel
to see any one prefer your smooth ways and even disposition?
And when he comes to-night, heed you, you must thank him
right civilly for bringing you the little spaniel; 'tis a great favor; the dog is one of value that many would prize—"

"I can not take it—I will not have it. 'Twas meant for you, Judith, as well you know," the other cried, in real distress.

"But you must and shall accept the gift," her friend said, with decision. "Ay, and show yourself grateful for his having singled you out withal. Neither himself nor his spaniel would go long a-begging in Stratford, I warrant you: give him friendly welcome, sweetheart."

"He went away without a word to you, Judith."

"I am content."

"But why should it be thus?" Prudence said, almost piteously.

"Why? Dear mouse, I have told you. He and I never did agree; 'twas ever something wrong on one side or the other; and wherefore should not he look around for a gentler companion? 'Twere a wonder should he do aught else; and now he hath shown more wisdom than ever I laid to his credit."

"But the ungraciousness of his going, Judith," said the gentle Prudence, who could in no wise understand the apparent coolness with which Judith seemed to regard the desperate thing that had taken place.

"Heaven have mercy! why should that trouble you if it harm not me?" was the instant answer. "My spirits are not like to be dashed down for want of a 'fare you well.' In good sooth he had given you so much of his courtesy and fair speeches that perchance he had none to spare for others."

By this time they were come to the little wooden gate leading into the garden; and it was no wonder they should pause in passing through that to regard the bewildering and glowing luxuriance of foliage and blossom, though this was but a cottage inclosure, and none of the largest. The air seemed filled with the perfume of this summer abundance; and the clear sunlight shone on the various masses of color—roses red and white, pansies, snapdragon, none-so-pretty, sweet-williams of every kind, to say nothing of the clustering honeysuckle that surrounded the cottage door.

"Was't not worth the trouble, sweetheart?" Judith said. "Indeed, the good dame does well to be proud of such a pageant."

As she spoke her grandmother suddenly made her appearance, glancing sharply from one to the other of them.

"Welcome, child, welcome," she said, "and to you, sweet Mistress Shawe."

And yet she did not ask them to enter the cottage; there was some kind of hesitation about the old dame's manner that was unusual.

"Well, grandmother," said Judith, gayly, "have you no grumbling? My cap I made myself; then must it be out of fashion. Or I did not make it myself; then it must have cost a mint of money. Or what say you to my petticoat—does not the color offend you? Shall I ever attain to the pleasing of you, think you, good grandmother?"

"Wench, wench, hold your peace!" the old dame said, in a lower voice. "There is one within that may not like the noise of strangers—though he be no stranger to you, as he says—"

"What, grandmother?" Judith exclaimed, and involuntarily she shrank back a little, so startled was she. "A stranger? In the cottage? You do not mean the young gentleman that is in hiding—that I met in the lane—"

"The same, Judith, the same," she said, quickly; "and I know not whether he would wish to be seen by more than needs be—"

She glanced at Judith, who understood: moreover, the latter had pulled together her courage again.

"Have no fear, good grandmother," said she; and she turned to Prudence. "You hear, good Prue, who is within."

"Yes," the other answered, but somewhat breathless.

"Now, then, is such an opportunity as may ne'er occur again," Judith said. "You will come with me, good Prue? Nay, but you must."

"Indeed I shall not!" Prudence exclaimed, stepping back in affright. "Not for worlds, Judith, would I have aught to do with such a thing. And you, Judith, for my sake, come away! We will go back to Stratford!—we will look at the garden some other time!—in truth, I can see your grandmother is of my mind too. Judith, for the love of me, come!—let us get away from this place!"

Judith regarded her with a strange kind of smile.

"I have had such courtesy and fair manners shown me to-day, sweet Prue," said she, with a sort of gracious calmness, "that I am fain to seek elsewhere for some other treatment, lest

I should grow vain. Will it please you to wait for me in the garden, then? Grandmother, I am going in with you to help you give your guest good welcome."

"Judith!" the terrified Prudence exclaimed, in a kind of despair.

But Judith, with her head erect, and with a perfect and proud self-possession, had followed her grandmother into the house.

CHAPTER XIII.

A HERALD MERCURY.

THE distance between this luxuriant garden, all radiant and glowing in light and color, and the small and darkened inner room of the cottage, was but a matter of a few yards; yet in that brief space, so alert was her brain, she had time to reconsider much. And, with her, pride or anger was always of short duration, the sunny cheerfulness of her nature refusing to harbor such uncongenial guests. Why, she asked herself, should she take umbrage at the somewhat too open neglect that had just been shown her? Was it not tending in the very direction she had herself desired? Had she not begged and prayed him to give Prudence the little spaniel-gentle? Nay, had she not willfully gone and buried in the church-yard the bit of rosemary that he had sent her to keep, putting it away from her with the chance of its summoning an unknown lover? So now, she said to herself, she would presently come out again to the poor affrighted Prudence, and would re-assure her, and congratulate her, moreover, with words of good cheer and comfort for the future.

And then again, in this lightning-like survey of the situation, she was conscious that she was becomingly dressed—and right glad indeed that she had chanced to put on the gray velvet cap with the brass beads and the curling feather; and she knew that the young gentleman would be courteous and civil, with admiring eyes. Moreover, she had a vague impression that he was somewhat too much given to speak of Ben Jonson; and she hoped for some opportunity to let him understand that her father was one of good estate, and much thought of by

every one around, whose daughter knew what was due to his
position, and could conduct herself not at all as a country
wench. And so it was that the next minute found her in the
twilight of the room; and there, truly enough, he was, standing
at the small window.

"Give ye good welcome, sir," said she.

"What! fair Mistress Judith?" he said, as he quickly turned
round. And he would have come forward and kissed her
hand, perchance, but that a moment's hesitation prevented him.

"It may be that I have offended you," said he, diffidently.

"In what, good sir?"

She was quite at her ease; the little touch of modest color in
her face could scarcely be attributed to rustic shyness; it was
but natural; and it added to the gentleness of her look.

"Nay, then, sweet lady, 'twas but a lack of courage that I
would ask you to pardon," said he—though he did not seem
conscious of heavy guilt, to judge by the way in which his
black and eloquent eyes regarded Judith's face and the prettinesses of her costume. "There was a promise that I should
communicate with you if I returned to this part of the country;
but I found myself not bold enough to take advantage of your
kindness. However, fortune has been my friend, since again
I meet you; 'tis the luckiest chance; I but asked your good
grandmother here for a cup of water as I passed, and she
would have me take a cup of milk instead; and then she bade
me to come in out of the heat for a space—which I was nothing loath to do, as you may guess; and here have I been
taking up the good lady's time with I know not what of idle
gossip—"

"But sit ye down, grandchild," the good dame said; "and
you, sir, pray sit you down. Here, wench," she called to the
little maid that was her sole domestic; "go fill this jug from
the best barrel."

And then she herself proceeded to get down from the high
wooden rail some of the pewter trenchers that shone there like
a row of white moons in the dusk; and these she placed on
the table, with one or two knives; and then she began to get
forth cakes, a cheese, a ham, some spiced bread, the half of a
cold gooseberry-tart, and what not.

"'Tis not every day we come by a visitor in these quiet

parts," said she—"ay, good sir, and one that is not afraid to
speak out his mind. Nay, nay, grandchild, I tell thee sit
thee down; thou art too fine a madam this morning to meddle
wi' kitchen matters. Tell the gentleman I be rather deaf; but
I thank him for his good company. Sit ye down, sweeting;
sooth, you look bravely this morning."

"Have I pleased you at last, grandmother?—'tis a miracle,
surely," she said, with a smile; and then she turned gravely
to entertain the old dame's visitor. "I hope your fortunes
have mended, sir," said she.

"In a measure—somewhat; but still I am forced to take
heed—"

"Perchance you have still the letter to my father?" she asked.

"Nay, madam, I considered it a prudent thing to destroy
it—little as that was in my heart."

"I had thought on your next coming to the neighborhood
that you would have taken the chance to make my father's
friendship," said she, and not without some secret disappointment; for she was anxious that this acquaintance of Ben Jonson's should see the New Place, with all its tapestries, and
carved wood, and silver-gilt bowls; with its large fair garden,
too, and substantial barns and stables. Perhaps she would
have had him carry the tale to London? There were some
things (she considered) quite as fine as the trumpery masques
and mummeries of the court that the London people seemed to
talk about. She would have liked him to see her father at the
head of his own table, with her mother's napery shining, and
plenty of good friends round the board, and her father drinking to the health of Bess Hall out of the silver-topped tankard
that Thomas Combe, and Russell, and Sadler, and Julius Shawe,
and the rest of them, had given him on his last birthday. Or
perchance she would have had him see her father riding through
the town of Stratford with some of these good neighbors (and
who the handsomest of all the company? she would make bold
to ask), with this one and that praising the Evesham roan,
and the wagoners as they passed touching their caps to "worthy
Mahster Shacksper." Ben Jonson! Well, she had seen Ben
Jonson. There was not a maid in the town would have looked his way. Whereas, if there were any secret enchantments
going forward on Hallowmas-eve (and she knew of such, if

the ministers did not), and if the young damsels were called on to form a shape in their brain as they prayed for the handsome lover that was to be sent them in the future, she was well aware what type of man they would choose from amongst those familiar to them; and also it had more than once reached her ears that the young fellows would jokingly say among themselves that right well it was that Master Shakespeare was married and in safe-keeping, else they would never have a chance. In the mean while, and with much courtesy, this young gentleman was endeavoring to explain to her why it was he dared not go near Stratford town.

"Truly, sweet Mistress Judith," said he, in his suave voice, and with modestly downcast eyes, "it is a disappointment to me in more regards than one; perchance I dare not say how much. But in these times one has to see that one's own misfortunes may not prove harmful to one's friends; and then again, ever since the French King's murder, they are becoming harder and harder against any one, however innocent he may be, that is under suspicion. And whom do they not suspect? The Parliament have entreated the King to be more careful of his safety; and the recusants—as they call those that have some regard for the faith they were brought up in—must not appear within ten miles of the court. Nay, they are ordered to betake themselves to their own dwellings; and by the last proclamation all Roman priests, Jesuits, and seminaries are banished the kingdom. I wonder not your good grandmother should have a word of pity for them that are harried this way and that for conscience' sake."

"I say naught, I say naught; 'twere well to keep a still tongue," the old dame said, being still busy with the table. "But I have heard there wur more peace and quiet in former days when there wur but one faith in the land; ay, and good tending of the poor folk by the monks and the rich houses."

However, the chance reference to the French King had suddenly recalled to Judith that Prudence was waiting her in the garden; and her conscience smote her for her neglect; while she was determined that so favorable an opportunity should not be lost of banishing once and forever her dear gossip's cruel suspicions. So she rose.

"I crave your pardon, good sir," said she, "if I leave you for

a moment to seek my gossip Prudence Shawe, that was to wait
for me in the garden. I would have you acquainted with each
other; but pray you, sir, forbear to say anything against the
Puritan section of the church, for she is well inclined that way,
and she has a heart that is easily wounded."

"And thank you for the caution, fair Mistress Judith," said
he; and he rose, and bowed low, and stood hat in hand until
she had left the apartment.

At first, so blinding was the glare of light and color, she
could hardly see; but presently, when her eyes were less dazzled, she looked everywhere, and found the garden quite empty. She called; there was no answer. She went down to the
little gate; there was no one in the road. And so, taking it
for granted that Prudence had sought safety in flight, and was
now back in Stratford town, or on the way thither, she returned into the cottage with a light heart, and well content to hear
what news was abroad.

"Pray you, sir," said old Mistress Hathaway, "sit in to the
table; and you, grandchild, come your ways. If the fare be
poor, the welcome is hearty. What, then, Judith? Dined already, sayst thou? Body o' me, a fresh-colored young wench
like you should be ready for your dinner at any time. Well,
well, sit thee in, and grace the table; and you shall sip a cup
of claret for the sake of good company."

Master Leofric Hope, on the other hand, was not at all backward in applying himself to this extemporized meal; on the
contrary, he did it such justice as fairly warmed the old dame's
heart. And he drank to her, moreover, bending low over his
cup of ale; but he did not do the like by Judith—for some reason or another. And all the while he was telling them of the
affairs of the town; as to how there was much talking of the
new river that was to bring water from some ten or twelve
miles off, and how one Middleton was far advanced with the
cutting of it, although many were against it, and would have
the project overthrown altogether. Of these and similar matters he spoke right pleasantly, and the old dame was greatly
interested; but Judith grew to think it strange that so much
should be said about public affairs, and what the people were
talking about, and yet no mention made of her father. And
so it came about, when he went on to tell them of the new ship

of war that so many were going to see at Woolwich, and that the King made so much of, she said:

"Oh, my father knows all about that ship. 'Twas but the other day I heard him and Master Combe speak of it; and of the King too; and my father said, 'Poor man, 'tis a far smaller ship than that he will make his last voyage in.'"

"Said he that of the King?"

She looked up in quick alarm.

"But as he would have said it of me, or of you, or of any one," she exclaimed. "Nay, my father is well inclined toward the King, though he be not as much at the court as some, nor caring to make pageants for the court ladies and their attendants and followers."

If there were any sarcasm in this speech, he did not perceive it; for it merely led him on to speak of the new masque that Ben Jonson was preparing for the Prince Henry; and incidentally he mentioned that the subject was to be Oberon, the Fairy Prince.

"Oberon?" said Judith, opening her eyes. "Why, my father hath writ about that!"

"Oh yes, as we all know," said he, courteously; "but there will be a difference—"

"A difference?" said she. "By my life, yes! There will be a difference. I wonder that Master Jonson was not better advised."

"Nay, in this matter, good Mistress Judith," said he, "there will be no comparison. I know 'tis the fashion to compare them—"

"To compare my father and Master Jonson?" she said, as if she had not heard aright. "Why, what comparison? In what way? Pray you remember, sir, I have seen Master Ben Jonson. I have seen him, and spoken with him. And as for my father, I'll be bound there is not his fellow for a handsome presence and gracious manners in all Warwickshire—no, nor in London town neither, I'll be sworn!"

"I meant not that, sweet lady," said he, with a smile; and he added, grimly: "I grant you our Ben looks as if he had been in the wars; he hath had a tussle with Bacchus on many a merry night, and bears the scars of these noble combats. No; 'tis the fashion to compare them as wits—"

6

"I'd as lief compare them as men, good sir," said she, with a touch of pride; "and I know right well which should have my choice."

"When it is my good fortune, dear lady," said the young man, "to have Master William Shakespeare's daughter sitting before me, I need no other testimony to his grace and bearing, even had I never set eyes on him." And with that he bowed low; and there was a slight flush on her face that was none of displeasure; while the old dame said:

"Ay, ay, there be many a wench in Warwickshire worse favored than she. Pray Heaven it turn not her head! The wench is a good wench, but ill to manage; and 'twere no marvel if the young men got tired of waiting."

To escape from any further discussion of this subject, Judith proposed that they should go out and look at her grandmother's roses and pansies, which was in truth the object of her visit; and she added that if Master Hope (this was the first time she had named him by his name) were still desirous of avoiding observation, they could go to the little bower at the upper hedgerow, which was sufficiently screened from the view of any passer-by. The old dame was right willing, for she was exceedingly proud of this garden, that had no other tending than her own; and so she got her knitting-needles and ball of wool, and preceded them out into the warm air and the sunlight.

"Dear, dear me," said she, stopping to regard two small shrubs that stood withered and brown by the side of the path. "There be something strange in that rosemary, now; in good sooth there be. Try as I may, I can not bring them along; the spring frost makes sure to kill them." And then she went on again.

"Strange indeed," said the young man to his companion, these two being somewhat behind, "that a plant that is so fickle and difficult to hold should be the emblem of constancy."

"I know not what they do elsewhere," said Judith, carelessly pulling a withered leaf or two to see if they were quite inodorous, "but hereabouts they often use a bit of rosemary for a charm, and the summoning of spirits."

He started somewhat, and glanced at her quickly and curiously. But there was clearly no subtle intention in the speech. She idly threw away the leaves.

"Have you faith in such charms, Mistress Judith?" said he, still regarding her.

"In truth I know not," she answered, as if the question were of but little moment. "There be some who believe in them, and others that laugh. But strange stories are told; marry, there be some of them that are not pleasant to hear of a winter's night, when one has to change the warm chimney-corner for the cold room above. There is my grandmother, she hath a rare store of them; but they fit not well with the summer-time and with such a show as this."

"A goodly show indeed," said he; and by this time they were come to a small arbor of rude lattice-work mostly smothered in foliage; and there was a seat within it, and also a tiny table; while in front they were screened from the gaze of any one going along the road by a straggling and propped-up wall of peas that were now showing their large white blossoms plentifully among the green.

"'Tis a quiet spot," said he, when they were seated, and the old dame had taken to her knitting; "'tis enough to make one pray never to hear more of the din and turmoil of London."

"I should have thought, sir," said Judith, "you would have feared to go near London, if there be those that would fain get to know of your whereabout."

"Truly," said he, "I have no choice. I must run the risk. From time to time I must seek to see whether the cloud that is hanging over me give signs of breaking. And surely such must now be the case, when fortune hath been so kind to me as to place me where I am at this moment—in such company— with such a quiet around. 'Tis like the work of a magician; though from time to time I remind me that I should rise and leave, craving your pardon for intruding on you withal."

"Trouble not yourself, young sir," the old dame said, in her matter-of-fact way, as she looked up from her knitting; "if the place content you, 'tis right well; we be in no such hurry in these country parts; we let the day go by as it lists, and thank God for a sound night's rest at the end of it."

"And you have a more peaceful and happy life than the London citizens, I'll be bound," said he, "with all their feasts and gayeties and the noise of drums and the like."

"We hear but the murmur of such things from a far distance," Judith said.   "Was there not a great to-do on the river when the citizens gave their welcome to the Prince?"

"Why, there, now," said he, brightening up at this chance of repaying in some measure the courtesy of his entertainers; "there was as wonderful a thing as London ever saw.   A noble spectacle, truly; for the Companies would not be outdone; and such bravery of apparel, and such a banqueting in the afternoon!   And perchance you heard of it but through some news-letter!   Shall I tell you what I saw on my own part?"

"If it be not too troublesome to you, good sir."

He was glad enough; for he had noticed, when he was describing such things, that Judith's eyes grew absent, and he could gaze at them without fear of causing her to start and blush.   Moreover, it was a pretty face to tell a story to; and the day was so still and shining; and all around them there was a scent of roses in the air.

"Why, it was about daybreak, as I should think," he said, "that the citizens began to come forth; and a bright fair morning it was; and all of them in their best array.   And you may be sure that when the Companies learned that the whole of the citizens were minded to show their love for the Prince Henry on his coming back from Richmond, they were not like to be behindhand ; and such preparations had been made as you would scarce believe.   Well, then, so active were they in their several ways that by eight of the clock the Companies were all assembled in their barges of state to wait the Lord Mayor and Aldermen; and such a sound of drums and trumpets and fifes was there; and the water covered with the fleet, and the banks all crowded with them that had come down to see. Then the Lord Mayor and the Aldermen being arrived, the great procession set forth in state; and such a booming of cannon there was, and cheering from the crowd.   'Twas a sight, on my life; for they bore the pageant with them—that was a huge whale and a dolphin ; and on the whale sat a fair and lovely nymph, Corinea she was called, the Queen of Cornwall; and she had a coronet of strange sea-shells, and strings of pearls around her neck and on her wrists; and her dress was of crimson silk, so that all could make her out from a distance; and she had a silver shield slung on to her left arm, and in her right hand a silver spear—oh, a wonderful sight she was; I marvel not the crowd cheered and cheered again. Then on the other animal—that is, the dolphin—sat one that represented Amphion—he was the father of music, as you must know; and a long beard he wore, and he also had a wreath of seashells on his head, and in his hand a harp of gold that shone in the sun. Well, away they set toward Chelsea; and there they waited for the Prince's approach—"

"And the young Prince himself," Judith said, quickly and eagerly; "he bears himself well, does he not? He bears himself like a prince? He would match such a pageant right royally, is't not so?"

"Why, he is the very model and mirror of princehood!— the pink of chivalry!—nor is there one of them at the court that can match him at the knightly exercises," said this enthusiastic chronicler, who had his reward in seeing how interested she was. "Well, when the young Prince was come to Chelsea, there he paused; and the Queen Corinea addressed him in a speech of welcome—truly, I could not hear a word of it, there was such a noise among the multitude; but I was told thereafter that it presented him with their love and loyal duty; and then they all set forth toward Whitehall again. By this time 'twas later in the day; and no man would have believed so many dwelt in the neighborhood of our great river; and that again was as naught to the crowd assembled when they were come again to the town. And here—as it must have been arranged beforehand, doubtless—the fleet of barges separated, and formed two long lines, so as to make a lane for the Prince to pass through, with great cheering and shouting, so that when they were come to the court steps, he was at the head of them all. And now it was that the dolphin approached, and Amphion, that was riding on his back, bid the Prince a loyal farewell in the name of all the citizens; and at the end of the speech—which, in truth, the people guessed at rather than heard—there was such a tumult of huzzas, and a firing of cannon, and the drums and the trumpets sounding, and on every hand you could hear nothing but 'Long live our Prince of Wales, the Royal Henry!'"

"And he bore himself bravely, I'll dare be sworn!" she exclaimed. "I have heard my father speak of him; he is one that will uphold the honor of England when he comes to the throne!"

"And there was such a feasting and rejoicing that evening," he continued, "within-doors and without; and many an honest man, I fear me, transgressed, and laid the train for a sore-distracted head next day. Then 'twas some two or three evenings after that, if I remember aright, that we had the great water-fight and the fire-works; but perchance you heard of these, sweet Mistress Judith?"

"In truth, good sir," she answered, "I heard of these, as of the welcome you speak of, but in so scant a way as to be worth naught. 'Tis not a kind of talking that is encouraged at our house; unless, indeed, when Julius Shawe and Master Combe and some of them come in of an evening to chat with my father; and then sometimes I contrive to linger, with the bringing in of a flagon of Rhenish or the like, unless I am chid and sent forth. I pray you, good sir, if I do not outwear your patience, to tell us of the water-fight, too."

"'Tis I that am more like to outwear your patience, fair Judith," said he. "I would I had a hundred fights to tell you of. But this one—well, 'twas a goodly pageant; and a vast crowd was come down to the water's edge to see what was going forward, for most of the business of the day was over, and both master and 'prentice were free. And very soon we saw how the story was going; for there was a Turkish pirate, with fierce men with blackened faces; and they would plunder two English merchantmen and make slaves of the crews. This was but the beginning of the fight; and there was great firing of guns and manœuvring of the vessels; and the merchantmen were like to fare badly, not being trained to arms like the pirate. In sooth they were sore bestead; but presently up came two ships of war to rescue; and then the coil began in good earnest, I warrant you; for there was boarding and charging and clambering over the bulwarks—ay, and many a man on both sides knocked into the sea; until in the end they had killed or secured all the pirates, and then there was naught to do but to blow up the pirate ship into the air, with a noise like thunder, and scarce a rag or spar of him remaining. 'Twas a right good ending, I take it, in the minds of the worthy citizens; doubtless they hoped that every Turkish rogue would

"THEN HE BOWED LOW AGAIN AND WITHDREW."

be served the like. And then it was that the blowing up of the pirate ship was a kind of signal for the beginning of the fire-works; and it had grown to dusk now; so that the blazes of red light and blue light and the whizzing of the squibs and what not seemed to fill all the air. 'Twas a rare climax to the destruction of the Turks; and the people cheered and cheered again when 'twas well done; and then at the end came a great discharge of guns and squibs and showers of stars, that one would have thought the whole world was on fire. Sure I am that the waters of the Thames never saw such a sight before. And the people went home right well content, and I doubt not drank to the confusion of all pirates, as well as to the health of the young Prince, that is to preserve the realm to us in years to come."

They talked for some time thereafter about that and other matters, and about his own condition and occupations at the farm; and then he rose, and there was a smile on his face.

"You know, fair Mistress Judith," said he, "that a wise man is careful not to outstay his welcome, lest it be not offered to him again; and your good grandmother has afforded me so pleasant an hour's gossip and good company that I would fain look forward to some other chance of the same in the future."

"Must you go, good sir?" said Judith, also rising. "I trust we have not overtaxed your patience. We country folk are hungry listeners."

"To have been awarded so much of your time, sweet Mistress Judith," said he, bowing very low, "is an honor I am not likely to forget."

And then he addressed the old dame, who had missed something of this.

"Give ye good thanks for your kindness, good Mistress Hathaway," said he.

"Good fortune attend ye, sir," said the old dame, contentedly, and without ceasing from her knitting.

Judith was standing there, with her eyes cast down.

"Sweet lady, by your leave," said he, and he took her hand and raised it and just touched her fingers with his lips. Then he bowed low again, and withdrew.

"Fare you well, good sir," Judith had said at the same moment, but without any word as to a future meeting. Then she returned into the little arbor and sat down.

"Is't not like a meteor, grandmother, shooting across the sky?" said she, merrily. "Beshrew me, but the day has grown dark since he left! Didst ever hear of such a gallymawfrey of dolphins and whales, and prince's barges, and the roaring of cannon, and fire-works? Sure 'tis well we live in the country quiet, our ears would be riven in twain else. And you, grandmother, that was ever preaching about prudent behavior, to be harboring one that may be an outlaw—a recusant; perchance he hath drawn his sword in the King's presence—"

"What know you of the young gentleman, Judith?" the old dame said, sharply.

"Marry, not a jot beyond what he hath doubtless told to yourself, good grandmother. But see you any harm in him? Have you suspicion of him? Would you have me think—as Prudence would fain believe—that there is witchcraft about him?"

"Truly I see no harm in the young gentleman," the old grandmother was constrained to say. "And he be fair-spoken, and modest withal. But look you to this, wench: should you chance to meet him again while he bideth here in this neighborhood—I trow 'twere better you did not—but should that chance, see you keep a still tongue in your head about church and King and Parliament. Let others meddle who choose; 'tis none of your affairs: do you hear me, child? These be parlous times, as the talk is; they do well that keep the by-ways, and let my lord's coaches go whither they list."

"Grandmother," said Judith, gravely, "I know there be many things in which I can not please you, but this sin that you would lay to my charge—nay, dear grandam, when have you caught me talking about church and King and Parliament? Truly I wish them well; but I am content if they go their own way."

The old dame glanced at her, to see what this demure tone of speech meant.

"Thou?" she said, in a sort of grumble. "Thy brain be filled with other gear, I reckon. 'Tis a bit of ribbon that hath hold of thee; or the report as to which of the lads shot best at the match; or perchance 'tis the purchase of some penny ballads, that you may put the pictures on your chamber wall, as if you were a farm wench just come in from the milking pail."

"Heaven have pity on me, good grandmother," said she, with much penitence, and she looked down at her costume, "but I can find no way of pleasing you. You scold me for being but a farm wench; and truly this petticoat, though it be pretty enough, methinks might have been made of a costlier stuff; and my cap—good grandmother, look at my cap—"

She took it off, and smoothed the gray velvet of it, and arranged the beads and the feather.

" —is the cap also too much of the fashion of a farm wench? or have I gone amiss the other way, and become too like a city dame? Would that I knew how to please you, grandam!"

" Go thy ways, child; get thee home!" the old woman said, but only half angrily. "Thy foolish head hath been turned by hearing of those court gambols. Get you to your needle: be your mother's napery all so well mended that you can spend the whole day in idleness?"

"Nay, but you are in the right there, good grandmother," said Judith, drawing closer to her, and taking her thin and wrinkled hand in her own warm, white, soft ones. "But not to the needle—not to the needle, good grandam; I have other eggs on the spit. Did not I tell you of the Portugal receipts that Prudence got for me?—in good sooth I did; well, the dishes were made; and next day at dinner my father was right well pleased. 'Tis little heed he pays to such matters; and we scarce thought of asking him how he liked the fare, when all at once he said: 'Good mother, you must give my thanks to Jane cook; 'twill cheer her in her work; nay, I owe them.' Then says my mother: 'But these two dishes were not prepared by the cook, good husband; 'twas one of the maids.' 'One of the maids?' he says. 'Well, which one of the maids? Truly, 'tis something rare to be found in a country house.' And then there was a laughing amongst all of them; and he fixes his eyes on me. 'What?' he says, 'that saucy wench? Is she striving to win her a husband at last?' And so, you see, good grandmother, I must waste no more time here, for Prudence hath one or two more of these receipts; and I must try them to see whether my father approves or not."

And so she kissed the old dame, and bade her farewell, refus-

ing at the same time to have the escort of the small maid across
the meadows to the town.

All the temporary annoyance of the morning was now
over and forgotten; she was wholly pleased to have had this
interview, and to have heard minutely of all the great doings
in London.   She walked quickly; a careless gladness shone in
her face; and she was lightly singing to herself, as she went
along the well-beaten path through the fields,

> "*Sigh no more, ladies, sigh no more,*
> *Men were deceivers ever.*"

But it was not in the nature of any complaint against the in-
constancy of man that this rhyme had come into her head.
Quite other thoughts came as well.   At one moment she was
saying to herself:

"Why, now, have I no spaniel-gentle with me to keep me
company ?"

And then the next minute she was saying, with a sort of
laugh:

"God help me, I fear I am none of the spaniel-gentle kind !"

But there was no deep smiting of conscience even when she
confessed so much.   Her face was radiant and content; she
looked at the cattle, or the trees, or the children, as it chanced,
as if she knew them all, and knew that they were friendly toward her; and then again the idle air would come into her
brain:

> "*Then sigh not so, but let them go,*
> *And be you blithe and bonny,*
> *Converting all your sounds of woe*
> *Into hey, nonny, nonny !*"

CHAPTER XIV.

A TIRE-WOMAN.

IT was not until after supper that evening that Judith was free to seek out her companion, who had fled from her in the morning; and when she did steal forth—carrying a small basket in her hand—she approached the house with much more caution than was habitual with her. She glanced in at the lower windows, but could see nothing. Then, instead of trying whether the latch was left loose, she formally knocked at the door.

It was opened by a little rosy-cheeked girl of eleven or twelve, who instantly bobbed a respectful courtesy.

"Is Mistress Prudence within, little Margery?" she said.

"Yes, if it please you," said the little wench, and she stood aside to let Judith pass.

But Judith did not enter; she seemed listening.

"Where is she?"

"In her own chamber, if it please you."

"Alone, then?"

"Yes, if it please you, Mistress Judith."

Judith patted the little maid in requital of her courtesy, and then stole noiselessly upstairs. The door was open. Prudence was standing before a small table ironing a pair of snow-white cuffs, the while she was repeating to herself verses of a psalm. Her voice, low as it was, could be heard distinctly:

" Open thou my lips, O Lord, and my mouth shall shew forth thy praise.
For thou desirest no sacrifice, though I would give it; thou delightest not in burnt-offering.
The sacrifices of God are a contrite spirit; a contrite and a broken heart, O God, thou will not despise.
Be favorable unto Zion for thy good pleasure; build the walls of Jerusalem.
Then shalt thou accept the sacrifices of righteousness, even the burnt-offering and oblation ; then shall they offer calves upon thine altar."

She happened to turn her head; and then she uttered a slight cry of surprise, and came quickly to Judith, and caught her by the hand.

"What said he?" she exclaimed, almost breathlessly. "You saw him? 'Twas the same, was it not? How came he there? Judith, tell me!"

"You timid mouse that ran away!" the other said, with a complacent smile. "Why, what should he say? But prithee go on with the cuffs, else the iron will be cold. And are you alone in the house, Prudence? There is no one below?"

"None but the maids, I trow; or Julius, perchance, if he be come in from the malt-house."

"Quick, then, with the cuffs," Judith said, "and get them finished. Nay, I will tell thee all about the young gentleman thereafter. Get thee finished with the cuffs, and put them on—"

"But I meant them not for this evening, Judith," said she, with her eyes turned away.

"'Tis this evening, and now, you must wear them," her friend said, peremptorily. "And more than these. See, I have brought you some things, dear mouse, that you must wear for my sake—nay, nay, I will take no denial—you must and shall—and with haste, too, must you put them on, lest any one should come and find the mistress of the house out of call. Is not this pretty, good Prudence?"

She had opened the basket and taken therefrom a plaited ruff that the briefest feminine glance showed to be of the finest cobweb lawn, tinged a faint saffron hue, and tied with silken strings. Prudence, who now divined the object of her visit, was overwhelmed with confusion. The fair and pensive face became rose red with embarrassment, and she did not even know how to protest.

"And this," said Judith, in the most matter-of-fact way, taking something else out of the basket, "will also become you well—nay, not so, good mouse, you shall be as prim and Puritanical as you please to-morrow; to-night you shall be a little braver; and is it not handsome, too?—'twas a gift to my mother —and she knows that I have it—though I have never worn it."

This second article that she held out and stroked with her fingers was a girdle of buff-colored leather, embroidered with flowers in silk of different colors, and having a margin of fili- gree silver-work both above and below, and a broad silver clasp.

"Come, then, let's try—"

"Nay, Judith," the other said, retreating a step; "I can not —indeed I can not—"

"Indeed you must, silly child!" Judith said, and she caught hold of her angrily. "I say you shall. What know you of such things? Must I teach you manners?"

And when Judith was in this authoritative mood, Prudence had but little power to withstand her. Her face was still burning with embarrassment, but she succumbed in silence, while Judith whipped off the plain linen collar that her friend wore, and set on in its stead this small but handsome ruff. She arranged it carefully, and smoothed Prudence's soft fair hair, and gave a finishing touch to the three-cornered cap; then she stepped back a pace or two to contemplate her handiwork.

"There!" she exclaimed (pretending to see nothing of Prudence's blushes). "A princess! On my life, a princess! And now for the girdle; but you must cast aside that housewife's pouch, sweetheart, and I will lend thee this little pomander of mine; in truth 'twill suit it well."

"No, no, dear Judith!" the other said, almost piteously. "Indeed I can not prank me out in these borrowed plumes. If you will have it so, I will wear the ruff; but not the girdle—not the girdle, dear cousin; that all would see was none of mine—"

"What's that?" Judith exclaimed, suddenly, for there was a noise below.

"'Tis Julius come in from the barn," Prudence said.

"Mercy on us," the other cried, with a laugh, "I thought 'twas the spaniel-gentle come already. So you will not wear the girdle? Well, the ruff becomes you right fairly: and—and those roses in your cheeks, good Prue—why, what is the matter? Is there aught wonderful in one of Julius's friends coming to see him in the evening? And as the mistress of the house you must receive him well and courteously; and be not so demure of speech and distant in manner, dearest heart, for youth must have a little merriment, and we can not always be at our prayers."

"I know not what you mean, Judith, unless it be something that is far away from any thought or wish of mine."

There was a touch of sincerity in this speech that instantly recalled Judith from her half-gibing ways. The truth was that

while she herself was free enough in confiding to this chosen
gossip of hers all about such lovers or would-be lovers as
happened to present themselves, Prudence had never volunteer-
ed any similar confidence in return; and the very fact that
there might be reasons for this reticence was enough to keep
Judith from seeking to remove the veil. Judith herself was
accustomed to make merry over the whole matter of sweethearts
and rhymed messages and little tender gifts; but Prudence was
sensitive, and Judith was careful not to wound her by indiscreet questioning. And at this moment, when Prudence was
standing there confused and abashed, some compunction seized
the heart of her friend. She took her hand.

"In good sooth, I meant not to tease you, sweetheart," said
she, in a kindly way; "and if I advise you in aught, 'tis but
that you should make your brother's house a pleasant resort
for them that would be friendly with him and visit him. What
harm can there be in receiving such with a cheerful welcome,
and having a pretty house-mistress, and all things neat and
comfortable? Dear mouse, you so often lecture me that I
must have my turn; and I do not find fault or cause of quarrel; 'tis but a wish that you would be less severe in your ways,
and let your kind heart speak more freely. Men, that have
the burden of the world's fight to bear, love to meet women-
folk that have a merry and cheerful countenance; 'twere a marvel else; and of an evening, when there is idleness and some
solace after the labors of the day, why should one be glum,
and thinking ever of that next world that is coming soon
enough of its own accord? Look you how well the ruff becomes you; and what sin is in it? The girdle, too; think you
my mother would have worn it had there been aught of evil in
a simple piece of leather and embroidery?"

"'Tis many a day since she put it aside, as I well remember,"
Prudence said, but with a smile, for she was easily won over.

"Truly," said Judith, with a touch of scorn, "the good
preachers are pleased to meddle with small matters when they
would tell a woman what she should wear, and order a maiden
to give up a finger ring or a bit of lace on peril of her losing
her soul. These be marvellous small deer to be so hunted and
stormed about with bell, book, and candle. But now, good
Prudence, for this one evening, I would have you please your

visitor and entertain him; and the spaniel-gentle—that, indeed, you must take from him—"

"I can not, dear Judith; 'twas meant for you," Prudence exclaimed.

"You can not go back from your promise, good cousin," Judith said, coolly, and with some slight inattention to facts. "'Twould be unmannerly of you to refuse the gift, or to refuse ample thanks for it either. And see you have plenty on the board, for men like good fare along with good company; and let there be no stint of wine or ale as they may choose, for your brother's house, Prudence, must not be niggard, were it only for appearance' sake."

"But you will stay, dear Judith, will you not?" the other said, anxiously. "In truth you can entertain them all wherever you go; and always there is such heart in the company—"

"Nay, I can not, sweet mouse," Judith said, lightly. "There is much for me to do now in the evenings since Susan has gone back to her own home. Now I must go, lest your visitor arrive and find you unprepared. You must wear the cuffs as they are, since I have hindered you in the ironing."

"But you can not go, Judith, till you have told me what happened to-day at the cottage," the other pleaded.

"What happened? Why, nothing," Judith said, brightly. "Only that my grandmother is of a mind with myself that a fairer-spoken young gentleman seldom comes into these parts, and that, when he does, he should be made welcome. Bless thy heart, hadst thou but come in and seen how attentive the good dame was to him! And she would press him to have some claret wine; but he said no: perchance he guessed that good grandam had but small store of that. Nay, but you should have come in, sweet mouse; then would you have been conscience-smitten about all your dark surmisings. A murderer, forsooth! a ghost! a phantom! Why, so civil was his manner that he but asked for a cup of water in passing, and my grandmother must needs have him come in out of the sun, and rest him, and have some milk. Was that like a ghost? I warrant you there was naught of the ghost about him when she put a solid repast before him on the table: ghosts make no such stout attacks on gooseberry tart and cheese, else they be sore belied."

"But who and what is this man, Judith?"

"Why, who can tell what any man is?" said the other. "They all of them are puzzles, and unlike other human creatures. But this one—well, he hath a rare store of knowledge as to what is going forward at the court—and among the players, too; and as we sat in the little bower there you would have sworn you could see before you the river Thames, with a wonderful pageant on it—dolphins, and whales, and crowned sea-queens, and the like; and in the midst of them all the young Prince Henry—'Long live the young Prince Henry!' they cried; and there was such a noise of drums and cannons and trumpets that you could scarce hear my grandmother's bees among the flowers. I warrant you the good dame was well repaid for her entertainment, and right well pleased with the young gentleman. I should not marvel to find him returning thither, seeing that he can remain there in secrecy, and have such gossip as pleases him."

"But, Judith, you know not what you do!" her friend protested, anxiously. "Do you forget—nay, you can not forget—that this was the very man the wizard prophesied that you should meet; and, more than that, that he would be your husband!"

"My husband?" said Judith, with a flush of color, and she laughed uneasily. "Nay, not so, good Prudence. He is not one that is likely to choose a country wench. Nay, nay, the, juggler knave failed me—that is the truth of it; the charm was a thing of naught; and this young gentleman, if I met him by accident, the same might have happened to you, as I showed you before. Marry, I should not much crave to see him again, if anything like that were in the wind. This is Stratford town, 'tis not the forest of Arden; and in this neighborhood a maiden may not go forth to seek her lover, and coax him into the wooing of her. My father may put that into a play, but methinks if he heard of his own daughter doing the like, the key would quickly be turned on her. Nay, nay, good Prue, you shall not fright me out of doing a civil kindness to a stranger, and one that is in misfortune, by flaunting his lovership before my eyes. There be no such thing: do not I know the tokens? By my life, this gentleman is too courteous to have a lover's mind within him!"

"And you will go and see him again, Judith?" her friend asked, quickly.

"Nay, I said not that," Judith answered, complacently. "'Tis not the forest of Arden; would to Heaven it were, for life would move to a pleasanter music! I said not that I would go forth and seek him; that were not maidenly; and belike there would come a coil of talking among the gossips or soon or late; but at this time of the year, do you see, sweet cousin, the country is fair to look upon, and the air is sweeter in the meadows than it is here in the town; and if a lone damsel, forsaken by all else, should be straying silent and forlorn along the pathway or by the river-side, and should encounter one that hath but lately made her acquaintance, why should not that acquaintance be permitted in all modesty and courtesy to ripen into friendship? The harm, good Prue—the harm of it? Tush! your head is filled with childish fears of the wizard; that is the truth; and had you but come into the house to-day, and had but five minutes' speech of the young gentleman, you would have been as ready as any one to help in the beguilement of the tedium of his hiding, if that be possible to two or three silly women. And bethink you, was't not a happy chance that I wore my new velvet cap this morning?"

But she had been speaking too eagerly. This was a slip; and instantly she added, with some touch of confusion,

"I mean that I would fain have my father's friends in London know that his family are not so far out of the world, or out of the fashion."

"Is he one of your father's friends, Judith?" Prudence said, gravely.

"He is a friend of my father's friends, at least," said she, "and some day, I doubt not, he will himself be one of these. Truly that will be a rare sight, some evening at New Place, when we confront you with him, and tell him how he was charged with being a ghost, or a pirate, or an assassin, or something of the like."

"Your fancy runs free, Judith," her friend said. "Is't a probable thing, think you, that one that dares not come forth into the day, that is hiding from justice, or perchance scheming in Catholic plots, should become the friend of your house?"

"You saw him not at my grandmother's board, good Prue,"

said Judith, coolly. "The young gentleman hath the trick of making himself at home wherever he cometh, I warrant you. And when this cloud blows away, and he is free to come to Stratford, there is none will welcome him more heartily than I, for methinks he holdeth Master Benjamin Jonson in too high consideration, and I would have him see what is thought of my father in the town, and what his estate is, and that his family, though they live not in London, are not wholly of Moll the milkmaid kind. And I would have Susan come over too; and were she to forget her preachers and her psalms for but an evening, and were there any merriment going forward, the young gentleman would have to keep his wits clear, I'll be bound. There is the house, too, I would have him see; and the silver-topped tankard with the writing on it from my father's good friends; nay, I warrant me Julius would not think of denying me the loan of the King's letter to my father— were it but for an hour or two—"

But here they were startled into silence by a knocking below; then there was the sound of a man's voice in the narrow passage.

"'Tis he, sweetheart," Judith said, quickly, and she kissed her friend, and gave a final touch to the ruff and the cap. "Get you down and welcome him; I will go out when that you have shut the door of the room. And be merry, good heart, be merry—be brave and merry, as you love me."

She almost thrust her out of the apartment, and listened to hear her descend the stairs; then she waited for the shutting of the chamber door; and finally she stole noiselessly down into the passage, and let herself out without waiting for the little maid Margery.

CHAPTER XV.

A FIRST PERFORMANCE.

"NAY, zur," said the sour-visaged Matthew, as he leaned his chin and both hands on the end of a rake, and spoke in his slow-drawling, grumbling fashion—"nay, zur, this country be no longer the country it wur; no, nor never will be again."

"Why, what ails the land ?" said Judith's father, turning from the small table in the summer-house, and lying back in his chair, and crossing one knee over the other, as if he would give a space to idleness.

"Not the land, zur," rejoined goodman Matthew, oracularly —"not the land; it be the men that live in it, and that are all in such haste to make wealth, with plundering of the poor and of each other, that there's naught but lying and cheating and roguery—God-a-mercy, there never wur the loike in any country under the sun! Why, zur, in my vather's time a pair o' shoes would wear you through all weathers for a year; but now, with their half-tanned leather, and their horse-hide, and their cat-skin for the inner sole, 'tis a marvel if the rotten leaves come not asunder within a month. And they be all aloike; the devil would have no choice among 'em. The cloth-maker he hideth his bad wool wi' liquid stuff; and the tailor, no matter whether it be doublet, cloak, or hose, he will filch you his quarter of the cloth ere you see it again; and the chandler—he be no better than the rest—he will make you his wares of stinking offal that will splutter and run over, and do aught but give good light; and the vintner, marry, who knoweth not his tricks and knaveries of mixing and blending, and the selling of poison instead of honest liquor ? The rogue butcher, too, he will let the blood soak in, ay, and puff wind into the meat—meat, quotha!—'tis as like as not to have been found dead in a ditch !"

"A bad case indeed, good Matthew, if they be all preying on each other so."

"'Tis the poor man pays for all, zur. Though how he liveth to pay no man can tell; what with the landlords racking the rents, and inclosing the commons and pasturages—nay, 'tis a noble pastime the making of parks and warrens, and shutting the poor man out that used to have his cow there and a pig or two; but no, now shall he not let a goose stray within the fence. And what help hath the poor man? May he go to the lawyers, with their leases and clauses that none can understand —ay, and their fists that must be well greased ere they set to the business? 'Tis the poor man pays for all, zur, I warrant ye; nor must he grumble when the gentleman goes a-hunting and breaks down his hedges and tramples his corn. Corn? 'Tis the last thing they think of, beshrew me else! They are busiest of all in sending our good English grain—ay, and our good English beef and bacon and tallow—beyond the seas; and to bring back what?—baubles of glass beads and amber, fans for my ladies, and new toys from Turkey! The proud dames—I would have their painted faces scratched!"

"What, what, good Matthew?" Judith's father said, laughing. "What know you of the city ladies and their painting?"

"Nay, nay, zur, the London tricks be spread abroad, I warrant ye; there's not a farmer's wife nowadays but must have her french-hood, and her daughter a taffeta cap—marry, and a grogram gown lined through with velvet! And there be other towns in the land than London to learn the London tricks; I have heard of the dames and their daughters; set them up with their pinching and girding with whalebone, to get a small waist withal!—ay, and the swallowing of ashes and candles, and whatever will spoil their stomach, to give them a pale bleak color. Lord, what a thing 'tis to be rich and in the fashion!—let the poor man suffer as he may. Corn, i' faith!— there be plenty of corn grown in the land, God wot; but 'tis main too dear for the poor man; the rack-rents for him, and a murrain on him; the corn for the forestallers and the merchants and gentlemen, that send it out of the country; and back come the silks and civets for proud madam and her painted crew!"

"God have mercy on us, man!" Judith's father exclaimed, and he drove him aside, and got out into the sunlight. At the same moment he caught sight of Judith herself.

"Come hither, wench, come hither!" he called to her.

She was nothing loath. She had merely been taking some

scraps to the Don; and seeing Matthew in possession there, she had not even staid to look into the summer-house. But when her father came out and called to her, she went quickly toward him; and her eyes were bright enough, on this bright morning.

"What would you, father?"

For answer he plucked off her cap and threw it aside, and took hold of her by a bunch of her now loosened and short sun-brown curls.

"Father!" she protested (but with no great anger). "There be twenty minutes' work undone!"

"Where bought you those roses?" said he, sternly. "Answer me, wench!"

"I bought no roses, father!"

"The paint? Is't not painted? Where got you such a face, madam?"

"Father, you have undone my hair; and the parson is coming to dinner."

"Nay, I'll be sworn 'tis as honest a face as good Mother Nature ever made. This goodman Matthew hath belied you!"

"What said he of me?" she asked, with a flash of anger in her eyes.

Her father put his hand on her neck, and led her away.

"Nay, nay, come thy ways, lass; thou shalt pick me a handful of raspberries. And as for thine hair, let that be as God made it; 'tis even better so; and yet, methinks"—here he stopped, and passed his hand lightly once or twice over her head, so that any half-imprisoned curls were set free—"methinks," said he, regarding the pretty hair with considerable favor, "if you would as lief have some ornament for it, I saw that in London that would answer right well. 'Twas a net-work kind of cap; but the netting so fine you could scarce see it; and at each point a bead of gold. Now, Madame Vanity, what say you to that? Would you let your hair grow free as it is now, and let the sunlight play with it, were I to bring thee a fairy cap all besprinkled with gold?"

"I will wear it any way you wish, father, and right gladly," said she, "and I will have no cap at all if it please you."

"Nay, but you shall have the gossamer cap, wench; I will not forget it when next I go to London."

"I would you had never to go to London again," said she, rather timidly.

He regarded her for a second with a scrutinizing look, and there was an odd sort of smile on his face.

"Why," said he, "I was but this minute writing about a man that had to use divers arts and devices for the attainment of a certain end—yea, and devices that all the world would not approve of, perchance; and that was ever promising to himself that when the end was gained he would put aside these spells and tricks, and be content to live as other men live, in a quiet and ordinary fashion. Wouldst have me live ever in Stratford, good lass?"

"The life of the house goes out when you go away from us," said she, simply.

"Well, Stratford is no wilderness," said he, cheerfully; "and I have no bitter feud with mankind that I would live apart from them. Didst ever think, wench," he added, more absently, "how sad a man must have been ere he could speak so:

"Happy were he could finish forth his fate
    In some unhaunted desert, most obscure
From all societies, from love and hate
    Of worldly folk; then might he sleep secure;
Then wake again, and ever give God praise,
    Content with hips and haws and bramble-berry;
In contemplation spending all his days,
    And change of holy thoughts to make him merry;
Where, when he dies, his tomb may be a bush,
Where harmless robin dwells with gentle thrush."

"Is it that you are writing now, father?"

"Nay, indeed," said he, slowly, and a cloud came over his face. "That was written by one that was my good friend in by-gone days; by one that was betrayed and done to death by lying tongues, and had but sorry favor shown him in the end by those he had served."

He turned away. She thought she heard him say, "My noble Essex," but she was mutely following him. And then he said,

"Come, lass; come pick me the berries."

He kept walking up and down, by himself, while her nimble fingers were busy with the bushes; and when she had collected a sufficiency of the fruit, and brought it to him, she found that he appeared to be in no hurry this morning, but was now grown cheerful again, and rather inclined to talk to her. And she was far from telling him that her proper place at this moment was within-doors, to see that the maids were getting things forward; and if she bestowed a thought of any kind on the good parson, it was to the effect that both he and the dinner would have to wait. Her father had hold of her by the arm. He was talking to her of all kinds of things, as they slowly walked up and down the path, but of his friends in Stratford mostly, and their various ways of living; and this she conceived to have some reference to his project of withdrawing altogether from London, and settling down for good amongst them. Indeed, so friendly and communicative was he on this clear morning—in truth, they were talking like brother and sister—that when at last he went into the summer-house, she made bold to follow; and when he chanced to look at some sheets lying on the table, she said,

"Father, what is the story of the man with the devices?"

For an instant he did not understand what she meant; then he laughed.

"Nay, pay you no heed to such things, child."

"And why should not I, father, seeing that they bring you so great honor?"

"Honor, said you?" but then he seemed to check himself. This was not Julius Shawe, to whom he could speak freely enough about the conditions of an actor's life in London. "Well, then, the story is of a banished duke, a man of great wisdom and skill, and he is living on a desert island with his daughter—a right fair maiden she is, too, and she has no other companion in the world but himself."

"But he is kind to her and good?" she said, quickly.

"Truly."

"What other companion would she have, then? Is she not content—ay, and right well pleased withal?"

"Methinks the story would lag with but these," her father said, with a smile. "Would you not have her furnished with a lover—a young prince and a handsome—one that would play chess with her, and walk with her while her father was busy?"

"But how on a desert island? How should she find such a one?" Judith said, with her eyes all intent.

"There, you see, is where the magic comes in. What if

her father have at his command a sprite, a goblin, that can
work all wonders—that can dazzle people in the dark, and
control the storm, and whistle the young prince to the very feet
of his mistress?"

Judith sighed, and glanced at the sheets lying on the table.

"Alas, good father, why did you aid me in my folly, and
suffer me to grow up so ignorant?"

"Folly, fond wench!" said he, and he caught her by the
shoulders and pushed her out of the summer-house. "Thank
God you have naught to do with any such stuff. There, go
you and seek out Prudence, and get you into the fields, and
give those pink roses in your cheeks an airing. Is't not a rare
morning? And you would blear your eyes with books, silly
wench? Get you gone—into the meadows with you—and you
may gather me a nosegay if your fingers would have work."

"I must go in-doors, father; good Master Blaise is coming to
dinner; but I will bring you the nosegay in the afternoon,
so please you. So fare you well," she added; and she glanced
at him, "and pray you, sir, be kind to the young prince."

He laughed and turned away; and she hurried quickly into
the house. In truth, all through that day she had plenty to
occupy her attention; but whether it was the maids that were
asking her questions, or her mother seeking her help, or good
Master Walter paying authoritative court to her, her eyes were
entirely distraught. For they saw before them a strange isl-
and, with magic surrounding it, and two young lovers, and a
grave and elderly man regarding them; and she grew to wonder how much more of that story was shut up in the summer-
house, and to lament her misfortune in that she could not go
boldly to her father and ask him to be allowed to read it. She
felt quite certain that could she but sit down within there, and
peruse these sheets for herself, he would not say her nay; and
from that conclusion to the next—that on the first chance
she would endeavor to borrow the sheets and have them read to
her—was but an obvious step, and one that she had frequently
taken before. Moreover, on this occasion the chance came to
her sooner than she could have expected. Toward dusk in
the evening her father went out, saying that he was going along
to see how the Harts were doing. Matthew gardener was gone
home; the parson had left hours before; and her mother was

in the brew-house, and out of hearing. Finally, to crown her good fortune, she discovered that the key had been left in the door of the summer-house; and so the next minute found her inside on her knees.

It was a difficult task. There was scarcely any light, for she dared not leave the door open; and the mark that she put on the sheets, to know which she had carried to Prudence, was minute. And yet the sheets seemed to have been tossed into this receptacle in fairly regular order; and when at length, and after much straining of her eyes, she had got down to the marked ones, she was rejoiced to find that there remained above these a large bulk of unperused matter, and the question was as to how much it would be prudent to carry off. Further, she had to discover where there was some kind of division, so that the story should not abruptly break off; and she had acquired some experience in this direction. In the end, the portion of the play that she resolved upon taking with her was modest and small; there would be the less likelihood of detection; and it was just possible that she would have no opportunity of returning the sheets that night.

And then she quickly got in-doors, and put on her hood and muffler, and slipped out into the dusk. She found Prudence alone in the lower room, sitting sewing, the candles on the table being already lit; and some distance off, curled up and fast asleep on the floor, lay the little spaniel-gentle.

"Dear heart," said Judith, brightly, as she glanced at the little dog, "you have shown good sense after all; I feared me you would fall away from my wise counsel."

"My brother was well inclined to the little creature," Prudence said, with some embarrassment.

"And you had a right merry evening, I'll be bound," Judith continued, blithely. "And was there singing?—nay, he can sing well when he is in the mood—none better. Did he give you

'There is a garden in her face
Where roses and white lilies grow,'

for Julius is more light-hearted in such matters than you are, dear mouse. And was there any trencher business—and wine? I warrant me Julius would not have his guest sit dry-throated. 'Twas a merry evening, in good sooth, sweetheart?"

7

"They talked much together," Prudence said, with her eyes cast down.

"*They* talked? Mercy on us, were you not civil to him? Did you not thank him prettily for the little spaniel?"

"In a measure I think 'twas Julius took the little creature from him," Prudence said, bashfully.

"Beshrew me now, but you know better!—'twas given to you, you know right well. A spaniel-gentle for your brother! As soon would he think of a farthingale and a petticoat! And what did he say? Had he aught special to say to you, dear mouse?"

"He would have me look at a book he had, with strange devices on the leaves," Prudence said. "Truly 'twas strange and wonderful, the ornamentation of it in gold and colors, though I doubt me 'twas the work of monks and priests. He would have me take it from him," she added, with a faint blush.

"And you would not, silly one?" Judith exclaimed, angrily.

"Would you have me place such Popish emblems alongside such a book as that that Dr. Hall gave me? Dear Judith, 'twould be a pollution and a sin!"

"But you gave him thanks for the offer, then?"

"Of a surety; 'twas meant in friendship."

"Well, well; right glad am I to see the little beast lying there; and methinks your gentleness hath cast a spell o'er it already, sweetheart, or 'twould not rest so soundly. And now, dear mouse, I have come to tax your patience once more: see, here is part of the new play; and we must go to your chamber, dear Prue, lest some one come in and discover us."

Prudence laughed in her quiet fashion.

"I think 'tis you that casteth spells, Judith, else I should not be aiding thee in this perilous matter."

But she took one of the candles in her hand nevertheless, and led the way upstairs; and then, when they had carefully bolted the door, Judith placed the roll of sheets on the table, and Prudence sat down to arrange and decipher them.

"But this time," Judith said, "have I less weight on my conscience; for my father hath already told me part of the story, and why should not I know the rest? Nay, but it promises well, I do assure thee, sweetheart. 'Tis a rare beginning: the desert island, and the sprite that can work wonders, and the poor banished duke and his daughter. Ay, and there comes a handsome young prince, too; marry, you shall hear of marvels! For the sprite is one that can work magic at the bidding of the duke, and be seen like a fire in the dark, and can lead a storm whither he lists—"

"'Tis with a storm that it begins," Prudence said, for now she had arranged the sheets.

And instantly Judith was all attention. It is true, she seemed to care little for the first scene and the squabbles between the sailors and the gentlemen; she was anxious to get to the enchanted island; and when at length Prudence introduced Prospero and Miranda, Judith listened as if a new world were being slowly opened before her. And yet not altogether with silence, for sometimes she would utter a few words of quick assent, or even explanation; but always so as not to interfere with the gentle-voiced reader. Thus it would go:

"Then Prospero says to her—

> 'Be collected:
> No more amazement: tell your piteous heart
> There's no harm done.
> *Miranda.*   Oh, woe the day!
> *Prospero.*   No harm.
> I have done nothing but in care of thee,
> Of thee, my dear one, thee, my daughter, who
> Art ignorant of what thou art, naught knowing
> Of whence I am, nor that I am more better
> Than Prospero, master of a full poor cell,
> And thy no greater father.
> *Miranda.*   More to know
> Did never meddle with my thoughts.' "

"A right dutiful daughter!" Judith would exclaim—but as apart. "A rare good wench, I warrant; and what a gentle father he is withal!"

And then, when the banished duke had come to the end of his story, and when he had caused slumber to fall upon his daughter's eyes, and was about to summon Ariel, Judith interposed to give the patient reader a rest.

"And what say you, Prudence?" said she, eagerly. "Is't not a beautiful story? Is she not a sweet and obedient maiden, and he a right noble and gentle father? Ah, there, now, they may talk about their masques and pageants of the court, and gods and goddesses dressed up to saw the air with long speeches: see you what my father can tell you in a few words, so that you can scarcely wait, but must on to hear the rest. And do I hurry you, good Prue ? Will you to it again ? For now the spirit is summoned that is to work the magic."

"Indeed, 'tis no heavy labor, Judith," her friend said, with a smile. "And now here is your Ariel:

> 'All hail! great master! grave sir, hail! I come
> To answer thy best pleasure; be't to fly,
> To swim, to dive into the fire, to ride
> On the curled clouds; to thy strong bidding task
> Ariel and all his quality!'

Then says Prospero:

> 'Hast thou, spirit,
> Performed to point the tempest that I bade thee?
> *Ariel.*   To every article.
> I boarded the King's ship; now on the beak,
> Now in the waist, the deck, in every cabin,
> I flamed amazement; sometimes I'd divide,
> And burn in many places; on the topmast,
> The yards and bowsprit, would I flame distinctly,
> Then meet and join. Jove's lightnings, the precursors
> O' the dreadful thunder-claps, more momentary
> And sight-outrunning were not. . . .
> *Prospero.*   My brave spirit!
> Who was so firm, so constant, that this coil
> Would not infect his reason?
> *Ariel.*   Not a soul
> But felt a fever of the mad, and played
> Some tricks of desperation. All but mariners
> Plunged in the foaming brine and quit the vessel,
> Then all afire with me: the King's son Ferdinand—'"

"The prince, sweetheart!—the prince that is to be brought ashore."

"Doubtless, Judith.

> 'The King's son Ferdinand,
> With hair up-staring—then like reeds, not hair—
> Was the first man that leaped: cried, "Hell is empty,
> And all the devils are here."
> *Prospero.*   Why, that's my spirit!
> But was not this nigh shore?
> *Ariel.*   Close by, my master.
> *Prospero.* But are they, Ariel, safe?
> *Ariel.*   Not a hair perished,
> On their sustaining garments not a blemish,
> But fresher than before; and, as thou badst me,
> The King's son have I landed by himself;
> Whom I left cooling of the air with sighs
> In an odd angle of the isle, and sitting,
> His arms in this sad knot.'"

"And hath he not done well, that clever imp!" Judith cried. "Nay, but my father shall reward him—that he shall—'twas bravely done and well. And now to bring him to the maiden that hath never seen a sweetheart—that comes next, good Prue? I marvel now what she will say?"

"'Tis not yet, Judith," her friend said, and she continued the reading, while Judith sat and regarded the dusky shadows beyond the flame of the candle as if wonder-land were shining there. Then they arrived at Ariel's song, "Come unto these yellow sands," and all the hushed air around seemed filled with music; but it was distant, somehow, so that it did not interfere with Prudence's gentle voice.

"Then says Prospero to her:

'The fringed curtains of thine eye advance,
And say what thou seest yond.
   Miranda.   What is't? a spirit?
Lord, how it looks about! Believe me, sir,
It carries a brave form. But 'tis a spirit.
   Prospero. No, wench; it eats and sleeps, and hath such senses
As we have, such. This gallant which thou seest
Was in the wreck; and but he's something stained
With grief, that's beauty's canker, thou might'st call him
A goodly person. He hath lost his fellows,
And strays about to find them.
   Miranda.   I might call him
A thing divine, for nothing natural
I ever saw so noble.'"

"And what says he? What thinks he of her?" Judith said, eagerly.

"Nay, first the father says—to himself, as it were:

'It goes on, I see,
As my soul prompts it. Spirit, fine spirit! I'll free thee
Within two days, for this.'

And then the Prince says:
'Most sure, the goddess
On whom these airs attend! Vouchsafe, my prayer
May know, if you remain upon this island;
And that you will some good instruction give,
How I may bear me here; my prime request,
Which I do last pronounce, is, O you wonder!
If you be maid or no?
   Miranda.   No wonder, sir,
But certainly a maid.
   Ferdinand.   My language! heavens!
I am the best of them that speak this speech,
Were I but where 'tis spoken.'"

"But would he take her away?" said Judith, quickly (but to herself, as it were). "Nay, never so! They must remain on the island—the two happy lovers—with Ariel to wait on them: surely my father will so make it?"

Then, as it appeared, came trouble to check the too swift anticipations of the Prince, though Judith guessed that the father of Miranda was but feigning in his wrath; and when Prudence finally came to the end of such sheets as had been brought her, and looked up, Judith's eyes were full of confidence and pride—not only because she was sure that the story would end happily, but also because she would have her chosen gossip say something about what she had read.

"Well?" said she.

"'Tis a marvel," Prudence said, with a kind of sigh, "that shapes of the air can so take hold of us."

Judith smiled; there was something in her manner that Prudence did not understand.

"And Master Jonson, good Prue—that they call Ben Jonson —what of him?"

"I know not what you mean, Judith."

"Sure you know they make so much of him at the court, and of his long speeches about Greece and Rome and the like; and when one comes into the country with news of what is going forward, by my life you'd think that Master Jonson were the only writer in the land! What say you, good Prue: could worthy Master Jonson invent you a scene like that?"

"In truth I know not, Judith; I never read aught of his writing."

Judith took over the sheets and carefully rolled them up.

"Why," said she, "'twas my father brought him forward, and had his first play taken in at the theatre!"

"But your father and he are great friends, Judith, as I am told; why should you speak against him?"

"I speak against him?" said Judith, as she rose, and there was an air of calm indifference on her face. "In truth, I have naught to say against the good man. 'Tis well that the court ladies are pleased with Demogorgons and such idle stuff, and 'tis passing well that he knows the trade. Now give ye good-night and sweet dreams, sweet mouse; and good thanks, too, for the reading."

But at the door below—Prudence having followed her with the candle—she turned, and said, in a whisper:

"Now tell me true, good cousin: think you my father hath ever done better than this magic island, and the sweet Miranda, and the rest?"

"You know I am no judge of such matters, Judith," her friend answered.

"But, dear heart, were you not bewitched by it? Were you not taken away thither? Saw you not those strange things before your very eyes?"

"In good sooth, then, Judith," said the other, with a smile, "for the time being I knew not that I was in Stratford town, nor in our own country of England either."

Judith laughed lightly and quickly, and with a kind of pride too. And when she got home to her own room, and once more regarded the roll of sheets, before bestowing them away in a secret place, there was a fine bravery of triumph in her eyes. "Ben Jonson!" she said, but no longer with any anger, rather with a sovereign contempt. And then she locked up the treasure in her small cupboard of boxes, and went down-stairs again to seek out her mother, her heart now quite recovered from its envy, and beating warm and equally in its disposition toward all mankind, and her mind full of a perfect and complacent confidence. "Ben Jonson!" she said.

CHAPTER XVI.

BY THE RIVER.

THE next morning she was unusually demure, and yet merry withal. In her own chamber, as she chose out a petticoat of pale blue taffeta, and laid on the bed her girdle of buff-colored leather, and proceeded to array herself in these and other braveries, it was to the usual accompaniment of thoughtless and quite inconsequent ballad-singing. At one moment it was "Green-sleeves was all my joy," and again "Fair, fair, and twice so fair," or perhaps—

"*An ambling nag, and a-down, a-down,*
We have borne her away to Dargison."

But when she came to take forth from the cupboard of boxes the portion of the play she had locked up there the night before, and when she carefully placed that in a satchel of dark blue velvet that she had attached to the girdle, she was silent; and when she went down-stairs and encountered her mother, there was a kind of anxious innocence on her face. The good parson (she explained) had remained so late on the previous afternoon, and there were so many things about the house she had to attend to, that she had been unable to get out into the fields, as her father had bade her, to bring him home some wild flowers. Besides, as every one knew, large dogs got weak in the hind-legs if they were kept chained up too continuously; and it was absolutely necessary she should take Don Roderigo out for a run with her through the meadows, if her father would permit.

"There be plenty of flowers in the garden, surely," her mother said, who was busy with some leather hangings, and wanted help.

"But he would liefer have some of the little wildlings, good mother," said Judith. "That I know right well; for he is pleased to see them lying on the table before him; and sometimes, too, he puts the names of them in his writing."

"How know you that?" was the quick and sharp question.

"As I have heard, good mother," Judith said, with calm equanimity.

And then she went to the small mirror to see that her gray velvet cap and starched ruff were all right.

"What can your father want with wild flowers if he is to remain the whole day at Warwick?" her mother said.

"Is my father going to Warwick?" she asked, quickly.

"If he be not already set forth."

She glanced at the window; there was neither horse nor serving-man waiting there. And then she hastily went out and through the back yard into the garden; and there, sure enough, was her father, ready booted for the road, and giving a few parting directions to his bailiff.

"Well, wench," he said, when he had finished with the man, "what would you?"

She had taken from her purse all the money she could find there.

"Good father," said she, "will you do this errand for me at Warwick?"

"More vanities?" said he. "I wonder you have no commissioner to dispatch to Spain and Flanders. What is't, then? —a muff of satin—a gimmal ring—"

"No, no, not so, father; I would have you buy for me a clasp-knife—as good a one as the money will get; and the cutler must engrave on the blade, or on the handle, I care not which, a message—an inscription, as it were; 'tis but three words—*For Judith's Sweetheart*. Could you remember that, good father? Is't too much of a trouble?"

"How now?" said he. "For whom do you wish me to bring you such a token?"

"Nay, sir," said she, "would you have me name names? The gift of a sweetheart to a sweetheart is a secret thing."

"You are a mad wench," said he (though doubtless he guessed for whom the knife was intended), and he called to Matthew gardener to go round and see if Master Shawe were not yet ready. "But now I bethink me, child, I have a message for thee. Good Master Walter spoke to me yesternight about what much concerns him—and you."

Instantly all her gay self-confidence vanished; she became confused, anxious, timid; and she regarded him as if she feared what his look or manner might convey.

"Yes, sir," she said, in rather a low voice.

"Well, you know what the good man wishes," her father said, "and he speaks fairly, and reasoneth well. Your mother, too, would be right well pleased."

"And you, sir?" she said, rather faintly.

"I?" said he. "Nay, 'tis scarce a matter that I can say ought in. 'Tis for yourself to decide, wench; but were you inclined to favor the young parson, I should be well pleased enough—indeed 'tis so—a good man and honest, as I take him to be, of fair attainment, and I know of none that bear him ill-will, or have ought to say against him. Nay, if your heart be set that way, wench, I see no harm; you are getting on in years to be still in the unmarried state; and, as he himself says, there would be security in seeing you settled in a home of your own, and your future no longer open and undecided. Nay, nay, I see no harm. He reasons well."

7*

"But, father, know you why he would have me become his wife?" Judith said, with a wild feeling overcoming her that she was drowning, and must needs throw out her hands for help. "'Tis for no matter of affection that I can make out—or that he might not as well choose any other in the town; but 'tis that I should help him in his work, and—and labor in the vineyard, as he saith. In truth I am all unfit for such a task—there be many another far better fitted than I; my mother must know that right well. There is little that I would not do to please her; but surely we might all of us have just as much of the good man's company without this further bond. But what say you, father? What is your wish?" she added, humbly. "Perchance I could bring my mind to it if all were anxious that it should be so."

"Why, I have told thee, wench, thou must choose for thyself. 'Twould please your mother right well, as I say; and as for the duties of a parson's wife—nay, nay, they are none so difficult. Have no fears on that score, good lass; I dare be sworn you are as honest and well-minded as most, though perchance you make less profession of it." (The gratitude that sprang to her eyes, and shone there, in spite of her downcast face!) "Nor must you think the good parson has but that end in view; 'tis not in keeping with his calling that he should talk the language of romances. Consider it, wench—consider. And there is more for you to think of. Even if Master Blaise be no vehement lover, as some of the young rattlepates might be, that is but a temporary thing; 'tis the long years of life that weigh for the most; and all through these you would be in an honorable station, well thought of, and respected. Nay, there be many, I can tell thee, lass, that might look askance now at the player's daughter, who would be right glad to welcome the parson's wife."

"What say you, father?" said she—and she was so startled that the blood forsook her lips for a moment. "That—that there be those—who scorn the player's daughter—and would favor the parson's wife?" And then she instantly added: "I pray you, sir, did not you say that I was to decide for myself?"

"Truly, child, truly," said he, somewhat wondering at her manner, for her face had grown quite pale.

"Then I have decided, father."

"And how? What answer will you have for Master Walter?"

She spoke slowly now, and with a distinctness that was almost harsh.

"This, so please you, sir—that the player's daughter shall not, and shall never, become the parson's wife, God helping her!"

"Why, how now? what a coil is this!" he exclaimed. "Good lass, 'twas not the parson that said ought of the kind. Lay not that to his charge, in fair honesty."

"I have decided," she said, proudly and coldly. "Father, the horses are brought round—I can hear them. You will not forget the knife, and the message on the blade?"

He looked at her, and laughed, but in a kindly way; and he took her by the shoulder.

"Nay, now, wench, thou shalt not throw over the good man for a matter that was none of his bringing forward. And why should you wish to have less than the respect of all your neighbors, all and sundry, whatever be their views? In good sooth I meant to speak for the parson, and not to harm him; and when I have more time I must undo the ill that I have done him. So soften your heart, you proud one, and be thankful for the honor he would do you; and think over it; and be civil and grateful."

"Nay, I will be civil enough to the good minister," said she, with a return to her ordinary placid humor, "if he speak no more of making me his wife."

"He will win you yet, for as stubborn as you are," her father said, with a smile. "He hath a rare gift of reason; do not say nay too soon, wench, lest you have to recall your words. Fare you well, lass, fare you well!"

"And forget not the knife, good father. 'With Judith's Love,' or 'For Judith's Sweetheart,' or what you will." And then she added, daringly: "'Tis for the young prince Mamillius, if you must know, good sir."

He was just going away; but this caused him to stop for a second; and he glanced at her with a curious kind of suspicion. But her eyes had become quite inscrutable. Whatever of dark mischief was within them was not to be made out but by further questioning, and for that he had now no time. So she

was left alone, mistress of the field, and rather inclined to
laugh at her own temerity; until it occurred to her that now
she could go leisurely forth for her stroll along the banks of the
Avon, taking the great dog with her.

Indeed, her anger was always short-lived. Or perhaps it
was the feeling that this danger was got rid of—that the decision was taken, and the parson finally and altogether left
behind her—that now raised her spirits. At all events, as she
went along the thoroughfare, and cheerfully greeted those that
met her, the neighbors said 'twas little wonder that Master
William Shakespeare's second daughter put off the choosing of
a mate for herself, for that she seemed to grow younger and
more winsome every day. And she knew all the children by
name, and had a word for them—scolding or merry, as the case
might be—when that she passed them by; and what with the
clear sunlight of the morning, and the fresher atmosphere as
she got out of the town, it seemed to herself as if all the air
were filled with music.

> " *Then sigh not so, but let them go,*
> *And be you blithe and bonny,*"

she said or sung to herself; and she had not a trace of ill-will
in her mind against the parson (although she did·not fail to
recollect that she was a player's daughter); and she was ad-
monishing the Don to take good care of her, for that phantom
conspirators and such like evil creatures might be about. And
so she got down to the river-side; but she did not cross; she
kept along by the path that followed the windings of the
stream, between the wide meadows and the luxurious vegeta-
tion that overhung the current.

This English-looking landscape was at its fairest on this fair
morning, for some heavy rain in the night had washed the atmosphere clear; everything seemed sharp and luminous; and
the rows of trees along the summits of the distant and low-lying hills were almost black against the white and blue sky.
Nearer her all the foliage of the wide-branching elms was
stirring and rustling before a soft westerly breeze; the flooded
river was of a tawny brown; while its banks were a wilderness
of wild flowers between the stems of the stunted willows—
straggling rose-bushes of white and red, tall masses of goose-

grass all powdered over with cream-white blossom, a patch of
fragrant meadow-sweet here and there, or an occasional blood-
red poppy burning among the dark dull greens. And as for
companions ? Well, she caught a glimpse of a brood of ducks
sidling along by the reeds, and tried to follow them, but the
bushes shut them out from her sight. A mare and her foal,
standing under the cool shadow of the trees, gazed blankly
at her as she passed. Further off there were some shorn sheep
in the meadows; but she could see no shepherd. The harsh
note of the corn-crake sounded somewhere in the long grass;
and the bees were busy; and now and again a blue-backed
swallow would swoop by her and over the stream; while all
around there was a smell of clover sweetening the westerly
wind. At this moment, she convinced herself, she bore no
ill-will at all against the good parson: only that she had it in
her mind that she would be well content to remain a player's
daughter. Her condition, she imagined, was one that she did
not desire to have bettered. Why, the air that touched her
cheek was like velvet; and there could be nothing in the world
fairer than the pink and white roses bestarring the bushes
there; and the very pulse of her blood seemed to beat to an
unheard and rhythmical and subtle tune. What was it her
father had said? "I dare be sworn you are as honest and
well-minded as most, though perchance you make less profession of it." She laughed to herself, with a kind of pride. And
she was so well content that she wished she had little Willie
Hart here, that she might put her hand on his shoulder and
pet him, and convey to him some little of that satisfaction that
reigned within her own bosom. No matter; he should have
the clasp-knife—"*With Judith's Love*"; and right proud he
would be of that, she made sure. And so she went idly on
her way, sometimes with,

> "*Fair, fair, and twice so fair,*
> *And fair as any may be,*"

coming uncalled-for into her head; and always with an eye to
the various wild flowers, to see what kind of a nosegay she
would be able to gather on her homeward walk.

But by-and-by her glances began to go further afield. Master Leofric Hope, in his brief references to his own habits and

condition at the farm, had incidentally remarked that of all
his walks abroad he preferred the following of the path by the
river-side; for there he was most secure from observation.
Nay, he said that sometimes, after continued solitude, a longing possessed him to see a town—to see a populated place filled
with a fair number of his fellow-creatures—and that he would
come within sight of Stratford itself and have a look at the
church, and the church spire, and the thin blue smoke rising
over the houses.   That, he said, was safer for him than coming over such an exposed thoroughfare as Bardon Hill; and
then again, when he was of a mind to read—for this time he
had brought one or two books with him—he could find many
a sheltered nook by the side of the stream, where even a passer-by would not suspect his presence.   Nor could Judith, on
this fresh, warm, breezy morning, conceal from herself the true
object of her coming forth.   If she had tried to deceive herself,
the contents of the blue velvet satchel would have borne
crushing testimony against her.   In truth she was now looking with some eagerness to find whether, on such a pleasant
morning, it was possible that he could have remained within-
doors, and with the very distinct belief that sooner or later
she would encounter him.

Nor was she mistaken, though the manner of the meeting
was unexpected.   The mastiff happened to have gone on a
yard or two in front of her, and she was paying but little attention to the beast, when all of a sudden it stopped, became
rigid, and uttered a low growl.   She sprang forward and seized
it by the collar.   At the same instant she caught sight of some
one down by the water's edge, where, but for this occurrence,
he would doubtless have escaped observation.   It was Leofric
Hope, without a doubt; for now he was clambering up through
the bushes, and she saw that he had a small book in his
hand.

"My good fortune pursues me, fair Mistress Judith," said he
(but with a watchful eye on the dog), "that I should so soon
again have an opportunity of meeting with you.   But perchance your protector is jealous?   He likes not strangers?"

"A lamb, sir—a very lamb!" Judith said, and she patted the
dog and coaxed him, and got him into a more friendly—or at
least neutral and watchful—frame of mind.

"I marvel not you have come forth on such a morning,"
said he, regarding the fresh color in her face. "'Tis a rare
morning; and 'tis a rare chance for one that is a prisoner,
as it were, that his dungeon is not four walls, but the wide
spaces of Warwickshire. Will you go further? May I attend you?"

"Nay, sir," said she, "I but came forth to look at the country, and see what blossoms I could carry back to my father; I
will go as far as the stile there, and rest a few minutes, and
return."

"'Tis like your kindness, sweet lady, to vouchsafe me a moment's conversation; a book is but a dull companion," said he,
as they walked along to the stile that formed part of a bound-
ary hedge. And when they reached it she seated herself on
the wooden bar with much content, and the mastiff lay down,
stretching out his paws, while the young gentleman stood idly
—but not carelessly—by. He seemed more than ever anxious
to interest his fair neighbor, and so to beguile her into remaining.

"A dull companion," he repeated, "it is. One would rather hear the sound of one's voice occasionally. When I came
along here this morning I should have been right glad even to
have had a she shepherd say 'Good-morrow' to me—"

"A what, good sir?" she asked.

He laughed.

"Nay, 'tis a book the wits in London have much merriment
over just now—a guide-book for the use of foreigners coming
to this country—and there be plenty of them at present, in
the train of the ambassadors. Marry, the good man's English is none of the best. '*For to ask the Way*' is a chapter of
the book; and the one traveller saith to the other, '*Ask of
that she shepherd*'—in truth the phrase hath been caught up
by the town. But the traveller is of a pleasant and courteous
turn; when that he would go to bed, he saith to the chamber-
maid: 'Draw the curtains, and pin them with a pin. My she
friend, kiss me once, and I shall sleep the better. I thank you,
fair maiden.' Well, their English may be none of the best,
but they have a royal way with them, some of those foreigners
that come to our court. When the Constable of Castile was
at the great banquet at Whitehall—doubtless you heard of

it, sweet Mistress Judith ?—he rose and drank the health of the
Queen from a cup of agate of extraordinary value, all set with
diamonds and rubies, and when the King had drank from the
same cup the Constable called a servant, and desired that the
cup should be placed on his Majesty's buffet, to remain there.
Was't not a royal gift ?   And so likewise he drank the health of
the King from a beautiful dragon-shaped cup of crystal all
garnished with gold; but he drank from the cover only, for the
Queen, standing up, drank the pledge from the cup itself; and
then he would have that in turn transferred to her buffet,
as he had given the other one to the King."

"My father," said she, with much complacent good-nature—
for she had got into the way of talking to this young gentleman with a marvellous absence of restraint or country shyness, "hath a tankard of great age and value, and on the silver
top of it is a tribute engraved from many of his friends—truly
I would that you could come and see it, good sir—and—and—
my father, too, he would make you welcome, I doubt not.
And what book is it," she continued, with a smile, "that you
have for companion, seeing that there be no she shepherd for
you to converse withal ?"

"'Tis but a dull affair," said he, scarce looking at it, for Judith's eyes were more attractive reading. "And yet if the
book itself be dull, there is that within its boards that is less so.
Perchance you have not heard of one Master Browne, a young
Devonshire gentleman; that hath but late come to London, and
that only for a space, as I reckon ?"

"No, sir," she said, hesitatingly.

"The young man hath made some stir with his poems," he
continued, "though there be none of them in the booksellers'
hands as yet.   And as it hath been my good fortune to see
one or two of them—marry, I am no judge, but I would call
them excellent, and of much modesty and grace—I took occasion to pencil down a few of the lines inside the cover of this
little book.   May I read them to you, Mistress Judith ?"

"If it please you, good sir."

He opened the book, and she saw that there were some lines
pencilled on the gray binding; but they must have been familiar to him, for he scarce took his eyes from Judith's face as he
repeated them.

HE OPENED THE BOOK, AND SHE SAW THAT THERE WERE SOME LINES PENCILLED ON THE GRAY BINDING.

"They are a description," said he, "of one that must have been fair indeed:

> *"'Her cheeks, the wonder of what eye beheld,*
> *Begot betwixt a lily and a rose,*
> *In gentle rising plains divinely swelled,*
> *Where all the graces and the loves repose.*
> *Nature in this piece all her works excelled,*
> *Yet showed herself imperfect in the close,*
> *For she forgot (when she so fair did raise her)*
> *To give the world a wit might duly praise her.*

> *"'When that she spoke, as at a voice from heaven,*
> *On her sweet words all ears and hearts attended;*
> *When that she sung, they thought the planets seven*
> *By her sweet voice might well their tunes have mended;*
> *When she did sigh, all were of joy bereaven;*
> *And when she smiled, heaven had them all befriended:*
> *If that her voice, sighs, smiles, so many thrilled,*
> *Oh, had she kissed, how many had she killed!'"*

"'Tis a description of a lady of the court?" Judith asked, timidly.

"No, by heavens," he said, with warmth; "the bonniest of our English roses are they that grow in the country air!"— and his glance of admiration was so open and undisguised, and the application of his words so obvious, that her eyes fell, and in spite of herself the color mounted to her cheeks. In her embarrassment she sought safety in the blue velvet satchel. She had contemplated some other way of introducing this latest writing of her father's; but now that had all fled from her brain. She knew that the town gentlemen were given to flattery; but then she was not accustomed to it. And she could not but swiftly surmise that he had written down these lines with the especial object of addressing them to her when he should have the chance.

"Good sir," said she, endeavoring to hide this brief embarrassment by assuming a merry air, "a fair exchange, they say, is no robbery. Methinks you will find something here that will outweigh good Master Browne's verses—in bulk, if not in merit."

He gazed in astonishment at the parcel of sheets she handed to him, and he but glanced at the first page when he exclaimed,

"Why, I have heard naught of this before."

"Nay, sir," said she, with a calm smile, "the infant is but

young—but a few weeks, as I take it; it hath had but little
chance of making a noise in the world as yet.   Will you say
what you think of it ?"

But now he was busy reading.   Then by-and-by she recollected something of the manner in which she had meant to in-
troduce the play.

"You see, sir, my father hath many affairs on his hands;
'tis not all his time he can give to such things.   And yet I
have heard that they be well spoken of in London—if not by
the wits, perchance, or by the court ladies, at least by the common people and the 'prentices.   We in these parts have but
little skill of learning; but—but methinks 'tis a pretty story—
is it not, good sir?—and perchance as interesting as a speech
from a goddess among the clouds ?"

"In truth it is a rare invention," said he, but absently, for
his whole and rapt attention was fixed on the sheets.

She, seeing him so absorbed, did not interfere further.   She
sat still and content—perhaps with a certain sedate triumph in
her eyes.   She listened to the rustling of the elms overhead,
and watched the white clouds slowly crossing the blue, and the
tawny-hued river lazily and noiselessly stealing by below the
bushes.   The corn-crake was silent now—there was not even
that interruption; and when the bell in the church tower began
to toll, it was so soft and faint and distant that she thought it
most likely he would not even hear it.   And at what point
was he now ?   At the story of how the sweet Miranda came to
grow up in exile ?   Or listening to Ariel's song ?   Or watching the prince approach this new wonder of the magic island ?
Her eyes were full of triumph.   "Ben Jonson!" she had said.

But suddenly he closed the sheets together.

"It were unmannerly so to keep you waiting," said he.

"Nay, heed not that, good sir," she said, instantly.   "I pray
you go on with the reading.   How like you it ?   'Tis a pretty
story, methinks; but my father hath been so busy of late—what
with acres, and tithes, and sheep, and malt, and the like—that
perchance he hath not given all his mind to it."

"It is not for one such as I, fair Mistress Judith," said he,
with much modesty, "to play the critic when it is your father's writing that comes forward.   Beshrew me, there be
plenty of that trade in London, and chiefly the feeble folk

that he hath driven from our stage. No, sweet lady; rather consider me one of those that crowd to see each new piece of his, and are right thankful for aught he pleaseth to give us."

"Is that so?" said she; and she regarded him with much favor, which he was not slow to perceive.

"Why," said he, boldly, "what needs your father to heed if some worshipful Master Scoloker be of opinion that the play of the Prince Hamlet belongeth to the vulgar sort, and that the prince was but moon-sick; or that some one like Master Greene—God rest his soul, wherever it be!—should call him an upstart crow, and a Johannes factotum, and the like? 'Tis what the people of England think that is of import; and right sure am I what they would say—that there is no greater writer than your father now living in the land."

"Ah, think you so?" she said, quickly, and her face grew radiant, as it were, and her eyes were filled with gratitude.

"This Master Greene," he continued, "was ever gibing at the players, as I have heard, and bidding them be more humble, for that their labor was but mechanical, and them attracting notice through wearing borrowed plumes. Nay, he would have it that your father was no more than that—poor man, he lived but a sorry life, and 'twere ill done to cherish anger against him; but I remember to have seen the apology that he that published the book made thereafter to your father—in good truth it was fitting and right that it should be printed and given to the world; and though I forget the terms of it, 'twas in fair praise of Master William Shakespeare's gentle demeanor, and his uprightness of conduct, and the grace of his wit."

"Could you get that for me, good sir?" said she, eagerly. "Is't possible that I could get it?"

And then she stopped in some embarrassment, for she remembered that it was not becoming she should ask this stranger for a gift. "Nay, sir, 'twould be of little use to me, that have no skill of reading."

"But I pray you, sweet Mistress Judith, to permit me to bring you the book; 'twill be something, at least, for you to keep and show to your friends—"

"If I might show it to Prudence Shawe, I could return it to you, good sir," said she. And then she added, "Not that she—

no, nor any one in Stratford town—would need any such testimony to my father's qualities, that are known to all."

"At least they seem to have won him the love and loyalty of his daughter," said he, gallantly; "and they know most about a man who live nearest him. Nay, but I will beg you to accept the book from me when I can with safety get to London again; 'twill be a charge I am not likely to forget. And in return, fair Mistress Judith, I would take of you another favor, and a greater."

"In what manner, gentle sir?"

"I have but glanced over this writing, for fear of detaining you, and but half know the value of it," said he. "I pray you let me have it with me to my lodging for an hour or two, that I may do it justice. When one hath such a chance come to him, 'tis not to be lightly treated; and I would give time and quiet to the making out the beauties of your father's latest work."

She was at first somewhat startled by this proposal, and almost involuntarily was for putting forth her hand to receive the sheets again into safe-keeping; but then she asked herself what harm there could be in acceding to his request. She was eagerly anxious that he should understand how her father —even amidst those multifarious occupations that were entailed on him by his prominent position in the town—could, when he chose, sit down and write a tale far exceeding in beauty and interest any of the mummeries that the court people seemed to talk about. Why should not he have a few hours' time to study this fragment withal? Her father was gone to Warwick for the day. Nay, more, she had taken so small a portion of what had been cast aside that she knew the absence of it would not be noticed, however long it might be kept. And then this young gentleman, who was so civil and courteous, and who spoke so well of her father, was alone, and to be pitied for that he had so few means of beguiling the tedium of his hiding.

"In the afternoon," said he, seeing that she hesitated, "I could with safety leave it at your grandmother's cottage, and then, perchance, you might send some one for it. Nay, believe me, sweet Mistress Judith, I know the value of that I ask; but I would fain do justice to such a treasure."

"You would not fail me, sir, in leaving it at the cottage?" said she.

"You do me wrong, Mistress Judith, to doubt—in good sooth you do. If you can find a trusty messenger—"

"Nay, but I will come for it myself, good sir, and explain to my grandmother the nature of the thing, lest she suspect me of meddling with darker plots. Let it be so, then, good sir, for now I must get me back to the town. I pray you forget not to leave the package; and so—farewell!"

"But my thanks to you, dear lady—"

"Nay, sir," said she, with a bright look of her eyes, "bethink you you have not yet fairly made out the matter. Tarry till you have seen whether these sheets be worth the trouble—whether they remind you in aught of the work of your friend Master Jonson—and then your thanks will be welcome. Give ye good-day, gentle sir."

There was no thought in her mind that she had done anything imprudent in trusting him with this portion of the play for the matter of an hour or two; it was but a small equivalent, she recollected, for his promise to bring her from London the retractation or apology of one of those who had railed at her father, or abetted in that, and found himself constrained by his conscience to make amends. And now it occurred to her that it would look ill if, having come out to gather some wild flowers for the little table in the summer-house, she returned with empty hands; so, as she proceeded to walk leisurely along the winding path leading back to the town, she kept picking here and there such blossoms as came within her reach. If the nosegay promised to be somewhat large and straggling, at least it would be sweet-scented, and she felt pretty sure that her father would be well content with it. At first she was silent, however; her wonted singing was abandoned; perchance she was trying to recall something of the lines that Master Leofric Hope had repeated to her with so marked an emphasis.

"And what said he of our English roses?" she asked herself, with some faint color coming into her face at the mere thought of it.

But then she forcibly dismissed these recollections, feeling that that was due to her own modesty, and busied herself with her blossoms and sprays; and presently, as she set out in good earnest for the town, she strove to convince herself that there was nothing more serious in her brain than the tune of "Green-sleeves":

> " *Green-sleeves, now farewell, adieu ;*
> *God I pray to prosper thee ;*
> *For I am still thy lover true—*
> *Come once again and love me !*"

CHAPTER XVII.

WILD WORDS.

HER light-heartedness did not last long.   In the wide clear landscape a human figure suddenly appeared, and the briefest turn of her head showed her that Tom Quiney was rapidly coming toward her across the fields.   For a second her heart stood still.   Had he been riding home from Ludington?   Or from Bidford?   Was it possible that he had come over Bardon Hill, and from that height espied the two down by the river? She could not even tell whether that was possible, or what he had done with his horse, or why he had not interfered sooner, if he was bent on interfering.   But she had an alarmed impression that this rapid approach of his boded trouble, and she had not long to wait before that fear was confirmed.

"Judith, who is that man?" he demanded, with a fury that was but half held in.

She turned and faced him.

"I knew not," she said, coldly and slowly, "that we were on a speaking platform."

"'Tis no time to bandy words," said he; and his face was pale, for he was evidently striving to control the passion with which his whole figure seemed to quiver from head to heel. "Who is that man? I ask.   Who is he, that you come here to seek him, and alone?"

"I know not by what right you put such questions to me," she said; but she was somewhat frightened.

"By what right?   And you have no regard, then, for your good name?"

There was a flash in her eyes.   She had been afraid: she was no longer afraid.

"My good name?" she repeated. "I thank God 'tis in none of your keeping!"

In his madness he caught her by the wrist.

"You shall tell me—"

"Unhand me, sir!" she exclaimed; and she threw off his grasp, while her cheeks burned with humiliation.

"Nay, I quarrel not with women," said he. "I crave your pardon. But, by God, I will get to know that man's name and purpose here if I rive it from his body!"

So he strode off in the direction that Leofric Hope had taken; and for a moment she stood quite terror-stricken and helpless, scarcely daring to think of what might happen. A murder on this fair morning? This young fellow, that was quite beside himself in his passion of jealous anger, was famed throughout the length and breadth of Warwickshire for his wrestling prowess. And the other—would he brook high words? These things flashed across her mind in one bewildering instant; and in her alarm she forgot all about her pride. She called to him,

"I pray you—stay!"

He turned and regarded her.

"Stay," said she, with her face afire. "I—I will tell you what I know of him—if you will have it so."

He approached her with seeming reluctance, and with anger and suspicion in his lowering look. He was silent, too.

"Indeed, there is no harm," said she (and still with her face showing her mortification that she was thus forced to defend herself). "'Tis a young gentleman that is in some trouble—his lodging near Bidford is also a hiding, as it were—and—and I know but little of him beyond his name, and that he is familiar with many of my father's friends in London."

"And how comes it that you seek him out here alone?" said he. "That is a becoming and maidenly thing!"

"I promised you I would tell you what I know of the young gentleman," said she, with scornful lips. "I did not promise to stand still and suffer your insolence."

"Insolence!" he exclaimed, as if her audacity bewildered him.

"How know you that I sought him out!" she said, indignantly. "May not one walk forth of a summer morning

without being followed by suspicious eyes—I warrant me, eyes
that are only too glad to suspect! To think evil is an easy
thing, it seems, with many: I wonder, sir, you are not ashamed."

"You brave it out well," said he, sullenly; but it was evident that her courage had impressed him, if it still left him angered and suspicious.

And then he asked:

"How comes it that none of your friends or your family
know ought of this stranger?"

"I marvel you should speak of my family," she retorted.
"I had thought you were inclined to remain in ignorance of
them of late. But had you asked of Prudence Shawe she
might have told you something of this young gentleman; or
had you thought fit to call in at my grandmother's cottage, you
might perchance have found him seated there, and a welcome
guest at her board. Marry, 'tis easier far to keep aloof and to
think evil, as one may see."

And then she added:

"Well, sir, are you satisfied? May I go home without farther threats?"

"I threatened you not, Judith," said he, rather more humbly. "I would have my threats kept for those that would
harm you."

"I know of none such," she said, distinctly. "And as for
this young gentleman—that is in misfortune—such as might
happen to any one—and not only in hiding, but having intrusted his secret to one or two of us that pity him and see no
harm in him—I say it were a cruel and unmanly thing to spy
out his concealment, or to spread the rumor of his being in
the neighborhood."

"Nay, you need not fear that of me, Judith," said he. "Man
to man is my way, when there is occasion. But can you marvel if I would have you for your own sake avoid any further
meetings with this stranger? If he be in hiding, let him remain there, in God's name; I for one will set no beagles to
hunt him out. But as for you, I would have you meddle with
no such dangerous traps."

"Good sir," said she, "I have my conduct in my own keeping, and can answer to those that have the guardianship of me."

He did not reply to this rebuke. He said:

"May I walk back to the town with you, Judith?"

"You forget," she said, coldly, "that if we were seen together the gossips might say I had come out hither to seek you, and alone."

But he paid no heed to this taunt.

"I care not," said he, with an affectation of indifference, "what the gossips in Stratford have to talk over. Stratford and I are soon to part."

"What say you?" said she, quickly—and they were walking on together now, the Don leisurely following at their heels.

"Nay, 'tis nothing," said he, carelessly; "there are wider lands beyond the seas, where a man can fight for his own and hold it."

"And you?" she said. "You have it in your mind to leave the country?"

"Marry, that have I!" said he, gayly. "My good friend Daniel Hutt hath gotten together a rare regiment, and I doubt not I shall be one of the captains of them ere many years be over."

Her eyes were downcast, and he could not see what impression this piece of news had made upon her—if, indeed, he cared to look. They walked for some time in silence.

"It is no light matter," said she at length, and in rather a low voice, "to leave one's native land."

"As for that," said he, "the land will soon be not worth the living in. Why, in former times, men spoke of the merry world of England. A merry world?—I trow the canting rogues of preachers have left but little merriment in it; and now they would seek to have all in their power, and to flood the land with their whining and psalm-singing, till we shall have no England left us, but only a vast conventicle. Think you that your father hath any sympathy with these? I tell you no; I take it he is an Englishman, and not a conventicle-man. 'Tis no longer the England of our forefathers when men may neither hawk nor hunt, and women are doomed to perdition for worshipping the false idol starch, and the very children be called in from their games of a Sunday afternoon. God-a-mercy, I have had enough of Brother Patience-in-suffering, and his dominion of grace!"

This seemed to Judith a strange reason for his going away,

8

for he had never professed any strong bias one way or the other
in these religious dissensions; his chief concern, like that of
most of the young men in Stratford, lying rather in the direction of butt-shooting, or wrestling, or having a romp with
some of the wenches to the tune of "Packington's Pound."

"Nay, as I hear," said he, "there be some of them in such
discontent with the King and the Parliament that they even
talk of transplanting themselves beyond seas, like those that
went to Holland: 'twere a goodly riddance if the whole gang
of the sour-faced hypocrites went, and left to us our own England.   And a fair beginning for the new country across the
Atlantic—half of them these Puritanical rogues, with their
fastings and preachments; and the other half the constable's
brats and broken men that such as Hutt are drafting out: a
right good beginning, if they but keep from seizing each other by the throat in the end!   No matter: we should have our
England purged of the double scum!"

"But," said Judith, timidly, "methought you said you were
going out with these same desperate men?"

"I can take my life in my hand as well as another," said he,
gloomily.   And then he added: "They be none so desperate,
after all.   Broken men there may be amongst them, and
many against whom fortune would seem to have a spite: perchance their affairs may mend in the new country."

"But your affairs are prosperous," Judith said—though she
never once regarded him.   "Why should you link yourself
with such men as these?"

"One must forth to see the world," said he; and he went on
to speak in a gay and reckless fashion of the life that lay before
him, and of its possible adventures and hazards and prizes.
"And what," said he, "if one were to have good fortune in
that far country, and become rich in land, and have good store
of corn and fields of tobacco; what if one were to come back
in twenty years' time to this same town of Stratford, and set
up for the trade of gentleman?"

"Twenty years?" said she, rather breathlessly.   "'Tis a long
time; you will find changes."

"None that would matter much, methinks," said he, indifferently.

"There be those that will be sorry for your going away,"

she ventured to say—and she forced herself to think only of Prudence Shawe.

"Not one that will care a cracked three-farthings!" was the answer.

"You do ill to say so—indeed you do!" said she, with just a touch of warmth in her tone. "You have many friends; you serve them ill to say they would not heed your going."

"Friends?" said he. "Yes, they will miss me at the shovel-board, or when there is one short at the catches."

"There be others than those," said she, with some little hesitation.

"Who, then?" said he.

"You should know yourself," she answered. "Think you that Prudence, for one, will be careless as to your leaving the country?"

"Prudence?" said he, and he darted a quick glance at her. "Nay, I confess me wrong, then; for there is one that hath a gentle heart, and is full of kindness."

"Right well I know that—for who should know better than I?" said Judith. "As true a heart as any in Christendom, and a prize for him that wins it, I warrant you. If it be not won already," she added, quickly. "As to that, I know not."

They were now nearing the town—they could hear the dull sound of the mill, and before them was the church spire among the trees, and beyond that the gray and red huddled mass of houses, barns, and orchards.

"And when think you of going?" she said, after a while.

"I know not, and I care not," said he, absently. "When I spoke of my acquaintances being indifferent as to what might befall me, I did them wrong, for in truth there be none of them as indifferent as I am myself."

"'Tis not a hopeful mood," said she, "to begin the making of one's fortunes in a new country withal. I pray you, what ails this town of Stratford, that you are not content?"

"It boots not to say, since I am leaving it," he answered. "Perchance in times to come, when I am able to return to it, I shall be better content. And you?"

"And I?" she repeated, with some surprise.

"Nay, you will be content enough," said he, somewhat bitterly. "Mother Church will have a care of you. You will be in the fold by then. The faithful shepherd will have a charge over you, to keep you from communication with the children of anger and the devil, that rage without like lions seeking to destroy."

"I know not what you mean," said she, with a hot face.

"Right well you know," said he, coolly; but there was an angry resentment running through his affected disdain as he went on: "There be those that protest, and go forth from the Church. And there be those that protest, and remain within, eating the fat things, and well content with the milk and the honey, and their stores of corn and oil. Marry, you will be well provided for—the riches of the next world laid up in waiting for you, and a goodly share of the things of this world to beguile the time withal. Nay, I marvel not; 'tis the wisdom of the serpent along with the innocence of the dove. What matters the surplice, the cross in baptism, and the other relics of popery, if conformity will keep the larder full? Better that than starvation in Holland, or seeking a home beyond the Atlantic, where, belike, the children of the devil might prove overrude companions. I marvel not, I; 'tis a foolish bird that forsakes a warm nest."

And now she well knew against whom his bitter speech was levelled; and some recollection of the slight he had put upon her in the church-yard came into her mind, with the memory that it had never been atoned for. And she was astounded that he had the audacity to walk with her now and here, talking as if he were the injured one. The sudden qualm that had filled her heart when he spoke of leaving the country was put aside; the kindly reference to Prudence was forgotten; she only knew that this sarcasm of his was very much out of place, and that this was far from being the tone in which he had any right to address her.

"I know not," said she, stiffly, "what quarrel you may have with this or that section of the Church; but it concerns me not. I pray you attack those who are better able to defend themselves than I am, or care to be. Methinks your studies in that line have come somewhat late."

"'Tis no greater marvel," said he, "than that you should have joined yourself to the assembly of the saints: it was not always so with you."

"I ?" she said; but her cheeks were burning; for well she knew that he referred to his having seen her with the parson on that Sunday morning, and she was far too proud to defend herself. "Heaven help me now, but I thought I was mistress of my own actions!"

"In truth you are, Mistress Judith," said he, humbly (and this was the first time that he had ever addressed her so, and it startled her, for it seemed to suggest a final separation between them—something as wide and irrevocable as that twenty years of absence beyond the seas). And then he said, "I crave your pardon if I have said ought to offend you; and would take my leave."

"God be wi' you," said she, civilly; and then he left, striking across the meadows toward the Bidford road, and, as she guessed, probably going to seek his horse from whomsoever he had left it with.

And as she went on, and into the town, she was wondering what Prudence had said to him that should so suddenly drive him to think of quitting the country. All had seemed going well. As for Master Leofric Hope, his secret was safe; this late companion of hers seemed to have forgotten him altogether in his anger against the good parson. And then she grew to think of the far land across the ocean, that she had heard vaguely of from time to time; and to think how twenty years could be spent there; and what Stratford would be like when that long space was over.

"Twenty years," she said to herself, with a kind of sigh. "There are many things will be settled, ere that time be passed, for good or ill."

CHAPTER XVIII.

A CONJECTURE.

WHEN she got back to New Place she found the house in considerable commotion. It appeared that the famous divine Master Elihu Izod had just come into the town, being on his way toward Leicestershire, and that he had been brought by the gentleman whose guest he was to pay a visit to Judith's mother. Judith had remarked ere now that the preachers and other godly persons who thus honored the New Place generally made their appearance a trifling time before the hour of dinner; and now, as she reached the house, she was not surprised to find that Prudence had been called in to entertain the two visitors—who were at present in the garden—while within-doors her mother and the maids were hastily making such preparations as were possible. To this latter work she quickly lent a helping hand; and in due course of time the board was spread with a copious and substantial repast, not forgetting an ample supply of wine and ale for those that were that way inclined. Then the two gentlemen were called in, Prudence was easily persuaded to stay, and, after a lengthened grace, the good preacher fell to, seasoning his food with much pious conversation.

At such times Judith had abundant opportunities for reverie, and for a general review of the situation of her own affairs. In fact, on this occasion she seemed in a manner to be debarred from participation in these informal services at the very outset. Master Izod, who was a tall, thin, dark, melancholy-visaged man—unlike his companion, Godfrey Buller, of the Leas, near to Hinckley, who, on the contrary, was a stout, yeoman-like person, whose small gray absent eyes remained motionless and vacant in the great breadth of his rubicund face—had taken for his text, as it were, a list he had found somewhere or other of those characters that were entitled to command the admiration and respect of all good people. These were: a young saint; an old martyr; a religious soldier; a conscionable statesman;

a great man courteous; a learned man humble; a silent woman; a merry companion without vanity; a friend not changed
with honor; a sick man cheerful; a soul departing with comfort and assurance. And as Judith did not make bold to claim
to be any one of these—nor, indeed, to have any such merits or
excellences as would extort the approval of the membership
of the saints—she gradually fell away from listening; and her
mind was busy with other things; and her imagination, which
was vivid enough, intent upon other scenes. One thing that
had struck her the moment she had returned was that Prudence
seemed in an unusually cheerful mood. Of course the arrival
of two visitors was an event in that quiet life of theirs; and
no doubt Prudence was glad to be appointed to entertain the
strangers—one of them, moreover, being of such great fame.
But so pleased was she, and so cheerful in her manner, that
Judith was straightway convinced there had been no quarrel
between her and Tom Quiney. Nay, when was there time for
that? He could scarcely have seen her that morning; while
the night before there had certainly been no mention of his
projected migration to America, else Prudence would have said
as much. What, then, had so suddenly driven him to the
conclusion that England was no longer a land fit to live in?
And why had he paid Prudence such marked attention—why
had he presented her with the spaniel-gentle and offered her
the emblazoned missal—one evening, only to resolve the next
morning that he must needs leave the country? Nay, why had
he so unexpectedly broken the scornful silence with which he
had recently treated herself? He had given her to understand
that, as far as he was concerned, she did not exist. He seemed determined to ignore her presence. And yet she could not
but remember that, if this contemptuous silence on his part
was broken by the amazement of his seeing her in the company
of a stranger, his suspicions in that direction were very speedily disarmed. A few words, and they fled. It was his far more
deadly jealousy of the parson that remained; and was like to
remain, for she certainly would not stoop to explain that the
meeting in the church-yard was quite accidental. But why
should he trouble his head about either her or the parson?
Had he not betaken himself elsewhere—and that with her
right good will? Nay, on his own confession he had discover-

ed how kind and gentle Prudence was: there was a fit mate for
him—one to temper the wildness and hot-headedness of his
youth. Judith had never seen the sea, and therefore had never seen moonlight on the sea; but the nearest to that she could
go, in thinking of what Prudence's nature was like, in its restful and sweet and serious beauty, was the moonlight she had
seen on the river Avon in the calm of a summer's night, the
water unbroken by a ripple, and not a whisper among the
reeds. Could he not perceive that too, and understand?

As for herself, she knew that she could at any moment cut
the knot of any complications that might arise by allowing
Master Walter to talk her over into marrying him. Her father had assured her that the clear-headed and energetic young
parson was quite equal to that. Well, it was about time she
should abandon the frivolities and coquetries of her youth;
and her yielding would please many good people, especially her
mother and sister, and obtain for herself a secure and estab-
lished position, with an end to all these quarrels and jealousies
and uncertainties. Moreover, there would be safety there.
For, if the truth must be told, she was becoming vaguely and
uncomfortably conscious that her relations with this young
gentleman who had come secretly into the neighborhood were
no longer what they had been at first. Their friendship had
ripened rapidly; for he was an audacious personage, with plenty
of self-assurance; and with all his professions of modesty and
deference, he seemed to know very well that he could make
his society agreeable. Then those lines he had repeated: why,
her face grew warm now as she thought of them. She could
not remember them exactly, but she remembered their purport;
and she remembered, too, the emphasis with which he had declared that the bonniest of our English roses were those that
grew in the country air. Now a young man cut off from his
fellows as he was might well be grateful for some little solace
of companionship, or for this or the other little bit of courtesy;
but he need not (she considered) show his gratitude just in that
way. Doubtless his flattery might mean little; the town gentlemen, she understood, talked in that strain; and perhaps it
was only by an accident that the verses were there in the book;
but still she had the uneasy feeling that there was something
in his manner and speech that, if encouraged, or suffered to

continue without check, might lead to embarrassment. That is to say, if she continued to see him; and there was no need for that. She could cut short this acquaintance the moment she chose. But on the one hand she did not wish to appear uncivil; and on the other she was anxious that he should see the whole of this play that her father had written—thrown off, as it were, amid the various cares and duties that occupied his time. If Master Leofric Hope talked of Ben Jonson when he came into the country, she would have him furnished with something to say of her father when he returned to town.

These were idle and wandering thoughts; and in one respect they were not quite honest. In reality she was using them to cloak and hide, or to drive from her mind altogether, a suspicion that had suddenly occurred to her that morning, and that had set her brain afire in a wild way. It was not only the tune of "Green-sleeves" that was in her head as she set off to walk home, though she was trying to force herself to believe that. The fact is this: when Master Leofric Hope made the pretty speech about the country roses, he accompanied it, as has been said, by a glance of only too outspoken admiration; and there was something in this look—apart from the mere flattery of it—that puzzled her. She was confused, doubtless; but in her confusion it occurred to her that she had met that regard somewhere before. She had no time to pursue this fancy further; for in order to cover her embarrassment she had betaken herself to the sheets in her satchel; and thereafter she was so anxious that he should think well of the play that all her attention was fixed on that. But after leaving him, and having had a minute or two to think over what had happened, she recalled that look, and wondered why there should be something strange in it. And then a startling fancy flashed across her mind—the wizard! Was not that the same look—of the same black eyes—that she had encountered up at the corner of the field above the Weir Brake?—a glance of wondering admiration, as it were? And if these two were one and the same man? Of course that train, being lit, ran rapidly enough: there were all kinds of parallels—in the elaborate courtesy, in the suave voice, in the bold and eloquent eyes. And she had no magical theory to account for the transformation—it did not even occur to her that the wizard could have

changed himself into a young man—there was no dismay or
panic in that direction: she instantly took it for granted that
it was the young man who had been personating the wizard.
And why?—to what end, if this bewildering possibility were
to be regarded for an instant? The object of the wizard's coming was to point out to her her future husband. And if this
young man were himself the wizard? A trick to entrap her?

Ariel himself could not have flashed from place to place
more swiftly than this wild conjecture; but the next moment
she had collected herself. Her common-sense triumphed. She
bethought her of the young man she had just left—of his respectful manners—of the letter he had brought for her father
—of the circumstances of his hiding. It was not possible that
he had come into the neighborhood for the deliberate purpose
of making a jest of her. Did he look like one that would play
such a trick; that would name himself as her future husband;
that would cozen her into meeting him? She felt ashamed
of herself for harboring such a thought for a single instant.
Her wits had gone wool-gathering! Or was it that Prudence's
fears had so far got hold of her brain that she could not regard
the young man but as something other than an ordinary mortal? In fair justice, she would dismiss this absurd surmise from
her mind forthwith; and so she proceeded with her gathering
of the flowers; and when she did set forth for home, she had
very nearly convinced herself that there was nothing in her
head but the tune of "Green-sleeves." Nay, she was almost inclined to be angry with Prudence for teaching her to be so suspicious.

Nevertheless, during this protracted dinner, while good Master Izod was enlarging upon the catalogue of persons worthy
of honor and emulation, Judith was attacked once more by the
whisperings of the demon. For a while she fought against
these, and would not admit to herself that any further doubt
remained in her mind; but when at last she found herself,
despite herself, going back and back to that possibility, she
took heart of grace and boldly faced it. What if it were true?
Supposing him to have adopted the disguise, and passed himself off as a wizard, and directed her to the spot where she
should meet her future husband—what then? What ought
she to do? How ought she to regard such conduct? As an

idle frolic of youth ? Or the device of one tired of the loneli-
ness of living at the farm, and determined at all hazards to
secure companionship ? Or a darker snare still—with what ul-
timate aims she could not divine ? Or again (for she was quite
frank), if this were merely some one who had seen her from
afar, at church, or fair, or market, and considered she was a
good-looking maid, and wished to have further acquaintance,
and could think of no other method than this audacious prank?
She had heard of lovers' stratagems in plenty; she knew of
one or two of such that had been resorted to in this same
quiet town of Stratford. And supposing that this last was the
case, ought she to be indignant ? Should she resent his bold-
ness in hazarding such a stroke to win her ? And then, when
it suddenly occurred to her that, in discussing this possibility,
she was calmly assuming that Master Leofric Hope was in love
with her—he never having said a word in that direction, and
being in a manner almost a stranger to her—she told herself
that no audacity on his part could be greater than this on hers;
and that the best thing she could do would be to get rid once
and forever of such unmaidenly conjectures. No; she would
go back to her original position. The facts of the case were
simple enough. He would have brought no letter to her father had he been bent on any such fantastic enterprise. Was
it likely he would suffer the thralldom of that farm-house,
and live away from his friends and companions, for the mere
chance of a few minutes' occasional talk with a Stratford
wench ? As for the similarity between his look and that of the
wizard, the explanation lay no doubt in her own fancy, which
had been excited by Prudence's superstitious fears. And if in
his courtesy he had applied to herself the lines written by the
young Devonshire poet—well, that was but a piece of civility
and kindness, for which she ought to be more than usually
grateful, seeing that she had not experienced too much of that
species of treatment of late from one or two of her would-be
suitors.

She was awakened from these dreams by the conversation
suddenly ceasing; and in its place she heard the more solemn
tones of the thanksgiving offered up by Master Izod:

"The God of glory and peace, who hath created, redeemed,

and presently fed us, be blessed forever and ever! So be it. The God of all power, who hath called from death that great pastor of the sheep, our Lord Jesus, comfort and defend the flock which He hath redeemed by the blood of the eternal testament; increase the number of true preachers; repress the rage of obstinate tyrants; mitigate and lighten the hearts of the ignorant; relieve the pains of such as be afflicted, but specially of those that suffer for the testimony of Thy truth; and finally, confound Satan by the power of our Lord Jesus Christ. Amen."

And then, as the travellers were continuing their journey forthwith, they proposed to leave; and Master Buller expressed his sorrow that Judith's father had not been at home to have made the friendship of a man so famous as Master Izod; and the good parson, in his turn, as they departed, solemnly blessed the house and all that dwelt therein, whether present or absent. As soon as they were gone, Judith besought her mother for the key of the summer-house, for she wished to lay on her father's table the wild flowers she had brought; and having obtained it, she carried Prudence with her into the garden, and there they found themselves alone, for goodman Matthew had gone home for his dinner.

"Dear mouse," said she, quickly, "what is it hath happened to Tom Quiney?"

"I know not, Judith," the other said, in some surprise.

"It is in his mind to leave the country."

"I knew not that."

"I dare be sworn you did not, sweetheart," said she, "else surely you would have told me. But why? What drives him to such a thing? His business prospers well, as I hear them say; and yet must he forsake it for the company of those desperate men that are going away to fight the Indians beyond seas. Nothing will content him. England is no longer England; Stratford is no longer Stratford. Mercy on us, what is the meaning of it all?"

"In truth I know not, Judith."

Then Judith regarded her.

"Good cousin, I fear me you gave him but a cold welcome yesternight."

"I welcomed him as I would welcome any of my brother's friends," said Prudence, calmly and without embarrassment. "But you do not understand," Judith said, with a touch of impatience. "Bless thy heart! young men are such strange creatures; and must have all to suit their humors; and are off and away in their peevish fits if you do not entertain them, and cringe, and say your worship to every sirrah of them! Oh, they be mighty men of valor in their own esteem; and they must have us poor handmaidens do them honor; and if all be not done to serve, 'tis boot and spur and off to the wars with them, and many a fine tale thereafter about the noble ladies that were kind to them abroad. Marry! they can crow loud enough; 'tis the poor hens that durst never utter a word; and all must give way before his worship! What, then? What did you do? Was not the claret to his liking? Did not your brother offer him a pipe of Trinidado?"

"Indeed, Judith, it can not be through ought that happened last night, if he be speaking of leaving the country," Prudence said. "I thought he was well content, and right friendly in his manner."

"But you do not take my meaning," Judith said. "Dear heart, bear me no ill-will; but I would have you a little more free with your favors. You are too serious, sweet mouse. Could you not pluck up a little of the spirit that the pretty Rosalind showed—do you remember?—when she was teasing Orlando in the forest? In truth these men are fond of a varying mood; when they play with a kitten they like to know it has claws. And again, if you be too civil with them, they presume, and would become the master all at once; and then must everything be done to suit their lordships' fantasies, or else 'tis up and away with them, as this one goes."

"I pray you, Judith," her friend said, and now in great embarrassment, "forbear to speak of such things: in truth, my heart is not set that way. Right well I know that if he be leaving the country, 'tis through no discontent with me, nor that he would heed in any way how I received him. Nay, 'tis far otherwise; it is no secret whom he would choose for wife. If you are sorry to hear of his going away from his home, you know that a word from you would detain him."

"Good mouse, the folly of such thoughts!" Judith exclaimed. "Why, when he will not even give me a 'Good-day to you, wench'!"

"You best know what reasons he had for his silence, Judith; I know not."

"Reasons ?" said she, with some quick color coming to her face. "We will let that alone, good gossip. I meddle not with any man's reasons, if he choose to be uncivil to me; God help us, the world is wide enough for all !"

"Did you not anger him, Judith, that he is going away from his home and his friends ?"

"Anger him? Perchance his own suspicions have angered him," was the answer; and then she said, in a gentler tone: "But in truth I hope he will change his mind. Twenty years is a long space to be away from one's native land; there would be many changes ere he came back. Twenty years, he said."

Judith rather timidly looked at her companion, but indeed there was neither surprise nor dismay depicted on the pale and gentle face. Her eyes were absent, it is true, but they did not seem to crave for sympathy.

"'Tis strange," said she. "He said nought of such a scheme last night, though he and Julius spoke of this very matter of the men who were preparing to cross the seas. I know not what can have moved him to such a purpose."

"Does he imagine, think you," said Judith, "that we shall all be here awaiting him at the end of twenty years, and as we are now ? Or is he so sure of his own life?—they say there is great peril in the new lands they have taken possession of beyond sea, and that there will be many a bloody fight ere they can reap the fruit of their labors in peace. Nay, I will confess to thee, sweet mouse, I like not his going. Old friends are old friends, even if they have wayward humors; and fain would I have him remain with us here in Stratford—ay, and settled here, moreover, with a sweet Puritan wife by his side, that at present must keep everything hidden. Well, no matter," she continued, lightly. "I seek no secrets—except those that be in the oaken box within here."

She unlocked the door of the summer-house, and entered, and put the flowers on the table. "Tell me, Prue," said she, "may we venture to take some more of the play, or must I wait till I have put back the other sheets ?"

"You have not put them back?"

"In truth, no," said Judith, carelessly. "I lent them to the young gentleman, Leofric Hope."

"Judith!" her friend exclaimed, with frightened eyes.

"What, then?"

"To one you know nothing of? You have parted with these sheets—that are so valuable?"

"Nay, nay, good mouse," said she; "you know the sheets are cast away as useless. And I but lent them to him for an hour or two to lighten the tedium of his solitude. Nor was that all, good Prue, if I must tell thee the truth: I would fain have him know that my father can do something worth speaking of as well as his friend Ben Jonson, and perchance even better: what think you?"

"You have seen him again, then?—this morning?"

"Even so," Judith answered, calmly.

"Judith, why will you run into such danger?" her friend said, in obvious distress. "In truth I know not what 'twill come to. And now there is this farther bond in this secret commerce—think you that all this can remain unknown? Your meeting with him must come to some one's knowledge—indeed it must, sweetheart."

"Nay, but this time you have hit the mark," said Judith, complacently. "If you would assure yourself, good Prue, that the young gentleman is no grisly ghost or phantom, methinks you could not do better than ask Tom Quiney, who saw him this very morning—and saw us speaking together, as I guess."

"He saw you!" Prudence exclaimed. "And what said he?"

"He talked large and wild for a space," said Judith, coolly, "but soon I persuaded him there was no great harm in the stranger gentleman. In sooth his mind was so full of his own affairs—and so bitter against all preachers, ministers, and pastors—and he would have it that England was no longer fit to live in—marry, he told me so many things in so few minutes that I have half forgotten them!"

And then it suddenly occurred to her that this fantasy that had entered her mind in the morning, and that had haunted her during Master Elihu Izod's discourse, would be an excellent thing with which to frighten Prudence. 'Twas but a chimera, she assured herself; but there was enough substance in it for that. And so, when she had carefully arranged the flowers on the table, and cast another longing look at the oaken chest, she locked the door of the summer-house, and put her arm within the arm of her friend, and led her away for a walk in the garden.

"Prudence," said she, seriously, "I would have you give me counsel. Some one hath asked me what a young maiden should do in certain circumstances that I will put before you; but how can I tell, how can I judge of anything, when my head is in a whirligig of confusion with parsons' arguments, and people leaving the country, and I know not what else? But you, good mouse—your mind is ever calm and equable —you can speak sweet words in Israel—you are as Daniel that was so excellent a judge even in his youth—"

"Judith!" the other protested; but indeed Judith's eyes were perfectly grave and apparently sincere.

"Well, then, sweetheart, listen: let us say that a young man has seen a young maiden that is not known to him but by name —perchance at church it may have been, or as she was walking home to her own door. And there may be reasons why he should not go boldly to her father's house, though he would fain do so; his fancy being taken with her in a small measure, and he of a gentle disposition, and ready to esteem her higher than she deserved. And again it might be that he wished for private speech with her—to judge of her manners and her inclinations—before coming publicly forward to pay court to her: but alack, I can not tell the story as my father would; 'tis the veriest skeleton of a story, and I fear me you will scarce understand. But let us say that the young man is bold and ingenious, and bethinks him of a stratagem whereby to make acquaintance with the damsel. He writes to her as a wizard that has important news to tell her; and begs her to go forth and meet him; and that on a certain morning he will be awaiting her at such and such a place. Now this maiden that I am telling you of has no great faith in wizards, but being curious to see the juggling, she goes forth to meet him as he asks—"

"Judith, I pray you speak plain; what is't you mean?" Prudence exclaimed; for she had begun to suspect.

"You must listen, good mouse, before you can give judgment," said Judith, calmly; and she proceeded: "Now you must understand that it was the young gentleman himself whom she met, though she knew it not; for he had dressed himself up as an ancient wizard, and he had a solemn manner, and Latin speech, and what not. Then says the wizard to her, 'I can show you the man that is to be your lover and sweetheart and husband; that will win you and wear you in the time coming; and if you would see him, go to such and such a cross-road, and he will appear.' Do you perceive, now, sweet mouse, that it was a safe prophecy, seeing that he had appointed himself to be the very one who should meet her?"

Prudence had gradually slipped her arm away from that of her friend, and now stood still, regarding her breathlessly, while Judith, with eyes quite placid and inscrutable, continued her story:

"'Twas a noteworthy stratagem, and successful withal; for the maiden goes to the cross-road, and there she meets the young gentleman—now in his proper costume. But she has no great faith in magic; she regards him not as a ghost summoned by the wizard; she would rather see in this meeting an ordinary accident; and the young man being most courteous and modest and civil-spoken, they become friends. Do you follow the story? You see, good mouse, there is much in his condition to demand sympathy and kindness—he being in hiding, and cut off from his friends; and she, not being too industrious, and fond rather of walking in the meadows and the like, meets him now here, now there, but with no other thought than friendliness. I pray you, bear that in mind, sweetheart; for though I esteem her not highly, yet would I do her justice: there was no thought in her mind but friendliness, and a wish to be civil to one that seemed grateful for any such communion. And then one morning something happens—beshrew me if I can tell thee how it happened, and that is the truth—but something happens—an idea jumps into her head—she suspects that this young gentleman is no other than the same who was the wizard, and that she has been entrapped by him, and that he, having played the wizard, would now fain play the lover—"

"Judith, is't possible!—is't possible!"

"Hold, cousin, hold; your time is not yet. I grant you 'tis a bold conjecture, and some would say not quite seemly and

becoming to a maiden, seeing that he had never spoken any
word to her of the kind; but there it was in her head—the suspicion that this young gentleman had tricked her, for his own
amusement, or perchance to secure her company. Now, sweet
judge in Israel, for your judgment! And on two points, please
you. First, supposing this conjecture to be false, how is she
to atone to the young gentleman? And how is she to punish
herself? And how is she to be anything but uneasy should
she chance to see him again? Nay, more, how is she to get this
evil suspicion banished from her mind, seeing that she dare
not go to him and confess, and beg him for the assurance that
he had never heard of the wizard? Then the second point:
supposing the conjecture to be true, ought she to be very indignant? How should she demean herself? Should she go
to him and reproach him with his treachery? She would never forgive it, dear mouse, would she, even as a lover's stratagem?"

"Judith, I can not understand you; I can not understand
how you can even regard such a possibility, and remain content and smiling—"

"Then I ought to be indignant?—good cousin, I but asked
for your advice," Judith said. "I must be angry; I must
fret and fume, and use hot language, and play the tragedy
part? In good sooth, when I think on't, 'twas a piece of bold-
ness to put himself forward as my future husband—it was indeed—though 'twas cunningly contrived. Marry, but I understand now why my goodman wizard would take no money from
me; 'twas myself that he would have in payment of his skill;
and 'gracious lady' and 'sweet lady,' these were the lures to
lead me on; and his shepherd's dial placed on the ground!
Then off go beard and cloak, and a couple of days thereafter
he is a gay young gallant; and 'sweet lady' it is again—or
'fair lady,' was't?—'know you one Master Shakespeare in the
town?' And such modesty, and such downcast eyes, and an
appeal for one in misfortune: Heaven save us, was it not well
done? Modesty! By my life, a rare modest gentleman! He
comes down to Stratford, armed with his London speech and
his London manners, and he looks around. Which one, then?
which of all the maidens will his lordship choose for wife?
'Oh!' saith he, 'there is Judith Shakespeare; she will do as

well as another; perchance better, for New Place is the fairest house in the town, and doubtless she will have a goodly marriage portion. So now how to secure her? how to charm her away from any clownish sweetheart she may chance to have? Easily done, i' faith!—a country wench is sure to believe in magic; 'tis but raising my own ghost out of the ground, and a summons to her, and I have her sure and safe, to win and to wear, for better or worse!'" She looked at Prudence. "Heaven's blessings on us all, good Prue, was there ever poor maiden played such a scurril trick?"

"Then your eyes are opened, Judith?" said Prudence, eagerly. "You will have no more to do with such a villain?"

Again Judith regarded her, and laughed.

"I but told a story to frighten thee, good heart," said she. "A desperate villain? Yes, truly; but 'tis I am a desperate' villain to let such rascal suspicions possess me for an instant. Nay, good mouse, think of it!—is't possible that one would dare so much for so poor a prize? · That the young gentleman hath some self-assurance, I know; and he can quickly make friends; but do you think, if any such dark design had been his, he would have entered my grandmother's cottage, and ate and drank there, and promised to renew his visit? Sweet judge in Israel, your decision on the other point, I pray you! What penance must I do for letting such cruel thoughts stray into my brain? How shall I purge them away? To whom must I confess? Nay, methinks I must go to the young gentleman himself, and say: 'Good sir, I have a friend and gossip that is named Prudence Shawe, who hath a strange belief in phantom-men and conspirators. I pray you pardon me that through her my brain is somewhat distraught; and that I had half a mind to accuse you of a plot for stealing me away—me, who have generally this stout mastiff with me. I speech you, sir, steal me not—nay, forgive me that I ever dreamed of your having any such purpose. 'Tis our rude country manners, good sir, that teach a maid to believe a man may not speak to her without intent to marry her. I pray you pardon me—my heart is kneeling to you, could you but see—and give me such assurance that you meditated no such thing as will bring me back my scattered senses.' Were not that well done? Shall that be my penance, good mouse?"

"Dear Judith, tell me true," her friend said, almost piteously, "do you suspect him of having played the wizard to cheat
you and entrap you?"

"Good cousin," said she, in her frankest manner, "I confess:
I did suspect—for an instant. I know not what put it into my
head. But sure I am I have done him wrong—marry, 'twere
no such deadly sin even had he been guilty of such a trick;
but I believe it not—nay, he is too civil and gentle for a jest of
the kind. When I see him again I must make him amends
for my evil thinking: do not I owe him as much, good gossip?"

This was all she could say at present, for Matthew gardener
here made his appearance, and that was the signal for their
withdrawing into the house. But that afternoon, as Judith
bethought her that Master Leofric Hope would be coming to
her grandmother's cottage with the manuscript he had promised to return, she became more and more anxious to see him
again. Somehow she thought she could more effectually
drive away this disquieting surmise if she could but look at
him, and regard his manner, and hear him speak. As it turned out, however, it was not until somewhat late on in the evening that she found time to seek out little Willie Hart, and propose to him that he should walk with her as far as Shottery.

CHAPTER XIX.

A DAUGHTER OF ENGLAND.

"SWEETHEART WILLIE," she said—and her hand lay lightly on his shoulder, as they were walking through the meadows in the quiet of this warm golden evening—"what mean you to be when you grow up?"

He thought for a second or two, and then he rather timidly regarded her.

"What would you have me to be, Cousin Judith?" he said.

"Why, then," said she, "methinks I would have you be part student and part soldier, were it possible, like the gallant Sir Philip Sidney, that Queen Elizabeth said was the jewel of her reign. And yet you know, sweetheart, that we can not all of us be of such great estate. There be those who live at the court, and have wealth and lands, and expeditions given them to fit out, so that they gain fame; that is not the lot of every one, and I know not whether it may be yours—though for brave men there is ever a chance. But this I know I would have you ready to do, whether you be in high position or in low, and that is to fight for England, if needs be, and defend her, and cherish her. Why," she said, "what would you think, now, of one brought up by a gentle mother, one that owes his birth and training to this good mother, and because there is something amiss in the house, and because everything is not to his mind, he ups and says he must go away and forsake her? Call you that the thought of a loyal son and one that is grateful? I call it the thought of a peevish, froward, fractious child. Because, forsooth, this thing or the other is not to his worship's liking, or all the company not such as he would desire, or others of the family having different opinions—as surely, in God's name, they have a right to have— why, he must needs forsake the mother that bore him, and be off and away to other countries! Sweetheart Willie, that shall never be your mind, I charge you. No, you shall re-

main faithful to your mother England, that is a dear mother
and a good mother, and hath done well by her sons and
daughters for many a hundred years; and you shall be proud
of her, and ready to fight for her, ay, and to give your life for
the love of her, if ever the need should be!"

He was a small lad, but he was sensitive and proud-spirited;
and he loved dearly this Cousin Judith who had made this appeal to him; so that for a second the blood seemed to forsake
his face.

"I am too young as yet to do aught, Cousin Judith," said
he, in rather a low voice, for his breath seemed to catch; "but
—but when I am become a man I know that there will be
one that will sooner die than see any Spaniard or Frenchman
seize the country."

"Bravely said, sweetheart, by my life!" she exclaimed (and
her approval was very sweet to his ears). "That is the spirit
that women's hearts love to hear of, I can tell thee." And she
stooped and kissed him in reward. "Hold to that faith. Be
not ashamed of your loyalty to your mother England!
Ashamed? Heaven's mercy! where is there such another country to be proud of? And where is there another mother that
hath bred such a race of sons? Why, times without number
have I heard my father say that neither Greece, nor Rome,
nor Carthage, nor any of them, were such a race of men as
these in this small island, nor had done such great things, nor
earned so great a fame, in all parts of the world and beyond
the seas. And mark you this, too: 'tis the men who are fiercest
to fight with men that are the gentlest to women; they make
no slaves of their women; they make companions of them;
and in honoring them they honor themselves, as I reckon.
Why, now, could I but remember what my father hath written about England, 'twould stir your heart, I know; that it
would; for you are one of the true stuff, I'll be sworn; and
you will grow up to do your duty by your gracious mother
England—not to run away from her in peevish discontent!"

She cast about for some time, her memory, that she could
not replenish by any book-reading, being a large and somewhat miscellaneous store-house.

"'Twas after this fashion," said she, "if I remember
aright:

' This royal throne of kings, this sceptred isle,
This earth of majesty, this seat of Mars,
This fortress, built by Nature for herself
Against infestion and the hand of war ;
This happy breed of men, this little world,
This precious stone set in the silver sea,
Which serves it in the office of a wall,
Or as a moat defensive to a house,
Against the envy of less happier lands—
This blessed plot, this earth, this realm, this England !'

Mark you that, sweetheart?—is't not a land worth fighting
for? Ay, and she hath had sons that could fight for her;
and she hath them yet, I dare be sworn, if the need were to
arise. And this is what you shall say, Cousin Willie, when
you are a man and grown:

' Come the three corners of the world in arms,
And we shall shock them. Naught shall make us rue,
If England to itself do rest but true !' "

These quotations were but for the instruction of this small
cousin of hers, and yet her own face was proud.

"Shall I be a soldier, then, Cousin Judith?" the boy said.
"I am willing enough. I would be what you would wish me
to be; and if I went to the wars, you would never have need
to be shamed of me."

"That know I right well, sweetheart," said she, and she
patted him on the head. "But 'tis not every one's duty to
follow that calling. You must wait and judge for yourself.
But whatever chances life may bring you, this must you ever
remain, if you would have my love, sweetheart, and that I
hope you shall have always—you must remain a good and
loyal son to your mother England, one not easily discontented
with small discomforts, and sent forth in a peevish fit. Where
is there a fairer country? Marry, I know of none. Look
around—is't not a fair enough country?"

And fair indeed on this quiet evening was that wide stretch
of Warwickshire, with its hedges and green meadows, and low-
lying wooded hills bathed in the warm sunset light. But it was
the presence of Judith that made it all magical and mystical
to him. Whatever she regarded with her clear-shining and
wondrous eyes was beautiful enough for him—while her hand
lay on his shoulder or touched his hair. He was a willing
pupil. He drank in those lessons in patriotism: what was it

he would not do for his cousin Judith? What was it he would not believe if it were she who told him, in that strange voice of hers, that thrilled him, and was like music to him, whether she spoke to him in this proud, admonitory way, or was in a teasing mood, or was gentle and affectionate toward him? Yes, this Warwickshire landscape was fair enough, under the calm sunset sky; but he knew not what made it all so mystical and wonderful, and made the far golden clouds seem as the very gateways to heaven.

"Or is there one with a prouder story?" she continued. "Or a land of greater freedom? Why, look at me, now. Here am I, a woman, easily frightened, helpless if there were danger, not able to fight any one. Why, you yourself, Cousin Willie, if you were to draw a dagger on me, I declare to thee I would run and shriek and hide. Well, look at me as I stand here: all the might and majesty of England can not harm me; I am free to go or to stay. What needs one more? None durst put a hand on me. My mind is as free as my footsteps. I may go this way or that as I choose; and no one may command me to believe this, that, or the other. What more? And this security—think you it had not to be fought for?— think you it was not worth the fighting for? Or think you we should forget to give good thanks to the men that faced the Spaniards, and drove them by sea and shore, and kept our England to ourselves? Or think you we should forget our good Queen Bess, that I warrant me had as much spirit as they, and was as much a man as any of them?"

She laughed.

"Perchance you never heard, sweetheart, of the answer that she made to the Spanish ambassador?"

"No, Judith," said he, but something in her manner told him that there had been no cowardice in that answer.

"Well," she said, "I will tell thee the story of what happened at Deptford. And now I bethink me, this must you do, Cousin Willie, when you are grown to be a man; and whether you be soldier or sailor, or merchant, or student, 'tis most like that some day or other you will be in London; and then must you not fail to go straightway to Deptford to see the famous ship of Sir Francis Drake lying there. I tell thee, 'twas a goodly thought to place it there; that was like our brave Queen

Bess; she would have the youth of the country regard with honor the ship that had been all round the world, and chased the Spaniards from every sea. Nay, so bad is my memory that I can not recall the name of the vessel—perchance 'twas the *Judith*—at least I have heard that he had one of that name; but there it lies, to signal the glory of England and the routing of Spain."

"The *Judith*?" said he, with wondering eyes. "Did he name the ship after you, cousin?"

"Bless the lad! All that I am going to tell thee happened ere I was born."

"No matter," said he, stoutly; "the first thing I will ask to see, if ever I get to London, is that very ship."

"Well, then, the story," she continued, shaping the thing in her mind (for being entirely destitute of book-learning, historical incidents were apt to assume a dramatic form in her imagination, and also to lose literal accuracy of outline). "You must know the Spaniards were sore vexed because of the doings of Francis Drake in all parts of the world, for he had plundered and harried them, and burned their ships and their towns, and made the very name of England a terror to them. 'Tis no marvel if they wished to get hold of him; and they declared him to be no better than a pirate; and they would have the Queen—that is, our last Queen—deliver him over to them that they might do with him what they willed. Marry, 'twas a bold demand to make of England! And the Queen, how does she take it, think you?—how is she moved to act in such a pass? Why, she goes down to Deptford, to this very ship that I told thee of—she and all her nobles and ladies, for they would see the famous ship. Then they had dinner on board, as I have heard the story; and the Queen's Majesty asked many particulars of his voyages from Master Drake, and received from him certain jewels as a gift, and was right proud to wear them. Then says she aloud to them all: 'My lords, is this the man the Spaniards would have me give over to them?' Right well she knew he was the man; but that was her way, and she would call the attention of all of them. 'Your Majesty,' they said, ''tis no other.' Then she swore a great oath that the Queen of England knew how to make answer to such a demand. 'Come hither, Master Drake,' says she, in a terrible voice. 'Kneel!' Then he knelt on his knee before her. 'My lord,' says she to one of the noblemen standing close by, 'your sword!' And then, when she had the sword in her hand, she says, in a loud voice, 'My lords, this is the man that Spain would have us give up to her; and this is the answer of England: Arise, Sir Francis!'—and with that she taps him on the shoulder—which is the way of making a knight, Cousin Willie; and I pray you may be brave and valiant, and come to the same dignity, so that all of us here in Stratford shall say, 'There, now, is one that knew how to serve faithfully his fair mother England!' But that was not all, you must know, that happened with regard to Sir Francis Drake. For the Spanish ambassador was wroth with the Queen; ay, and went the length even of speaking with threats. ''Twill come to the cannon,' says he. 'What?' says she, turning upon him. 'Your Majesty,' says he, 'I fear me this matter will come to the cannon.' And guess you her answer?—nay, they say she spoke quite calmly, and regarded him from head to foot, and that if there were anger in her heart there was none in her voice. 'Little man, little man,' says she, 'if I hear any more such words from thee, by God I will clap thee straight into a dungeon!'"

Judith laughed, in a proud kind of way.

"That was the answer that England gave," said she, "and that she is like to give again, if the Don or any other of them would seek to lord it over her."

Three-fourths of these details were of her own invention, or rather—for it is scarcely fair to say that—they had unconsciously grown up in her mind from the small seed of the true story. But little Willie Hart had no distrust of any legend that his cousin Judith might relate to him. Whatever Judith said was true, and also luminous in a strange kind of fashion: something beautiful and full of color, to be thought over and pondered over. And now as they walked along toward the village, idly and lazily enough—for she had no other errand than to fetch back the manuscript that would be lying at the cottage—his eyes were wistful. His fancies were far away. What was it, then, that he was to do for England—that Judith should approve in the after-years? And for how long should he be away—in the Spanish Main, perchance, of which he had heard many stories, or fighting in the lowlands of Holland, or whatever he was called to do—and what was there at the end? Well, the end that he foresaw and desired—the reward of all his toil—was nothing more nor less than this: that he should be sitting once again in a pew in Stratford church, on a quiet Sunday morning, with Judith beside him as of old, they listening to the singing together. He did not think of his being grown up, or that she would be other than she was now. His mind could form no other or fairer consummation than that—that would be for him the final good—to come back to Stratford town to find Judith as she had ever been to him, gentle, and kind, and soft-handed, and ready with a smile from her beautiful and lustrous eyes.

"Yes, sweetheart Willie," said she, as they were nearing the cottages, "look at the quiet that reigns all around, and no priests of the Inquisition to come dragging my poor old grandmother from her knitting. What has she to do but look after the garden, and scold the maid, and fetch milk for the cat? And all this peace of the land that we enjoy we may have to fight for again; and then, if the King's Majesty calls either for men or for money, you shall have no word but obedience. Heard you never of the Scotch knight, Sir Patrick Spens?—that the Scotch King would send away to Norroway at an evil time of the year? Did he grumble? Did he say his men were ill content to start at such a time? Nay, as I have heard, when he read the King's letter the tears welled in his eyes; but I'll be sworn that was for the companions he was taking with him to face the cruel sea.

'The King's daughter from Norroway,
'Tis we must fetch her home,'

he says; and then they up with their sails, and set out from the land that they never were to see more. What of that? They were brave men; they did what was demanded of them; though the black seas of the north were too strong for them in the end. 'Twas a sad tale, in good sooth: •

'O lang, lang may the ladies sit,
Wi' the fans into their hand,
Before they see Sir Patrick Spens
Come sailing to the strand!

'And lang, lang may the maidens sit,
    Wi' their gold combs in their hair,
All waiting for their ain dear loves,
    For them they'll see nae mair.

'Half owre, half owre to Aberdour,
    'Tis fifty fathoms deep,
And there lies good Sir Patrick Spens
    Wi' the Scots lords at his feet.'

But what then ? I tell thee, sweetheart, any maiden that
would be worth the winning would a hundred times liefer wail
for a lover that had died bravely than welcome him back safe
and sound as a coward. You shall be no coward, I warrant
me, when you are grown up to be a man; and above all, as I
say, shall you be gentle and forgiving with your mother England, even if your own condition be not all you wish; and
none the less for that shall you be willing to fight for her
should she be in trouble. Nay, I'll answer for thee, lad: I
know thee well."

"But, Judith," said he, "who are they you speak of, that
are discontented, and would go away and leave the country ?"

Well, it is probable she might have found some embarrassment in answering this question (if she had been pressed to
name names) but that what she now beheld deprived her of
the power of answering altogether. She had come over from
the town with no other thought than to pay a brief visit to her
grandmother, and fetch back the portion of the play, and she
had not the slightest expectation of encountering Master Leofric Hope. But there unmistakably he was, though he did not
see her, for he was standing at the gate of her grandmother's
cottage, and talking to the old dame, who was on the other side.
There was no pretense of concealment. Here he was in the
public path, idly chatting, his hand resting on the gate. And
as Judith had her cousin Willie with her, her first thought was
to hurry away in any direction in order to escape an interview;
but directly she saw that this was impossible, for her grandmother had descried her, if Leofric Hope had not. The consequence was that, as she went forward to the unavoidable
meeting, she was not only surprised and a trifle confused and
anxious, but also somewhat and vaguely resentful; for she had
been intending, before seeing him again, to frame in her mind
certain tests which might remove or confirm one or two sus-

picions that had caused her disquietude. And now—and un-
fairly, as she thought—she found herself compelled to meet him
without any such legitimate safeguard of preparation. She
had no time to reflect that it was none of his fault. Why
had not he left the play earlier? she asked herself. Why had
not he departed at once? Why, with all his professions of
secrecy, should he be standing in the open highway, carelessly
talking? And what was she to say to little Willie Hart that
would prevent his carrying back the tale to the school and
the town? When she went forward, it was with considerable
reluctance; and she had a dim, hurt sense of having been im-
posed upon, or somehow or another injured.

CHAPTER XX.

VARYING MOODS.

But the strange thing was that the moment he turned and
saw her—and the moment she met the quick look of friendliness
and frank admiration that came into his face and his eloquent
dark eyes—all her misgivings, surmises, suspicions, and half-
meditated safeguards instantly vanished. She herself could
not have explained it; she only knew that, face to face with
him, she had no longer any doubt as to his honesty; and consequently that vague sense of injury vanished also. She had
been taken unawares, but she did not mind. Everything, indeed, connected with this young man was of a startling, unusual character; and she was becoming familiar with that,
and less resentful at being surprised.

"Ah, fair Mistress Judith," said he, "you come opportune-
ly: I would thank you from the heart for the gracious company I have enjoyed this afternoon through your good-will;
in truth, I was loath to part with such sweet friends, and perchance detained them longer than I should."

"I scarce understand you, sir," said she, somewhat bewildered.

"Not the visions that haunt a certain magic island?" said he.
Her face lit up.

"Well, sir?" she asked, with a kind of pride; but at this

point her grandmother interposed, and insisted—somewhat to
Judith's surprise—that they should come in and sit down, if not
in the house, at least in the garden. He seemed willing
enough; for without a word he opened the gate to let Judith
pass; and then she told him who her cousin was; and in this
manner they went up to the little arbor by the hedge.

"Well, good sir, and how liked you the company?" said she,
cheerfully, when she had got within and sat down.

Her grandmother had ostensibly taken to her knitting; but
she managed all the same to keep a sharp eye on the young
man; for she was curious, and wanted to know something further of the parcel that he had left with her. It was not merely hospitality or a freak of courtesy that had caused her to give
him this sudden invitation. Her granddaughter Judith was a
self-willed wench and mischievous; she would keep an eye
on her too; she would learn more of this commerce between
her and the young gentleman who had apparently dropped, as
it were, from the skies. As for little Willie Hart, he remained
outside, regarding the stranger with no great good-will; but
perhaps more with wonder than with anger, for he marvelled
to hear Judith talk familiarly with this person, of whom he had
never heard a word, as though she had known him for years.

"'Tis not for one such as I," said Master Leofric Hope, modestly—and with such a friendly regard toward Judith that she
turned away her eyes and kept looking at this and that in the
garden—"to speak of the beauties of the work; I can but tell
you of the delight I have myself experienced. And yet how
can I even do that? How can I make you understand that—or
my gratitude either, sweet Mistress Judith—unless you know
something of the solitude of the life I am compelled to lead?
You would have yourself to live at Bassfield Farm; and watch
the monotony of the days there; and be scarcely able to pass
the time: then would you know the delight of being introduced
to this fair region that your father hath invented, and being
permitted to hear those creatures of his imagination speak
to each other. Nay, but 'tis beautiful! I am no critical judge;
but I swear 'twill charm the town."

"You think so, sir?" said she, eagerly, and for an instant
she withdrew her eyes from the contemplation of the flowers.
But immediately she altered her tone to one of calm indiffer-

ence. "My father hath many affairs to engage him, you must understand, good sir; perchance, now, this play is not such as he would have written had he leisure, and—and had he been commanded by the court, and the like. Perchance 'tis too much of the human kind for such purposes ?"

"I catch not your meaning, sweet lady," said he.

"I was thinking," said she, calmly, "of the masques you told us of—at Theobald's and elsewhere—that Master Benjamin Jonson has written, and that they all seem to prize so highly: perchance these were of a finer stuff than my father hath time to think of, being occupied, as it were, with so many cares. 'Tis a rude life, having regard to horses, and lands, and malt, and the rest; and—and the court ladies—they would rather have the gods and goddesses marching in procession, would they not ? My father's writing is too much of the common kind, is it not, good sir ?—'tis more for the 'prentices, one might say, and such as these ?"

He glanced at her. He was not sure of her.

"The King, sweet lady," said he, "is himself learned, and would have the court familiar with the ancient tongues; and for such pageants 'tis no wonder they employ Master Jonson, that is a great scholar. But surely you place not such things —that are but as toys—by the side of your father's plays, that all marvel at, and applaud, and that have driven away all others from our stage ?"

"Say you so ?" she answered, with the same indifferent demeanor. "Nay, I thought that Master Scoloker—was that his worship's name ?—deemed them to be of the vulgar sort. But perchance he was one of the learned ones. The King, they say, is often minded to speak in the Latin. What means he by that, good sir, think you ? Hath he not yet had time to learn our English speech ?"

"Wench, what would you ?" her grandmother interposed, sharply. "Nay, good sir, heed her not; her tongue be an unruly member, and maketh sport of her, as I think; but the wench meaneth no harm."

"The King is proud of his learning, no doubt," said he; and he would probably have gone on to deprecate any comparison between the court masques and her father's plays but that she saw here her opportunity, and interrupted him.

"I know it," she said, "for the letter that the King sent to my father is writ in the Latin."

"Nay, is it so?" said he.

She affected not to observe his surprise.

"'Twas all the same to my father," she continued, calmly, "whether the letter was in one tongue or the other. He hath one book now—how is it called?—'tis a marvellous heap of old stories—the Jests—"

"Not the *Gesta Romanorum*?" he said.

"The same, as I think. Well, he hath one copy that is in English, and of our own time, as I am told; but he hath also another and a very ancient copy, that is in the Latin tongue; and this it is—the Latin one, good sir—that my father is fondest of; and many a piece of merriment he will get out of it, when Julius Shawe is in the house of an evening."

"But the *Gesta* are not jests, good Mistress Judith," said he, looking somewhat puzzled.

"I know not; I but hear them laughing," said she, placidly. "And as for the book itself, all I know of it is the outside; but that is right strange and ancient, and beautiful withal: the back of it white leather stamped with curious devices; and the sides of parchment printed in letters of red and black; and the silver clasps of it with each a boar's head. I have heard say that that is the crest of the Scotch knight that gave the volume to my father when they were all at Aberdeen; 'twas when they made Laurence Fletcher a burgess; and the knight said to my father, 'Good sir, the honor to your comrade is a general one, but I would have you take this book in particular, in the way of thanks and remembrance for your wit and pleasant company'—that, or something like that, said he; and my father is right proud of the book, that is very ancient and precious; and often he will read out of it—though it be in the Latin tongue. Oh, I assure you, sir," she added, with a calm and proud air, "'tis quite the same thing to him. If the King choose to write to him in that tongue, well and good. Marry, now I think of it, I make no doubt that Julius Shawe would lend me the letter, did you care to see it."

He looked up quickly and eagerly.

"Goes your goodness so far, sweet Mistress Judith? Would you do me such a favor and honor?"

"Nay, young sir," the grandmother said, looking up from her knitting, "tempt not the wench; she be too ready to do mad things out of her own mind. And you, grandchild, see you meddle not in your father's affairs."

"Why, grandam," Judith cried, "'tis the common property of Stratford town. Any one that goeth into Julius Shawe's house may see it. And why Julius Shawe's friends only? Beshrew me, there are others who have as good a title to that letter—little as my father valueth it."

"Nay, I will forego the favor," said he at once, "though I owe you none the less thanks, dear lady, for the intention of your kindness. In truth, I know not how to make you sensible of what I already owe you; for, having made acquaintance with those fair creations, how can one but long to hear of what further befell them? My prayer would rather go in that direction—if I might make so bold."

He regarded her now with a timid look. Well, she had not undertaken that he should see the whole of the play, nor had she ever hinted to him of any such possibility; but it had been in her mind, and for the life of her she could not see any harm in this brief loan of it. Harm? Had not even this brief portion of it caused him to think of her father's creations as if they were of a far more marvellous nature than the trumpery court performances that had engrossed his talk when first she met him?

"There might be some difficulty, good sir," said she, "but methinks I could obtain for you the further portions, if my good grandmother here would receive them and hand them to you when occasion served."

"What's that, wench?" her grandmother said, instantly.

"'Tis but a book, good grandam, that I would lend Master Hope to lighten the dullness of his life at the farm withal: you can not have any objection, grandmother?"

"'Tis a new trade to find thee in, wench," said her grandmother. "I'd 'a thought thou wert more like to have secret commerce in laces and silks."

"I am no peddler, good madam," said he, with a smile; "else could I find no pleasanter way of passing the time than in showing to you and your fair granddaughter my store of braveries. Nay, this that I would beg of you is but to keep

9*

the book until I have the chance to call for it; and that is a kindness you have already shown in taking charge of the little package I left for Mistress Judith here."

"Well, well, well," said the old dame, "if 'tis anything belonging to her father, see you bring it back, and let not the wench get into trouble."

"I think you may trust me so far, good madam," said he, with such simplicity of courtesy and sincerity that even the old grandmother was satisfied.

In truth she had been regarding the two of them with some sharpness during these few minutes to see if she could detect anything in their manner that might awaken suspicion. There was nothing. No doubt the young gentleman regarded Judith with an undisguised wish to be friendly with her, and say pretty things; but was that to be wondered at? 'Twas not all the lads in Stratford that would be so modest in showing their admiration for a winsome lass. And this book-lending commerce was but natural in the circumstances. She would have been well content to hear that his affairs permitted him to leave the neighborhood, and that would happen in good time; meanwhile there could be no great harm in being civil to so well-behaved a young gentleman. So now, as she had satisfied herself that the leaving of the package meant nothing dark or dangerous, she rose and hobbled away in search of the little maid, to see that some ale were brought out for the refreshment of her visitor.

"Sweetheart Willie," Judith called, "what have you there? Come hither!"

Her small cousin had got hold of the cat, and was vainly endeavoring to teach it to jump over his clasped hands. He took it up in his arms, and brought it with him to the arbor, though he did not look in the direction of the strange gentleman.

"We shall be setting forth for home directly," said she. "Wilt thou not sit down and rest thee?"

"'Tis no such distance, cousin," said he.

He seemed unwilling to come in; he kept stroking the cat, with his head averted. So she went out to him, and put her arm round his neck.

"This, sir," said she, "is my most constant companion, next

to Prudence Shawe; I know not to what part of all this neighborhood we have not wandered together. And such eyes he
hath for the birds' nests; when I can see naught but a cloud of
leaves he will say, why, 'tis so and so, or so and so; and up
the tree like a squirrel, and down again with one of the eggs,
or perchance a small naked birdling, to show me. But we always put them back, sweetheart, do we not?—we leave no bereft
families, or sorrowing mother bird to find an empty nest. We
do as we would be done by; and 'tis no harm to them that we
should look at the pretty blue eggs, or take out one of the small
chicks with its downy feathers and its gaping bill. And for the
fishing, too—there be none cleverer at setting a line, as I hear,
or more patient in watching: but I like not that pastime, good
Cousin Willie, for or soon or late you are certain to fall
through the bushes into the river, as happened to Dickie Page
last week, and there may not be some one there to haul you out,
as they hauled out him."

"And how fares he at the school?" said the young gentleman in the arbor.

"Oh, excellent well, as I am told," said she, "although I be
no judge of lessons myself. Marry, I hear good news of his
behavior; and if there be a bloody nose now and again, why,
a boy that's attacked must hold his own, and give as good as he
gets—'twere a marvel else—and 'tis no use making furious over
it, for who knows how the quarrel began? Nay, I will give
my cousin a character for being as gentle as any, and as reasonable; and if he fought with Master Crutchley's boy, and
hit him full sore, I fear, between the eyes—well, having heard
something of the matter, I make no doubt it served young
Crutchley right, and that elder people should have a care in
condemning when they can not know the beginning of the
quarrel. Well, now I bethink me, sweetheart, tell me how
it began, for that I never heard. How began the quarrel?"

"Nay, 'twas nothing," he said, shamefacedly.

"Nothing? Nay, that I will not believe. I should not
wonder now if it were about some little wench. What? Nay,
I'll swear it now! 'Twas about the little wench that has come
to live at the Vicarage—what's her name?—Minnie, or Win-
nie?"

"'Twas not, then, Judith," said he. "If you must know,

I will tell you; I had liefer say naught about it. But 'twas not the first time he had said so—before all of them—that my uncle was no better than an idle player, that ought to be put in the stocks and whipped."

"Why, now," said she, "to think that the poor lad's nose should be set a-bleeding for nothing more than that!"

"It had been said more than once, Cousin Judith; 'twas time it should end," said he, simply.

At this moment Master Leofric Hope called to him.

"Come hither, my lad," said he. "I would hear how you get on at school."

The small lad turned and regarded him, but did not budge. His demeanor was entirely changed. With Judith he was invariably gentle, submissive, abashed: now, as he looked at the stranger, he seemed to resent the summons.

"Come hither, my lad."

"Thank you, no, sir," he said; "I would as lief be here."

"Sweetheart, be these your manners?" Judith said.

But the young gentleman only laughed good-naturedly.

"Didst thou find any such speeches in the *Sententiæ Pueriles?*" said he. "They were not there when I was at school."

"When go we back to Stratford, Judith?" said the boy.

"Presently, presently," said she (with some vague impression that she could not well leave until her grandmother's guest showed signs of going also). "See, here is my grandam coming with various things for us; and I warrant me you shall find some gingerbread amongst them."

The old dame and the little maid now came along, bringing with them ale and jugs and spiced bread and what not, which were forthwith put on the small table; and though Judith did not care to partake of these, and was rather wishful to set out homeward again, still, in common courtesy, she was compelled to enter the arbor and sit down. Moreover, Master Hope seemed in no hurry to go. It was a pleasant evening, the heat of the day being over; the skies were clear, fair, and lambent with the declining golden light: why should one hasten away from this quiet bower, in the sweet serenity and silence, with the perfume of roses all around, and scarce a breath of air to stir the leaves? He but played with this slight refection; nevertheless, it was a kind of excuse for the starting of fresh talk;

and his talk was interesting and animated. Then he had discovered a sure and easy way of pleasing Judith, and instantly
gaining her attention. When he spoke of the doings in London, her father was no longer left out of these: nay, on the
contrary, he became a central figure; and she learned more
now of the Globe and Blackfriars theatres than ever she had
heard in her life before. Nor did she fail to lead him on with
questions. Which of her father's friends were most constant
attendants at the theatre? Doubtless they had chairs set for
them on the stage? Was there any one that her father singled
out for especial favor? When they went to the tavern in the
evening, what place had her father at the board? Did any of the
young lords go with them? How late sat they? Did her father outshine them all with his wit and merriment, or did he
sit quiet and amused?—for sometimes it was the one and sometimes the other with him here in Stratford. Did they in London know that he had such a goodly house, and rich lands, and
horses? And was there good cooking at the tavern—Portugal
dishes and the like? Or perchance (she asked, with an inquir-
ing look from the beautiful, clear eyes) it was rather poor?
And the napery, now: it was not always of the cleanest? And
instead of neat-handed maids, rude serving-men, tapsters, drawers, and so forth? And the ale—she could be sworn 'twas no
better than the Warwickshire ale; no, nor was the claret likely
to be better than that brought into the country for the gentle-
folk by such noted vintners as Quiney. Her father's lodging—
that he said was well enough, as he said everything was well
enough, for she had never known him utter a word of discontent with anything that happened to him—perchance 'twas
none of the cleanliest? for she had heard that the London
housewives were mostly slovens, and would close you doors and
windows against the air, so that a countryman going to that
town was like to be sickened. And her father—did he ever
speak of his, family when he was in London? Did they know
he had belongings? Nay, she was certain he must have talked to his friends and familiars of little Bess Hall, for how
could he help that?

"You forget, sweet Mistress Judith," said he, in his pleasant
way, "that I have not the honor of your father's friendship,
nor of his acquaintance even, and what I have told you is all

of hearsay, save with regard to the theatre, where I have seen him often. And that is the general consent: that this one may have more learning, and that one more sharpness of retort, but that in these encounters he hath a grace and a brilliancy far outvying them all, and, moreover, with such a gentleness as earns him the general good-will. Such is the report of him; I would it had been in my power to speak from my own experience."

"But that time will come, good sir," said she, "and soon, I trust."

"In the mean while," said he, "bethink you what a favor it is that I should be permitted to come into communion with those fair creations of his fancy; and I would remind you once more of your promise, sweet Mistress Judith; and would beseech your good grandmother to take charge of anything you may leave for me. Nay, 'twill be for no longer than an hour or two that I would detain it; but that brief time I would have free from distractions, so that the mind may dwell on the picture. Do I make too bold, sweet lady? Or does your friendship go so far?"

"In truth, sir," she answered, readily, "if I can I will bring you the rest of the play—but perchance in portions, as the occasion serves; 'twere no great harm should you carry away with you some memory of the Duke and his fair daughter on the island."

"The time will pass slowly until I hear more of them," said he.

"And meanwhile, good grandmother," said she, "if you will tell me where I may find the little package, methinks I must be going."

At this he rose.

"I beseech your pardon if I have detained you, sweet lady," said he, with much courtesy.

"Nay, sir, I am indebted to you for welcome news," she answered, "and I would I had longer opportunity of hearing. And what said you—that he outshone them all?—that it was the general consent?"

"Can you doubt it?" he said, gallantly.

"Nay, sir, we of his own household—and his friends in Stratford—we know and see what my father is: so well esteemed, in truth, as Julius Shawe saith, that there is not a man in Warwickshire would cheat him in the selling of a horse, which they are not slow to do, as I hear, with others. But I knew not he had won so wide and general a report in London, where they might know him not so well as we."

"Let me assure you of that, dear lady," he said, "and also that I will not forget to bring or send you the printed tribute to his good qualities that I spoke of, when that I may with safety go to London. 'Tis but a trifle; but it may interest his family; marry, I wonder he hath not himself spoken of it to you."

"He speak of it!" said she, regarding him with some surprise, as if he ought to have known better. "We scarce know aught of what happeneth to him in London. When he comes home to Warwickshire it would seem as if he had forgotten London and all its affairs, and left them behind for good.".

"Left them behind for good, say you, wench?" the old dame grumbled, mostly to herself, as she preceded them down the path. "I would your father had so much sense. What hath he to gain more among the players and dicers and tavern brawlers and that idle crew? Let him bide at home, among respectable folk. Hath he not enough of gear gathered round him, eh? It be high time he slipped loose from those mummers that play to please the cutpurses and their trulls in London. Hath he not enough of gear?"

"What say you, grandmother? You would have my father come away from London and live always in Warwickshire? Well, now, that is nearer than you think, or my guesses are wrong."

But her grandmother had gone into the cottage; and presently she returned with the little package. Then there was a general leave-taking at the gate; and Leofric Hope, after many expressions of his thanks and good-will, set out on his own way, Judith and her cousin taking the path through the meadows.

For some time they walked in silence; then, as soon as the stranger was out of ear-shot, the lad looked up and said,

"Who is that, Judith?"

"Why," said she, lightly, "I scarcely know myself; but that he is in misfortune and hiding, and that he knoweth cer-

tain of my father's friends, and that he seems pleased to have
a few words with one or other of us to cheer his solitude.
You would not begrudge so much, sweetheart? Nay, there is
more than that I would have you do: his safety depends on
there being no talk about him in the town; and I know you can
keep a secret, Cousin Willie; so you must not say a word to
any one—whether at school, or at home, or at New Place—of
your having seen him. You will do as much for my sake,
sweetheart?"

"Yes; but why for your sake, cousin?" said the boy, looking up. "Why should you concern yourself?"

"Nay, call it for anybody's sake, then," said she. "But I
would not have him betrayed by any one that I had aught to
do with—and least of all by you, sweetheart, that I expect to
show nothing but fair and manly parts. Nay, I trust you.
You will not blab."

And then, as they walked on, it occurred to her that this
young gentleman's secret—if he wished it kept—was becoming
somewhat widely extended in his neighborhood. In her own
small circle how many already knew of his presence?—her
grandmother, Prudence Shawe, herself, Tom Quiney, and now
this little Willie Hart. And she could not but remember that
not much more than half an hour ago she had seen him at the
garden gate, carelessly chatting, and apparently not heeding
in the least what passers-by might observe him. But that was
always the way: when she left him, when she was with her
own thoughts, curious surmises would cross her mind; whereas, when she met him, these were at once discarded. And so
she took to arguing with herself as to why she should be so
given to do this young man injustice in his absence, when,
every time she encountered him face to face she was more than
ever convinced of his honesty. Fascination? Well, she liked
to hear of London town and the goings on there; and this
evening she had been particularly interested in hearing about
the Globe Theatre, and the spectators, and the tavern to which
her father and his friends repaired for their supper; but surely that would not blind her if she had any reason to think
that the young man was other than he represented? And
then, again, this evening he had been markedly deferential.
There was nothing in his manner of that somewhat too open

gallantry he had displayed in the morning when he made his
speech about the English roses. Had she not wronged him,
then, in imagining even for a moment that he had played a
trick upon her in order to make her acquaintance? It is true,
she had forgotten to make special remark of his eyes, as to
whether they were like those of the wizard; for indeed the
suspicion had gone clean out of her mind. But now she
tried to recall them; and she could not fairly say to herself
that there was a resemblance. Nay, the wizard was a solemn
person, who seemed to rebuke her light-heartedness; he spoke
gravely and slow; whereas this young man, as any one could
see, had a touch of merriment in his eye that was ready to declare itself on further acquaintance, only that his deference
kept him subdued, while his talk was light and animated and
rapid. No, she would absolve him from this suspicion; and
soon, indeed, as she guessed, he would absolve himself by removing from the neighborhood, and probably she would hear
no more of him, unless, perchance, he should remember to
send her that piece of print concerning her father.

And then her thoughts went far afield. She had heard
much of London that evening; and London, in her mind, was
chiefly associated with her father's plays, or such as she knew
of them; and these again were represented to her by a succession of figures, whose words she thought of, whose faces she
saw, when, as now, her fancies were distant. And she was
more silent than usual as they went on their way across the
meadows, and scarce addressed a word to her companion; insomuch that at last he looked up into her face, and said,

"Judith, why are you so sad this evening?"

"Sad, sweetheart? Surely no," she answered; and she put
her hand on his head. "What makes thee think so?"

"Did Dame Hathaway speak harshly to you?" said he.
"Methought I heard her say something. Another time I will
bid her hold her peace."

"Nay, nay, not so," said she; and as they were now come
to a stile, she paused there, and drew the boy toward her.

Not that she was tired; but the evening was so quiet and still,
and the whole world seemed falling into a gentle repose.
There was not a sound near them; the earth was hushed as it
sank to sleep; far away they could hear the voices of children

going home with their parents, or the distant barking of a
dog. It was late, and yet the skies seemed full of light, and all
the objects around them were strangely distinct and vivid.
Behind them, the northwestern heavens were of a pale luminous gold; overhead and in front of them, the great vault
was of a beautiful lilac-gray, deepening to blue in the sombre
east; and into this lambent twilight the great black elms rose
in heavy masses. The wide meadows still caught some of the
dying radiance; and there was a touch of it on the westward-
looking gables of one or two cottages; and then through this
softened glow there came a small keen ray of lemon yellow—a
light in one of the far-off windows that burned there like a
star. So hushed this night was, and so calm and beautiful,
that a kind of wistfulness fell over her mind—scarcely sadness,
as the boy had imagined—but a dull longing for sympathy,
and some vague wonder as to what her life might be in the
years to come.

"Why, sweetheart," said she, absently, and her hand lay af-
fectionately on his shoulder, "as we came along here this
evening we were speaking of all that was to happen to you in
after-life; and do you never think you would like to have the
picture unrolled now, and see for yourself, and have assurance ?
Does not the mystery of it make you impatient, or restless, or
sad—so that you would fain have the years go by quick, and
get to the end ? Nay, I trow not; the day and the hour are
sufficient for thee; and 'tis better so. Keep as thou art, sweetheart, and pay no heed to what may hereafter happen to thee."

"What is't that troubles you, Judith ?" said he, with an instinctive sympathy, for there was more in her voice than in
her words.

"Why, I know not myself," said she, slowly, and with her
eyes fixed vacantly on the darkening landscape. "Nothing,
as I reckon. 'Tis but beating one's wings against the invisible
to seek to know even to-morrow. And in the further years
some will have gone away from Stratford, and some to far
countries, and some will be married, and some grown old;
but to all the end will be the same; and I dare say now that,
hundreds of years hence, other people will be coming to Stratford, and they will go into the church-yard there, and walk
about and look at the names—that is, of you and me and all

the rest of us—and they will say, 'Poor things, they vexed themselves about very small matters while they were alive, but they are all at peace at last.' "

"But what is it that troubles you, Judith?" said he; for this was an unusual mood with her, who generally was so thoughtless and merry and high-hearted.

"Why, nothing, sweetheart, nothing," said she, seeming to rouse herself. "'Tis the quiet of the night that is so strange, and the darkness coming. Or will there be moonlight? In truth, there must be, and getting near to the full, as I reckon. A night for Jessica! Heard you ever of her, sweetheart?"

"No, Judith."

"Well, she was a fair maiden that lived long ago, somewhere in Italy, as I think. And she ran away with her lover, and was married to him, and was very happy; and all that is now known of her is connected with music and moonlight and an evening such as this. Is not that a fair life to lead after death: to be in all men's thoughts always as a happy bride, on such a still night as this is now? And would you know how her lover spoke to her?—this is what he says:

> 'How sweet the moonlight sleeps upon this bank!
> Here will we sit, and let the sounds of music
> Creep to our ears; soft stillness and the night
> Become the touches of sweet harmony.
> Sit, Jessica: Look, how the floor of heaven
> Is thick inlaid with patines of bright gold;
> There's not the smallest orb which thou behold'st
> But in his motion like an angel sings,
> Still quiring to the young-eyed cherubims:
> Such harmony is in immortal souls;
> But, whilst this muddy vesture of decay
> Doth grossly close it in, we can not hear it.—
> Come, ho, and wake Diana with a hymn;
> With sweetest touches pierce your mistress' ear,
> And draw her home with music.'

Is not that a gentle speech? And so shall you speak to your bride, sweetheart, in the years to come, when you have wooed her and won her. And then you will tell her that if she loves you not—ay, and if she loves you not dearly and well—then is she not like one that you knew long ago, and that was your cousin, and her name Judith Shakespeare. Come, sweetheart," said she, and she rose from the stile and took his hand in hers.

"Shall I draw thee home? But not with sweet music, for I have not Susan's voice. I would I had, for thy sake."

"You have the prettiest voice in the whole world, Cousin Judith," said he.

And so they walked on and into the town, in silence mostly. The world had grown more solemn now: here and there in the lilac-gray deeps overhead a small silver point began to appear. And sure he was that whatever might happen to him in the years to come, no sweetheart or any other would ever crush out from his affection or from his memory this sweet cousin of his; for him she would always be the one woman, strange and mystical and kind; there never would be any touch like the touch of her hand, so gentle was it as it rested on his hair; and there never would be anything more wonderful and gracious to look forward to than the old and familiar sitting in the church pew by Judith's side, with the breathless fascination of knowing that she was so near, and the thrill of hearing her join (rather timidly, for she was not proud of her voice) in the singing of the choir.

CHAPTER XXI.

A DISCOVERY.

"THAT be so as I tell ye, zur," said Matthew gardener, as he slowly sharpened a long knife on the hone that he held in his hand; "it all cometh of the pampering of queasy stomachs nowadays that can not hold honest food. There be no such folk now as there wur in former days, when men wur hardy, and long-lived, and healthy; and why, zur?—why, but that they wur content wi' plain dishes of pulse or herbs, and for the most worshipful no more than a dish of broth and a piece of good wholesome beef withal. But nowadays, Lord! Lord!—dish after dish, with each his several sauce; and this from Portugal and that from France, so that gluttony shall have its swing, and never a penny be kept for the poor. Nay, I tell ye, zur, rich and poor alike wur stronger and healthier when there wur no such waste in the land; when a man would wear his frieze coat and hosen of the color of the sheep that bore them; and have his shirt of honest hemp or flax, and could sleep well with his head on a block of wood and a sheep-skin thrown o'er it. But nowadays must he have his shirt of fine lawn and needle-work; ay, and his soft pillow to lie on, so that his lily-white body shall come to no scratching; nor will he drink any longer small drink, no, nor water, but heavy ales and rich wines; and all goeth to the belly, and naught to his poorer neighbor. And what cometh of this but tender stomachs, and riot, and waste?—and lucky if Bocardo be not at the end of it all."

As it chanced on this fine morning, Judith's father had strolled along to look at some trained apple-trees at the further end of the garden, and finding goodman Matthew there, and having a mind for idleness, had sat down on a bench to hear what news of the condition of the land Matthew might have to lay before him.

"Nay, but, good Matthew," said he, "if these luxuries work such mischief, 'tis the better surely that the poor have none of them. They, at least, can not have their stomachs ruined with sauces and condiments."

"Lord bless ye, zur," said the ancient, with a wise smile, "'tis not in one way, but in all ways, that the mischief is done; for the poorest, seeing such waste and gluttony everywhere abroad, have no continence of their means, but will spend their last penny on any foolishness. Lord! Lord! they be such poor simple creatures! they that have scarce a rag to their backs will crowd at the mops and fairs, and spend their money—on what? Why, you must ha' witnessed it, zur—the poor fools!—emptying their pouches to see a woman walking on a rope, or a tumbler joining his hands to his heels, or a hen with two heads. The poor simple creatures!—and yet I warrant me they be none so poor but that the rascal doctor can make his money out o' them: 'tis a foine way o' making a fortune that, going vagrom about the country with his draughts and pills—not honest medicines that a body might make out o' wholesome herbs, but nauseous stinking stuff that robs a man of his breath in the very swallowing of it. And the almanac-makers, too—marry, that, now, is another thriving trade!—the searching of stars, and the prophesying of dry or wet weather! Weather? what know they of the weather, the town-bred rogues, that lie and cheat to get at the poor country folks' money? God 'a mercy, a whip to their shoulders would teach them more o' the weather than ever they are like to get out of the stars! And yet the poor fools o' countrymen—that scarce know a B from a battledoor—will sit o' nights puzzling their brains o'er the signs o' the heavens; and no matter what any man with eyes can see for himself—ay, and fifty times surer, as I take it—they will prophesy you a dry month or a wet month, because the almanac saith so; and they will swear to you that Taurus—that is a lion—and the virgin scales have come together, therefore there must be a blight on the pear-trees! Heard you ever the like, zur?—that a man in Lunnon, knowing as much about husbandry and farm-work as a cat knows about quoit-throwing, is to tell me the weather down here in Warwickshire? God help us, they be poor weak creatures that think so; I'd liefer look at the cover of a penny ballad, if I wanted to know when there was to be frost o' nights."

At this juncture the old man grinned, as if some secret joke were tickling his fancy.

"Why, zur," said he, looking up from the hone, "would you believe this, zur—they be such fools that a rogue will sell them a barren cow for a milch-cow if he but put a strange calf to her? 'Tis done, zur—'tis done, I assure ye."

"In truth, a scurvy trick!" Judith's father said. He was idly drawing figures on the ground with a bit of stick he had got hold of. Perhaps he was not listening attentively; but at all events he encouraged Matthew to talk. "But surely with years comes wisdom. The most foolish are not caught twice with such a trick."

"What of that, zur?" answered Matthew. "There be plenty of other fools in the land to make the trade of roguery thrive. 'Tis true that a man may learn by his own experience; but what if he hath a son that be growing up a bigger fool than himself? And that's where 'tis nowadays, zur; there be no waiting and prudence; but every saucy boy must match on to his maid, and marry her ere they have a roof to put over their heads. 'Tis a fine beginning, surely! No waiting, no prudence—as the rich are wasteful and careless, so are the poor heedless of the morrow; and the boy and the wench they must have their cottage at the lane end, run up of elder poles, and forthwith begin the begetting of beggars to swarm over the land. A rare beginning! Body o' me, do they think they can live on nettles and grass, like Nebuchadnezzar?"

And so the old man continued to rail and grumble and bemoan, sometimes with a saturnine grin of satisfaction at his own wit coming over his face; and Judith's father did not seek to controvert; he listened, and drew figures on the ground, and merely put in a word now and again. It was a pleasant morning—fresh, and clear, and sunny; and this town of Stratford was a quiet place at that hour, with the children all at school. Sometimes Judith's father laughed; but he did not argue; and goodman Matthew, having it all his own way, was more than ever convinced not only that he was the one wise man among a generation of fools, but also that he was the only representative and upholder of the Spartan virtues that had characterized his forefathers. It is true that on more than one occasion he had been found somewhat overcome with ale; but this, when he had recovered from his temporary confusion, he declared was entirely due to the rascal brewers of those degenerate days—and especially of Warwickshire—who put all manner of abominations into their huff-cap, so that an honest Worcestershire stomach might easily be caught napping, and take no shame.

And meanwhile what had been happening in another part of the garden? As it chanced, Judith had been sent by her mother to carry to the summer-house a cup of wine and some thin cates; and in doing so she of course saw that both her father and goodman Matthew were at the further end of the garden, and apparently settled there for the time being. The opportunity was too good to be lost. She swiftly went back to the house, secured the portion of the play that was secreted there, and as quickly coming out again, exchanged it for an equal number of new sheets. It was all the work of a couple of minutes; and in another second she was in her own room, ready to put the precious prize into her little cupboard of boxes. And yet she could not forbear turning over the sheets, and examining them curiously, and she was saying to herself: "You cruel writing, to have such secrets, and refuse to give them up! If it were pictures, now, I could make out something with a guess; but all these little marks, so much alike, what can one

make of them ?—all alike—with here and there a curling, as if
my father had been amusing himself—and all so plain and
even, too, with never a blot: marry, I marvel he should make
the other copy, unless with intent to alter as he writes.   And
those words with the big letters at the beginning—these be the
people's names—Ferdinand, and sweet Miranda, and the Duke,
and the ill beast that would harm them all.   Why, in Heaven's
mercy, was I so fractious ?   I might even now be learning all
the story—here by myself—the only one in the land: I might
all by myself know the story that will set the London folk agog
in the coming winter.   And what a prize were this, now, for
Master Ben Jonson!   Could one but go to him and say, 'Good
sir, here be something better than your masques and mummeries, your Greeks and clouds and long speeches: put your
name to it, good sir—nay, my father hath abundant store of
such matter, and we in Warwickshire are no niggards—put
your name to it, good sir, and you will get the court ladies to
say you have risen a step on the ladder, else have they but a
strange judgment!'   What would the goodman do ?   Beshrew
me, Prudence never told me the name of the play!   But let
us call it *The Magic Island.   The Magic Island, by Master
Benjamin Jonson.*   What would the wits say ?"

But here she heard some noise on the stair; so she quickly
hid away the treasure in the little drawer, and locked it up
safe there until she should have the chance of asking Prudence
to read it to her.

That did not happen until nearly night-fall; for Prudence
had been away all day helping to put the house straight of a
poor woman that was ill and in bed.   Moreover, she had been
sewing a good deal at the children's clothes and her eyes looked tired—or perhaps it was the wan light that yet lingered in
the sky that gave her that expression, the candles not yet being
lit.   Judith regarded her, and took her hands tenderly, and
made her sit down.

"Sweet mouse," said she, "you are wearing yourself out in
the service of others; and if you take such little heed of yourself, you will yourself fall ill.   And now must I demand of
you further labor.   Or will it be a refreshment for you after
the fatigue of the day ?   See, I have brought them all with me
—the sprite Ariel, and the sweet prince, and Miranda; but in

"AND NOW SHE BEGAN READING."

good sooth I will gladly wait for another time if you are tired—"

"Nay, not so, Judith," she answered. "There is nothing I could like better—but for one thing."

"What, then ?"

"Mean you to show this also to the young gentleman that is at Bidford ?"

"And wherefore not, good Prue ? He hath seen so much of the story, 'twere a pity he should not have the rest. And what a small kindness—the loan but for an hour or two; and I need not even see him, for I have but to leave it at my grandmother's cottage. And if you heard what he says of it— and how grateful he is: marry, it all lies in this, sweet Prue, that you have not seen him, else would you be willing enough to do him so small a favor."

By this time Prudence had lit the candles; and presently they made their way upstairs to her own room.

"And surely," said Judith, as her gentle gossip was arranging the manuscript, "the story will end well, and merrily for the sweet maiden, seeing how powerful her father is ? Will he not compel all things to her happiness—he that can raise storms, and has messengers to fly round the world for him ?"

"And yet he spoke but harshly to the young man when last we saw them," Prudence said. "Why, what's this ?"

She had run her eye down the first page; and now she began reading:

Enter FERDINAND *bearing a log.*

Ferdinand. There be some sports are painful, and their labor
Delight in them sets off. This my mean task
Would be as heavy to me as odious, but
The mistress which I serve quickens what's dead,
And makes my labors pleasures. Oh, she is
Ten times more gentle than her father's crabbed;
And he's composed of harshness. I must remove
Some thousands of these logs and pile them up,
Upon a sore injunction. My sweet mistress
Weeps when she sees me work; and says such baseness
Had never like executor.

Judith's face had gradually fallen.

"Why, 'tis cruel," said she; "and 'tis cruel of my father to put such pain on the sweet prince, that is so gentle, and so unfortunate withal."

10

But Prudence continued the reading:

Enter MIRANDA.

Miranda.   Alas, now, pray you,
Work not so hard: I would the lightning had
Burnt up those logs, that you are enjoined to pile!
Pray, set it down and rest yon: when this burns,
'Twill weep for having wearied you. My father
Is hard at study; pray, now, rest yourself;
He's safe for these three hours.
   Ferdinand.   O most dear mistress,
The sun will set before I shall discharge
What I must strive to do.
   Miranda.   If you'll sit down,
I'll bear your logs the while: pray give me that—
I'll carry it to the pile.

At this point Judith's eyes grew proud and grateful (as
though Miranda had done some brave thing), but she did not
speak.

   Ferdinand.   No, precious creature;
I had rather crack my sinews, break my back,
Than you should such dishonor undergo,
While I sit lazy by.
   Miranda.   You look wearily.
   Ferdinand. No, noble mistress; 'tis fresh morning with me,
When you are by at night. I do beseech you
(Chiefly that I may set it in my prayers),
What is your name?
   Miranda.   Miranda.—O my father,
I have broke your hest to say so!
   Ferdinand.   Admired Miranda:
Indeed, the top of admiration; worth
What's dearest to the world! Full many a lady
I have eyed with best regard; and many a time
The harmony of their tongues hath into bondage
Brought my too diligent ear: for several virtues
Have I liked several women; never any
With so full soul but some defect in her
Did quarrel with the noblest grace she owed,
And put it to the foil. But you, O you,
So perfect and so peerless, are created
Of every creature's best!
   Miranda.   I do not know
One of my sex: no woman's face remember,
Save, from my glass, mine own; nor have I seen
More that I may call men than you, good friend,
And my dear father: how features are abroad,
I am skill-less of; but, by my modesty
(The jewel in my dower), I would not wish
Any companion in the world but you;
Nor can imagination form a shape,
Besides yourself, to like of: But I prattle
Something too wildly, and my father's precepts
I therein do forget.

"Nay, is she not fair and modest!" Judith exclaimed—but apart; and, as the reading proceeded, she began to think of how Master Leofric Hope would regard this maiden. Would he not judge her to be right gentle, and timid, and yet womanly withal, and frank in her confiding? And he—supposing that he were the young prince—what would he think of such a one? Was it too submissive that she should offer to carry the logs? Ought she to so openly confess that she would fain have him to be her companion? And then, as Judith was thus considering, this was what she heard, in Prudence's gentle voice:

Miranda. Do you love me?
Ferdinand. O heaven, O earth, bear witness to this sound,
And crown what I profess with kind event,
If I speak true; if hollowly, invert
What best is boded me, to mischief! I,
Beyond all limit of what else i' the world,
Do love, prize, honor you.
Miranda. I am a fool
To weep at what I am glad of.
Ferdinand. Wherefore weep you?
Miranda. At mine unworthiness, that dare not offer
What I desire to give; and much less take
What I shall die to want: But this is trifling;
And all the more it seeks to hide itself,
The bigger bulk it shows. Hence, bashful cunning!
And prompt me, plain and holy innocence!
I am your wife, if you will marry me;
If not, I'll die your maid; to be your fellow
You may deny me; but I'll be your servant,
Whether you will or no.
Ferdinand. My mistress, dearest;
And I thus humble ever.
Miranda. My husband, then?
Ferdinand. Ay, with a heart as willing
As bondage e'er of freedom: here's my hand.
Miranda. And mine, with my heart in't; and now farewell,
Till half an hour hence.
Ferdinand. A thousand thousand!

She clapped her hands and laughed, in delight and triumph. "Why, sure her father will relent," she cried. "But, Judith, Judith, stay," Prudence said, quickly, and with scarce less gladness. "'Tis so set down; for this is what her father says:

'So glad of this as they I can not be,
Who are surprised withal; but my rejoicing
At nothing can be more.'

Nay, I take it he will soon explain to us why he was so harsh
with the young prince—perchance to try his constancy ?"

Well, after that the reading went on as far as the sheets that
Judith had brought; but ever her mind was returning to the
scene between the two lovers, and speculating as to how Leofric Hope would look upon it.   She had no resentment against
Ben Jonson now; her heart was full of assurance and triumph,
and was therefore generous.   Her only vexation was that the
night must intervene before there could be a chance of the
young London gentleman calling at the cottage; and she looked forward to the possibility of seeing him some time or other
with the determination to be more demure than ever.   She
would not expect him to praise this play.   Perchance 'twas
good enough for simple Warwickshire folk; but the London
wits might consider it of the vulgar kind.   And she laughed
to herself at thinking how awkward his protests would be if
she ventured to hint anything in that direction.

Prudence put the sheets carefully together again.

"Judith, Judith," she said, with a quiet smile, "you lead me
far astray.   I ought to find such things wicked and horrible to
the ear; but perchance 'tis because I know your father, and see
him from day to day, that I find them innocent enough.   They
seem to rest the mind when one is sorrowful."

"Beware of them, good Prue; they are the devil himself
come in the guise of an angel to snatch thee away.   Nay, but,
sweetheart, why should you be sorrowful ?"

"There is Martha Hodgson," said she, simply, "and her
children, nigh to starving; and I can not ask Julius for more—"

Judith's purse was out in an instant.

"Why," said she, "my father did not use half of what I
gave him for the knife he bought at Warwick—marry, I guess
he paid for it mostly himself; but what there is here you shall
have."

And she emptied the contents on to the table, and pushed
them over to her friend.

"You do not grudge it, Judith ?" said Prudence.   "Nay,
I will not ask thee that.   Nor can I refuse it either, for the
children are in sore want.   But why should you not give it
to them yourself, Judith ?"

"Why ?" said Judith, regarding the gentle face with kindly

eyes. "Shall I tell thee why, sweetheart? 'Tis but this: that if I were in need, and help to be given me, I would value it thrice as much if it came from your hand. There is a way of doing such things, and you have it: that is all."

"I hear Julius is come in," Prudence said, as she took up the two candles. "Will you go in and speak with him?"

There was some strange hesitation in her manner, and she did not go to the door. She glanced at Judith somewhat timidly. Then she set the candles down again.

"Judith," said she, "your pity is quick, and you are generous and kind; I would you could find it in your heart to extend your kindness."

"How now, good cousin?" Judith said, in amazement. "What's this?"

Prudence glanced at her again, somewhat uneasily, and obviously in great embarrassment.

"You will not take it ill, dear Judith?"

"By my life, I will not! Not from you, dear heart, whatever it be. But what is the dreadful secret?"

"Tom Quiney has spoken to me," she said, diffidently.

Judith eagerly caught both her hands.

"And you! What said you? 'Tis all settled, then!" she exclaimed, almost breathlessly.

"It is as I imagined, Judith," said Prudence, calmly—and she withdrew her hands, with a touch of maidenly pride, perhaps, from what she could not but imagine to be a kind of felicitation. "He hath no fault to find with the country. If he goes away to those lands beyond seas, 'tis merely because you will say no word to hold him back."

"I!" said Judith, impatiently; and then she checked herself. "But you, sweetheart, what said he to you?"

Prudence's cheeks flushed red.

"He would have me intercede for him," she said, timidly.

"Intercede? with whom?"

"Why, you know, Judith; with whom but yourself? Nay, but be patient—have some kindness. The young man opened his heart to me; and I know he is in trouble. 'Twas last night as we were coming home from the lecture; and he would have me wait till he left a message at his door, so that thus we fell behind; and then he told me why it was that Stratford had grown distasteful to him, and not to be borne, and why he was going away. How could I help saying that that would grieve you ?—sure I am you can not but be sorry to think of the young man banishing himself from his own people. . And he said that I was your nearest friend; and would I speak for him ? And I answered that I was all unused to such matters, but that if any pleading of mine would influence you I would right gladly do him that service; and so I would, dear Judith; for how can you bear to think of the youth going away with these godless men, and perchance never to return to his own land, when a word from you would restrain him ?"

Judith took both her hands again, and looked with a kindly smile into the timid, pleading eyes.

"And 'tis you, sweet mouse, that come to me with such a prayer? Was there ever so kind a heart? But that is you ever and always—never a thought for yourself, everything for oth⸗ ers. And so he had the cruelty to ask you—you—to bring this message ?"

"Judith," said the other, with the color coming into her face again, "you force me to speak against my will. Nay, how can I hide from myself, dear friend, that you have plans and wish⸗ es—perchance suspicions—with regard to me? And if what I guess be true—if that is your meaning—indeed 'tis all built on a wrong foundation : believe me, Judith, it is so. I would have you assured of it, sweetheart. You know that I like not speaking of such matters; 'tis not seemly and becoming to a maiden; and fain would I have my mind occupied with far other things; but, Judith, this time I must speak plain; and I would have you put away from you all such intentions and surmises—dear heart, you do me wrong !"

"In good sooth, am I all mistaken ?" Judith said, glancing keenly at her.

"Do you doubt my word, Judith ?" said she.

"And yet," her friend said, as if to herself, and musingly, "there were several occasions: there was the fortune-teller at Hampton Lucy that coupled you, and Quiney seemed right merry withal; and then again when he would have us play kiss-in-the-ring on the evening after Mary Sadler's marriage, and I forbade it chiefly for your sake, sweet mouse, then me⸗ thought you seemed none overpleased with my interference—"

But here she happened to look at Prudence, and she could not fail to see that the whole subject was infinitely distressing to her. There was a proud, hurt expression on the gentle face, and a red spot burning in each cheek. So Judith took hold of her and kissed her.

"Once and forever, dearest heart," said she, "I banish all such thoughts. And I will make no more plans for thee, nor suspect thee, but let thee go in thine own way, in the paths of charity and goodness. But I mean not to give up thy friendship, sweet Prue; if I can not walk in the same path, at least I may stretch a hand over to thee; and if I but keep so near so true a saint, marry, I shall not go so far wrong."

She took up one of the candles.

"Shall we go down and see Julius?" said she.

"But Tom Quiney, Judith—what shall I say?" Prudence asked, anxiously.

"Why, say nothing, sweetheart," was the immediate answer. "'Twas a shame to burden you with such a task. When he chooses he can at any moment have speech of me, if his worship be not too proud or too suspicious. In Stratford we can all of us speak the English tongue, I hope."

"But, Judith," said the other, slowly and wistfully, "twenty years is a long space for one to be away from his native land."

"Marry is it, sweet mouse," Judith answered, as she opened the door and proceeded to go down the narrow wooden steps. "'Tis a long space indeed, and at the end of it many a thing that seemeth of great import and consequence now will be no better than an old tale, idle and half forgotten."

CHAPTER XXII.

PORTENTS.

IT was somewhat hard on little Bess Hall that her aunt Judith was determined she should grow up as fearless as she herself was, and had, indeed, charged herself with this branch of her niece's education. The child, it is true, was not more timid than others of her age, and could face with fair equanimity beggars, school-boys, cows, geese, and other dangerous creatures; while as for ghosts, goblins, and similar nocturnal terrors, Judith had settled all that side of the question by informing the maids of both families, in the plainest language, that any one of them found even mentioning such things to this niece of hers would be instantaneously and without ceremony shot forth from the house. But beyond and above all this Judith expected too much, and would flout and scold when Bess Hall declined to perform the impossible, and would threaten to go away and get a small boy out of the school to become her playmate in future. At this moment, for example, she was standing at the foot of the staircase in Dr. Hall's house. She had come round to carry off her niece for the day, and she had dressed her up like a small queen, and now she would have her descend the wide and handsome staircase in noble state and unaided. Bess Hall, who had no ambition to play the part of a queen, but had, on the other hand, a wholesome and instinctive fear of breaking her neck, now stood on the landing, helpless amid all her finery, and looking down at her aunt in a beseeching sort of way.

"I shall tumbie down, Aunt Judith; I know I shall," said she, and budge she would not.

"Tumble down, little stupid! Why, what should make you tumble down? Are you going forever to be a baby? Any baby can crawl down-stairs by holding on to the balusters."

"I know I shall tumbie down, Aunt Judith—and then I shall cry."

But even this threat was of no avail.

"Come along, little goose; 'tis easy enough when you try it. Do you think I have dressed you up as a grown woman to see you crawl like a baby? A fine woman—you! Come along, I say!"

But this lesson, happily for the half-frightened pupil, was abruptly brought to an end. Judith was standing with her face to the staircase, and her back to the central hall and the outer door, so that she could not see any one entering, and indeed the first intimation she had of the approach of a stranger was a voice behind her:

"Be gentle with the child, Judith."

And then she knew that she was caught. For some little time back she had very cleverly managed to evade the good parson, or at least to secure the safety of company when she saw him approach. But this time she was as helpless as little Bess herself. Dr. Hall was away from home; Judith's sister was ill of a cold, and in bed; there was no one in the house, besides the servants, but herself. The only thing she could do was to go up to the landing, swing her niece on to her shoulder, and say to Master Walter that they were going round to New Place, for that Susan was ill in bed, and unable to look after the child.

"I will walk with you as far," said he, calmly, and, indeed, as if it were rather an act of condescension on his part.

She set out with no good-will. She expected that he would argue, and she had an uncomfortable suspicion that he would get the best of it. And if she had once or twice rather wildly thought that in order to get rid of all perplexities, and in order to please all the people around her, she would in the end allow Master Walter Blaise to win her over into becoming his wife, still she felt that the time was not yet. She would have the choosing of it for herself. And why should she be driven into a corner prematurely? Why be made to confess that her brain could not save her? She wanted peace. She wanted to play with Bess Hall, or to walk through the meadows with Willie Hart, teaching him what to think of England. She did not want to be confronted with clear, cold eyes, and arguments like steel, and the awful prospect of having to labor in the vineyard through the long, long, gray, and distant years. She grew to think it was scarcely fair of her father to hand her
10*

over.   He at least might have been on her side.   But he seemed as willing as any that she should go away among the
saints, and forsake forever (as it seemed to her) the beautiful,
free, and clear-colored life that she had been well content to
live.

And then, all of a sudden, it flashed upon her mind that she
was a player's daughter, and a kind of flame went to her face.

"I pray you, good Master Blaise," said she, with a lofty and
gracious courtesy, "bethink you, ere you give us your company through the town."

"What mean you, Judith ?" said he, in some amazement.

"Do you forget, then, that I am the daughter of a player ?—
and this his granddaughter ?" said she.

"In truth, I know not what you mean, Judith," he exclaimed.

"Why," said she, "may not the good people who are the
saints of the earth wonder to see you consort with such as
we ?—or, rather, with one such as I, who am impenitent, and
take no shame that my father is a player—nay, God's my
witness, I am wicked enough to be proud of it, and I care not
who knows it, and they that hope to have me change my
thoughts on that matter will have no lack of waiting."

Well, it was a fair challenge; and he answered it frankly,
and with such a reasonableness and charity of speech that, despite herself, she could not but admit that she was pleased, and
also, perhaps, just a little bit grateful.   He would not set up
to be any man's judge, he said; nor was he a Pharisee; the Master that he served was no respecter of persons—He had welcomed all when He was upon the earth—and it behooved His
followers to beware of pride and the setting up of distinctions;
if there was any house in the town that earned the respect of
all, it was New Place; he could only speak of her father as
he found him, here, in his own family, among his own friends
—and what that was all men knew; and so forth.   He spoke
well, and modestly; and Judith was so pleased to hear what he
said of her father that she forgot to ask whether all this was
quite consistent with his usual denunciations of plays and
players, his dire prophecy as to the fate of those who were
not of the saints, and his sharp dividing and shutting off of
these.   He did not persecute her at all.   There was no argu-

ment. What he was mostly anxious about was that she should not tire herself with carrying Bess Hall on her shoulder.

"Nay, good sir," said she, quite pleasantly, "'tis a trick my father taught me; and the child is but a feather-weight."

He looked at her—so handsome and buxom, and full of life and courage; her eyes lustrous, the rose-leaf tint of health in her cheeks; and always at the corner of her mouth what could only be called a disposition to smile, as if the world suited her fairly well, and that she was ready at any moment to laugh her thanks.

"There be many, Judith," said he, "who might envy you your health and good spirits."

"When I lose them, 'twill be time enough to lament them," said she, complacently.

"The hour that is passing seems all in all to you; and who can wonder at it?" he continued. "Pray Heaven your carelessness of the morrow have reason in it! But all are not so minded. There be strange tidings in the land."

"Indeed, sir; and to what end?" said she.

"I know not whether these rumors have reached your house," he said, "but never at any time I have read of have men's minds been so disturbed—with a restlessness and apprehension of something being about to happen. And what marvel! The strange things that have been seen and heard of throughout the world of late—meteors, and earthquakes, and visions of armies fighting in the heavens. Even so was Armageddon to be foreshadowed. Nay, I will be honest with you, Judith, and say that it is not clear to my own mind that the great day of the Lord is at hand; but many think so; and one man's reading of the Book of Revelation is but a small matter to set against so wide a belief. Heard you not of the vision that came to the young girl at Chipping Camden last Monday?"

"Indeed, no, good sir."

"I marvel that Prudence has not heard of it, for all men are speaking of it. 'Twas in this way, as I hear. The maiden is one of rare piety and grace, given to fasting, and nightly vigils, and searching of the heart. 'Twas on the night of Sunday last—or perchance toward Monday morning—that she was awakened out of her sleep by finding her room full of light;

and looking out of the window she beheld in the darkness a figure of resplendent radiance—shining like the sun, as she said, only clear white, and shedding rays around; and the figure approached the window, and regarded her; and she dropped on her knees in wonder and fear, and bowed her head and worshipped. And as she did so, she heard a voice say to her: 'Watch and pray: Behold, I come quickly.' And she durst not raise her head, as she says, being overcome with fear and joy. But the light slowly faded from the room; and when at last she rose she saw something afar off in the sky, that was now grown dark again. And ever since she has been trembling with the excitement of it, and will take no food; but from time to time she cries in a loud voice, 'Lord Jesus, come quickly! Lord Jesus, come quickly!' Many have gone to see her, as I hear, and from all parts of the country; but she heeds them not; she is intent with her prayers; and her eyes, the people say, look as if they had been dazzled with a great light, and are dazed and strange. Nay, 'tis but one of many things that are murmured abroad at present; for there have been signs in the heavens seen in sundry places, and visions, and men's minds grow anxious."

"And what think you yourself, good sir? You are one that should know."

"I?" said he. "Nay, I am far too humble a worker to take upon myself the saying ay or no at such a time; I can but watch and pray and wait. But is it not strange to think that we here at this moment, walking along this street in Stratford, might within some measurable space—say, a year, or half a dozen years or so—that we might be walking by the pure river of water that John saw flowing from the throne of God and of the Lamb? Do you not remember how the early Christians, with such a possibility before their eyes, drew nearer to each other, as it were, and rejoiced together, parting with all their possessions, and living in common, so that the poorest were even as the rich? 'Twas no terror that overtook them, but a happiness; and they drew themselves apart from the world, and lived in their own community, praying with each other, and aiding each other. 'All that believed,' the Bible tells us, 'were in one place, and had all things common. And they sold their possessions and goods, and parted them to all

men, as every one had need. And they continued daily in the
Temple, and, breaking bread at home, did eat their meat together with gladness and singleness of heart, praising God, and had
favor with all the people; and the Lord added to the Church
from day to day such as should be saved.' Such a state of
spiritual brotherhood and exaltation may come among us once
more; methinks I see the symptoms of its approach even now.
Blessed are they who will be in that communion with a pure
soul and a humble mind, for the Lord will be with them as
their guide, though the waters should arise and overflow, or
fire consume the earth."

"Yes, but, good sir," said she, "when the early Christians
you speak of thought the world was near to an end they were
mistaken. And these, now, of our day—"

"Whatever is prophesied must come to pass," said he, "or
soon or late, though it is possible for our poor human judgment to err as to the time. But surely we ought to be prepared; and what preparation, think you, is sufficient for so
great and awful a change? Joy there may be in the trivial
things of this world—in the vanities of the hour, that pass
away and are forgotten; but what are these things to those
whose heart is set on the New Jerusalem—the shining city?
The voice that John heard proclaimed no lie: 'twas the voice
of the Lord of heaven and earth—a promise to them that wait
and watch for his coming. 'And God shall wipe away all
tears from their eyes; and there shall be no more death, neither
sorrow, neither crying, neither shall there be any more pain,
for the first things are passed. . . . . And there shall be no more
curse; but the throne of God and of the Lamb shall be in it,
and His servants shall serve Him. And they shall see His
face, and His name shall be in their foreheads. And there shall
be no night there; and they need no candle, neither light of
the sun, for the Lord God giveth them light, and they shall
reign for evermore.'"

She sighed.

"'Tis too wonderful a thing for poor sinful creatures to expect," she said.

But by this time they were at the house, and he could not say
anything further to her; indeed, when he proposed that she
should come into the sitting-room, and that he would read to

her a description of the glories of the New Jerusalem, out of
the Book of Revelation, she excused herself by saying that she
must carry Bess Hall to see her father. So he went in and sat
down, waiting for Judith's mother to be sent for; while aunt
and niece went out and through the back yard to the garden.

"Bess," said Judith, on the way, "heardst thou aught of a
white figure?"

"No, Judith," said the child, who had been engaged all the
way in examining the prettinesses of her aunt's velvet cap,
and ruff, and what not.

"That is well," said she.

When she got into the garden, she could see that goodman
Matthew eyed their approach with little favor—for Bess Hall,
when her grandfather had charge of her, was allowed to tear
flowers, and walk over beds, or do anything she choose; but Judith did not mind that much. On the other hand, she would
not go deliberately and disturb her father. She would give
him his choice—to come forth or not as he pleased. And so,
quite noiselessly, and at a little distance off, she passed the
summer-house. There was no sign. Accordingly, she went
on idly to the further end of the garden, and would doubtless
have remained there (rather than return within-doors) amusing the child somehow, but that the next minute her father appeared.

"Come hither, Bess! Come hither, wench!" he called.

Nay, he came to meet them; and as he lifted the child down
from Judith's shoulder, something—perhaps it was the touch
of the sunlight on the soft brown of her short curls—seemed
to attract his notice.

"Why, wench," said he to Judith, "methinks your hair
grows prettier every day. And yet you keep it overshort—yes,
'tis overshort—would you have them think you a boy?"

"I would I were a man," said she, glancing at him rather
timidly.

"How, then? What, now?"

"For then," said she, "might I help you in your work, so
please you, sir."

He laughed, and said:

"My work? What know you of that, wench?"

The blood rushed to her face.

"Nay, sir, I but meant the work of the fields—in going about with the bailiff and the like. The maids say you were abroad at five this morning."

"Well, is't not the pleasantest time of the day in this hot weather?" he said—and he seemed amused by her interference.

"But why should you give yourself so many cares, good father?" she made bold to say (for she had been meditating the saying of it for many a day back). "You that have great fame, and land, and wealth. We would fain see you rest a little more, father; and 'tis all the harder to us that we can give you no help, being but women-folk."

There was something in the tone of her voice—or perhaps in her eyes—that conveyed more than her words. He put his hand on her head.

"You are a good lass," said he. "And listen. You can do something for me that is of far more value to me than any help in any kind of work: nay, I tell thee 'tis of greater value to me than all of my work; and 'tis this: keep you a merry heart, wench—let me see your face right merry and cheerful as you go about—that is what you can do for me; I would have you ever as you are now, as bright and glad as a summer day."

"'Tis an easy task, sir, so long as you are content to be pleased with me," she managed to answer; and then little Bess Hall—who could not understand why she should have been so long left unnoticed—began to scramble up his knees, and was at last transferred to his arms.

Judith's heart was beating somewhat quickly—with a kind of pride and gladness that was very near bringing tears to her eyes; but, of course, that was out of the question, seeing that he had enjoined her to be cheerful. And so she forced herself to say, with an odd kind of smile, .

"I pray you, sir, may I remain with you for a space—if Bess and I trouble you not?"

"Surely," said he, regarding her; "but what is it, then?"

"Why," said she, pulling herself together, "good Master Blaise is within-doors, and his last belief is enough to frighten a poor maiden—let alone this small child. He says the world is nigh unto its end."

"Nay, I have heard of some such talk being abroad," said he, "among the country folk. But why should that frighten thee ? Even were it true, we can make it nor better nor worse."

"Only this, father," said she, and she looked at him with the large, clear-shining gray eyes no longer near to tears, but rather suggesting some dark mystery of humor, "that if the end of the world be so nigh at hand, 'twould be an idle thing for the good parson to think of taking him a wife."

"I ask for no secrets, wench," her father said, as he sat little Bess Hall on the branch of an apple-tree.

"Nay, sir, he but said that as many were of opinion that something dreadful was about to happen, we should all of us draw nearer together. That is well, and to be understanded; but if the world be about to end for all of us, surely 'twere a strange thing that any of us should think of taking husband or wife."

"I'll meddle not," her father said. "Go thine own ways. I have heard thou hast led more than one honest lad in Stratford a madcap dance. Take heed; take heed—as thy grandmother saith—lest thou outwear their patience."

And then something—she could scarce tell what—came into her head: some wild wish that he would remain always there at Stratford: would she not right willingly discard all further thoughts of lovers or sweethearts if only he would speak to her sometimes as he had just been speaking; and approve of her hair; and perchance let her become somewhat more of a companion to him ? But she durst not venture to say so much. She only said, very modestly and timidly,

"I am content to be as I am, sir, if you are content that I should bide with you."

"Content?" said he, with a laugh that had no unkindness in it. "Content that thou shouldst bide with us ? Keep that pretty face of thine merry and glad, good lass—and have no fear."

CHAPTER XXIII.

A LETTER.

WHEN she should get back from Master Leofric Hope the last portion of the yet unnamed play, there remained (as she considered) but one thing more—to show him the letter written by the King to her father, so that when the skies should clear over the young gentleman's head, and he be permitted to return among his friends and acquaintances, he might have something else occasionally to talk of than Ben Jonson and his masques and his favor at court. Nor had she any difficulty in procuring the letter; for Prudence was distinctly of opinion that by right it belonged to Judith, who had coveted it from the beginning. However, Judith only now wanted the loan of it for a day or two, until, in her wanderings, she might encounter Master Hope.

That opportunity soon arrived; for whether it was that the young gentleman kept a sharp lookout for her, or whether she was able to make a shrewd guess as to his probable whereabouts at certain hours of the day, she had scarcely ever failed to meet him when she went over to Shottery for the successive installments of the play that he had left for her there. On this occasion she had found the last of these awaiting her at the cottage; and when she had put it into her velvet satchel, and bade goodby to her grandmother, she set out for home with a pretty clear foreknowledge that sooner or later the young gentleman would appear. Was it not his duty?—to say what he thought of all this romance that he had been allowed to see; and to thank her; and say farewell? For she had a vague impression that she had done as much as could reasonably be expected of her in the way of cheering the solitude of one in misfortune: and she had gathered, moreover, that he was likely soon to leave the neighborhood. But she would not have him go without seeing the King's letter.

Well, when he stepped forth from behind some trees, she was not surprised; and even the Don had grown accustomed to these sudden appearances.

"Give ye good-day, sweet lady," said he.

"And to you, sir," she said.   "I thank you for your care in leaving me these pages; I would not have had any harm come to them, even though my father will in time throw them away."

"And my thanks to you, sweet Mistress Judith," said he— "how can I express them?"—and therewith he entered upon such a eulogy of the story he had just been reading as she was not likely to hear from any Stratford-born acquaintance.   Indeed, he spoke well, and with obvious sincerity; and although she had intended to receive these praises with indifference (as though the play were but a trifle that her father had thrown off easily amid the pressure of other labors), she did not quite succeed.   There was a kind of triumph in her eyes; her face was glad and proud; when he quoted a bit of one of Ariel's songs, she laughed lightly.

"He is a clever musician, that merry imp, is he not?" said she.

"I would I had such a magic-working spirit to serve me," said he, looking at her.   "One could shape one's own course then.   'Under the blossom that hangs on the bough,' would be my motto; there would be no going back to London or any other town.   And what think you: might he not find out for me some sweet Miranda?—not that I am worthy of such a prize, or could do aught to deserve her, except in my duty and humble service to her.   The Miranda, I think, could be found," he said, glancing timidly at her; "nay, I swear I know myself where to find just such a beautiful and gentle maiden; but where is the Ariel that would charm her heart and incline her to pity and kindness?"

"Here, sir," said she, quickly, "is the letter I said I would bring you, that the King wrote to my father."

He did not look at the blue velvet satchel; he looked at her— perhaps to see whether he had gone too far.   But she did not show any signs of confusion or resentment; at all events she pretended not to be conscious; and, for one thing, her eyes were lowered, for the satchel seemed for a second or so difficult to open.   Then she brought forth the letter.

"Perchance you can tell me the English of it, good sir?" said she.   "'Tis some time since Master Blaise read it for us, and I would hear it again."

"Nay, I fear my Latin will scarce go so far," said he—"'tis but little practice in it I have had since my school-days; but I will try to make out the sense of it."

She carefully opened the large folded sheet of paper, and handed it to him. This was what he found before him:

"JACOBUS D. G. Rex Anglorum et Scotorum poetæ nostro fideli et bene dilecto GULIELMO SHAKESPEARE, S. P. D.

"Cum nuper apud Londinium commorati comœdiam tuam nobis inductam spectâssemus, de manu viri probi Eugenii Collins fabulæ libro accepto, operam dedimus ut eam diligenter perlegeremus. Subtilissima illa quidem, multisque ingenii luminibus et artis, multis etiam animi oblectamentis, excogitata, nimis tamen accommodata ad cacchinationem movendam vulgi imperiti, politioris humanitatis expertis. Quod vero ad opera tua futura attinet, amicissime te admonemus ut multa commentatione et meditatione exemplaria verses antistitum illorum artis comœdicæ, Menandri scilicet Atheniensis et Plauti et Terentii Romani, qui minus vulgi plausum captabant quam vitiis tanquam flagellis castigandis studebant. Qui optimi erant arte et summa honestate et utilitate, qualem te etiam esse volumus; virtutum artium et exercitationum doctores, atque illustrium illorum a Deo ad populum regendum præpositorum adminicula. Quibus fac ne te minorem præstes; neque tibi nec familiaribus tuis unquam deerimus quin, quum fiat occasio, munere regali fungamur. Te interea Deus opt. max. feliciter sospitet.

"Datum ex regia nostra apud Greenwich X. Kal. Jun."

He began his translation easily:

"'To our trusty and well-beloved poet, William Shakespeare: Health and greeting.'" But then he began to stammer. "'When formerly—when recently—tarrying in London—thy comedy—thy comedy'—nay, fair Mistress Judith, I beseech your pardon; I am grown more rusty than I thought, and would not destroy your patience. Perchance, now, you would extend your favor once more, and let me have the letter home with me, so that I might spell it out in school-boy fashion?"

She hesitated; but only for a second.

"Nay, good sir, I dare not. These sheets were thrown aside, and so far of little account; but this—if aught were to come amiss to this letter, how should I regard myself? If my father value it but slightly, there be others who think more of it; and —and they have intrusted it to me; I would not have it go out of my own keeping, so please you, and pardon me."

It was clear that she did not like to refuse this favor to so courteous and grateful a young gentleman. However, her face instantly brightened.

"But I am in no hurry, good sir," said she. "Why should you not sit you on the stile there, and take time to master the letter, while I gather some wild flowers for my father? In truth, I am in no hurry; and I would fain have you know what the King wrote."

"I would I were a school-boy again for five minutes," said he, with a laugh; but he went obediently to the stile, and sat down, and proceeded to pore over the contents of the letter.

And then she wandered off by herself (so as to leave him quite undisturbed), and began to gather here and there a wild rose from the hedge, or a piece of meadow-sweet from the bank beneath, or a bit of yarrow from among the grass. It was a still, clear, quiet day, with some rainy clouds in the sky; and beyond these, near to the horizon, broad silver shafts of sunlight striking down on the woods and the distant hills. It looked as if a kind of mid-day sleep had fallen over the earth; there was scarce a sound; the birds were silent; and there was not even enough wind to make a stirring through the wide fields of wheat or in the elms. The nosegay grew apace, though she went about her work idly—kneeling here and stretching a hand there; and always she kept away from him, and would not even look in his direction; for she was determined that he should have ample leisure to make out the sense of the letter, of which she had but a vague recollection, only that she knew it was complimentary.

Even when he rose and came toward her she pretended not to notice. She would show him she was in no hurry. She was plucking the heads of red clover, and sucking them to get at the honey; or she was adding a buttercup or two to her nosegay; or she was carelessly humming to herself:

" O stay and hear; your true love's coming,
That can sing both high and low."

"Well, now, Mistress Judith," said he, with an air of apology, "methinks I have got at the meaning of it, however imperfectly; and your father might well be proud of such a commendation from so high a source—the King, as every one knows, being a learned man, and skilled in the arts. And I have not heard that he has written to any other of the poets of our day—"

"No, sir?" said she, quickly. "Not to Master Jonson?"

"Not that I am aware of, sweet lady," said he, "though he hath sometimes messages to send, as you may suppose, by one coming from the court. And I marvel not that your father should put store by this letter that speaks well of his work—"

"Your pardon, good sir, but 'tis not so," said Judith, calmly. "Doubtless if the King commend my father's writing, that showeth that his Majesty is skilled and learned, as you say; and my father was no doubt pleased enough—as who would not be?—by such a mark of honor; but as for setting great value on it, I assure you he did not: nay, he gave it to Julius Shawe. And will you read it, good sir?—I remember me there was something in it about the ancients."

"'Tis but a rough guess that I can make," said he, regarding the paper. "But it seems that the King had received at the hands of one Eugene Collins the book of a comedy of your father's that had been presented before his Majesty when he was recently in London. And very diligently, he says, he has read through the same; and finds it right subtly conceived, with many beauties and delights, and such ornaments as are to be approved by an ingenious mind. It is true his Majesty hints that there may be parts of the play more calculated than might be to move the laughter of the vulgar; but you would not have a critic have nothing but praise?—and the King's praise is high indeed. And then he goes on to say that as regards your father's future work, he would in the most friendly manner admonish him to study the great masters of the comic art; that is, Menander the Athenian, and the Romans Plautus and Terentius, who—who—what says the King?—less studied to capture the applause of the vulgar than to lash the vices of the day as with whips. And these he highly commends as being of great

service to the state; and would have your father be the like:
teachers of virtue, and also props and aids to those whom God
hath placed to rule over the people. He would have your father be among these public benefactors; and then he adds that,
when occasion serves, he will not fail to extend his royal favor
to your father and his associates; and so commends him to the
protection of God. Nay, 'tis a right friendly letter; there is
none in the land that would not be proud of it; 'tis not every
day nor with every one that King James would take such trouble and play the part of tutor."

He handed her the letter, and she proceeded to fold it up
carefully again and put it in her satchel. She said nothing,
but she hoped that these phrases of commendation would remain fixed in his mind when that he was returned to London.

And then there was a moment of embarrassment—or at least
of constraint. He had never been so near the town with her
before (for his praise of her father's comedy, as they walked
together, had taken some time), and there before them were
the orchards and mud walls, and, further off, the spire of the
church among the trees. She did not like to bid him go, and
he seemed loath to say farewell, he probably having some dim
notion that, now he had seen the end of the play and also this
letter, there might be some difficulty in finding an excuse for
another meeting.

"When do you return to London?" said she, for the sake of
saying something. "Or may you return? I hope, good sir,
your prospects are showing brighter; it must be hard for one
of your years to pass the time in idleness."

"The time that I have spent in these parts," said he, "has
been far more pleasant and joyful to me than I could have
imagined—you may easily guess why, dear Mistress Judith.
And now, when there is some prospect of my being able to
go, I like it not; so many sweet hours have been passed here,
the very fields and meadows around have acquired a charm—"

"Nay, but, good sir," said she, a little breathlessly, "at your
time of life you would not waste the days in idleness."

"In truth it has been a gracious idleness!" he exclaimed.

"At your time of life," she repeated, quickly, "why, to be
shut up in a farm—"

"The Prince Ferdinand," said he, "though I would not

compare myself with him, found the time pass pleasantly and sweetly enough, as I reckon, though he was shut up in a cave. But then there was the fair Miranda to be his companion. There is no Ariel to work such a charm for me, else do you think I could ever bring myself to leave so enchanting a neighborhood ?"

"Good sir," said she (in some anxiety to get away), "I may not ask the reason of your being in hiding, though I wish you well, and would fain hear there was no further occasion for it. And I trust there may be none when next you come to Warwickshire, and that those of our household who have a better right to speak for it than I, will have the chance of entertaining you. And now I would bid you farewell."

"No, dear Judith!" he exclaimed, with a kind of entreaty in his voice. "Not altogether ? Why, look at the day!—would you have me say farewell to you on such a day of gloom and cloud ? Surely you will let me take away a brighter picture of you, and Warwickshire, and of our brief meetings in these quiet spots—if go I must. In truth I know not what may happen to me; I would speak plainer; but I am no free agent; I can but beg of you to judge me charitably, if ever you hear aught of me—"

And here he stopped abruptly and paused, considering, and obviously irresolute and perplexed.

"Why," said he at length, and almost to himself—"why should I go away at all ? I will carry logs—if needs be—or anything. Why should I go ?"

She knew instantly what he meant; and knew, also, that it was high time for her to escape from so perilous a situation.

"I pray you pardon me, good sir; but I must go. Come, Don."

"But one more meeting, sweet Mistress Judith," he pleaded, "on a fairer day than this—you will grant as much ?"

"I may not promise," said she; "but indeed I leave with you my good wishes; and so, farewell!"

"God shield you, dearest lady," said he, bowing low; "you leave with me also a memory of your kindness that will remain in my heart."

Well, there was no doubt that she felt very much relieved when she had left him and was nearing the town; and yet she had a kind of pity for him too, as she thought of his going away by himself to that lonely farm: one so gentle, and so grateful for company, being shut up there on this gloomy day. Whereas she was going back to a cheerful house; Prudence was coming round to spend the afternoon with them, and help to mark the new napery; and then in the evening the whole of them, her father included, were going to sup at Dr. Hall's, who had purchased a dishful of ancient coins in one of his peregrinations, and would have them come and examine them. Perhaps, after all, that reference to Miranda was not meant to apply to her. It was but natural he should speak of Miranda, having just finished the play. And carrying logs: he could not mean carrying logs for her father; that would be a foolish jest. No, no; he would remain at the farm and spend the time as best he could; and then, when this cloud blew over, he would return to London, and carry with him (as she hoped) some discreet rumor of the new work of her father's that he had praised so highly, and perchance some mention of the compliments paid by the King; and if, in course of time, the young gentleman should make his way back to Stratford again, and come to see them at New Place, and if his pleasant manner and courtesy proved to be quite irresistible, so that she had to allow the wizard's prophecy to come true in spite of herself, why, then, it was the hand of fate, and none of her doing, and she would have to accept her destiny with as good a grace as might be.

As she was going into the town she met Tom Quiney. He was on the other side of the roadway, and after one swift glance at her, he lowered his eyes, and would have passed on without speaking. And then it suddenly occurred to her that she would put her pride in her pocket. She knew quite well that her maidenly dignity had been wounded by his suspicions, and that she ought to let him go his own way if he chose. But, on the other hand (and this she did not know), there was in her nature an odd element of what might be called boyish generosity—of frankness and common-sense and good comradeship. And these two had been very stanch comrades in former days, each being in a curious manner the protector of the other; for while she many a time came to his aid—being a trifle older than he, and always ready with her quick feminine wit and ingenuity when they were both of them likely to get into trouble—he, on his side, was her shield and bold champion by reason of his superior stature and his strength, and his terrible courage in face of bulls or barking dogs and the like. For the moment she only thought of him as her old companion; and she was a good-natured kind of creature, and frank and boyish in her ways, and so she stepped across the road, though there was some mud about.

"Why can't we be friends?" said she.

"You have enough of other friends," said he.

It was a rebuff; but still—she would keep down her girlish pride.

"I hope you are not going away from the country?" said she.

He did not meet her look; his eyes were fixed on the ground.

"What is there to keep me in it?" was his answer.

"Why, what is there to keep any of us in it?" she said. "Heaven's mercy, if we were all to run away when we found something or another not quite to our liking, what a fine thing that would be! Nay, I hope there is no truth in it," she continued, looking at him, and not without some memories of their escapades together when they were boy and girl. "'Twould grieve many—indeed it would. I pray you think better of it. If for no other, for my sake: we used to be better friends."

There were two figures now approaching.

"Oh, here come Widow Clemms and her daughter," she said; "a rare couple. 'Twill be meat and drink to them to carry back a story. No matter. Now, fare you well; but pray think better of it; there be many that would grieve if you went away."

He stole a look at her as she passed on: perhaps there was a trifle more than usual of color in her radiant and sunny face, because of the approach of the two women. It was a lingering kind of look that he sent after her; and then he, too, turned and went on his way—cursing the parson.

11

CHAPTER XXIV.

A VISITOR.

MASTER LEOFRIC HOPE, on leaving Judith, returned to the farm, but not to the solitude that had awakened her commiseration. When he entered his room, which was at the back of the house, and facing the southern horizon (that alone showed some streaks of sunlight on this gloomy day), he found a stranger there—and a stranger who had evidently some notion of making himself comfortable, for he had opened the window, and was now sitting on the sill, and had just begun to smoke his pipe. His hat, his sword, and sword-belt he had flung on the table.

For a second the proper owner of the apartment knew not who this new tenant might be—he being dark against the light; but the next second he had recognized him, and that with no good grace.

"What the devil brings you here?" said he, sulkily.

"A hearty welcome, truly!" the other said, with much complacency. "After all my vexation in finding thee out! A goodly welcome for an old friend! But no matter, Jack—come, hast naught to offer one to drink? I have ridden from Banbury this morning; and the plague take me if I had not enough trouble ere I found the hare in her form. But 'tis snug—'tis snug. The place likes me; though I thought by now you might have company, and entered with care. Come, man, be more friendly! Will you not ask me to sit? Must I call the landlady—or the farmer's wife—myself, and beg for a cup of something on so hot a day? Where be your manners, Gentleman Jack?"

"What the devil brings you into Warwickshire?" the other repeated, as he threw his hat on the table, and dropped into a chair, and stretched out his legs, without a further look at his companion.

"Nay, 'tis what the devil keeps thee here—that is the graver question—though I know the answer right well. Come, Jack, be reasonable! 'Tis for thy good I have sought thee out.

AN UNWELCOME VISITOR.

What, man, would you ruin us both ?—for I tell thee, the end
is pressing and near."

Seeing that his unwilling host would not even turn his eyes
toward him, he got down from the window-sill, and came along
to the table, and took a chair. He was a short, stout young
man, of puffy face and red hair, good-natured in look, but
with a curious glaze in his light blue-gray eyes that told of the
tavern and himself being pretty close companions. His dress
had some show of ornament about it, though it was rather
travel-stained and shabby; he wore jewelled rings in his ears;
and the handkerchief which he somewhat ostentatiously displayed, if the linen might have been whiter, was elaborately embroidered with thread of Coventry blue. For the rest, he spoke
pleasantly and good-humoredly, and was obviously determined
not to take offense at his anything but hearty reception.

"Hoy-day," said he, with a laugh, "what a·bother I had
with the good dame here, that would scarce let me come in!
For how knew I what name you might be dancing your latest
galliard in ?—not plain Jack Orridge, I'll be bound!—what is't,
your worship ?—or your lordship, perchance?—nay, but a lord
would look best in the eyes of a daughter of Will Shakespeare,
that loveth to have trumpets and drums going, and dukes and
princes stalking across his boards. But 'fore Heaven, now,
Jack," said he, interrupting himself, and sending an appealing
look round the room, "have you naught to drink in the house?
Came you ever to my lodging and found such scurvy entertainment ?"

The reluctant host left the apartment for a second or two,
and presently returned, followed by the farmer's wife, who
placed on the table a jug of small beer, and some bread and
cheese. The bread and cheese did not find much favor with
the new-comer, but he drank a large horn of the beer, and took
to his pipe again.

"Come, Jack, be friendly," said he; "'tis for thine own
good I have sought thee out."

"I would you would mind your own business," the other
said, with a sullen frown remaining on his face.

"Mine and yours are one, as I take it, good coz," his companion said, coolly; and then he added, in a more friendly way:
"Come, come, man, you know we must sink or swim together.

And sinking it will be, if you give not up this madcap chase. Nay, you carry the jest too far, *mon ami.* 'Twas a right merry tale at the beginning—the sham wizard, and your coquetting with Will Shakespeare's daughter to while away the time; 'twas a prank would make them roar at the Cranes in the Vintry; and right well done, I doubt not—for, in truth, if you were not such a gallant gentleman, you might win to a place in the theatres as well as any of them; but to come back here again— to hide yourself away again—and when I tell you they will no longer forbear, but will clap thee into jail if they have not their uttermost penny—why, 'tis pure moonshine madness to risk so much for a jest!"

"I tell thee 'tis no jest at all!" the other said, angrily. "In Heaven's name, what brought you here?"

"Am I to have no care of myself, then, that am your surety, and have their threats from hour to hour?"

He laughed in a stupid kind of way, and filled out some more beer and drank it off thirstily.

"We had a merry night, last night, at Banbury," said he. "I must pluck a hair of the same wolf to-day. And what say you? No jest? Nay, you look sour enough to be virtuous, by my life, or to get into a pulpit and preach a sermon against fayles and tick-tack, as wiles of the devil. No jest? Have you been overthrown at last—by a country wench? Must you take to the plough, and grow turnips? Why, I should as soon expect to see Gentleman Jack consort with the Finsbury archers, or go a-ducking to Islington ponds! Our Gentleman Jack a farmer! The price of wheat, goodman Dickon?—how fatten your pigs?—will the fine weather last, think you? Have done with this foolery, man! If all comes to the worst, 'twere better we should take to the road, you and I, and snip a purse when chance might serve."

"You?" said his companion, with only half-concealed contempt. "The first click of a pistol would find you behind a hedge."

"Why, old lad," said the other (who did not seem to have heard that remark, during his pouring out of another hornful of beer), "I know you better than you know yourself. This time, you say, 'tis serious—ay, but how many times before hast thou said the same? And ever the wench is the fairest

of her kind, and a queen! For how long?—a fortnight!—
perchance three weeks. Oh, the wonder of her! And 'tis all
a love-worship; and the praising of her hands and ankles; and
Tom Morley's ditty about a lover and his lass,

> 'That through the green corn fields did pass
> In the pretty spring-time,
> Ring-a-ding-ding!'

Ay, for a fortnight; and then Gentleman Jack discovers that
some wench of the Bankside hath brighter eyes and freer favors than the country beauty, and you hear no more of him
until he has ne'er a penny left, and comes begging his friends
to be surety for him, or to write to his grandam at Oxford,
saying how virtuous a youth he is, and in how sad a plight.
Good Lord, that were an end!—should you have to go back
to the old dame at last, and become tapster—no more acting of
your lordship and worship—what ho, there! thou lazy knave,
a flask of Rhenish, and put speed into thy rascal heels!"

The cloud on his companion's face had been darkening.

"Peace, drunken fool!" he muttered—but between his teeth,
for he did not seem to wish to anger this stranger.

"Come, come, man," the other said, jovially, "unwitch
thee! unwitch thee! Fetch back thy senses. What?—
wouldst thou become a jest and by-word for every tavern table
between the Temple and the Tower? Nay, I can not believe it
of thee, Jack. Serious? Ay, as you have been twenty times
before. Lord, what a foot and ankle!—and she the queen o' the
world—the rose and crown and queen o' the world—and the
sighing o' moonlight nights—

> '*Mignonne, tant je vous aime,*
> *Mais vous ne m'aimez pas*'—

and we are all to be virtuous and live cleanly for the rest
of our lives; but the next time you see Gentleman Jack, lo,
you, now!—'tis at the Bear-house; his pockets lined with
angels wrung from old Ely of Queenhithe; and as for his company—Lord! Lord! And as it hath been before, so 'twill be
again, as said Solomon the wise man; only that this time—
mark you now, Jack—this time it were well if you came to
your senses at once; for I tell thee that Ely and the rest of
them have lost all patience, and they know this much of thy

Stratford doings, that if they can not exactly name thy whereabout, they can come within a stone's-cast of thee. And if
I come to warn thee—as is the office of a true friend and an old
companion—why shouldst thou sit there with a sulky face,
man? Did I ever treat thee so in Fetter Lane?"

While he had been talking, a savory odor had begun to
steal into the apartment, and presently the farmer's wife appeared, and proceeded to spread the cloth for dinner. Her
lodger had given no orders; but she had taken his return as
sufficient signal, and naturally she assumed that his friend
would dine with him. Accordingly, in due course, there was
placed on the board a smoking dish of cow-heel and bacon,
with abundance of ale and other garnishings; and as this
fare seemed more tempting to the new-comer than the bread
and cheese, he needed no pressing to draw his chair to the table.
It was not a sumptuous feast; but it had a beneficial effect on
both of them—sobering the one, and rendering the other somewhat more placable. Master Leofric Hope—as he had styled
himself—was still in a measure taciturn; but his guest—whose
name, it appeared, was Francis Lloyd—had ceased his uncomfortable banter; and indeed all his talk now was of the charms
and wealth of a certain widow who lived in a house near to
Gray's Inn, on the road to Hampstead. He had been asked to
dine with the widow; and he gave a magniloquent description
of the state she kept—of her serving-men, and her furniture,
and her plate, and the manner in which she entertained her
friends.

"And why was I," said he—"why was poor Frank Lloyd—
that could scarce get the wherewithal to pay for a rose for his
ear—why was he picked out for so great a favor? Why, but
that he was known to be a friend of handsome Jack Orridge.
'Where be your friend Master Orridge, now?' she says, for she
hath sometimes a country trick in her speech, hath the good
lady. 'Business, madam—affairs of great import,' I say to her,
'keep him still in the country.' Would I tell her the wolves
were waiting to rend you should you be heard of anywhere
within London city? 'Handsome Jack, they call him, is't not
so?' says she. Would I tell her thou wert called 'Gentleman
Jack?' as if thou hadst but slim right to the title. Then says
she to one of the servants, 'Fill the gentleman's cup.' Lord,

Jack, what a sherris that was!—'twas meat and drink; a thing
to put marrow in your bones—cool and clear it was, and rich
withal—cool on the tongue and warm in the stomach. 'Fore
Heaven, Jack, if thou hast not ever a cup of that wine ready for
me when I visit thee, I will say thou hast no more gratitude
than a toad. And then says she to all the company (raising
her glass the while), 'Absent friends'; but she nods and smiles
to me, as one would say: 'We know whom we mean; we know.'
Lord, that sherris, Jack! I have the taste of it in my mouth
now; I dream o' nights there is a jug of it by me."

"Dreaming or waking, there is little else in thy head," said
the other; "nor in thy stomach, either."

"Is it a bargain, Jack?" he said, looking up from his plate
and regarding his companion with a fixed look.

"A bargain?"

"I tell thee 'tis the only thing will save us now." This
Frank Lloyd said with more seriousness than he had hitherto
shown. "Heavens, man, you must cease this idling; I tell
thee they are not in the frame for further delay. 'Tis the
Widow Becket or the King's highway, one or t'other, if you
would remain a free man; and as for the highway, why, 'tis an
uncertain trade, and I know that Gentleman Jack is no lover
of broken heads. What else would you? Live on in a hole
like this? Nay, but they would not suffer you. I tell you
they are ready to hunt you out at this present moment. Go
beyond seas? Ay, and forsake the merry nights at the Cranes
and the Silver Hind? When thy old grandam is driven out
of all patience, and will not even forth with a couple of shillings to buy you wine and radish for your breakfast, 'tis a bad
case. Wouldst go down to Oxford and become tapster?—Gentleman Jack, that all of them think hath fine fat acres in the
west country, and a line of ancestors reaching back to Noah
the sailor or Adam gardener. Come, man, unwitch thee!
Collect thy senses. If this sorry jest of thine be growing serious
—and I confess I had some thought of it, when you would
draw on Harry Condell for the mere naming of the wench's
name—then, o' Heaven's name, come away and get thee out of
such foolery! I tell thee thou art getting near an end, o' one
way or another; and wouldst thou have me broken too, that
have ever helped thee, and shared my last penny with thee?"

"Broken?" said his friend, with a laugh. "If there be any
in the country more broken than you and I are at this moment,
Frank, I wish them luck of their fortunes. But still there is
somewhat for you. You have not pawned those jewels in your
ears yet. And your horse—you rode hither, said you not?—
well, I trust it is a goodly beast, for it may have to save thee
from starvation ere long."

"Nay, ask me not how I came by the creature," said he,
"but 'tis not mine, I assure ye."

"Whose, then?"

Master Frank Lloyd shrugged his shoulders.

"If you can not guess my errand," said he, "you can not
guess who equipped me."

"Nay," said his friend, who was now in a much better humor, "read me no riddles, Frank. I would fain know who
knew thee so little as to lend thee a horse and see thee ride forth
with it. Who was't, Frank?"

His companion looked up and regarded him.

"The Widow Becket," he answered, coolly.

"What?" said the other, laughing. "Art thou so far in the
good dame's graces, and yet would have me go to London and
marry her?"

"'Tis no laughing matter, Master Jack, as you may find out
ere long," the other said. "The good lady lent me the horse,
'tis true; else how could I have come all the way into Warwickshire?—ay, and lent me an angel or two to appease the
villain landlords. I tell thee she is as bountiful as the day.
Lord, what a house!—I'll take my oath that Master Butler hath
a good fat capon and a bottle of claret each evening for his supper—if he have not, his face belieth him. And think you she
would be niggard with Handsome Jack? Nay, but a gentleman must have his friends; ay, and his suppers at the tavern,
when the play is over; and store of pieces in his purse to
make you good company. Why, man, thy fame would spread
through the Blackfriars, I warrant you: where is the hostess
that would not simper and ogle and court'sy to Gentleman Jack,
when that he came among them, slapping the purse in his
pouch?"

"'Tis a fair picture," his friend said. "Thy wits have been
sharpened by thy long ride, Frank. And think you the buxom

widow would consent, were one to make bold and ask her? Nay, nay; 'tis thy dire need hath driven thee to this excess of fancy."

For answer Master Lloyd proceeded to bring forth a small box, which he opened, and took therefrom a finger ring. It was a man's ring, of massive setting; the stone of a deep blood red, and graven with an intaglio of a Roman bust. He pushed it across the table.

"The horse was lent," said he, darkly. "That—if it please you—you may keep and wear."

"What mean you?" Leofric Hope said, in some surprise.

"'I name no thing, and I mean no thing,'" said he, quoting a phrase from a popular ballad. "If you understand not, 'tis a pity. I may not speak more plainly. But bethink you that poor Frank Lloyd was not likely to have the means of purchasing thee such a pretty toy, much as he would like to please his old friend. Nay, canst thou not see, Jack? 'Tis a message, man! More I may not say. Take it and wear it, good lad; and come back boldly to London; and we will face the harpies, and live as free men, ere a fortnight be over. What?—must I speak? Nay, an' you understand not, I will tell no more."

He understood well enough; and he sat for a second or two moodily regarding the ring; but he did not take it up. Then he rose from the table, and began to walk up and down the room.

"Frank," said he, "couldst thou but see this wench—"

"Nay, nay, spare me the catalogue," his friend answered, quickly. "I heard thee declare that Ben Jonson had no words to say how fair she was: would you better his description and overmaster him? And fair or not fair, 'tis all the same with thee; any petticoat can bewitch thee out of thy senses: Black Almaine or New Almaine may be the tune, but 'tis ever the same dance; and such a heaving of sighs and despair!—

> 'Thy gown was of the grassy green,
> Thy sleeves of satin hanging by;
> Which made thee be our harvest queen—
> And yet thou wouldst not love me.'

'Tis a pleasant pastime, friend Jack; but there comes an end. I know not which be the worse, wenches or usurers, for land-

11*

ing a poor lad in jail; but both together, Jack—and that is
thy case—they are not like to let thee escape. 'Tis not to every
one in such a plight there cometh a talisman like that pretty
toy there: beshrew me, what a thing it is in this world to have
a goodly presence!"

He now rose from the table and went to the door, and called
aloud for some one to bring him a light. When that was
brought, and his pipe set going, he sat him down on the bench
by the empty fire-place, for the seat seemed comfortable, and
there he smoked with much content, while his friend continued
to pace up and down the apartment, meditating over his own
situation, and seemingly not over well pleased with the survey.

Presently something in one of the pigeon-holes over the fire-
place attracted the attention of the visitor; and having nothing
better to do (for he would leave his friend time to ponder over
what he had said), he rose and pulled forth a little bundle of
sheets of paper that opened in his hand as he sat down again.

"What's this, Jack?" said he. "Hast become playwright?
Surely all of this preachment is not in praise of the fair damsel's
eyebrows?"

His friend turned round; saw what he had got hold of, and
laughed.

"That, now," said he, "were something to puzzle the wits
with, were one free to go to London. I had some such jest
in mind; but perchance 'twas more of idleness that made
me copy out the play."

"'Tis not yours, then? Whose?" said Master Frank Lloyd,
looking over the pages with some curiosity.

"Whose? Why, 'tis by one Will Shakespeare, that you
may have heard of. Would it not puzzle them, Frank?
Were it not a good jest, now, to lay it before some learned critic and ask his worship's opinion? Or to read it at the Silver
Hind as of thy writing? Would not Dame Margery weep with
joy? Out upon the Mermaid!—have we not poets of our own?"

He had drawn near, and was looking down at the sheets
that his friend was examining.

"I tell thee this, Jack," the latter said, in his cool way,
"there is more than a jest to be got out of a play by Will
Shakespeare. Would not the booksellers give us the price of
a couple of nags for it if we were pressed so far?"

"Mind thine own business, fool!" was the angry rejoinder; and ere he knew what had happened his hands were empty.

And at that same moment, away over there in Stratford town, Judith was in the garden, trying to teach little Bess Hall to dance, and merrily laughing the while. And when the dancing lesson was over she would try a singing lesson; and now the child was on Judith's shoulder, and had hold of her bonny sun-brown curls.

"Well done, Bess; well done! Now again—

> ' *The hunt is up—the hunt is up—*
> *Awake, my lady dear!*
> *O a morn in spring is the sweetest thing*
> *Cometh in all the year!*'

Well done indeed! Will not my father praise thee, lass; and what more wouldst thou have for all thy pains?"

CHAPTER XXV.

AN APPEAL.

GREAT changes were in store. To begin with, there were rumors of her father being about to return to London. Then Dr. Hall was summoned away into Worcestershire by a great lady living there, who was continually fancying herself at the brink of death, and manifesting on such occasions a terror not at all in consonance with her professed assurance that she was going to a happier sphere. As it was possible that Dr. Hall would seize this opportunity to pay several other professional visits in the neighboring county, it was proposed that Susan and her daughter should come for a while to New Place, and that Judith should at the same time go and stay with her grandmother at Shottery, to cheer the old dame somewhat. And so it happened, on this July morning, that Judith's mother having gone round to see her elder daughter about all these arrangements, Judith found herself not only alone in the house, but, as rarely chanced, with nothing to do.

She tried to extract some music from her sister's lute, but that was a failure; she tried half a dozen other things; and

then it occurred to her—for the morning was fine and clear,
and she was fond of the meadows and of open air and sunlight
—that she would walk round to the grammar school and beg
for a half-holiday for Willie Hart. He, as well as Bess Hall,
was under her tuition; and there were things she could teach
him of quite as much value (as she considered) as anything to
be learned at a desk. At the same time, before going to meet
the staring eyes of all those boys, she thought she might as
well repair to her own room and smarten up her attire—even
to the extent, perhaps, of putting on her gray beaver hat with
the row of brass beads.

That was not at all necessary. Nothing of the kind was
needful to make Judith Shakespeare attractive and fascinating
and wonderful to that crowd of lads. The fact was, the whole
school of them were more or less secretly in love with her;
and this, so far from procuring Willie Hart such bumps and
thrashings as he might have received from a solitary rival,
gained for him, on the contrary, a mysterious favor and good-
will that showed itself in a hundred subtle ways. For he
was in a measure the dispenser of Judith's patronage. When
he was walking along the street with her he would tell her the
name of this one or that of his companions (in case she had
forgotten), and she would stop and speak to him kindly, and
hope he was getting on well with his tasks. Also the other
lads, on the strength of Willie Hart's intermediation, would
now make bold to say, with great politeness, "Give ye good-
morrow, Mistress Judith," when they met her, and sometimes
she would pause for a moment and chat with one of them, and
make some inquiries of him as to whether her cousin did not
occasionally need a little help in his lessons from the bigger
boys. Then there was a kind of fury of assistance instantly
promised; and the youth would again remember his good manners, and bid her formally farewell, and go on his way, with
his heart and his cheeks alike afire, and his brain gone a-dan-
cing. Even that dread being, the head-master, had no frown
for her when she went boldly up to his desk, in the very middle
of the day's duties, to demand some favor. Nay, he would
rather detain her with a little pleasant conversation, and
would at times become almost facetious (at sight of which the
spirits of the whole school rose into a seventh heaven of equa-

nimity). And always she got what she wanted; and generally, before leaving, she would give one glance down the rows of oaken benches, singling out her friends here and there, and, alas! not thinking at all of the deadly wounds she was thus dealing with those lustrous and shining eyes.

Well, on this morning she had no difficulty in rescuing her cousin from the dull captivity of the school-room; and hand in hand they went along and down to the river-side and to the meadows there. But seemingly she had no wish to get much farther from the town; for the truth was that she lacked assurance as yet that Master Leofric Hope had left that neighborhood; and she was distinctly of a mind to avoid all further communications with him until, if ever, he should be able to come forward openly and declare himself to the small world in which she lived. Accordingly she did not lead Willie Hart far along the river-side path; they rather kept to seeking about the banks and hedge-rows for wild flowers—the pink and white bells of the bind-weed she was mostly after, and these did not abound there—until at last they came to a stile; and there she sat down, and would have her cousin sit beside her, so that she should give him some further schooling as to all that he was to do and think and be in the coming years. She had far other things than Lilly's Grammar to teach him. The Sententiæ Pueriles contained no instructions as to how, for example, a modest and well-conducted youth should approach his love-maiden to discover whether her heart was well inclined toward him. And although her timid-eyed pupil seemed to take but little interest in the fair creature that was thus being · provided for him in the future, and was far more anxious to know how he was to win Judith's approval, either now or then, still he listened contentedly enough, for Judith's voice was soft and musical. Nay, he put that imaginary person out of his mind altogether. It was Judith, and Judith alone, whom he saw in these forecasts. Would he have any other supplant her in his dreams and visions of what was to be? This world around him—the smooth-flowing Avon, the wooded banks, the wide white skies, the meadows and fields and low-lying hills: was not she the very spirit and central life and light of all these? Without her, what would these be?—dead things; the mystery and wonder gone out of them; a world in darkness.

But he could not think of that; the world he looked forward to was filled with light, for Judith was there, the touch of her hand as gentle as ever, her eyes still as kind.

"So must you be accomplished at all points, sweetheart," she was continuing, "that you shame her not in any company, whatever the kind of it may be. If they be grave, and speak of the affairs of the realm, then must you know how the country is governed, as becomes a man (though, being a woman, alack! I can not help you there), and you must have opinions about what is best for England, and be ready to uphold them, too. Then, if the company be of a gayer kind, again you shall not shame her, but take part in all the merriment; and if there be dancing, you shall not go to the door, and hang about like a booby; you must know the new dances, every one; for would you have your sweetheart dance with others, and you standing by? That were a spite, I take it, for both of you!—nay, would not the wench be angry to be so used? Let me see, now—what is the name of it?—the one that is danced to the tune of 'The Merchant's Daughter went over the Field'?—have I shown you that, sweetheart?"

"I know not, Cousin Judith," said he.

"Come, then," said she, blithely; and she took him by the hand and placed him opposite her in the meadow. "Look you, now, the four at the top cross hands—so (you must imagine the other two, sweetheart); and all go round once—so; and then they change hands, and go back the other way—so; and then each takes his own partner, and away they go round the circle, and back to their place. Is it not simple, cousin? Come, now, let us try properly."

And so they began again; and for music she lightly hummed a verse of a song that was commonly sung to the same tune:

> *Maid, will you love me, yes or no?*
> *Tell me the truth, and let me go.*

"The other hand, Willie—quick!"

> *It can be no less than a sinful deed*
> *(Trust me truly)*
> *To linger a lover that looks to speed*
> *(In due time duly).*

"Why, is it not simple!" she said, laughing. "But, now,

instead of crossing hands, I think it far the prettier way that they should hold their hands up together—so: shall we try it, sweetheart?"

And then she had to sing another verse of the ballad:

> Consider, sweet, what sighs and sobs
> Do nip my heart with cruel throbs,
> And all, my dear, for the love of you
> (*Trust me truly*);
> But I hope that you will some mercy show
> (*In due time duly*).

"And then," she continued, when they had finished that laughing rehearsal, "should the fiddles begin to squeal and screech—which is as much as to say, 'Now, all of you, kiss your partners!'—then shall you not bounce forward and seize the wench by the neck, as if you were a ploughboy besotted with ale, and have her hate thee for destroying her head-gear and her hair. No, you shall come forward in this manner, as if to do her great courtesy, and you shall take her hand and bend one knee—and make partly a jest of it, but not altogether a jest—and then you shall kiss her hand, and rise and retire. Think you the maiden will not be proud that you have shown her so much honor and respect in public?—ay, and when she and you are thereafter together, by yourselves, I doubt not but that she may be willing to make up to you for your forbearance and courteous treatment of her. Marry, with that I have naught to do; 'tis as the heart of the wench may happen to be inclined; though you may trust me she will be well content that you show her other than ale-house manners; and if 'tis but a matter of a kiss that you forego, because you would pay her courtesy in public, why, then, as I say, she may make that up to thee, or she is no woman else. I wonder, now, what the Bonnybel will be like—or tall, or dark, or fair—"

"I wish never to see her, Judith," said he, simply.

However, there was to be no further discussion of this matter, nor yet greensward rehearsals of dancing; for they now descried coming to them the little maid who waited on Judith's grandmother. She seemed in a hurry, and had a basket over her arm.

"How now, little Cicely?" Judith said, as she drew near.

"I have sought you everywhere, so please you, Mistress

Judith," the little maid said, breathlessly, "for I was coming in to the town—on some errands—and—and I met the stranger gentleman that came once or twice to the house—and—and he would have me carry a message to you—"

"Prithee, good lass," said Judith, instantly, and with much composure, "go thy way back home. I wish for no message."

"He seemed in sore distress," the little maid said, diffidently.

"How, then? Did a gentleman of his tall inches seek help from such a mite as thou?"

"He would fain see you, sweet mistress, and but for a moment," the girl answered, being evidently desirous of getting the burden of the message off her mind. "He bid me say he would be in the lane going to Bidford, or thereabout, for the next hour or two, and would crave a word with you—out of charity, the gentleman said, or something of the like—and that it might be the last chance of seeing you ere he goes, and that I was to give his message to you very secretly."

Well, she scarcely knew what to do. At their last interview he had pleaded for another opportunity of saying farewell to her, and she had not definitely refused; but, on the other hand, she would much rather have seen nothing further of him in these present circumstances. His half-reckless references to Prince Ferdinand undergoing any kind of hardship for the sake of winning the fair Miranda were of a dangerous cast. She did not wish to meet him on that ground at all, even to have her suspicions removed. But if he were really in distress? And this his last day in the neighborhood? It seemed a small matter to grant.

"What say you, Cousin Willie?" said she, good-naturedly. "Shall we go and see what the gentleman would have of us? I can not, unless with thee as my shield and champion."

"If you wish it, Cousin Judith," said he: what would he not do that she wished?

"And Cicely—shall we all go?"

"Nay, so please you, Mistress Judith," the girl said; "I have to go back for my errands. I have been running everywhere to seek you."

"Then, Willie, come along," said she, lightly. "We must get across the fields to the Evesham road."

And so the apple-cheeked little maiden trudged back to the

town with her basket, while Judith and her companion went on their way across the meadows. There was a kind of good-humored indifference in her consent, though she felt anxious that the interview should be as brief as possible. She had had more time of late to think over all the events that had recently happened—startling events enough in so quiet and even a life; and occasionally she bethought her of the wizard, and of the odd coincidence of her meeting this young gentleman at the very spot that had been named. She had tried to laugh aside certain recurrent doubts and surmises, and was only partially successful. And she had a vivid recollection of the relief she had experienced when their last interview came to an end.

"You must gather me some flowers, sweetheart," said she, "while I am speaking to this gentleman; perchance he may have something to say of his own private affairs."

"I will go on to your grandmother's garden," said he, "if you wish it, Cousin Judith, and get you the flowers there."

"Indeed, no," she answered, patting him on the shoulder. "Would you leave me without my champion? Nay, but if you stand aside a little, that the gentleman may speak in confidence, if that be his pleasure, surely that will be enough."

They had scarcely entered the lane when he made his appearance, and the moment she set eyes on him she saw that something had happened. His face seemed haggard and anxious—nay, his very manner was changed: where was the elaborate courtesy with which he had been wont to approach her?

"Judith," said he, hurriedly, "I must risk all now. I must speak plain. I—I scarce hoped you would give me the chance."

But she was in no alarm.

"Now, sweetheart," said she, calmly, to the little lad, "you may get me the flowers; and if you find any more of the bindweed bells and the St. John's wort, so much the better."

Then she turned to Master Leofric Hope.

"I trust you have had no ill news," said she, but in a kind way.

"Indeed, I have. Well, I know not which way to take it," he said, in a sort of desperate fashion. "It might be good news. But I am hard pressed; 'twill be sink or swim with me presently. Well, there is one way of safety open to me: 'tis for you to say whether I shall take it or not."

"I, sir?" she said; and she was so startled that she almost
recoiled a step.

"Nay, but first I must make a confession," said he, quickly,
"whatever comes of it. Think of me what you will, I will
tell you the truth. Shall I beg for your forgiveness beforehand?"

He was regarding her earnestly and anxiously, and there
was nothing but kindness and a dim expression of concern in
the honest, frank face and in the beautiful eyes.

"No, I will not," he said. "Doubtless you will be angry,
and with just cause; and you will go away. Well, this is the
truth. The devils of usurers were after me; I had some friends
not far from here; I escaped to them; and they sought out this
hiding for me. Then I had heard of you—you will not forgive me, but this is the truth—I had heard of your beauty;
and Satan himself put it into my head that I must see you. I
thought it would be a pastime, to while away this cursed hiding, if I could get to know you without discovering myself.
I sent you a message. I was myself the wizard. Heaven is
my witness that when I saw you at the corner of the field up
there, and heard you speak, and looked on your gracious and
gentle ways, remorse went to my heart; but how could I forego
seeking to see you again? It was a stupid jest. It was begun
in thoughtlessness; but now the truth is before you: I was myself the wizard; and—and my name is not Leofric Hope, but
John Orridge—a worthless poor devil that is ashamed to stand
before you."

Well, the color had mounted to her face; for she saw clearly the invidious position that this confession had placed her in;
but she was far less startled than he had expected. She had
already regarded this trick as a possible thing, and she had
also fully considered what she ought to do in such circumstances. Now, when the circumstances were actually laid before her, she made no display of wounded pride, or of indignant anger, or anything of the kind.

"I pray you," said she, with a perfect and simple dignity,
"pass from that. I had no such firm belief in the wizard's
prophecies. I took you as you represented yourself to be, a
stranger, met by chance, one who was known to my father's
friends, and who was in misfortune; and if I have done aught

beyond what I should have done in such a pass, I trust you
will put it down to our country manners, that are perchance
less guarded than those of the town."

For an instant—there was not the slightest doubt of it—actual tears stood in the young man's eyes.

"By heavens," he exclaimed, "I think you must be the noblest creature God ever made! You do not drive me away in
scorn; you have no reproaches? And I—to be standing here
—telling you such a tale—"

"I pray you, sir, pass from that," said she. "What of your
own fortunes? You are quitting the neighborhood?"

"But how can you believe me in anything, since you know
how I have deceived you?" said he, as if he could not understand how she should make no sign of her displeasure.

"'Twas but a jest, as you say," she answered, good-naturedly, but still with a trifle of reserve. "And no harm has come
of it. I would leave it aside, good sir."

"Harm?" said he, regarding her with a kind of anxious timidity. "That may or may not be, sweet lady, as time will
show. If I dared but speak to you—well, bethink you of my
meeting you here from day to day, in these quiet retreats, and
seeing such a sweetness and beauty and womanliness as I have
never met in the world before—such a wonder of gentleness and
kindness—"

"I would ask you to spare me these compliments," said she,
simply. "I thought 'twas some serious matter you had in
hand."

"Serious enough, i' faith!" he said, in an altered tone, as if
she had recalled him to a sense of the position in which he
stood. "But there is the one way out of it, after all. I can
sell my life away for money to pacify those fiends; nay, besides
that, I should live in abundance, doubtless, and be esteemed a
most fortunate gentleman, and one to be envied. A gilded
prison-house and slavery; but what would the fools think of
that if they saw me with a good fat purse at the tavern?"

Again he regarded her.

"There is another way yet, however, if I must needs trouble
you, dear Mistress Judith, with my poor affairs. What if I
were to break with that accursed London altogether, and go
off and fight my way in another country, as many a better

man hath done? ay, and there be still one or two left who
would help me to escape if they saw me on the way to reform,
as they would call it.   And what would I not do in that way—
ay, or in any way—if I could hope for a certain prize to be won
at the end of it all?"

"And that, good sir?"

"That," said he, watching her face—"the reward that would
be enough and more than enough for all I might suffer would
be just this—to find Judith Shakespeare coming to meet me
in this very lane."

"Oh, no, sir," was her immediate and incoherent exclama-
tion; and then she promptly pulled herself together, and said,
with some touch of pride: "Indeed, good sir, you talk wildly.
I scarce understand how you can be in such grave trouble."

"Then," said he, and he was rather pale, and spoke slowly,
"it would be no manner of use for any poor Ferdinand of
these our own days to go bearing logs or suffering any hard-
ships that might arise?   There would be no Miranda waiting
for him, after all?"

She colored deeply; she could not affect to misunderstand the
repeated allusion; and all she had in her mind now was to
leave him and get away from him, and yet without unkindness or anger.

"Good sir," said she, with such equanimity as she could
muster, "if that be your meaning—if that be why you wished
to see me again—and no mere continuance of an idle jest,
plain speech will best serve our turn.   I trust no graver matters occupy your mind; as for this, you must put that away.
It was with no thought of any such thing that I—that I met
you once or twice, and—and lent you such reading as might
pass the time for you.   And perchance I was too free in that,
and in my craving to hear of my father and his friends in
London, and the rest.   But what you say now, if I understand
you aright—well, I had no thought of any such thing.   Indeed,
good sir, if I have done wrong in listening to you about my
father's friends, 'twas in the hope that soon or late you would
continue the tale in my father's house.   But now—what you
say—bids me to leave you—and yet in no anger—for in truth I
wish you well."

She gave him her hand, and he held it for a moment.

"Is this your last word, Judith?" said he.

"Yes, yes, indeed," she answered, rather breathlessly and earnestly. "I may not see you again. I pray Heaven your troubles may soon be over; and perchance you may meet my father in London, and become one of his friends; then might I hear of your better fortunes. 'Twould be welcome news, believe me. And now fare you well."

He stooped to touch her hand with his lips; but he said not a word; and she turned away without raising her eyes. He stood there, motionless and silent, watching her and the little boy as they walked along the lane toward the village—regarding them in an absent kind of way, and yet with no great expression of sadness or hopelessness in his face. Then he turned and made for the highway to Bidford; and he was saying to himself as he went along:

"Well, there goes one chance in life, for good or ill. And what if I had been more persistent? What if she had consented, or even half consented, or said that in the future I might come back with some small modicum of hope? Nay: the devil only knows where I should get logs to carry for the winning of so fair a reward. Frank Lloyd is right. My case is too desperate. So fare you well, sweet maiden; keep you to your quiet meadows and your wooded lanes: and the clown that will marry you will give you a happier life than ever you could have had with Jack Orridge and his broken fortunes."

Indeed, he seemed in no downcast mood. As he walked along the highway he was absently watching the people in the distant fields, or idly whistling the tune of "Calen o Custure me." But by-and-by, as he drew near the farm, his face assumed a more sombre look; and when, coming still nearer, he saw Frank Lloyd calmly standing at the door of the stables, smoking his pipe, there was a sullen frown on his forehead that did not promise well for the cheerfulness of that journey to London which Master Lloyd had sworn he would not undertake until his friend was ready to accompany him.

CHAPTER XXVI.

TO LONDON TOWN.

BUT that was not the departure for London which was soon to bring Judith a great heaviness of heart, and cause many a bitter fit of crying when that she was lying awake o' nights. She would rather have let all her lovers go, and welcome, a hundred times over. But, as the days passed, it became more and more evident, from certain preparations, that her father was about to leave Stratford for the south, and finally the very moment was fixed. Judith strove to keep a merry face (for so she had been bid), but again and again she was on the point of going to him and falling on her knees and begging him to remain with them. She knew that he would laugh at her; but did he quite know what going away from them meant? And the use of it? Had they not abundance? Still, she was afraid of being chid for meddling in matters beyond her; and so she went about her duties with as much cheerfulness as she could assume; though, when in secret conclave with Prudence, and talking of this, and what the house would be like when he was gone, quiet tears would steal down her face in the dusk.

To suit the convenience of one or two neighbors, who were also going to London, the day of departure had been postponed; but at last the fatal morning arrived. Judith, from an early hour, was on the watch, trying to get some opportunity of saying good-by to her father by herself (and not before all the strangers who would soon be gathering together), but always she was defeated, for he was busy in-doors with many things, and every one was lending a helping hand. Moreover, she was in an excited and trembling state; and more than once she had to steal away to her chamber and bathe her eyes with water lest that they should tell any tale when he regarded her. But the climax of her misfortunes was this. When the hour for leaving was drawing nigh she heard him go out and into the garden, doubtless with the intention of locking up the cupboard in the summer-house; and so she presently and swiftly stole out after him, thinking that now would be her chance. Alas! the instant she had passed through the back-court door she saw that Matthew gardener had forestalled her; and not only that, but he had brought a visitor with him—the master constable, Grandfather Jeremy, whom she knew well. Anger filled her heart; but there was no time to stand on her dignity. She would not retire from the field. She walked forward boldly, and stood by her father's side, as much as to say: "Well, this is my place. What do you want? Why this intrusion at such a time?"

Grandfather Jeremy was a little, thin, round-shouldered ancient, with long, straggling gray hair, and small, shrewd, ferret-like eyes that kept nervously glancing from Judith's father to goodman Matthew, who had obviously introduced him on this occasion. Indeed, the saturnine visage of the gardener was overspread with a complacent grin, as though he were saying, "Look you there, zur, there be a rare vool." Judith's father, on the other hand, showed no impatience over this interruption; he kept waiting for the old man to recover his power of speech.

"Well, now, master constable, what would you?" he said, gently.

"Why can't 'ee tell his worship, Jeremy?" Matthew gardener said, in his superior and facetious fashion. "Passion o' me, man, thy tongue will wag fast enough at Mother Tooley's alehouse."

"It wur a contrevarsie, so please your worship," the ancient constable said, but with a kind of vacant stare, as if he were half lost in looking back into his memory.

"Ay, and with whom?" said Judith's father, to help him along.

"With my poor old woman, so please your worship. She be a poor, mean creature in your honor's eyes, I make no doubt; but she hath wisdom, she hath, and a strength in contrevarsie past most. Lord, Lord, why be I standing here now—and holding your worship—and your worship's time and necessities—but that she saith, 'Jeremy, put thy better leg avore;' 'speak out,' saith she; ''twur as good for thee as a half-ox in a pie, or a score of angels in thy pouch.' 'Speak out,' she saith, 'and be not afraid, Jeremy.'"

"But, master constable," said Judith's father, "if your good dame be such a Mary Ambree in argument, she should have furnished you with fewer words and more matter. What would you?"

"Nay, zur, I be as bold as most," said the constable, pulling up his courage, and also elevating his head somewhat with an air of authority. "I can raise hue and cry in the hundred, that can I; and if the watch bring me a rogue, he shall lie by the heels, or I am no true man. But Lord, zur, have pity on a poor man that be put forward to speak for a disputation. When they wur talking of it at furst, your worship—this one and the other, and all of them to once—and would have me go forward to speak for them, 'Zure,' says I, 'I would as lief go to a bride-ale with my legs swaddled in wisps as go avore Mahster Shaksper without a power o' voine words.' But Joan, she saith, 'Jeremy, fear no man, howsoever great, for there be but the one Lord over us all; perzent thyself like a true countryman and an honest officer; take thy courage with thee,' saith she; 'and remember thou speakest vor thy friends as well as vor thyself. 'Tis a right good worshipful gentleman,' she saith, meaning yourself, sweet Mahster Shaksper; 'and will a not give us a share?'"

"In Heaven's name, man," said Judith's father, laughing, "what would you? Had Joan no clearer message to give you?"

"I but speak her words, so please your worship," said the ancient constable, with the air of one desperately trying to recall a lesson that had been taught him. "And all of them—they wur zaying as how she hath a power o' wisdom—and, 'Jeremy,' she saith, 'be not overbold with the worthy gentleman; 'tis but a share; and he be a right worthy and civil gentleman; speak him fair, Jeremy,' she saith, 'and put thy better leg avore, and acquit thee as a man. Nay, be bold,' she saith, 'and think of thy vriends, that be waiting without for an answer. Think of them, Jeremy,' she saith, 'if thy speech fail thee. 'Tis but a share; 'tis but a share; and he a right worshipful and civil gentleman.'"

Judith's father glanced at the sun-dial on the gable of the barn.

"My good friend," said he, "I hear that your wife Joan is ailing; 'tis through no lack of breath, I warrant me. An you come not to the point forthwith, I must be gone. What would you? Or what would your good dame have of me?—for there we shall get to it more quickly."

"So please you, zur," said Matthew, with his complacent grin, "the matter be like this, now: this worthy master constable and his comrades of the watch, they wur laying their heads together like; and they have heard say that you have written of them, and taken of their wisdom the couple o' nights they wur brought in to supper; and they see as how you have grown rich, so please you, zur, with such writing—"

"A vast o' money—a vast o' money and lands," the other murmured.

"And now, zur, they would make bold to ask for their share, for the help that they have given you. Nay, zur," continued Matthew gardener, who was proud of the ease with which he could put into words the inarticulate desires of this good constable, "be not angry with worthy Jeremy; he but speaketh for the others, and for his wife Joan too, that be as full of courage as any of them, and would have come to your worship but that she be sore troubled with an ague. Lord, zur, I know not how much the worthy gentlemen want. Perchance good Jeremy would be content wi' the barn and the store of malt in the malt-house—"

At this the small deep eyes of the ancient began to twinkle nervously; and he glanced in an anxious way from one to the other.

"And the watch, now," continued Matthew, grinning, and regarding the old constable: "why, zur, they be poor men; 'twould go well with them to divide amongst them the store of good wine in the cellar, and perchance also the leather hangings that be so much talked of in the town. But hark you, good Jeremy, remember this, now—that whoever hath the garden and orchard fall to his lot must pay me my wages, else 'tis no bargain."

For the first time in her life Judith saw her father in a passion of anger. His color did not change; but there was a strange look about his mouth, and his eyes blazed.

"Thou cursed fool," he said to the gardener, "'tis thou hast led these poor men into this folly." And then he turned to the bewildered constable, and took him by the arm. "Come,

12

good friend," said he, in a kindly way, "come into the house
and I will explain these matters to thee. Thou hast been mis-
led by that impudent knave—by my life, I will settle that score
with him ere long; and in truth the aid that you and your comrades have given me is chiefly that we have passed a pleasant
evening or two together, and been merry or wise as occasion
offered. And I would have you spend such another to-night
among yourselves, leaving the charges at the ale-house to me;
and for the present, if I may not divide my store of wine among
you, 'tis no reason why you and I should not have a parting
cup ere I put hand to bridle—"

That was all that Judith heard; and then she turned to the
ancient wise man and said, coolly,

"Were I in thy place, good Matthew, I would get me out of
this garden, and out of Stratford town too, ere my father come
back." And Matthew was too frightened to answer her.

The outcome of all this, however, was that Judith's father
did not return to the garden; and when she went into the house
she found that he had taken such time to explain to Jeremy
constable how small a share in his writings had been contributed by these good people that certain of the members of the
expedition bound for London had already arrived. Indeed,
their horses and attendants were at the door; and all and
everything was in such a state of confusion and uproar that
Judith saw clearly she had no chance of saying a quiet good-by
to her father all by herself. But was she to be again balked
by good-man Matthew? She thought not. She slipped away
by the back door and disappeared.

There was quite a little crowd gathered to see the cavalcade
move off. Dr. Hall was not there, but Tom Quiney was—
bringing with him as a parting gift for Judith's father a handsome riding-whip; and the worthy Parson Blaise had also appeared, though there was no opportunity for his professional
services amid so much bustle. And then there were hand-shak-
ings and kissings and farewells; and Judith's father was just
about to put his foot in the stirrup, when Susanna called out:

"But where is Judith? Is she not coming to say good-by to
my father?"

Then there were calls for Judith, here, there, and everywhere, but no answer; and her mother was angry that the girl

should detain all this assemblage. But her father, not having mounted, went rapidly through the house, and just opened the door leading into the garden. The briefest glance showed him that the mastiff was gone. Then he hurried back.

"'Tis all well, good mother," said he, as he got into the saddle. "I shall see the wench ere I go far. I know her tricks."

So the company moved away from the house, and through the streets, and down to Clopton's bridge. Once over the bridge, they struck to the right, taking the Oxford road by Shipston and Enstone; and ere they had gone far along the highway, Judith's father, who seemed less to join in the general hilarity and high spirits of the setting out than to be keeping a watch around, perceived something in the distance—at a corner where there was a high bank behind some trees—that caused him to laugh slightly, and to himself. When they were come near this corner the figure that had been on the sky-line had disappeared; but down by the road-side was Judith herself, looking very tremulous and ashamed as all these people came along, and the great Don standing by her. Her father, who had some knowledge of her ways, bade them all ride on, and then he turned his horse, and sprang down from the saddle.

"Well, wench," said he, and he took her by the shoulders, "what brings you here ?"

In answer she could only burst into tears, and hide her face in his breast.

"Why, lass," said he, "what is a journey to London ? And have you not enough left to comfort you ? Have you not sweethearts a plenty ?"

But she could not speak; she only sobbed and sobbed.

"Come, come, lass, I must be going," said he, stroking the soft brown hair. "Cheer up. Wouldst thou spoil the prettiest eyes in Warwickshire ? Nay, an thou have not a right merry and beaming face when I am come again, I will call thee no daughter of mine."

Then she raised her head—for still she could not speak—and he kissed her.

"Heaven's blessings on thee, good wench! I think 'tis the last time I shall ever have the courage to leave thee. Fare you

well, sweetheart; keep your eyes bright and your face happy—
to draw me home again."

Then she kissed him on each cheek, and he got into the saddle and rode on. She climbed up to the top of the bank, and
watched him and his companions while they were still in sight,
and then she turned to go slowly homeward.

And it seemed to her, when she came in view of Stratford,
and looked down on the wide meadows and the placid river and
the silent homesteads, that a sort of winter had already fall-
en over the land. That long summer had been very beautiful to her—full of sunlight and color and the scent of flowers;
but now a kind of winter was come, and a sadness and lone-
liness; and the days and days that would follow each other
seemed to have no longer any life in them.

CHAPTER XXVII.

EVIL TIDINGS.

But a far sharper winter than any she had thought of was
now about to come upon her, and this was how it befell:

After the departure of her father, good Master Walter Blaise
became more and more the guide and counsellor of these women-folk; and indeed New Place was now given over to meetings for prayer and worship, and was also become the head-
quarters in the town for the entertainment of travelling preachers, and for the institution of all kinds of pious and charitable
undertakings. There was little else for the occupants of it to
do: the head of the house was in London; Judith was at Shottery with her grandmother; Susanna was relieved from much
of her own domestic cares by the absence of her husband in
Worcestershire; and the bailiff looked after all matters pertaining to the farm. Indeed, so constant were these informal
services and ministerings to pious travellers that Julius Shawe
(though not himself much given in that direction, and perhaps
mostly to please his sister) felt bound to interfere and offer to
open his house on occasion, or pay part of the charges incurred
through this kindly hospitality. Nay, he went privately to
Master Blaise and threw out some vague hints as to the doubt-

ful propriety of allowing a wife, in the absence of her husband, to be so ready with her charity. Now Master Blaise was an honest and straightforward man, and he met this charge boldly and openly. He begged of Master Shawe to come to New Place that very afternoon, when two or three of the neighbors were to assemble to hear him lecture; and both Prudence and her brother went. But before the lecture, the parson observed that he had had a case of conscience put before him—as to the giving of alms and charity, by whom, for whom, and on whose authority—which he would not himself decide. The whole matter, he observed, had been pronounced upon in the holiday lectures of that famous divine Master William Perkins, who was now gone to his eternal reward; these lectures having recently been given to the world by the aid of one Thomas Pickering, of Emmanuel College, Cambridge. And very soon it appeared, as the young parson read from the little parchment-covered book, that the passages he quoted had been carefully chosen and were singularly pertinent. For after a discourse on the duty of almsgiving, as enjoined by Scripture (and it was pointed out that Christ himself had lived on alms—" not by begging, as the Papists affirm, but by the voluntary ministration and contribution of some to whom he preached"), Master Blaise read on, with an occasional glance at Julius Shawe: " 'It may be asked whether the wife may give alms without the consent of her husband, considering that she is in subjection to another, and therefore all that she hath is another's, and not her own. *Answer.* The wife may give alms of some things, but with these cautions: as, first, she may give of those goods that she hath excepted from marriage. Secondly, she may give of those things which are common to them both, provided it be with the husband's consent, at least general and implicit. Thirdly, she may not give without or against the consent of her husband. And the reason is, because both the law of nature and the word of God command her obedience to her husband in all things. If it be alleged that Joanna, the wife of Chuza, Herod's steward, with others, did minister to Christ of their goods (Luke, viii. 3), I answer: It is to be presumed that it was not done without all consent. Again, if it be said that Abigail brought a present to David for the relief of him and his young men, whereof she made not Nabal, her husband, acquainted

(1 Sam., xxv. 19), I answer, it is true, but mark the reason. Nabal was generally of a churlish and unmerciful disposition, whereupon he was altogether unwilling to yield relief to any, in how great necessity soever; whence it was that he railed on the young men that came to him, and drove them away, ver. 14. Again, he was a foolish man, and given to drunkenness, so as he was not fit to govern his house or to dispense his alms. Besides, that Abigail was a woman of great wisdom in all her actions, and that which she now did was to save Nabal's and her own life—yea, the lives of his whole family; for the case was desperate, and all that they had were in present hazard. The example, therefore, is no warrant for any woman to give alms, unless it be in the like case.' " And then he summed up in a few words, saying, in effect, that as regards the question which had been put before him, it was for the wife to say whether she had her husband's general and implied consent to her pious expenditure, and to rule her accordingly.

This completely and forever shut Julius Shawe's mouth. For he knew, and they all knew, that Judith's father was well content that any preachers or divines coming to the house should be generously received; while he on his part claimed a like privilege in the entertainment of any vagrant person or persons (especially if they were making a shift to live by their wits) whom he might chance to meet. Strict economy in all other things was the rule of the household; in the matter of hospitality the limits were wide. And if Judith's mother half guessed, and if Susanna Hall shrewdly perceived, why this topic had been introduced, and why Julius Shawe had been asked to attend the lecture, the subject was one that brought no sting to their conscience. If the whole question rested on the general and implied consent of the husband, Judith's mother had naught to tax herself with.

After that there was no further remonstrance (of however gentle and underhand a kind) on the part of Julius Shawe; and more and more did Parson Blaise become the guide, instructor, and mainstay of the household. They were women-folk, some of them timid, all of them pious, and they experienced a sense of comfort and safety in submitting to his spiritual domination. As for his disinterestedness, there could be no doubt of that; for now Judith was away at Shottery, and he could no longer pay court to her in that authoritative fashion of his. It seemed as if he were quite content to be with these others, bringing them the news of the day, especially as regarded the religious dissensions that were everywhere abroad, arranging for the welcoming of this or that faithful teacher on his way through the country, getting up meetings for prayer and profitable discourse in the afternoon, or sitting quietly with them in the evening while they went on with their tasks of dressmaking or embroidery.

And so it came about that Master Walter was in the house one morning—they were seated at dinner, indeed, and Prudence was also of the company—when a letter was brought in and handed to Judith's mother. It was an unusual thing; and all saw by the look of it that it was from London; and all were eager for the news, the good parson as well as any. There was not a word said as Judith's mother, with fingers that trembled a little from mere anticipation, opened the large sheet, and began to read to herself across the closely written lines. And then, as they waited, anxious for the last bit of tidings about the King or the Parliament or what not, they could not fail to observe a look of alarm come into the reader's face.

"Oh, Susan," she said, in a way that startled them, "what is this?"

She read on, breathless and stunned, her face grown quite pale now; and at last she stretched out her shaking hand with the letter in it.

"Susan, Susan, take it. I can not understand it. I can not read more. Oh, Susan, what has the girl done?"

And she turned aside her chair, and began to cry stealthily: she was not a strong-nerved woman, and she had gathered but a vague impression that something terrible and irrevocable had occurred.

Susan was alarmed, no doubt; but she had plenty of self-command. She took the letter, and proceeded as swiftly as she could to get at the contents of it. Then she looked up in a frightened way at the parson, as if to judge in her own mind as to how far he should be trusted in this matter. And then she turned to the letter again—in a kind of despair.

"Mother," said she at last, "I understand no more than yourself what should be done. To think that all this should have

been going on, and we knowing naught of it! But you see
what my father wants; that is the first thing. Who is to go to
Judith?"

At the mere mention of Judith's name a flash of dismay
went to Prudence's heart. She knew that something must
have happened ; she at once bethought her of Judith's interviews with the person in hiding; and she was conscious of her
own guilty connivance and secrecy; so that the blood rushed
to her face, and she sat there dreading to know what was coming.

"Mother," Susan said again, and rather breathlessly, "do
you not think, in such a pass, we might beg Master Blaise to
give us of his advice? The Doctor being from home, who else
is there?"

"Nay, if I can be of any service to you or yours, good Mistress Hall, I pray you have no scruple in commanding me,"
said the parson—with his clear and keen gray eyes calmly waiting for information.

Judith's mother was understood to give her consent; and then
Susan (after a moment's painful hesitation) took up the letter.

"Indeed, good sir," said she, with an embarrassment that
she rarely showed, "you will see there is reason for our perplexity, and—and I pray you be not too prompt to think ill
of my sister. Perchance there may be explanations, or the
story wrongly reported. In good truth, sir, my father writes
in no such passion of anger as another might in such a pass,
though 'tis but natural he should be sorely troubled and vexed."

Again she hesitated, being somewhat unnerved and bewildered by what she had just been reading. She was trying to
recall things, to measure possibilities, to overcome her amazement, all at once. And then she knew that the parson was
coolly regarding her, and she strove to collect her wits.

"This, good sir, is the manner of it," said she, in as calm a
way as she could assume, "that my father and his associates
have but recently made a discovery that concerns them much,
and is even a disaster to them; 'tis no less than that a copy
of my father's last-written play—the very one, indeed, that he
finished ere leaving Stratford—hath lately been sold, they
scarce know by whom as yet, to a certain bookseller in London, and that the bookseller is either about to print it and sell
it, or threatens to do so. They all of them, my father says,

are grievously annoyed by this, for that the publishing of the play will satisfy many who will read it at home instead of coming to the theatre, and that thus the interests of himself and his associates will suffer gravely. I am sorry, good sir, to trou‑ ble you with such matters," she added, with a glance of apology, "but they come more near home to us than you might think."

"I have offered to you my service in all things—that befit my office," said Master Walter, but with a certain reserve, as if he did not quite like the course that matters were taking.

"And then," continued Susan, glancing at the writing be‑ fore her, "my father says that they were much perplexed (hav‑ ing no right at law to stop such a publication), and made in‑ quiries as to how any such copy could have found its way into the bookseller's hands; whereupon he discovered that which hath grieved him far more than the trouble about the play. Prudence, you are her nearest gossip; it can not be true!" she exclaimed; and she turned to the young maiden, whose face was no longer pale and thoughtful, but rose-colored with shame and alarm. "For he says 'tis a story that is now every‑ where abroad in London—and a laugh and a jest at the tav‑ erns—how that one Jack Orridge came down to Warwickshire, and made believe to be a wizard, and cozened Judith—Judith, Prudence, our Judith!—heard ye ever the like?—into a secret love affair; and that she gave him a copy of the play as one of her favors—"

"Truly, now, that is false on the face of it," said Master Blaise, appositely. "That is a tale told by some one who knows not that Judith hath no skill of writing."

"Oh, 'tis too bewildering!" Susan said, as she turned again to the letter in a kind of despair. "But to have such a story going about London—about Judith—about my sister Judith— how can you wonder that my father should write in haste and in anger? That she should meet this young man day after day at a farm-house near to Bidford, and in secret, and listen to his stories of the court, believing him to be a worthy gen‑ tleman in misfortune! A worthy gentleman truly!—to come and make sport of a poor country maiden, and teach her to de‑ ceive her father and all of us, not one of us knowing—not one—"

"Susan! Susan!" Prudence cried, in an agony of grief, "'tis

not as you think. 'Tis not as it is written there. I will confess the truth. I myself knew of the young man being in the
neighborhood, and how he came to be acquainted with Judith.
And she never was at any farm-house to meet him, that I know
well, but—but he was alone, and in trouble, he said, and she
was sorry for him, and durst not speak to any one but me.
Nay, if there be aught wrong, 'twas none of her doing, that I
know: as to the copy of the play, I am ignorant; but 'twas
none of her doing. Susan, you think too harshly — indeed
you do."

"Sweetheart, I think not harshly," said the other, in a bewildered way. "I but tell the story as I find it."

"'Tis not true, then. On her part, at least, there was no
whit of any secret love affair, as I know right well," said Prudence, with a vehemence near to tears.

"I but tell thee the story as my father heard it. Poor
wench, whatever wrong she may have done, I have no word
against her," Judith's sister said.

"I pray you continue," interposed Master Blaise, with his
eyes calmly fixed on the letter; he had scarcely uttered a word.

"Oh, my father goes on to say that this Orridge—this person
representing himself as familiar with the court, and the great
nobles, and the like—is none other than the illegitimate son of
an Oxfordshire gentleman who became over well acquaint
with the daughter of an innkeeper in Oxford town; that the
father meant to bring up the lad, and did give him some smat-
tering of education, but died; that ever since he hath been de-
pendent on his grandmother, a widow, who still keeps the inn;
and that he hath lived his life in London in any sort of company he could impose upon by reason of his fine manners.
These particulars, my father says, he hath had from Ben Jonson, that seems to know something of the young man, and
maintains that he is not so much vicious or ill-disposed as reckless and idle, and that he is as likely as not to end his days
with a noose round his neck. This, saith my father, is all
that he can learn, and he would have us question Judith as
to the truth of the story, and as to how the copy of the play
was made, and whether 'twas this same Orridge that carried
it to London. And all this he would have inquired into at
once, for his associates and himself are in great straits because

of this matter, and have urgent need to know as much as can be known. Then there is this further writing toward the end —'I can not explain all to thee at this time; but 'tis so that we have no remedy against the rascal publisher. Even if they do not register at the Stationers' Company, they but offend the Company; and the only punishment that might at the best befall them would be his Grace of Canterbury so far misliking the play as to cause it to be burned—a punishment that would fall heavier on us, I take it, than on them; and that is in no case to be anticipated.'"

"I can not understand these matters, good sir," Judith's mother said, drying her eyes. "'Tis my poor wench that I think of. I know she meant no harm—whatever comes of it. And she is so gentle and so proud-spirited that a word of rebuke from her father will drive her out of her reason. That she should have fallen into such trouble, poor wench! poor wench!—and you, Prudence, that was ever her intimate, and seeing her in such a coil—that you should not have told us of it!"

Prudence sat silent under this reproach: she knew not how to defend herself. Perhaps she did not care, for all her thoughts were about Judith.

"Saw you ever the young man?" Susan said, scarcely concealing her curiosity.

"Nay, not I," was Prudence's answer. "But your grandmother hath seen him, and that several times."

"My grandmother!" she exclaimed.

"For he used to call at the cottage," said Prudence, "and pass an hour or two—being in hiding, as he said, and glad to have a little company. And he greatly pleased the old dame, as I have heard, because of his gracious courtesy and goodbreeding; and when they believed him to be in sad trouble, and pitied him, who would be the first to speak and denounce a stranger so helpless? Nay, I know that I have erred. Had I had more courage I should have come to you, Susan, and begged you to draw Judith away from any further communication with the young man; but I—I know not how it came about; she hath such a winning and overpersuading way, and is herself so fearless."

"A handsome youth, perchance?" said Susan, who seemed to wish to know more about this escapade of her sister's.

"Right handsome, as I have heard; and of great courtesy and gentle manners," Prudence answered. "But well I know what it was that led Judith to hold communication with him after she would fain have had that broken off." And then Prudence, with such detail as was within her knowledge, explained how Judith had come to think that the young stranger talked overmuch of Ben Jonson, and was anxious to show that her father could write as well as he (or better, as she considered). And then came the story of the lending of the sheets of the play, and Prudence had to confess how that she had been Judith's accomplice on many a former occasion in purloining and studying the treasures laid by in the summer-house. She told all that she knew openly and simply and frankly; and if she was in distress, it was with no thought of herself; it was in thinking of her dear friend and companion away over there at Shottery, who was all in ignorance of what was about to befall her.

Then the three women, being somewhat recovered from their first dismay, but still helpless and bewildered, and not knowing what to do, turned to the parson. He had sat calm and collected, silent for the most part, and reading in between the lines of the story his own interpretation. Perhaps, also, he had been considering other possibilities—as to the chances that such an occasion offered for gathering back to the fold an errant lamb.

"What your father wants done, that is the first thing, sweetheart," Judith's mother said, in a tremulous and dazed kind of fashion. "As to the poor wench, we will see about her afterward. And not a harsh word will I send her; she will have punishment enough to bear—poor lass! poor lass! So heedless and so headstrong she hath been always, but always the quickest to suffer if a word were spoken to her; and now if this story be put about, how will she hold up her head—she that was so proud? But what your father wants done, Susan, that is the first thing—that is the first thing. See what you can do to answer the letter as he wishes: you are quicker to understand such things than I."

And then the parson spoke, in his clear, incisive, and authoritative way:

"Good madam, 'tis little I know of these matters in London;

but if you would have Judith questioned—and that might be somewhat painful to any one of her relatives—I will go and see her for you, if you think fit. If she have been the victim of knavish designs, 'twill be easy for her to acquit herself; carelessness, perchance, may be the only charge to be brought against her. And as I gather from Prudence that the sheets of manuscript lent to the young man were in his possession for a certain time, I make no doubt that the copy—if it came from this neighborhood at all—was made by himself on those occasions, and that she had no hand in the mischief, save in over-trusting a stranger. Doubtless your husband, good madam, is desirous of having clear and accurate statements on these and other points; whereas, if you, or Mistress Hall, or even Prudence there, were to go and see Judith, natural affection and sympathy might blunt the edge of your inquiries. You would be so anxious to excuse (and who would not, in your place?) that the very information asked for by your husband would be lost sight of. Therefore I am willing to do as you think fitting. I may not say that my office lends any special sanction to such a duty, for this is but a worldly matter; but friendship hath its obligations; and if I can be of service to you, good Mistress Shakespeare, 'tis far from repaying what I owe of godly society and companionship to you and yours. These be rather affairs for men to deal with than for women, who know less of the ways of the world; and I take it that Judith, when she is made aware of her father's wishes, will have no hesitation in meeting me with frankness and sincerity."

It was this faculty of his of speaking clearly and well and to the point that in a large measure gave him such an ascendency over those women; he seemed always to see a straight path before him; to have confidence in himself, and a courage to lead the way.

"Good sir, if you would have so much kindness," Judith's mother said. "Truly, you offer us help and guidance in a dire necessity. And if you will tell her what it is her father wishes to know, be sure that will be enough; the wench will answer you, have no fear, good sir."

Then Susan said, when he was about to go:

"Worthy sir, you need not say to her all that you have heard concerning the young man. I would liefer know what

she herself thought of him; and how they came together; and
how he grew to be on such friendly terms with her. For hitherto she hath been so sparing of her favor; though many have
wished her to change her name for theirs; but always the wench
hath kept roving eyes. Handsome was he, Prudence? And of
gentle manners, said you? Nay, I warrant me 'twas something
far from the common that led Judith such a dance."

But Prudence, when he was leaving, stole out after him; and
when he was at the door, she put her hand on his arm. He
turned, and saw that the tears were running down her face.

"Be kind to Judith," she said—not heeding that he saw her
tears, and still clinging to his arm; "be kind to Judith, from
my heart I beg it of you—I pray you be kind and gentle with
her, good Master Blaise; for indeed she is like an own sister
to me."

CHAPTER XXVIII.

RENEWALS.

As yet she was all unconscious; and indeed the dullness
following her father's departure was for her considerably light-
ened by this visit to her grandmother's cottage, where she
found a hundred duties and occupations awaiting her. She
was an expert needle-woman, and there were many arrears in
that direction to be made up;-she managed the cooking, and introduced one or two cunning dishes, to the wonder of the little
Cicely; she even tried her hand at carpentering, where a shelf,
or the frame of a casement, had got loose; and as a reward she
was occasionally invited to assist her grandmother in the garden. The old dame herself grew wonderfully amiable and
cheerful in the constant association with this bright young
life; and she had a great store of ballads with which to beguile
the tedium of sewing—though, in truth, these were for the most
part of a monotonous and mournful character, generally recit-
ing the woes of some poor maiden in Oxfordshire or Lincoln-
shire who had been deceived by a false lover, and yet was willing to forgive him even as she lay on her death-bed. As for
Judith, she took to this quiet life quite naturally and happily;
and if she chanced to have time for a stroll along the wooded

lanes or through the meadows, she was now right glad that there was no longer any fear of her being confronted by Master Leofric Hope—or Jack Orridge, as he had called himself. Of course she thought of him often, and of his courteous manners, and his eloquent and yet modest eyes, and she hoped all was going well with him, and that she might perchance hear of him through her father. Nor could she forget (for she was but human) that the young man, when disguised as a wizard, had said that he had heard her named as the fairest maid in Warwickshire; and subsequently, in his natural character, that he had heard Ben Jonson speak well of her looks, and she hoped that if ever he recalled these brief interviews, he would consider that she had maintained a sufficiency of maidenly dignity, and had not betrayed the ignorance or awkwardness of a farm-bred wench. Nay, there were certain words of his that she put some store by—as coming from a stranger. For the rest, she was in no case likely to undervalue her appearance: her father had praised her hair, and that was enough.

One morning she had gone down to the little front gate, for some mischievous boys had lifted it off its hinges, and she wanted to get it back again on the rusty iron spikes. But it had got jammed somehow, and would not move; and in her pulling, some splinter of the wood ran into her hand, causing not a little pain. Just at this moment—whether he had come round that way on the chance of catching a glimpse of her it is hard to say—Tom Quiney came by; but on the other side of the road, and clearly with no intention of calling at the cottage.

"Good-morrow, Judith," said he, in a kind of uncertain way, and would have gone on.

Well, she was vexed and impatient with her fruitless efforts, and her hand smarted not a little; so she looked at him and said, half angrily,

"I wish you would come and lift this gate."

It was but a trifling task for the tall and straight-limbed young fellow who now strode across the highway. He jerked it up in a second, and then set it down again on the iron spikes, where it swung in its wonted way.

"But your hand is bleeding, Judith!" he exclaimed.

"'Tis nothing," she said. "It was a splinter. I have pulled it out."

But he snatched her hand peremptorily, before she could draw it away, and held it firmly and examined it.

"Why, there's a bit still there; I can see it."

"I can get it out for myself," said she.

"No, you can not," he answered. "'Tis far easier for some one else. Stay here a second, and I will fetch out a needle."

He went into the cottage, and presently re-appeared, not only with a needle, but also with a tin vessel holding water, and a bit of linen and a piece of thread. Then he took Judith's soft hand as gently as he could in his muscular fingers, and began to probe for the small fragment of wood just visible there. He seemed a long time about it: perhaps he was afraid of giving her pain.

"Do I hurt you, Judith?" he said.

"No," she answered, with some color of embarrassment in her face. "Be quick."

"But I must be cautious," said he. "I would it were my own hand; I would make short work of it."

"Let me try myself," said she, attempting to get away her hand from his grasp.

But he would not allow that; and in due time he managed to get the splinter out. Then he dipped his fingers in the water and bathed the small wound in that way; and then he must needs wrap the piece of linen round her hand—very carefully, so that there should be no crease—and thereafter fasten the bandage with the bit of thread. He did not look like one who could perform a surgical operation with exceeding delicacy; but he was as gentle as he could be, and she thanked him—in an unwilling kind of way.

Then all at once her face brightened.

"Why," said she, "I hear that you gave my father a riding-whip on his going."

"Did you not see it, Judith?" he said, with some disappointment. "I meant you to have seen it. The handle was of ivory, and of a rare carving."

"I was not at the door when they went away—I met my father as they passed along the road," said she. "But I shall see it, doubtless, when he comes home again. And what said he? Was he pleased? He thanked you right heartily, did he not?"

"Yes, truly; but 'twas a trifling matter."

"My father thinks more of the intention than of the value of such a gift," said she—"as I would."

It was an innocent and careless speech, but it seemed to suddenly inspire him with a kind of wild wish.

"Ah," said he, regarding her, "if you, Judith, now, would but take some little gift from me—no matter what—that would be a day I should remember all my life."

"Will you not come into the house?" said she, quickly. "My grandam will be right glad to see you."

She would have led the way ; but he hesitated.

"Nay, I will not trouble your grandmother, Judith," said he. "I doubt not but that she hath had enough of visitors since you came to stay with her."

"Since I came?" she said, good-naturedly—for she refused to accept the innuendo. "Why, let me consider, now. The day before yesterday my mother walked over to see how we did; and before that—I think the day before that—Mistress Wyse came in to tell us that they had taken a witch at Abbots Morton ; and then yesterday Farmer Bowstead called to ask if his strayed horse had been seen anywhere about these lanes. There, now, three visitors since I have come to the cottage: 'tis not a multitude."

"There hath been none other?" said he, looking at her with some surprise.

"Not another foot hath crossed the threshold to my knowledge," said she, simply, and as if it were a matter of small concern.

But this intelligence seemed to produce a very sudden and marked alteration in his manner. Not only would he accompany her into the house, but he immediately became most solicitous about her hand.

"I pray you be careful, Judith," said he, almost as if he would again take hold of her wrist.

"'Tis but a scratch," she said.

"Nay, now, if there be but a touch of rust, it might work mischief," said he, anxiously. "I pray you be careful; and I would bathe it frequently, and keep on the bandage until you are sure that all is well. Nay, I tell you this, Judith: there are more than you think of that would liefer lose a finger than that you should have the smallest hurt."

And in-doors, moreover, he was most amiable and gentle and anxious to please, and bore some rather sharp sayings of the old dame with great good-nature; and whatever Judith said, or suggested, or approved of, that was right, once and for all. She wished to hear more of the riding-whip also. Where was the handle carved? Had her father expressed any desire for such ornamentation?

"Truly 'twas but a small return for his kindness to us the other day," said the young man, who was half bewildered with delight at finding Judith's eyes once more regarding him in the old frank and friendly fashion, and was desperately anxious that they should continue so to regard him (with no chilling shadow of the parson intervening). "For Cornelius Greene being minded to make one or two more catches," he continued —and still addressing those eyes that were at once so gentle and so clear and so kind—" he would have me go to your father and beg him to give us words for these, out of any books he might know of. Not that we thought of asking him to write the words himself—far from that—but to choose them for us: and right willingly he did so. In truth, I have them with me," he added, searching for and producing a paper with some written lines on it. "Shall I read them to you, Judith?"

He did not notice the slight touch of indifference with which she assented; for when once she had heard that these compositions (whatever they might be) were not her father's writing, she was not anxious to become acquainted with them. But his concern, on the other hand, was to keep her interested and amused and friendly; and Cornelius Greene and his doings were at least something to talk about.

"The first one we think of calling 'Fortune's Wheel,'" said he; "and thus it goes:

> ' *Trust not too much, if prosperous times do smile,*
> *Nor yet despair of rising, if thou fall:*
> *The Fatal Lady mingleth one with th' other,*
> *And lets not fortune stay, but round turns all.*'

And the other one—I know not how to call it yet—but Cornelius takes it to be the better of the two for his purpose; thus it is:

> ' *Merrily sang the Ely monks*
> *When rowed thereby Canute the King.*
> " *Row near, my Knights, row near the land,*
> *That we may hear the good monks sing.*"'

See you now how well it will go, Judith—*Merrily sang—merrily sang—the Ely monks—the Ely monks—when rowed thereby*—CANUTE THE KING!" said he, in a manner suggesting the air. "'Twill go excellent well for four voices, and Cornelius is already begun. In truth, 'twill be something new at our merry-meetings—"

"Ay, and what have you to say of your business, good Master Quiney?" the old dame interrupted, sharply. "Be you so busy with your tavern catches and your merry-makings that you have no thought of that?"

"Indeed, I have enough regard for that, good Mistress Hathaway," said he, in perfect good-humor; "and it goes forward safely enough. But methinks you remind me that I have tarried here as long as I ought; so now I will get me back to the town."

He half expected that Judith would go to the door with him; and when she had gone so far, he said,

"Will you not come a brief way across the meadows, Judith?—'tis not well you should always be shut up in the cottage—you that are so fond of out-of-doors."

He had no cause for believing that she was too much within-doors; but she did not stay to raise the question; she good-naturedly went down the little garden path with him, and across the road, and so into the fields. She had been busy all the morning; twenty minutes' idleness would do no harm.

Then, when they were quite by themselves, he said, seriously:

"I pray you take heed, Judith, that you let not the blood flow too much to your hand, lest it inflame the wound, however slight you may deem it. See, now, if you would but hold it so, 'twould rest on mine, and be a relief to you."

He did not ask her to take his arm, but merely that she should rest her hand on his; and this seemed easy to do, and natural (so long as he was not tired). But also it seemed very much like the time when they used to go through those very meadows as boy and girl together, the tips of their fingers intertwined: and so she spoke in a gentle and friendly kind of fashion to him.

"And how is it with your business, in good sooth?" she asked. "I hope there be no more of these junketings, and dancings, and brawls."

"Dear Judith," said he, "I know not who carries such tales of me to you. If you knew but the truth, I am never in a brawl of mine own making or seeking; but one must hold one's own, and the more that is done, the less are any likely to interfere. Nay," he continued, with a modest laugh, "I think I am safe for quiet now with any in Warwickshire; 'tis only a strange lad now and again that may come among us and seek cause of quarrel; and surely 'tis better to have it over and done with, and either he or we to know our place? I seek no fighting for the love of it; my life on that; but you would not have any stranger come into Stratford a-swaggering, and biting his thumb at us, and calling us rogues of fiddlers?"

"Mercy on us, then," she cried, "are you champion for the town—or perchance for all of Warwickshire? A goodly life to look forward to! And what give they their watch-dog? Truly they must reward him that keeps such guard, and will do battle for them all?"

"Nay, I am none such, Judith," said he: "I but take my chance like the others."

He shifted her hand on his that it might rest the more securely, and his touch was gentle.

"And your merchandise—pray you who is so kind as to look after that when you are engaged in those pastimes?" she asked.

"I have no fault to find with my merchandise, Judith," said he. "That I look after myself. I would I had more inducement to attend to it, and to provide for the future. But it goes well; indeed it does."

"And Daniel Hutt?"

"He has left the country now."

"And his vagabond crew: have they all made their fortunes?"

"Why, Judith, they can not have reached America yet," said he.

"I am glad that you have not gone," she remarked, simply.

"Well," he said, "why should I strive to push my fortunes there more than here? To what end? There be none that I could serve either way."

And then it seemed to him that this was an ungracious speech, and he was anxious to stand well with her, seeing that she was disposed to be friendly.

"Judith," he said, suddenly, "surely you will not remain

over at Shottery to-morrow, with all the merriment of the
fair going on in the town? Nay, but you must come over—I
could fetch you, at any hour that you named, if it so pleased
you. There is a famous juggler come into the town, as I hear,
that can do the most rare and wonderful tricks, and hath a
dog as cunning as himself; and you will hear the new ballads,
to judge which you would have; and the peddlers would show
you their stores. Now, in good sooth, Judith, may not I come
for you?—why, all the others have some one to go about with
them; and she will choose this or that posy or ribbon, and
wear it for the jest of the day; but I have no one to walk
through the crowd with me, and see the people, and hear the
bargainings and the music. I pray you, Judith, let me come
for you. It can not be well for you always to live in such
dullness as is over there at Shottery."

"If I were to go to the fair with you," said she, and not
unkindly, "methinks the people would stare, would they not?
We have not been such intimate friends of late."

"You asked me not to go to America, Judith," said he.

"Well, yes," she admitted. "Truly I did so. Why should
you go away with those desperate and broken men? Surely
'tis better you should stay among your own people."

"I staid because you bade me, Judith," said he.

She flushed somewhat at this; but he was so eager not to em-
barrass or offend her that he instantly changed the subject.

"May I, then, Judith? If you would come but for an hour!"
he pleaded; for he clearly wanted to show to everybody that
Judith was under his escort at the fair; and which of all the
maidens (he asked himself) would compare beside her? "Why,
there is not one of them but hath his companion, to buy for her
some brooch, or pretty coif, or the like—"

"Are they all so anxious to lighten their purses?" said
she, laughing. "Nay, but truly I may not leave my grandmother, lest the good dame should think that I was wearying
of my stay with her. Pray you get some other to go to the fair
with you—you have many friends, as I know, in the town—"

"Oh, do you think 'tis the fair I care about?" said he,
quickly. "Nay, now, Judith, I would as lief not go to the
fair at all—or but for a few minutes—if you will let me bring
you over some trinket in the afternoon. Nay, a hundred

times would I rather not go, if you would grant me such a favor. 'Tis the first I have asked of you for many a day."

"Why," she said, with a smile, "you must all of you be prospering in Stratford, since you are all so eager to cast abroad your money. The peddlers will do a rare trade to-morrow, as I reckon."

This was almost a tacit permission, and he was no such fool as to press her for more. Already his mind ran riot—he saw himself ransacking all the packs and stalls in the town.

"And now," she said, as she had come within sight of the houses—"I will return now, or the good dame will wonder."

"But I will walk back with you, Judith," said he, promptly.

She regarded him, with those pretty eyes of hers clearly laughing.

"Methought you came away from the cottage," said she, "because of the claims of your business; and now you would walk all the way back again?"

"Your hand, Judith," said he, shame-facedly—"you must not let it hang down by your side."

"Nay, for such a dangerous wound," said she, with her eyes gravely regarding him, "I will take precautions; but can not I hold it up myself—so—if need were?"

He was so well satisfied with what he had gained that he would yield to her now as she wished. And yet he took her hand once more—gently and timidly—and as if unwilling to give up his charge of it.

"I hope it will not pain you, Judith," he said.

"I trust it may not lead me to death's door," she answered, seriously; and if her eyes were laughing, it was with no unkindness.

And then they said good-by to each other, and she walked away back to Shottery, well content to have made friends with him again, and to have found him for the time being quit of his dark suspicions and jealousies of her; while as for him, he went on to the town in a sort of foreknowledge that all Stratford Fair would not have anything worthy to be offered to Judith, and wondering whether he could not elsewhere, and at once, and by any desperate effort, procure something fine and rare and beautiful enough to be placed in that poor wounded hand.

CHAPTER XXIX.

"THE ROSE IS FROM MY GARDEN GONE."

Now when Parson Blaise set forth upon the mission that had been intrusted to him, there was not a trace of anger or indignation in his mind. He was not even moved by jealous wrath against the person with whom Judith had been holding these clandestine communications; nor had he any sense of having been himself injured by her conduct. For one thing, he knew enough of Judith's pride and self-reliance to be fairly well satisfied that she was not likely to have compromised herself in any serious way; and for another, his own choice of her, from among the Stratford maidens, as the one he wished to secure for helpmate, was the result not so much of any overmastering passion as of a cool and discriminating judgment. Nay, this very complication that had arisen—might he not use it to his own advantage? Might it not prove an argument more powerful than any he had hitherto tried? And so it was that he set out, not as one armed to punish, but with the most placable intentions; and the better to give the subject full consideration, he did not go straight across the meadows to the cottage, but went through the town, and away out the Alcester road, before turning round and making for Shottery.

Nor did it occur to him that he was approaching this matter with any mean or selfish ends in view. Far from that. The man was quite honest. In winning Judith over to be his wife, by any means whatever, was he not adding one more to the number of the Lord's people? Was he not saving her from her own undisciplined and wayward impulses, and from all the mischief that might arise from these? What was for his good was for her good, and the good of the Church also. She had a winning way; she was friends with many who rather kept aloof from the more austere of their neighbors; she would be a useful go-between. Her cheerfulness, her good temper, nay, her comely presence and bright ways—all these would be profitably employed. Nor did he forget the probability of a

handsome marriage portion, and the added domestic comfort
and serenity that that would bring himself. Even the marriage portion (which he had no doubt would be a substantial
one) might be regarded as coming into the Church in a way;
and so all would work together for good.

When he reached the cottage he found the old dame in the
garden, busy with her flowers and vegetables, and was told that
Judith had just gone within-doors. Indeed, she had but that
minute come back from her stroll across the fields with Quiney,
and had gone in to fetch a jug so that she might have some fresh
water from the well in the garden. He met her on the threshold.

"I would say a few words with you, Judith, and in private,"
said he.

She seemed surprised, but was in no ill-humor; so she said,
"As you will, good sir," and led the way into the main apartment, where she remained standing.

"I pray you be seated," said he.

She was still more surprised; but she obeyed him, taking her
seat under the window, so that her face was in shadow, while the
light from the small panes fell full on him, sitting opposite her.

"Judith," said he, "I am come upon a serious errand, and
yet would not alarm you unnecessarily. Nay, I think that
when all is done, good may spring out of the present troubles—"

"What is it?" she said, quickly. "Is any one ill?—my
mother—"

"No, Judith," he said. "'Tis no trial of that kind you are
called to face. The Lord hath been merciful to you and yours
these several years; while others have borne the heavy hand of
affliction, and lost their dearest at untimeous seasons, you have
been spared for many years now all but such trials as come in
the natural course: would I could see you as thankful as you
ought to be to the Giver of all good. And yet I know not but
that grief over such afflictions is easier to bear than grief over
the consequences of our own wrong-doing: memory preserves
this last the longer; sorrow is not so enduring, nor cuts so
deep, as remorse. And then to think that others have been
made to suffer through our evil-doing—that is an added sting:
when those who have expected naught but filial obedience and
duty, and the confidence that should exist between children
and their parents—"

But this phrase about filial obedience had struck her with a sudden fear.

"I pray you what is it, sir? What have I done?" she said, almost in a cry.

Then he saw that he had gone too fast and too far.

"Nay, Judith," he said, "be not over-alarmed. 'Tis perchance but carelessness and a disposition to trust yourself in all circumstances to your own guidance that have to be laid to your charge. I hope it may be so; I hope matters may be no worse; 'tis for yourself to say. I come from your mother and sister, Judith," he continued, in measured tones. "I may tell you at once that they have learned of your having been in secret communication with a stranger who has been in these parts, and they would know the truth. I will not seek to judge you beforehand, nor point out to you what perils and mischances must ever befall you so long as you are bent on going your own way, without government or counsel; that you must now perceive for yourself, and I trust the lesson will not be brought home to you too grievously."

"Is that all?" Judith had said, quickly, to herself, and with much relief.

"Good sir," she said to him, coolly, "I hope my good mother and Susan are in no bewilderment of terror. 'Tis true, indeed, that there was one in this neighborhood whom I met and spoke with on several occasions. If there was secrecy, 'twas because the poor young gentleman was in hiding; he dared not even present the letter that he brought commending him to my father. Nay, good Master Blaise, I pray you comfort my mother and sister, and assure them there was no harm thought of by the poor young man."

"I know not that, Judith," said he, with his clear, observant eyes trying to read her face in the dusk. "But your mother and sister would fain know what manner of man he was, and what you know of him, and how he came to be here."

Then the fancy flashed across her mind that this intervention of his was but the prompting of his own jealousy, and that he was acting as the spokesman of her mother and sister chiefly to get information for himself.

"Why, sir," said she, lightly, "I think you might as well ask these questions of my grandmother, that knoweth about as I do

13

concerning the young man, and was as sorry as I for his ill fortunes."

"I pray you take not this matter so heedlessly, Judith," he said, with some coldness. "'Tis of greater moment than you think. No idle curiosity has brought me hither to-day; nay, it is with the authority of your family that I put these questions to you; and I am charged to ask you to answer them with all of such knowledge as you may have."

"Well, well," said she, good-naturedly; "his name—"

She was about to say that his name was Leofric Hope; but she checked herself, and some color rose to her face—though he could not see that.

"His name, good sir, as I believe, is John Orridge," she continued, but with no embarrassment; indeed, she did not think that she had anything very serious either to conceal or to confess; "and I fear me the young man is grievously in debt, or otherwise forced to keep away from those that would imprison him; and being come to Warwickshire, he brought a letter to my father, but was afraid to present it. He hath been to the cottage here certain times, for my grandmother, as well as I, was pleased to hear of the doings in London; and right civil he was, and well-mannered; and 'twas news to us to hear about the theatres and my father's way of living there. But why should my mother and Susan seek to know aught of him?—surely Prudence hath not betrayed the trust I put in her? —for indeed the young man was anxious that his being in the neighborhood should not be known to any in Stratford. However, as he is now gone away, and that some weeks ago, 'tis of little moment, as I reckon; and if ever he cometh back here, I doubt not but that he will present himself at New Place, that they may judge of him as they please. That he can speak for himself, and to advantage and goodly showing, I know right well."

"And that is all you can say of this man, Judith," said he, with some severity in his tone—"of this man that you have been thus familiar with?"

"Marry is it!" she said, lightly. "But I have had guesses, no doubt; for first I thought him a gentleman of the court, he being apparently acquainted with all the doings there; and then methought he was nearer to the theatres, from his knowledge of the players. But you would not have had me ask the young man as to his occupation and standing, good sir? 'Twould have been unseemly in a stranger, would it not? Could I dare venture on questions, he being all unknown to any of us?"

And now a suspicion flashed upon him that she was merely befooling him, so he came at once and sharply to the point.

"Judith," said he, endeavoring to pierce with his keen eyes the dusk that enshrouded her, "you have not told me all. How came he to have a play of your father's in his possession?"

"Now," said she, with a quick anger, "that is ill done of Prudence. No one but Prudence knew; and for so harmless a secret—and that all over and gone, moreover, and the young man himself away I know not where—nay, by my life, I had not thought that Prudence would serve me so. And to what end? Why, good sir, I myself lent the young man the sheets of my father's writing—they were the sheets that were thrown aside—and I got each and all of them safely back, and replaced them. Prudence knew what led me to lend him my father's play; and where was the harm of it? I thought not that she would go and make trouble out of so small a thing."

By this time the good parson had come to see pretty clearly how matters stood—what with Prudence's explanations and Judith's present confessions. And he made no doubt that this stranger—whether from idleness, or for amusement, or with some more sinister purpose, he had no means of knowing—had copied the play when he had taken the sheets home with him to the farm; while as to the appearance in London of the copy so taken, it was sufficiently obvious that Judith was in complete ignorance, and could afford no information whatever. So that now the first part of his mission was accomplished. He asked her a few more questions, and easily discovered that she knew nothing whatever about the young man's position in life, or whether he had gone straight from the farm to London, or whether he was in London now. As to his being in possession, or having been in possession, of a copy of her father's play, it was abundantly evident that she had never dreamed of any such thing.

And now he came to the more personal part of his mission; that was for him much more serious.

"Judith," said he, "'tis not like you should know what sad

and grievous consequences may spring from errors apparently
small. How should you? You will take no heed or caution.
The advice of those who would be nearest and dearest to you is
of no account with you. You will go your own way, as if one
of your years and experience could know the pitfalls that lie
in a young maiden's path. The whole of life is but a jest to
you—a tale without meaning—something to pass the hour withal. And think you that such blindness and willfulness bring
no penalty? Nay, sooner or later the hour strikes; you look
back and see what you have done, and the offers of safe guidance that you have neglected or thrust aside."

"I pray you, sir, what is it now?" she said, indifferently
(and with a distinct wish that he would go away and release
her, and let her get out into the light again). "Methought I
had filled up the measure of my iniquities."

"Thus it is—thus it will be always," said he, with a kind of
hopelessness, "so long as you harden your heart, and have no
thought but for the vanities of the moment." And then he addressed her more pointedly. "But even now methinks I can
tell you what will startle you out of your moral sloth, which
is an offense in the eyes of the Lord, as it is a cause for pity
and almost despair to all who know you. It was a light matter, you think, that you should hold this secret commerce with
a stranger, careless of the respect due to your father's house,
careless of the opinion and the anxious wishes of your friends,
careless even of your good name—"

"My good name?" said she, quickly and sharply. "I pray
you, sir, have heed what you say."

"Have heed to what I have to tell you, Judith," said he,
sternly. "Ay, and take warning by it. Think you that I
have pleasure in being a bearer of evil tidings?"

"But what now, sir? What now? Heaven's mercy on us,
let us get to the end of the dreadful deeds I have done!" she
exclaimed, with some anger and impatience.

"I would spare you, but may not," said he, calmly. "And
now, what if I were to tell you that this young man whom
you encouraged into secret conversation—whose manners seemed to have had so much charm for you—was a rascal thief and
villain? How would your pride bear it if I told you that he
had cozened you with some foolish semblance of a wizard?"

"Good sir, I know it," she retorted. "He himself told me as much."

"Perchance. Perchance 'twas part of his courteous manners to tell you as much!" was the scornful rejoinder. "But he did not tell you all—he did not tell you that he had copied out every one of those sheets of your father's writing; that he was about to carry that stolen copy to London, like the knave and thief that he was; that he was to offer it for money to the booksellers? He did not tell you that soon your father and his associates in the theatre would be astounded by learning that a copy of the new play had been obtained in some dark fashion, and sold; that it was out of their power to recover it; that their interests would be seriously affected by this vile conspiracy; or that they would by-and-by discover that this purloined play, which was like to cause them so much grievous loss and vexation of mind, had been obtained here, in this very neighborhood, and by the aid of no other than your father's daughter."

"Who—told—you—this?" she asked, in a strange, stunned way: her eyes were terror-stricken, her hands all trembling.

"A good authority," said he. "Your father. A letter is but now come from London."

She uttered a low, shuddering cry; it was a moan almost.

"See you now," said he (for he knew that all her bravery was struck down, and she entirely at his mercy), "what must ever come of your willfulness and your scorn of those who would aid and guide you? Loving counsel and protection are offered you—the natural shield of a woman; but you must needs go your own way alone. And to what ends? Think you that this is all? Not so. For the woman who makes to herself her own rule of conduct must be prepared for calumnious tongues. And bethink you what your father must have thought of you—the only daughter of his household now—when he learned the story of this young man coming into Warwickshire, and befooling you with his wizard's tricks, and meeting you secretly, and cozening you of the sheets of your father's play. These deeds that are done in the dark soon reach the daylight; and can you wonder, when your father found your name abroad in London—the heroine of a common jest, a by-word—that his vexation and anger should overmaster

him? What marvel that he should forthwith send to Stratford demanding to know what further could be learned of
the matter, perchance fondly trusting—who knows?—to find
that rumor had lied? But there is no such hope for him—
nor for you. What must your mother say in reply? What excuse can she offer? Or how make reparation to those associates
of your father who suffer with him? And how get back your
good name, that is being bandied about the town as the heroine
of a foolish jest? Your father may regain possession of his
property—I know not whether that be possible or no—but can
he withdraw the name of his daughter from the ribald wit of
the taverns? And I know which he valueth the more highly, if his own daughter know it not."

He had struck hard; he knew not how hard.

"My father wrote thus?" she said; and her head was bent,
and her hands covering her face.

"I read the letter no more than an hour ago," said he.
"Your mother and sister would have me come over to see
whether such a story could be true; but Prudence had already
admitted as much—"

"And my father is angered," she said, in that low strange
voice.

"Can you wonder at it?" he said.

Again there came an almost inarticulate moan, like that of an
animal stricken to death.

As for him, he had now the opportunity of pouring forth the
discourse to her that he had in a measure prepared as he came
along the highway. He knew right well that she would be
sorely wounded by this terrible disclosure; that the proud
spirit would be in the dust; that she would be in a very bewilderment of grief. And he thought that now she might
consent to gentle leading, and would trust herself to the only
one (himself, to wit) capable of guiding her through her sor-
rows; and he had many texts and illustrations apposite. She
heard not one word. She was as motionless as one dead; and
the vision that rose before her burning brain was the face of
her father as she had seen it—for a moment—in the garden on
the morning of his departure. That terrible swift look of anger toward old Matthew she had never forgotten—the sudden
lowering of the brows, the flash in the eyes, the strange con-

traction of the mouth; and that was what she saw now—that was how he was regarding her; and that, she knew, would be the look that would meet her always and always as she lay and thought of him in the long wakeful nights. She could not go to him. London was far away. She could not go to him, and throw herself at his feet, and beg and pray with outstretched and trembling hands for but one word of pity. The good parson had struck hard.

And yet in a kind of way he was trying to administer consolation—at all events, counsel. He was enlarging on the efficacy of prayer. And he said that if the Canaanitish woman of old had power to intercede for her daughter, and win succor for her, surely that would not be denied to such a one as Judith's mother, if she sought for her daughter strength and fortitude in trouble where alone these could be found.

"The Canaanitish woman," said he, "had but the one saving grace—but that an all-powerful one—of faith; and even when the disciples would have her sent away, she followed, worshipping, and saying, 'Lord, help me.' And the Lord himself answered and said, 'It is not good to take the children's bread, and to cast it to whelps.' But she said, 'Truth, Lord; yet indeed the whelps eat of the crumbs which fall from their master's table.' Then our Lord answered and said, 'O woman, great is thy faith: be it to thee as thou desirest.' And her daughter was made whole at that hour."

Judith started up—she had not heard a single word.

"I pray you pardon me, good sir," she said—for she was in a half-frantic state of misery and despair—"my—my grandmother will speak with you. I—I pray you pardon me—"

She got up into her own little chamber—she scarce knew how. She sat down on the bed. There were no tears in her eyes; but there was a terrible weight on her chest that seemed to stifle her, and she was breathless, and could not think aright, and her trembling hands were clinched. Sometimes she wildly thought she wanted Prudence to come to her, and then a kind of shudder possessed her, and a wish to go away—she cared not where—and be seen no more. That crushing weight increased, choking her; she could not rest; she rose and went quickly down the stair, and through the garden into the road.

"Judith, wench!" called her grandmother, who was talking to the parson.

She took no heed. She went blindly on; and all these familiar things seemed so different now. How could the children laugh so? She got into the Bidford road; she did not turn her eyes toward any whom she met, to see whether she knew them or no: there was enough within her own brain for her to think of. She made her way to the summit of Bardon Hill; and there she looked over the wide landscape; but it was toward London that she looked—and with a strange and trembling fear. And then she seemed anxious to hide away from being seen, and went down by hedge-rows and field paths; and at last she was by the river. She regarded it, flowing so stealthily by, in the sad and monotonous silence. Here was an easy means of slipping away from all this dread thing that seemed to surround her and overwhelm her—to glide away as noiselessly and peacefully as the river itself, to any unknown shore, she cared not what. And then she sat down—still looking vaguely and absently at the water—and began to think of all that had happened to her on the banks of this stream; and she looked at these visionary pictures and at herself in them as if they were apart and separated from her, and she never to be like that again. Was it possible that she ever could have been so careless and so happy, with no weight at all resting on her heart, but singing out of mere thoughtlessness, and teaching Willie Hart the figures of dances, herself laughing the while? It seemed a long time ago now; and that he was cut off from her too, and all of them, and that there was to be no expiation for evermore for this that she had done.

How long she sat there she knew not. Everything was a blank to her but this crushing consciousness that what had happened could never be recalled; that her father and she were forever separated now—and his face regarding her with the terrible look she had seen in the garden; that all the happy past was cut away from her, and she an outcast, and a by-word, and a disgrace to all that knew her. And then she thought, in the very weariness of her misery, that if she could only walk away anywhere—anywhere alone, so that no one should meet her or question her—until she was broken and exhausted with fatigue, she would then go back to her own small room, and lie

down on the bed, and try if sleep would procure some brief
spell of forgetfulness, some relief from her aching head and far
heavier heart. But when she rose she found that she was
trembling from weakness; and a kind of shiver as of cold went
through her, though the autumn day was warm enough. She
walked slowly, and almost dragged herself, all the way home.
Her hand shook so that she could scarce undo the latch of the
gate. She heard her grandmother in the inner apartment; but
she managed to creep noiselessly upstairs into her own little
chamber; and there she sank down on the bed, and lay in a
kind of stupor, pressing her hands on her throbbing brow.

It was some two hours afterward that her grandmother,
who did not know that Judith had returned, was walking along
the little passage, and was startled by hearing a low moaning
above—a kind of dull cry of pain, so slight that she had to listen
again ere she could be sure that it was not mere fancy. Instantly she went up the few wooden steps and opened the door.
Judith was lying on the bed, with all her things on, just as she
had seen her go forth. And then—perhaps the noise of the
opening of the door had wakened her—she started up, and
looked at her grandmother in a wild and dazed kind of way, as
if she had just shaken off some terrible dream.

"Oh, grandmother," she said, springing to her and clinging
to her like a child, "it is not true—it is not true—it can not
be true!"

But then she fell to crying—crying as if her heart would
break. The whole weight of her misery came back upon
her; and the hopelessness of it; and her despair.

"Why, good lass," said her grandmother, smoothing the sun-
brown hair that was buried in her bosom, and trying to calm
the violence of the girl's sobbing, "thou must not take on
so. Thy father may be angered, 'tis true; but there will come
brighter days for thee. Nay, take not on so, good lass."

"Oh, grandmother, you can not understand," she said, and
her whole frame was shaken with her sobs. "You can not
understand. Grandmother, grandmother, there was—there
was but the one rose—in my garden—and that is gone now."

13*

CHAPTER XXX.

IN TIME OF NEED.

LATE that night, in the apartment below, Tom Quiney was seated by the big fire-place, staring moodily into the chips and logs that had been lit there, the evenings having grown somewhat chill now.   There was a little parcel lying unopened and unheeded on the table.   He had not had patience to wait for the fair of the morrow; he had ridden all the way to Warwick to purchase something worthy of Judith's acceptance; and he had come over to the cottage in high hopes of her being still in that kindly mood that reminded him of other days. Then came the good dame's story of what had befallen, and how that the parson had been over, bringing with him these terrible tidings; and how that since then Judith would not hear of any one being sent for, and would take no food, but was now lying there, alone in the dark, moaning to herself at times.   And the good dame—as this tall young fellow sat there listening to her, with his fists clinched, and the look on his face ever growing darker—went on to express her fear that the parson had been over-hard with her grandchild; that probably he could not understand how her father had been the very idol of her life-long worship; that the one thing she was ever thinking of was how to win his approval, to be rewarded by even a nod of encouragement.

"Nay, I liked not the manner of his speaking, when he wur come to me in the garden," the old dame continued.   "I liked it not.   He be sharp of tongue, the young pahrson; and there wur too much to my mind of discipline, and chastening of proud spirits, and the like o' that.   To my mind he have not years enough to be placed in such authority."

"The Church is behind him," said this young fellow, almost to himself, and his eyes were burning darkly as he spoke.   "I may not put hand on him.   The Church is behind him.   Marry, 'tis a goodly shelter for men that be of the woman kind."

Then he looked up quickly, and his words were savage.

"What think you, good grandmother, were one to seize him by neck and heel and break his back on the rail of Clopton's bridge? Were it not well done?—by my life, I think it were well done!"

"Nay, nay, now," said she, quickly, for she was somewhat alarmed, seeing his face set hard with passion and his eyes afire. "I would have no brawling. There be plenty of harm done already. Perchance the good pahrson hath not spoken so harshly after all. In good sooth, now, none but her own people can understand how the wench hath ever looked up to her father for a word or a nod commending her, as I say, and when she be told now that she hath wrought mischief, and caused herself to be talked about, and her father vexed, and all the rest of the tale, why, 'tis like to drive her out of her mind. And now this be all her cry—that she may see no one of her people any more; she would bide with me here. 'Grandmother, grandmother,' she saith, 'I will bide with you, if you will suffer me. I will show myself in Stratford no more; they shall have no shame through me.' Nay, but the wench be half out of her senses, as I think; and saith wild things—that she would go and sell herself to be a slave in the Indies, could she restore the money to her father or bring him back this that he hath lost. 'Tis a terrible plight for the poor wench; and always she saith, 'Grandmother, grandmother, let me bide with you; I will never go back to New Place; grandmother, I can work as well as any, and you will let me bide with you.' Poor lass—poor lass!"

"But how came the parson to interfere?" Quiney said, hotly. "I'll be sworn Judith's father did not write to him. How came he to be preaching his discipline and chastisement? How came he to be intrusted with the task of abusing her and crushing the too proud spirit? By heavens, now, there may be occasion ere long to tame some one's proud spirit, but not the spirit of a defenseless young maid—marry, that is work fit only for parsons. Man to man is the better way, and it will come ere long."

"Nay, softly, softly, good Master Quiney," said the old dame, in her gentlest tones. "Would you mar all the good opinion that Judith hath of you? Why, to-day, now, just ere the pahrson came, I wur in the garden, putting things straight a bit, and as she came through she says to me, quite pleasant like, 'I

have just been across the fields, grandmother, with Master Quiney'—or Tom Quiney, as she said, being friendly and pleasant
like—'and I hear less now of his quarrelling and fighting among
the young men; and his business goeth on well; and to-morrow,
grandmother, he is going to buy me something at the fair.'"

"Said she all that?" he asked, quickly, and with a flush of
color rushing to his face.

"Marry, did she; and looked pleased; for 'tis a right friendly wench and good-natured withal," the old dame said, glad
to see that these words had for the moment scattered his wrath
to the winds; and she went on for some little time talking to
him in her garrulous easy fashion about Judith's frank and
honest qualities, and her good-hearted ways, and the pretty
daintinesses of her coaxing when she was so inclined. It was
a story he was not loath to listen to, and yet it seemed so
strange: they were talking of her almost as of one passed
away—as if the girl lying there in that darkened room, instead
of torturing her brain with incessant and lightning-like visions
of all the harm she had caused in London, were now far removed from all such troubles, and hushed in the calm of death.

He went to the table and opened the box, and took out the
little present he had brought for Judith. It was a pair of lace
cuffs, with a slender silver circle at the wrist; the lace going
back from that in a succession of widening leaves. It was not
only a pretty present, it was also (in proportion to his means)
a costly one, as the old dame's sharp eyes instantly saw.

"I think she would have been pleased with them," he said,
absently.

And then he said,

"Good grandmother, it were of no use to lay them near her
in the morning—on a chair or at the window—that perchance
she might look at them?"

"Nay, nay," the grandmother said, shaking her head:
"'tis no child's trouble that hath befallen the poor wench;
that she can be comforted with pretty trifles."

"I meant not that," said he, flushing somewhat. "'Tis
that I would have her know that—that there were friends
thinking of her all the same; those that would rather have her
gladdened and tended and made much of rather than—than—
chidden with any chastisement."

This word chastisement seemed to recall his anger.

"I say that Judith hath done no wrong at all," he said, as if he were confronting some one not there; "and that I will maintain; and let no man in my hearing say aught else. Why, now, the story as you tell it, good grandmother—'tis as plain as daylight—a child can see it: all that she did was done to magnify her father and his writing; and if the villain sold the play, or let it slip out of his hands, was that her doing? Doubtless it is a sore mischance; but I see not that Judith is to be blamed for it; and right well I know that if her father were to hear how she is smitten down with grief, he would be the first to say: 'Good lass, there is no such harm done. A greater harm would be your falling sick; get you up and out; seek your friends again; and be happy as you were before.' That is what he would say, I will take my oath of it; and if the parson and his chastisements were to come across him, by my life I would not seek to be in the parson's shoes!"

"I must make another trial with the poor wench," said the good grandmother, rising, "that hath eaten nothing all the day. In truth, her only cry is to be left alone now, and that hereafter I am to let her bide with me. It be a poor shelter, I think, for one used to live in a noble house; but there 'tis, so long as she wisheth it."

"Nay, but this can not be suffered to go on, good Mistress Hathaway," said he, as he rose and got his cap. "For if Judith take no food, and will see no one, and be alone with her trouble, of a surety she will fall ill. Now to-morrow morning I will bring Prudence over. If any can comfort her, Prudence can; and that she will be right willing, I know. They have been as sisters."

"That be well thought of, Master Quiney," said the grandmother, as she went to the door with him. "Take care o' the ditch the other side of the way; it be main dark o' nights now."

"Good-night to you, good grandmother," said he, as he disappeared in the darkness.

But it was neither back home nor yet to Stratford town that Tom Quiney thought of going all that long night. He felt a kind of constraint upon him (and yet a constraint that kept his heart warm with a secret satisfaction) that he should play the part of watch-dog, as it were—as if Judith were sorely ill, or in danger, or in need of protection somehow; and he kept wandering about in the dark, never at any great radius from the cottage.   His self-imposed task was the easier now that as the black clouds overhead slowly moved before the soft westerly wind, gaps were opened, and here and there clusters of stars were visible, shedding a faint light down on the sombre roads and fields and hedges.   Many strange fancies occurred to him during that long and silent night as to what he could do, or would like to do, for Judith's sake.   Breaking the parson's neck was the first and most natural, and the most easily accomplished; but fleeing the country, which he knew must follow, did not seem so desirable a thing.   He wanted to do something—he knew not what.   He wished he had been less of a companion with the young men, and less careful to show, with them, that Stratford town, and the county of Warwick, could hold their own against all comers.   If he had been more considerate and gentle with Judith, perhaps she would not have sought the society of the parson ?   He knew he had not the art of winning her over, like the parson.   He could not speak so plausibly.   Nor had he the authority of the Church behind him.   It was natural for women to think much of that, and to be glad of the shelter of authority.   Parsons themselves (he considered) were a kind of half-women, being in women's se- crets, and entitled to speak to them in ghostly confidence.   But if Judith, now—wanted some one to do something for her, no matter what, in his rough-and-ready way—well, he wondered what that could be that he would refuse.   And so the dark hours went by.

With the gray of the dawn he began to cast his eyes abroad, as if to see if any one were stirring, or approaching the cluster of cottages nestled down there among the trees.   The daylight widened and spread up in the trembling east; the fields and the woods became clear; here and there a small tuft of blue smoke began to arise from a cottage chimney.   And now he was on Bardon Hill, and could look abroad over the wide landscape lying between Shottery and Stratford town; and if any one—any one bringing lowering brows and further cruel speech to a poor maid already stricken down and defenseless—had been in sight, what then ?   Watchfully and slowly he went down from the hill, and back to the meadows lying between the hamlet and Stratford, there to interpose, as it were, and question all comers. And well it was, for the sake of peace and charity, that the good parson did not chance to be early abroad on this still morning; and well it was for the young man himself. There was no wise-eyed Athene to descend from the clouds and bid this wrathful Achilles calm his heart. He was only an English country youth—though sufficiently Greek-like in form; and he was hungry, and gray-faced with his vigil of the night, and not in a placable mood. Nay, when a young man is possessed with the consciousness that he is the defender of some one behind him—some one who is weak, and feminine, and suffering—he is apt to prove a dangerous antagonist; and it was well for all concerned that he had no occasion to pick a quarrel on this morning in these quiet meadows. In truth, he might have been more at rest had he known that the good parson was in no hurry to follow up his monitions of the previous day; he wished these to sink into her mind and take root there, so that thereafter might spring up such wholesome fruits as repentance, and humility, and the desire of godly aid and counsel.

By-and-by he slipped away home, plunged his head into cold water to banish the dreams of the night; and then, having swallowed a cup of milk to stay his hunger, he went along to Chapel Street, to see if he could have speech of Prudence. He found that not only were all of the household up and doing, but that Prudence herself was ready to go out, being bent on one of her charitable errands. And it needed but a word to alter the direction of her kindness: of course she would at once go to see Judith.

"Truly I had fears of it," said she, as they went through the fields, the pale, calm face having grown more and more anxious as she listened to all that he had to tell her. "Her father was as the light of the world to her. With the others of us she hath ever been headstrong in a measure and careless —and yet so lovable withal and merry that I for one could never withstand her: nay, I confess I tried not to withstand her, for never knew I of any willfulness of hers springing from anything but good-nature and her kind and generous ways. But that she was ever ready to brave our opinions I know, and perchance make light of our anxieties, we not having her courage; and in all things she seemed to be a guide unto herself, and to walk sure, and have no fear. In all things but one. Indeed, 'tis true what her grandmother told you, and who should know better than I, who was always with her? The slightest wish of her father's—that was law to her. A word of commending from him, and she was happy for days. And think what this must be now—she that was so proud of his approval—that scarce thought of aught else. Nay, for myself, I can see that they have told him all a wrong story in London, that know I well; and 'tis no wonder that he is vexed and angry; but Judith—poor Judith—"

She could say no more just then; she turned aside her face somewhat.

"Do you know what she said to her grandmother, Prudence, when she fell a-crying?—that there had been but the one rose in her garden, and that was gone now."

"'Tis what Susan used to sing," said Prudence, with rather trembling lips. "'The rose is from my garden gone,' 'twas called. Ay, and hath she that on her mind now? Truly I wish that her mother and Susan had let me break this news to her; none know as well as I what it must be to her."

And here Tom Quiney quickly asked her whether it was not clear to her that the parson had gone beyond his mission altogether, and that in a way that would have to be dealt with afterward, when all these things were amended. Prudence, with some faint color in her pale face, defended Master Blaise to the best of her power, and said she knew he could not have been unduly harsh; nay, had she not herself, just as he was setting forth, besought him to be kind and considerate with Judith? Hereupon Quiney rather brusquely asked what the good man could mean by phrases about discipline and chastenings and chastisements; to which Prudence answered gently that these were but separate words, and that she was sure Master Blaise had fulfilled what he undertook in a merciful spirit, which was his nature. After that there was a kind of silence between these two; perhaps Quiney considered that no good end could be served at present by stating his own ideas on that subject. The proper time would come in due course.

At length they reached the cottage. But here, to their amazement, and to the infinite distress of Prudence, when

Judith's grandmother came down the wooden steps again, she shook her head, saying that the wench would see no one.

"I thought as 'twould be so," she said.

"But me, good grandmother!—me!" Prudence cried, with tears in her eyes. "Surely she will not refuse to see me!"

"No one, she saith," was the answer. "Poor wench, her head do ache so bad! And when one would cheer her or comfort her a morsel, 'tis another fit of crying—that will wear her to skin and bone, if she do not pluck up better heart. She hath eaten naught this morning neither; 'tis for no willfulness, poor lass, for she tried an hour ago; and now 'tis best, as I think, to leave her alone."

"By your leave, good grandmother," said Prudence, with some firmness, "that will I not. If Judith be in such trouble, 'tis not likely that I should go away and leave her. It hath never been the custom between us two."

"As you will, Prudence," the grandmother said. "Young hearts have their confidences among themselves. Perchance you may be able to rouse her."

Prudence went up the stairs silently, and opened the door. Judith was lying on the bed, her face turned away from the light, her hands clasped over her forehead.

"Judith!"

There was no answer.

"Judith," said her friend, going near, "I am come to see you." There was a kind of sob—that was all.

"Judith, is your head so bad? Can I do nothing for you?"

She put over her hand—the soft and cool and gentle touch of which had comforted many a sick-bed—and she was startled to find that both Judith's hands and forehead were burning hot.

"No, sweetheart," was the answer, in a low and broken voice, "you can do nothing for me now."

"Nay, nay, Judith, take heart," Prudence said, and she gently removed the hot fingers from the burning forehead, and put her own cooler hand there, as if to dull the throbbing of the pain. "Sweetheart, be not so cast down. 'Twill be all put right in good time."

"Never—never," the girl said, without tears, but with an abject hopelessness of tone. "It can never be undone now. He said my name was become a mockery among my father's friends. For myself, I would not heed that—nay, they might say of me what they pleased; but that my father should hear of it—a mockery and scorn—and they think I cared so little for my father that I was ready to give away his papers to any one pretending to be a sweetheart and befooling me—and my father to know it all, and to hear such things said—no, that can never be undone now. I used to count the weeks and the days and the very hours when I knew he was coming back; that was the joy of my life to me; and now if I were to know that he were coming near to Stratford I should fly, and hide somewhere—anywhere—in the river as lief as not. Nay, I make no complaint. 'Tis my own doing, and it can not be undone now."

"Judith! Judith! you break my heart!" her friend cried. "Surely to all troubles there must come an end."

"Yes, yes," was the answer, in a low voice, and almost as if she were speaking to herself. "That is right. There will come an end. I would it were here now."

All Prudence's talking seemed to be of no avail. She reasoned and besought, oftentimes with tears in her eyes; but Judith remained quite listless and hopeless; she seemed to be in a stunned and dazed condition after the long sleeplessness of the night, and Prudence was afraid that further entreaties would only aggravate her headache.

"I will go and get you something to eat now," said she. "Your grandmother says you have had nothing since yesterday."

"Do not trouble; 'tis needless, sweetheart," Judith said. And then she added, with a brief shiver, "But if you could fetch a thick cloak, dear Prudence, and throw it over me—surely the day is cold somewhat."

A few minutes after (so swift and eager was everybody in the house), Judith was warmly wrapped up; and by the side of the bed, on a chair, was some food the good grandmother had been keeping ready, and also a flask of wine that Quiney had brought with him.

"Look you, Judith," said Prudence, "here is some wine that Thomas Quiney hath brought for you—'tis of a rare quality, he saith—and you must take a little—nay, you must and shall, sweetheart; and then perchance you may be able to eat."

She sipped a little of the wine—it was but to show her grat-

itude and send him her thanks. She could not touch the food.
She seemed mostly anxious for rest and quiet; and so Prudence
noiselessly left her, and stole down the stair again.

Prudence was terribly perplexed, and in a kind of despair
almost.

"I know not what to do," she said. "I would bring over
her mother and Susan, but that she begs and prays me not to
do that—nay, she can not see them, she says. And there is no
reasoning with her. 'It can not be undone now'—that is her
constant cry. What to do I can not tell. For surely, if she
remain so, and take no comfort, she will fall ill."

"Ay, and if that be so, who is to blame?" said Quiney, who
was walking up and down in considerable agitation. "I say
that letter should never have been put into the parson's hands.
Was it meant to be conveyed to Judith? I warrant me it was
not! Did her father say that he wished her chidden? did
he ask any of you to bid the parson go to her with his up-
braidings? would he himself have been so quick and eager to
chasten her proud spirit? I tell you no. He is none of the
parson kind. Vexed he might have been; but he would have
taken no vengeance. What?—on his own child? By heavens, I'll be sworn, now, that if he were here, at this minute, he
would take the girl by the hand, and laugh at her for being so
afraid of his anger—ay, I warrant me he would—and would
bid her be of good cheer, and brighten her face, that was ever
the brightest in Warwickshire, as I have heard him say. That
would he—my life on it!"

"Ah," said Prudence, wistfully, "if you could only persuade Judith of that!"

"Persuade her?" said he. "Why, I would stake my life
that is what her father would do!"

"You could not persuade her," said Prudence, with a hopeless air. "No; she thinks it is all over now between her father and her. She is disgraced and put away from him. She
hath done him such injury, she says, as even his enemies have
never done. When he comes back again, she says, to Stratford, she will be here; and she knows that he will never come
near this house; and that will be better for her, she says, for
she could never again meet him face to face."

Well, all that day Judith lay there in that solitary room,

desiring only to be left alone, taking no food, the racking
pains in her head returning from time to time; and now and
again she shivered slightly as if from cold. Tom Quiney kept
coming and going to hear news of her, or to consult with Prudence as to how to rouse her from this hopelessness of grief;
and as the day slowly passed he grew more and more disturbed
and anxious and restless. Could nothing be done? could nothing be done? was his constant cry.

He remained late that evening, and Prudence staid all
night at the cottage. In the morning he was over again early,
and more distressed than ever to hear that the girl was wearing
herself out with this agony of remorse—crying stealthily when
that she thought no one was near, and hiding herself away
from the light, and refusing to be comforted.

But during the long and silent watches he had been taking
counsel with himself.

"Prudence," said he, regarding her with a curious look,
"do you think, now, if some assurance were come from her father himself—some actual message from him—a kindly message—some token that he was far indeed from casting her away
from him—think you Judith would be glad to have that?"

"'Twould be like giving her life back to her," said the girl,
simply. "In truth, I dread what may come of this: 'tis not in
human nature to withstand such misery of mind. My poor
Judith, that was ever so careless and merry!"

He hesitated for a second or two, and then he said, looking
at her, and speaking in a cautious kind of way:

"Because, when next I have need to write to London, I
might beg of some one—my brother Dick, perchance, that is
now in Bucklersbury, and would have small trouble in doing
such a service—I say I might beg of him to go and see Judith's father, and tell him the true story, and show him that
she was not so much to blame. Nay, for my part, I see not
that she was to blame at all, but for overkindness and confidence, and the wish to exalt her father. The mischief that
hath been wrought is the doing of the scoundrel and villain, on
whose head I trust it may fall ere long; 'twas none of hers.
And if her father were to have all that now put fairly and
straight before him, think you he would not be right sorry to
hear that she had taken his anger so much to heart, and was ly-

ing almost as one dead at the very thought of it? I tell you, now, if all this be put before him, and if he send her no comfortable message—ay, and that forthwith and gladly—I have far misread him. And as for her, Prudence, 'twould be welcome, say you?"

"'Twould be of the value of all the world to her," Prudence said, in her direct and earnest way.

Well, he almost immediately thereafter left (seeing that he could be of no further help to these women-folk), and walked quickly back to Stratford, and to his house, which was also his place of business. He seemed to hurry through his affairs with speed; then he went upstairs and looked out some clothing; he took down a pair of pistols and put some fresh powder in the pans; and made a few other preparations. Next he went round to the stable, and the stout little Galloway nag whinnied when she saw him at the door.

"Well, Maggie, lass," said he, going into the stall, and patting her neck and stroking down her knees, "what sayst thou? Wouldst like a jaunt that would carry thee many a mile away from Stratford town? Nay, but if you knew the errand, I warrant me you would be as eager as I! What, then— a bargain, lass? By my life, you shall have many a long day's rest in clover when this sharp work is done!"

CHAPTER XXXI.

A LOST ARCADIA.

IT was on this same morning that Judith made a desperate effort to rouse herself from the prostration into which she had fallen. All through that long darkness and despair she had been wearily and vainly asking herself whether she could do nothing to retrieve the evil she had wrought. Her good name might go — she cared little for that now; but was there no means of making up to her father the actual money he had lost? It was not forgiveness she thought of, but restitution. Forgiveness was not to be dreamed of; she saw before her always that angered face she had beheld in the garden; and her wish was to hide away from that, and be seen of it no more. Then there was another thing: if she were to be permitted to remain at the cottage, ought she not to show herself willing to take a share of the humblest domestic duties? Might not the good dame begin to regard her as but a useless encumbrance? If it were so that no work her ten fingers could accomplish would ever restore to her father what he had lost through her folly, at least it might win her grandmother's forbearance and patience. And so it was on the first occasion of her head ceasing to ache quite so badly she struggled to her feet (though she was so languid and listless and weak that she could scarcely stand), and put round her the heavy cloak that had been lying on the bed, and smoothed her hair somewhat, and went to the door. There she stood for a minute or two listening; for she would not go down if there were any strangers about.

The house seemed perfectly still. There was not a sound anywhere. Then, quite suddenly, she heard little Cicely begin to sing to herself—but in snatches, as if she were occupied with other matters—some well-known rhymes to an equally familiar tune—

"By the moon we sport and play ;
With the night begins our day ;
As we drink, the dew doth fall—
Trip it, dainty urchins all !

Lightly as the little bee,
Two by two, and three by three,
And about go we, go we"

—and she made no doubt that the little girl was alone in the kitchen. Accordingly she went down. Cicely, who was seated near the window, and busily engaged in plucking a fowl, uttered a slight cry when she entered, and started up. "Dear Mistress Judith," she said, "can I do aught for you? Will you sit down? Dear, dear, how ill you do look!"

"I am not at all ill, little Cicely," said Judith, as cheerfully as she could, and she sat down. "Give me the fowl—I will do that for you; and you can go and help my grandmother in whatever she is at."

"Nay, not so," said the little maid, definitely refusing. "Why should you?"

"But I wish it," Judith said. "Do not vex me now. Go and seek my grandmother, like a good little lass."

The little maid was thus driven to go; but it was with another purpose. In about a couple of minutes she had returned, and preceding her was Judith's grandmother.

"What, art come down, wench?" the old dame said, patting her kindly on the shoulder. "That be so far well—ay, ay, I like that, now; that be better for thee than lying all alone. But what would you with the little maid's work, that you would take it out of her hands?"

"Why, if I am idle and do nothing, grandmother, you will be for turning me out of the house," the girl answered, looking up with a strange kind of smile.

"Turn thee out of the house?" said her grandmother, who had just caught a better glimpse of the wan and tired face. "Ay, that will I—and now. Come thy ways, wench; 'tis time for thee to be in the fresh air. Cicely, let be the fowl now. Put some more wood on the fire, and hang on the pot—there's a clever lass. And thou, grandchild, come thy ways with me into the garden; and I warrant me, when thou comest back, a cupful of barley broth will do thee no harm."

Judith obeyed, though she would fain have sat still. And then, when she reached the front door, what a bewilderment of light and color met her eyes! She stood as one dazed for a second or two. The odors of the flowers and the shrubs were

so strange, moreover—pungent, and strange, and full of memories.   It seemed so long a time since she had seen this wonderful glowing world, and breathed this keen air, that she
paused on the stone flag to collect her senses, as it were.   And
then a kind of faintness came over her, and perhaps she might
have sunk to the ground but that she laid hold of her grandmother's arm.

"Ay, ay, come thy ways and sit thee down, dearie," the old
dame said, imagining that the girl was but begging for a little
assistance in her walking.   "I be main glad to see thee out
again.   I liked not that lying there alone—nay, I wur feared
of it, and I bade Prudence send your mother and Susan to see
you—"

"No, no, good grandmother—no, no," Judith pleaded, with
all the effort that remained to her.

"But yea, yea," her grandmother said, sharply.   "Foolish
wench, that would hide away from them that can best aid thee!
Ay, and knowest thou how the new disease, as they call it,
shows itself at the beginning?—why, with a pinching of the
face, and sharp pains in the head.   Wouldst thou have me let
thee lie there, and perchance go from bad to worse, and not
send for them — ay, and for Susan's husband, if need were?
Nay, but let not that fright thee, good wench," she said, in
a gentler way.   "'Tis none so bad as I thought, else you would
not be venturing down the stairs—nay, nay, there be no harm
done as yet, I warrant me; 'tis a breath of fresh air to sharpen
thee into a hungry fit that will be the best doctor for thee.
Here, sit thee down and rest, now; and when the barley broth
be warm enough, Cicely shall bring thee out a dish of it.   Nay,
I see no harm done.   Keep up thy heart, lass; thou wert ever
a brave one: ay, what was there ever that could daunt thee?—
and not the boldest of the youths but was afraid of thy laugh
and thy merry tongue!   Heaven save us, that thou should take
on so!   And if you would sell yourself to work in slavery in
the Indies, think you they would buy a poor weak trembling
creature?   Nay, nay; we will have to fetch back the roses to
your cheeks ere you make for that bargain, I warrant me!"

They were now seated in the little arbor.   On entering, Judith had cast her eyes round it in a strange and half-frightened
fashion; and now, as she sat there, she was scarcely listening

to the good-natured garrulity of the old dame, which was wholly meant to cheer her spirits.

"Grandmother," said she, in a low voice, "think you 'twas really he that took away with him my father's play?"

"I know not how else it could have been come by," said the grandmother; "but I pray you, child, heed not that for the present. What be done and gone can not be helped—let it pass. There, there, now, what a lack of memory have I, that should have shown thee the pretty lace cuffs that Thomas Quiney left for thee—fit for a queen, they be, to be sure—ay, and the fine lace of them, and the silver too. He hath a free hand, he hath; 'tis a fair thing for any that will be in life-partnership with him; 'twill not away—marry 'twill not; 'twill bide in his nature—that will never out of the flesh that's bred in the bone, as they say; and I like to see a young man that be none of the miser kind, but ready forth with his money where 'tis to please them he hath a fancy for. A brave lad he is, too, and one that will hold his own; and when I told him you were pleased that his business went forward well, why, saith he, as quick as quick, 'Said she that?'—and if my old eyes fail me not, I know of one that setteth greater share by your good word than you imagine, wench."

She but half heard; she was recalling all that had happened in this very summer-house.

"And think you, grandmother," said she, slowly, and with absent eyes, "that when he was sitting here with us, and telling us all about the court doings, and about my father's friends in London, and when he was so grateful to us, or saying that he was so, for our receiving of him here—think you that all the time he was planning to steal my father's play and to take it and sell it in London? Grandmother, can you think it possible? Could any one be such a hypocrite? I know that he deceived me at the first; but 'twas only a jest, and he confessed it all, and professed his shame that he had so done. But, grandmother, think of him—think of how he used to speak, and ever so modest and gentle: is't possible that all the time he was playing the thief, and looking forward to the getting away to London to sell what he had stolen?"

"For love's sake, sweetheart, heed that man no more!—'tis all done and gone; there can come no good of vexing thyself

14

about it," her grandmother said. "Be he villain or not, 'twill be well for all of us that we never hear his name more. In good sooth I am as much to blame as thou thyself, child, for the encouraging him to come about, and listening to his gossip —beshrew me, that I should have meddled in such matters, and not bade him go about his business! But 'tis all past and gone now, as I say—there be no profit in vexing thyself—"

"Past and gone, grandmother!" she exclaimed, and yet in a listless way. "Yes—but what remains? Good grandmother, perchance you did not hear all that the parson said. 'Tis past and gone, truly, and more than you think."

The tone in which she uttered these words somewhat startled the good dame, who looked at her anxiously. And then she said:

"Why, now I warrant me the barley broth will be hot enough by this time. I will go fetch thee a cupful, wench. 'Twill put warmth in thy veins, it will—ay, and cheer thy heart too."

"Trouble not, good grandmother," she said. "I would as lief go back to my room now. The light hurts my eyes strangely."

"Back to your room?—that shall you not!" was the prompt answer, but not meant unkindly. "You shall wait here, wench, till I bring thee that will put some color in thy white face—ay, and some of Thomas Quiney's wine withal; and if the light hurt thee, sit further back, then: of a truth 'tis no wonder, after thou hast hid thyself like a dormouse for so long."

And so she went away to the house. But she was scarcely gone when Judith—in this extreme silence that the rustling of a leaf would have disturbed—heard certain voices; and listening more intently, she made sure that the new-comers must be Susan and her mother, whom Prudence had asked to walk over. Instantly she got up, though she had to steady herself for a moment by resting her hand on the table; and then, as quickly as she could, and as noiselessly, she stole along the path to the cottage, and entered, and made her way up to her own room. She fancied she had not been heard. She would rather be alone. If they had come to accuse her, what had she to answer? Why, nothing: they might say of her what they pleased now; it was all deserved: only the one denunciation of her that she had listened to—the one she had heard from the

parson—seemed like the ringing of her death-knell. Surely
there was no need to repeat that? They could not wish to repeat it, did they but know all it meant to her.

Then the door was quietly opened, and her sister appeared,
bearing in one hand a small tray.

"I have brought you some food, Judith, and a little wine,
and you must try and take them, sweetheart," said she. "'Twas
right good news to us that you had come down, and gone into
the garden for a space. In truth, making yourself ill will not
mend matters; and Prudence was in great alarm."

She put the tray on a chair, for there was no table in the
room; but Judith, finding that her sister had not come to accuse her, but was in this gentle mood, said, quickly and eagerly:

"Oh, Susan, you can tell me all that I would so fain know!
You must have heard, for my father speaks to you of all his
affairs; and at your own wedding you must have heard, when
all these things were arranged. Tell me, Susan—I shall have
a marriage portion, shall I not?—and how much, think you?
Perchance not so large as yours, for you are the elder, and
Doctor Hall was ever a favorite with my father. But I shall
have a marriage portion, Susan, shall I not?—nay, it may already be set aside for me?"

And then her sister glanced somewhat reproachfully at her.

"I wonder you should be thinking of such things, Judith,"
said she.

"Ah, but 'tis not as you imagine," the girl said, with the
same pathetic eagerness. "'Tis in this wise, now: would my
father take it in a measure to repay him for the ill that I have
done? Would it make up the loss, Susan, or a part of it?
Would he take it, think you? Ah, but if he would do that!"

"Why, that were an easy way out of the trouble, assuredly!" her sister exclaimed. "To take the marriage portion that
is set aside for thee—and if I mistake not, 'tis all provided; ay,
and the Rowington copyhold, which will fall to thee, if 'tis
not thine already—truly, 'twere a wise thing to take these to
make good this loss, and then, when you marry, to have to give
you your marriage portion all the same!"

"Nay, nay, not so, Susan," her sister cried, quickly. "What
said you? The Rowington copyhold also? and perchance
mine already? Susan, would it make good the loss? Would all

taken together make good the loss? For, as Heaven is my witness, I will never marry—nor think of marrying—but rejoice
all the days of my life, if my father would but take these to
satisfy him of the injury I have done him. Nay, but is't possible, Susan? Will he do that for me?—as a kindness to me?
I have no right to ask for such; but—but if only he knew!—if
only he knew!"

The tears were running down her face; her hands were clasped in abject entreaty.

"Sweetheart, you know not what you ask," her sister said,
but gently. "When you marry, your marriage portion will
have to be in accordance with our position in the town; my father would not have it otherwise. Were you to surrender that
now, would he let one of his daughters go forth from his house
as a beggar, think you? Or what would her husband say, to
be so treated? You might be willing to give up these, but my
father could not, and your husband would not."

"Susan, Susan, I wish for no marriage," she cried; "I will
stay with my grandmother here; she is content that I should
bide with her; and if my father will take these, 'twill be the
joy of my life; I shall wish for no more, and New Place shall
come to no harm by me; 'tis here that I am to bide. Think
you he would take them, Susan?—think you he would take
them?" she pleaded; and in her excitement she got up and
tried to walk about a little, but with her hands still clasped.
"If one were to send to London, now—a message—or I would
walk every foot of the way did I but think he would do this
for me—oh, no! no! no! I durst not—I durst never see him
more; he has cast me off, and—and I deserve no less!"

Her sister went to her and took her by the hand.

"Judith, you have been in sore trouble, and scarce know
what you say," she said, in that clear, calm way of hers. "But
this is now what you must do. Sit down and take some of this
food. As I hear, you have scarce tasted anything these two
days. You have always been so wild and wayward: now must
you listen to reason and suffer guidance."

She made her sit down. The girl took a little of the broth,
some of the spiced bread, and a little of the wine; but it was
clear that she was forcing herself to it. Her thoughts were
elsewhere. And scarcely had she finished this make-believe of

a repast when she turned to her sister and said, with a pathetic pleading in her voice:

"And is it not possible, Susan? Surely I can do something! It is so dreadful to think of my father imagining that I have done him this injury, and gone on the same way, careless of what has happened. That terrifies me at night!—oh, if you but knew what it is in the darkness, in the long hours, and none to call to, and none to give you help; and to think that these are the thoughts he has of me—that it was all for a sweetheart I did it, that I gave away his writing to please a sweetheart, and that I care not for what has happened, but would do the like again to-morrow! It is so dreadful in the night!" ·

"I would comfort you if I could, Judith," said her sister, "but I fear me you must trust to wiser counsel than mine. In truth I know not whether all this can be undone, or how my father regards it at the moment; for at the time of the writing they were all uncertain. But surely now you would do well to be ruled by some one better able to guide you than any of us women-folk: Master Blaise hath been most kind and serviceable in this, as in all other matters, and hath written to your father in answer to his letter, so that we have had trust and assurance in his direction. And you also—why should you not seek his aid and counsel?"

At the mere mention of the parson's name, Judith shivered instinctively, she scarce knew why.

"Judith," her sister continued, regarding her watchfully, "to-morrow, as I understand, Master Blaise is coming over here to see you."

"May not I be spared that? He hath already brought his message," the girl said, in a low voice.

"Nay, he comes but in kindness—or more than kindness, if I guess aright. Bethink you, Judith," she said, "'tis not only the loss of the money—or great or small I know not—that hath distressed my father. There was more than that. Nay, do not think I am come to reproach you; but will it not be ever thus so long as you will be ruled by none, but must always go your own way? There was more than merely concerned money affairs in my father's letter, as doubtless Master Blaise hath told you; and then, think of it, Judith, how 'twill be when the bruit of the story comes down to Stratford."

"I care not," was the perfectly calm answer. "That is for me to bear. Can Master Blaise tell me how I may restore to my father this that he hath lost? Then his visit might be more welcome, Susan."

"Why will you harden your heart so?" the elder sister said, with some touch of entreaty in her tone. "Nay, think of it, Judith! Here is an answer to all. If you but listen to him, and favor him, you will have one always with you as a sure guide and counsellor; and who then may dare say a word against you?"

"Then he comes to save my good name?" the girl said, with a curious change of manner. "Nay, I will give him no such tarnished prize."

And here it occurred to the elder sister, who was sufficiently shrewd and observant, that her intercession did not seem to be producing good results; and she considered it better that the parson should speak for himself. Indeed, she hoped she had done no mischief; for this that she now vaguely suggested had for long been the dream and desire of both her mother and herself; and at this moment, if ever, there was a chance of Judith's being obedient and compliant. Not only did she forthwith change the subject, but also she managed to conquer the intense longing that possessed her to learn something further about the young man who (as she imagined) had for a time captured Judith's fancies. She gave her sister what news there was in the town. She besought her to take care of herself, and to go out as much as possible, for that she was looking far from well. And finally, when the girl confessed that she was fain to lie down for a space (having slept so little during these two nights), she put some things over her, and quietly left, hoping that she might soon get to sleep.

Judith did not rest long, however. The question whether the sacrifice of her marriage portion might not do something toward retrieving the disaster she had caused was still harassing her mind; and then, again, there was the prospect of the parson coming on the morrow. By-and-by, when she was certain that her mother and sister were gone, she went down-stairs, and began to help in doing this or the other little thing about the house. Her grandmother was out-of-doors, and so did not know to interfere, though the small maid-servant remonstrated as best she might. Luckily, however, nature was a more imperative monitress; and again and again the girl had to sit down from sheer physical weakness.

But there came over a visitor in the afternoon who restored to her something of her old spirit. It was little Willie Hart, who, having timidly tapped at the open door without, came along the passage, and entered the dusky chamber where she was.

"Ah, sweetheart," said she (but with a kind of sudden sob in her throat), "have you come to see me?"

"I heard that you were not well, cousin," said he, and he regarded her with troubled and anxious eyes as she stooped to kiss him.

"Nay, I am well enough," said she, with as much cheerfulness as she could muster. "Fret not yourself about that. What a studious scholar you are, Cousin Willie, that must needs bring your book with you! Were I not so ignorant myself, I should hear you your tasks; but you would but laugh at me—"

"'Tis no task-book, Judith," said he, diffidently. "'Twas Prudence who lent it to me."

And then he hesitated, through shyness.

"Why, you know, Judith," he said, "you have spoken to me many a time about Sir Philip Sidney; and I was asking this one and the other at times; and Prudence said she would show me a book he had written, that belongs to her brother. And then to-day, when I went to her, she bade me bring the book to you, and to read to you, for that you were not well, and might be pleased to hear it, she not being able to come over till the morrow."

"In truth, now, that was well thought of and friendly," said she; and she put her hand in a kindly fashion on his shoulder. "And you have come all the way over to read to me—see you how good a thing it is to be wise and instructed! Well, then, we will go and sit by the door, that you may have more of light; and if my grandmother catch us at such idleness, you shall have to defend me—you shall have to defend me, sweetheart—for you are the man of us two, and I must be shielded."

So they went to the door, and sat down on the step, the various-colored garden and the trees and the wide heavens all shining before them.

"And what is the tale, Cousin Willie?" said she, quite pleasantly (for indeed she was glad to see the boy, and to chat with one who had no reproaches for her, who knew nothing against her, but was ever her true lover and slave). "Nay, if it be by Sir Philip Sidney,'twill be of gallant and noble knights assuredly."

"I know not, Cousin Judith," said he; "I but looked at the beginning as I came through the fields. And this is how it goes."

He opened the book, and began to read:

"It was in the time that the Earth begins to put on her new apparel against the approach of her lover, and that the sun, running a most even course, becomes an indifferent arbiter between the night and the day, when the hopeless shepherd Strephon was come to the sands which lie against the island of Cithera, where, viewing the place with a heavy kind of delight, and sometimes casting his eyes to the isleward, he called his friendly rival the pastor Claius unto him; and, setting first down in his darkened countenance a doleful copy of what he would speak, 'O my Claius,' said he—"

Thus he went on; and as he read, her face grew more and more wistful. It was a far-off land that she heard of; and beautiful it was; it seemed to her that she had been dwelling in some such land, careless and all unknowing.

"The third day after," she vaguely heard him say, "in the time that the morning did strew roses and violets in the heavenly floor against the coming of the sun, the nightingales, striving one with the other which could in most dainty variety recount their wrong-caused sorrow, made them put off their sleep; and, rising from under a tree, which that night had been their pavilion, they went on their journey, which by-and-by welcomed Musidorus' eyes with delightful prospects. There were hills which garnished their proud heights with stately trees; humble valleys whose base estate seemed comforted with the refreshing of silver rivers; meadows enamelled with all sorts of eye-pleasing flowers; thickets which, being lined with most pleasant shade, were witnessed so to by the cheerful disposition of many well-tuned birds; each pasture stored with sheep, feeding with sober security, while the pretty lambs, with bleating oratory, craved the dams' comfort: here a shepherd's boy piping, as though he should never be old; there a young shepherdess knitting, and withal singing: and it seemed that her voice comforted her hands to work, and her hands kept time to her voice-music."

Surely she had herself been living in some such land of pleasant delights, without a thought that ever it would end for her, but that each following day would be as full of mirth and laughter as its predecessor. She scarcely listened to the little lad now. She was looking back over the years. So rare and bright and full of light and color were they—and always a kind of music in them, and laughter at the sad eyes of lovers. She had never known how happy she had been. It was all distant now—the idle flower-gathering in the early spring-time; the afternoon walking in the meadows, she and Prudence together (with the young lads regarding them askance); the open casements on the moon-lit nights, to hear the madrigal-singing of the youths going home; or the fair and joyous mornings that she was allowed to ride away, in the direction of Oxford, to meet her father and his companions coming in to Stratford town. And now, when next he should come, to all of them, and all of them welcoming him—even neighbors and half-strangers—and he laughing to them all, and getting off his horse, and calling for a cup of wine as he strode into the house, where should she be? Not with all of these, not laughing and listening to the merry stories of the journey, but away by herself, hiding herself, as it were, and thinking, alone.

"Dear Judith, but why are you crying?" said the little lad, as he chanced to look up; and his face was of an instant and troubled anxiety.

"Why, 'tis a fair land—oh, indeed, a fair land!" said she, with an effort at regarding the book, and pretending to be wholly interested in it. "Nay, I would hear more of Musidorus, sweetheart, and of that pretty country. I pray you continue the reading—continue the reading, sweetheart Willie. Nay, I never heard of a fairer country, I assure thee, in all the wide world!"

14*

CHAPTER XXXII.

A RESOLVE.

THEN that night, as she lay awake in the dark, her incessant imaginings shaped themselves toward one end. This passion of grief she knew to be unavailing and fruitless. Something she would try to do, if but to give evidence of her contrition; for how could she bear that her father should think of her as one having done him this harm and still going on light-hearted and unconcerned? The parson was coming over on the morrow. And if she were to put away her maidenly pride (and other vague dreams that she had sometimes dreamed), and take it that her consent would re-establish her in the eyes of those who were now regarding her askance, and make her peace with her own household? And if the surrender of her marriage portion and her interest in the Rowington copyhold (whatever it might be) were in a measure to mitigate her father's loss? It was the only thing she could think of. And if at times she looked forward with a kind of shudder (for in the night-time all prospects wear a darker hue) to her existence as the parson's wife, again there came to her the reflection that it was not for her to repine. Some sacrifice was due from her. And could she not be as resolute as the daughter of the Gileadite? Oftentimes she had heard the words read out in the still afternoon: "Now when Iphtah came to Mizpeh unto his house, behold his daughter came out to meet him with timbrels and dances: which was his only child; he had none other son nor daughter. And when he saw her he rent his clothes, and said, Alas, my daughter! thou has brought me low, and art of them that trouble me." The Jewish maiden had done no ill, and yet was brave to suffer: why should she repine at any sacrifice demanded of her to atone for her own wrong-doing? What else was there? She hoped that Susan and her mother would be pleased now, and that her father and his friends in London would not have any serious loss to regret. There was but the one way, she said to herself again and again. She was almost anxious for the parson to come over, to see if he would approve.

With the daylight her determination became still more clear; and also she saw more plainly the difficulties before her. For it could not be deemed a very seemly and maidenly thing that she, on being asked to become a bride (and she had no doubt that was his errand), should begin to speak of her marriage portion. But would he understand? Would he help her over her embarrassment? Nay, she could not but reflect, here was an opportunity for his showing himself generous and large-minded. He had always professed, or at least intimated, that his wish to have her for wife was based mostly on his care for herself and his regard for the general good of the pious community to which he belonged. She was to be a helpmeet for one laboring in the Lord's vineyard; she was to be of service in the church; she was to secure for herself a constant and loving direction and guidance. And now, if he wished to prove all this—if he wished to show himself so noble and disinterested as to win for himself her life-long gratitude—what if he were to take over all her marriage portion, as that might be arranged, and forthwith and chivalrously hand it back again, so that her grievous fault should so far be condoned? If the girl had been in her usual condition of health and spirits, it is probable that she would have regarded this question with a trifle of skepticism (for she was about as shrewd in such matters as Susan herself)—nay, it is just probable that she might have experienced a malicious joy in putting him to the proof. But she was in despair; her nerves were gone, through continual wakefulness and mental torture; this was the only direction in which she saw light, and she regarded it, not with her ordinary faculty of judgment, but with a kind of pathetic hope.

Master Blaise arrived in the course of the morning. His reception was not auspicious; for the old dame met him at the gate, and made more than a show of barring the way.

"Indeed, good sir," said she, firmly, "the wench be far from well now, and I would have her left alone."

He answered that his errand was of some importance, and that he must crave a few minutes' interview. Both her mother and sister, he said, were aware he was coming over to see her, and had made no objection.

" No, no, perchance not," the grandmother said, though without budging an inch, " but she be under my care now, and I will
have no harm befall her—"

" Harm, good Mistress Hathaway ?" said he.

"Well, she be none so strong as she were, and—and perchance there hath been overmuch lecturing of the poor lass.
Nay, I doubt not 'twas meant in kindness, but there hath been
overmuch of it, as I reckon; and what I say is, if the wench
have done amiss, let those that have the right to complain
come to her. Nay, 'twas kindness, good sir; 'twas well meant,
I doubt not; and 'tis your calling belike to give counsel and
reproof; I say naught against that; but I am of a mind to have
my grandchild left alone at present."

" If you refuse me, good Mistress Hathaway," said he, quite
courteously and calmly, " there is no more to be said. But I
imagine that her mother and sister will be surprised. And as
for the maiden herself—go you by her wishes ?"

" Nay, not I," was the bold answer. " I know better than
all of them together. For to speak plain with you, good master parson, your preaching must have been oversharp when
last you were within here, and was like to have brought the
wench to death's door thereafter—marry, she be none so far
recovered as to risk any further of such treatment. Perchance
you meant no harm; but she is proud and high-spirited, and,
by your leave, good sir, we will see her a little stronger and
better set up ere she have any more of the discipline of the
church bestowed on her."

It was well that Judith appeared at this juncture; for the
tone of the old dame's voice was growing more and more tart.

"Grandmother," said she, "I would speak with Master
Blaise."

" Get thee within-doors at once, I tell thee, wench !" was the
peremptory rejoinder.

" No, good grandmother, so please you," Judith said, " I
must speak with him. There is much of importance that I
have to say to him. Good sir, will you step into the garden ?"

The old dame withdrew, sulky and grumbling, and evidently inclined to remain within ear-shot, lest she should deem it
necessary to interfere. Judith preceded Master Blaise to the
door of the cottage, and asked the little maid to bring out a

couple of chairs. As she sat down, he could not but observe
how wan and worn her face was, and how listless she was in
manner; but he made no comment on that: he only remarked
that her grandmother seemed in no friendly mood this morning, and that only the fact that his mission was known to Susan and her mother had caused him to persist.

It was clear that this untoward reception had disconcerted
him somewhat; and it was some little time before he could recover that air of mild authority with which he was accustomed
to convey his counsels. At first he confined himself to telling
Judith what he had done on behalf of her mother and Susan
—in obedience to their wishes; but by-and-by he came to herself, and her own situation; and he hoped that this experience
through which she had passed, though it might have caused
her bitter distress for the time, would eventually make for good.
If the past could not be recalled, at least the future might be
made safe. Indeed, one or two phrases he used sounded as if
they had done some previous service; perhaps he had consult-
ed with Mistress Hall ere making this appeal; but in any case
Judith was not listening so particularly as to think of that—
she seemed to know beforehand what he had to say.

To tell the truth, he was himself a little surprised at her tacit
acquiescence. He had always had to argue with Judith; and
many a time he had found that her subtle feminine wit was capable of extricating herself from what he considered a defenseless position. But now she sat almost silent. She seemed to
agree to everything. There was not a trace left of the old audacious self-reliance, nor yet of those saucy rejoinders which
were only veiled by her professed respect for his cloth. She
was at his mercy.

And so, growing bolder, he put in his own personal claim.
He said little that he had not said, or hinted, on previous occasions; but now all the circumstances were changed; this heavy
misfortune that had befallen her was but another and all too
cogent reason why she should accept his offer of shelter and
aid and counsel, seeing into what pitfalls her own unguided
steps were like to lead her.

"I speak the words of truth and soberness," said he, as he
sat and calmly regarded her downcast face, "and make no appeal to the foolish fancies of a young and giddy-headed girl, for

that you are no longer, Judith. The years are going by.
There must come a time in life when the enjoyment of the
passing moment is not all in all; when one must look to the
future, and make provision for sickness and old age. Death
strikes here and there; friends fall away; what a sad thing it
were to find one's self alone, the dark clouds of life thickening
over, and none by to help and cheer! Then your mother and
sister, Judith—"

"Yes, I know," she said, almost in despair—"I know 'twould
please them."

And then she reflected that this was scarcely the manner in
which she should receive his offer, that was put before her so
plainly and with so much calm sincerity.

"I pray you, good sir," said she, in a kind of languid way,
"forgive me if I answer you not as frankly as might be. I
have been ill; my head aches now; perchance I have not followed all you said. But I understand it—I understand it; and
in all you say there is naught but good intention."

"Then it is yes, Judith?" he exclaimed, and for the first time
there was a little brightness of ardor—almost of triumph—in
this clearly conceived and argued wooing.

"It would please my mother and sister," she repeated, slowly. "They are afraid of some story coming from London
about—about what is passed. This would be an answer, would
it not?"

"Why, yes," he said, confidently, for he saw that she was
yielding (and his own susceptibilities were not likely to be
wounded in that direction). "Think you we should heed any
tavern scurrility? I trow not! There would be the answer
plain and clear—if you were my wife, Judith."

"They would be pleased," again she said, and her eyes were
absent. And then she added: "I pray you pardon me, good
sir, if I speak of that which you may deem out of place; but—
but if you knew—how I have been striving to think of some
means of repairing the wrong I have done my father, you would
not wonder that I should be anxious, and perchance indiscreet.
You know of the loss I have caused him and his companions.
How could I ever make that good with the work of my own
hands? That is not possible; and yet when I think of how he
hath toiled for all of us, late and early, as it were—why, good

sir, I have myself been bold enough to chide him, or to wish
that I were a man, to ride forth in the morning in his stead
and look after the land: and then that his own daughter should
be the means of taking from him what he hath earned so hardly—that I should never forget; 'twould be on my mind year
after year, even if he were himself to try to forget it."

She paused for a second; the mere effort of speaking seemed
to fatigue her.

"There is but the one means, as I can think, of showing him
my humble sorrow for what hath been done—of making him
some restitution. I know not what my marriage portion may
be—but 'twill be something—and Susan saith there is a part of
the manor of Rowington, also, that would fall to me. Now,
see you, good Master Blaise, if I were to give these over to my
father in part quittance of this injury, or if belike—my—my
—husband would do that—out of generosity and nobleness—
would not my father be less aggrieved?"

She had spoken rather quickly and breathlessly (to get over
her embarrassment), and now she regarded him with a strange
anxiety, for so much depended on his answer! Would he understand her motives? Would he pardon her bluntness?
Would he join her in this scheme of restitution?

He hesitated only for a moment.

"Dear Judith," he said, with perfect equanimity, "such matters are solely within the province of men, and not at the disposition of women, who know less of the affairs of the world.
Whatever arrangements your father may have made in respect
of your marriage portion—truly I have made no inquiry in
that direction—he will have made with due regard to his own
circumstances, and with regard to the family, and to your future. Would he be willing to upset these in order to please a
girlish fancy? Why, in all positions in life pecuniary losses
must happen, and a man takes an account of these; and is he
likely to recover himself at the expense of his own daughter?"

"Nay, but if she be willing! If she would give all that she
hath, good sir!" she cried, quickly.

"'Twould be but taking it from one pocket to put it in the
other," said he, in his patient and forbearing way. "I say
not, if a man were like to become bankrupt, that his family
might not forego their expectations in order to save him; but

your father is one in good position. Think you that the loss is so great to him? In truth, it can not be."

The eagerness fell away from her face. She saw too clearly that he could not understand her at all. She did not reckon her father's loss in proportion to his wealth—in truth she could not form the faintest notion of what that loss might be: all her thought was of her winning back (in some remote day, if that were still possible to her) to her father's forgiveness, and the regarding of his face as no longer in dread wrath against her.

"Why," said he, seeing that she sat silent and distraught (for all the hope had gone out of her), "in every profession and station in life a man must have here or there a loss, as I say; but would he rob his family to make that good? Surely not. Of what avail might that be? 'Tis for them that he is working; 'tis not for himself; why should he take from them to build up a property which must in due course revert and become theirs? I pray you put such fancies out of your head, Judith. Women are not accustomed to deal with such matters; 'tis better to have them settled in the ordinary fashion. Were I you I would leave it in your father's hands."

"And have him think of me as he is thinking now!" she said, in a kind of wild way. "Ah, good sir, you know not!— you know not! Every day that passes is but the deeper misery; for—for he will be hardened in the belief—'twill be fixed in his mind forever—that his own daughter did him this wrong, and went on lightly, not heeding, perchance to seek another sweetheart. This he is thinking now; and I—what can I do?—being so far away, and none to help!"

"In truth, dear Judith," said he, "you make too much of your share in what happened. 'Tis not to you your father should look for reparation of his loss, but to the scoundrel who carried the play to London. What punishment would it be for him, or what gain to your father, that your father should upset the arrangements he has made for the establishment and surety of his own family? Nay, I pray you put aside such a strange fancy, dear heart, and let such things take their natural course."

"In no wise! in no wise!" she exclaimed, almost in despair. "In truth, I can not. 'Twould kill me were nothing to be done to appease my father's anger; and I thought that if he were to learn that you had sought me in marriage, and—and

agreed that such restitution as I can make should be made
forthwith—or afterward, as might be decided—but only that he
should know now that I give up everything he had intended
for me—then I should have greater peace of mind."

"Indeed, Judith," said he, somewhat coldly, "I could be no
party to any such foolish freak—nay, not even in intention,
whatever your father might say to it. The very neighbors
would think I was bereft of my senses. And 'twould be an ill
beginning of our life together—in which there must ever be
authority and guidance as well as dutiful obedience—if I were
to yield to what every one must perceive to be an idle and fantastic wish. I pray you consult your own sober judgment: at
present you are ailing and perturbed; rest you awhile until
these matters have calmed somewhat, and you will see them
in their true light."

"No, no," she said, hurriedly and absently—"no, no, good
sir; you know not what you ask. Rest? Nay, one way or the
other, this must be done, and forthwith. I know not what he
may have intended for me, but be it large or small, 'tis all
that I have to give him—I can do no more than that; and then,
then there may be some thoughts of rest."

She spoke as if she were scarcely aware of the good parson's
presence; and in truth, though he was not one to allow any
wounded self-love to mar his interests, he could not conceal
from himself that she was considering the proposal he had put
before her mainly, if not wholly, with a view to the possible
settlement of these troubles and the appeasing of her friends.
Whether, in other circumstances, he might not have calmly
overlooked this slight need not now be regarded; in the present circumstances—that is to say, after her announced determination to forego every penny of her marriage portion—he
did take notice of it, and with some sharpness of tone, as if he
were truly offended.

"Indeed, you pay me no compliment, Judith," said he. "I
come to offer you the shelter of an honest man's home, an
honorable station as his wife, a life-long guidance and protection; and what is your answer?—that perchance you may make
use of such an offer to please your friends, and to pay back to
your father what you foolishly think you owe him. If these
be the only purposes you have in view—and you seem to think

of none other—'twould be a sorry forecast for the future, as I
take it. At the very beginning an act of madness! Nay, I
could be no party to any such thing. If you refuse to be
guided by me in great matters, how could I expect you to be
guided in small?"

These words, uttered in his clear and precise and definite
manner, she but vaguely understood (for her head troubled her
sorely, and she was tired and anxious to be at rest) to be a
withdrawal of his proposal; but that was enough; and perhaps
she even experienced some slight sense of relief. As for his
rebuking of her, she heeded not that.

"As you will, sir—as you will," she said, listlessly; and she
rose from her chair.

And he rose too. Perhaps he was truly offended; perhaps
he only appeared to be; but at all events he bade her farewell
in a cold and formal manner, and as if it were he who had
brought this interview to an end, and that for good.

"What said he, wench, what said he?" her grandmother
asked (who had been pretending all the time to be gathering
peas, and now came forward). "Nay, I caught but little—a
word here or there—and yet methinks 'tis a brave way of wooing they have nowadays, that would question a maid about her
marriage portion. Heaven's mercy! did ever any hear the
like? 'Twas not so when I was young—nay, a maid would
have bade him go hang that brought her such a tale. Oh, the
good parson!—his thoughts be not all bent on heaven, I warrant me! Ay, and what said he? And what saidst thou,
wench? Truly you be in no fit state to answer him; were you
well enough, and in your usual spirits, the good man would
have his answer—ay, as sharp as need be. But I will say no
more; Master Quiney hath a vengeful spirit, and perchance he
hath set me too much against the good man; but as for thyself, lass, there be little cause for talking further of thy offenses,
if 'tis thy marriage portion the parson be after, now!"

"Good grandmother, give me your arm," Judith said, in a
strange way. "My head is so strange and giddy. I know
not what I have said to him—I scarce can recollect it: if I have
offended, bid him forgive me; but—but I would have him remain away."

"As I am a living woman," said the old dame (forgetting

her resolve to speak smooth words), "he shall not come within the door, nor yet within that gate, while you bide with me
and would have him kept without! What, then? More talk
of chastenings? Marry, now, Thomas Quiney shall hear of
this—that shall he—by my life he shall!"

"No, no, no, good grandmother; pray you blame no one,"
the girl said; and she was trembling somewhat. "'Tis I that
have done all the harm to every one. But I know not what I
said. I—I would fain lie down, grandmother, if you will give
me your arm so far; 'tis so strangely cold—I understand it not
—and I forget what was't he said to me, but I trust I offended
him not—"

"Nay, but what is it, then, my dearie?" the old woman said,
taking both the girl's hands in hers. "What is it that you
should fret about? Nay, fret not, fret not, good wench; the
parson be well away, and there let him bide. And would you
lie down?—well, come, then; but sure you shake as if 'twere
winter. Come, lass—nay, fret not; we will keep the parson
away, I warrant, if 'tis that that vexes thee!"

"No, grandmother, 'tis not so," the girl said, in a low voice.
"'Twas down by the river, as I think; 'twas chilly there—I
have felt it ever since from time to time—but 'twill pass away
when I am lain down and become warm again."

"Heaven grant it be no worse!" the old dame said to herself,
as she shrewdly regarded the girl; but of course her outward
talk, as she took her within-doors, was ostensibly cheerful.
"Come thy ways, then, sweeting, and we shall soon make thee
warm enough. Ay, ay, and Prudence be coming over this
afternoon, as I hear; and no doubt Thomas Quiney too; and
thou must get thyself dressed prettily, and have supper with
us all, though 'tis no treat to offer to a man of his own wine.
Nay, I warrant me he will think naught of that, so thou be
there, with a pleasant look for him; he will want nor wine
nor aught else if he have but that, and a friendly word from
thee, as I reckon; ay, and thou shalt put on the lace cuffs, now,
to do him fair service for his gift to thee—that shalt thou, and
why not?—I swear to thee, my brave lass, they be fit for a
queen!"

And she would comfort her and help her (just as if this
granddaughter of hers, that always was so bright and gay and

radiant, so self-willed and self-reliant, with nothing but laughter for the sad eyes of the stricken youths, was now but a weak
and frightened child, that had to be guarded and coaxed and
caressed), and would talk as if all her thinking was of that visit
in the afternoon; but the only answer was:

"Will you send for Prudence, grandmother? Oh, grandmother, my head aches so! I scarce know what I said."

Swiftly and secretly the old dame sent across to the town;
and not to Prudence only, but also (for she was grown anxious)
to Mistress Hall, to say that if her husband were like to return
soon to Stratford, he might come over and see Judith, who was
far from well. As for Prudence, a word was sufficient to bring
her; she was there straightway.

She found Judith very much as she had left her, but somewhat more restless and feverish perhaps, and then again hope-
lessly weak and languid, and always with those racking pains
in the head. She said it was nothing—it would soon pass
away; it was but a chill she had caught in sitting on the river-
bank: would not Prudence now go back to her duties and her
affairs in the house?

"Judith," said her friend, leaning over her and speaking
low, "I have that to tell thee will comfort thee, methinks."

"Nay, I can not listen to it now," was the answer—and it
was a moan almost. "Dear mouse, do not trouble about me;
but my head is so bad that I—that I care not now. And the
parson is gone away thinking that I have wronged him also.
'Tis ever the same now— Oh, sweetheart, my head! my head!"

"But listen, Judith," the other pleaded. "Nay, but you
must know what your friends are ready to do for you—this
surely will make thee well, sweetheart. Think of it, now: do
you know that Quiney is gone to see your father?"

"To my father?" she repeated, and she tried to raise her
head somewhat, so that her eyes might read her friend's face.

"I am almost sure of it, dear heart," Prudence said, taking
her hot hand in hers. "Nay, he would have naught said of it.
None of his family know whither he is gone; and I but guess.
But this is the manner of it, dear Judith—that he and I were
talking, and sorely vexed he was that your father should be
told a wrong story concerning you—ay, and sorry to see you
so shaken, Judith, and distressed; and said he, 'What if I were

to get a message to her from her father—that he was in no such mood of anger, and had not heard the story aright, and that he was well disposed to her, and grieved to hear she had taken it so much to heart—would not that comfort her?' he said. And I answered that assuredly it would, and even more, perchance, than he thought of; and I gathered from him that he would write to some one in London to go and see your father and pray him to send you assurance of that kind. But now—nay, I am certain of it, dear Judith—I am certain that he himself is gone all the way to London to bring thee back that comfort; and will not that cheer thee, now, sweetheart?"

"He is doing all that for me?" the girl said, in a low voice, and absently.

"Ah, but you must be well and cheerful, good mouse, to give him greeting when he comes back," said Prudence, striving to raise her spirits somewhat. "Have I not read to thee many a time how great kings were wont to reward the messengers that brought them good news?—a gold chain round their neck, or lands, perchance. And will you have no word of welcome for him? Will you not meet him with a glad face? Why, think of it, now—a journey to London, and the perils and troubles by the way, and all done to please thee! Nay, he would say naught of it to any one, lest they might wonder at his doing so much for thee, belike; but when he comes back 'twere a sorry thing that you should not give him a good and gracious welcome."

Judith lay silent and thinking for a while; and then she said, but as if the mere effort to speak were too much for her:

"Whatever happens, dear Prudence—nay, in truth, I think I am very ill—tell him this, that he did me wrong: he thought I had gone to meet the parson that Sunday morning in the church-yard. 'Twas not so—tell him it was not so; 'twas but a chance, dear heart; I could not help it."

"Judith, Judith," her friend said, "these be things for thine own telling. Nay, you shall say all that to himself; and you must speak him fair—ay, and give him good welcome and thanks that hath done so much for thee."

Judith put her head down on the pillow again, languidly; but presently Prudence heard her laugh to herself in a strange way.

"Last night," she said, "'twas so wonderful, dear Prue. I thought I was going about in a strange country, looking for my little brother Hamnet, and I knew not whether he would have any remembrance of me. Should I have to tell him my name, I kept asking myself. And 'Judith, Judith,' I said to him when I found him; but he scarce knew; I thought he had forgotten me; 'tis so long ago now. 'Judith, Judith,' I said; and he looked up, and he was so strangely like little Willie Hart that I wondered whether it was Hamnet or no."

But Prudence was alarmed by these wanderings, and did her best to hush them. And then, when at length the girl lay silent and still, Prudence stole down-stairs again and bade the grandmother go to Judith's room, for that she must at once hurry over to Stratford to speak with Susan Hall.

CHAPTER XXXIII.

ARRIVALS.

SOME few mornings after that, two travellers were standing in the spacious archway of the inn at Shipston, chatting to each other, and occasionally glancing toward the stable-yard, as if they were expecting their horses to be brought round.

"The wench will thank thee for this service done her," the elder of the two said; and he regarded the younger man in a shrewd and not unkindly way.

"Nay, I am none well pleased with the issue of it all," the young man said, moodily.

"What, then?" his companion said. "Can nothing be done and finished but with the breaking of heads? Must that ever crown the work? Mercy on us!—how many would you have slaughtered? Now 'tis the parson that must be thrown into the Avon; again it is Gentleman Jack you would have us seek out for you; and then it is his friend—whose very name we know not—that you would pursue through the dens and stews of London town. A hopeful task, truly, for a Stratford youth! What know you of London, man? And to pursue one whose very name you know not—and all for the further breaking of heads, that never did any good anywhere in the world."

"You are right, sir," the younger man said, with some bitterness. "I can brag and bluster as well as any. But I see not that much comes of it. 'Tis easy to break the heads of scoundrels—in talk. Their bones are none the worse."

"And better so," the other said, gravely. "I would have no blood shed. What, man, are you still fretting that I would not leave you behind in London?"

"Nay, sir, altogether I like not the issue of it," he said, but respectfully enough. "I shall be told, I doubt not, that I might have minded my own business. They will blame me for bringing you all this way, and hindering your affairs."

"Heaven bless us!" said the other, "may not a man come to see his daughter without asking leave of the neighbors?"

"'Tis as like as not that she herself will be the first to chide me," the younger man answered. "A message to her was all I asked of you, sir. I dreamt not of hindering your affairs so."

"Nay, nay," said Judith's father, good-naturedly. "I can make the occasion serve me well. Trouble not about that, friend Quiney. If we can cheer up the wench and put her mind at rest—that will be a sufficient end of the journey; and we will have no broken heads withal, so please you. And if she herself should have put aside these idle fears, and become her usual self again, why, then, there is no harm done either. I mind me that some of them wondered that I should ride down to see my little Hamnet when he lay sick; for 'twas no serious illness that time, as it turned out; but what does that make for now? Now, I tell you, I am right glad I went to see the little lad; it cheered him to be made so much of; and such small services or kindnesses are pleasant things for ourselves to think of when those that are dearest to us are no longer with us. So cease your fretting, friend Quiney. For the hindering of my affairs I take it that I am answerable to myself, and not to the good gossips of Stratford town. And if 'tis merely to say a kind word to the lass—if that is all that need be done—well, there are many things that are of different value to different people; and the wench and I understand each other shrewdly well."

The horses were now brought round; but, ere they mounted, Judith's father said, again regarding the youth in that observant way,

"Nay, I see how it is with you, good lad; you are anxious as to how Judith may take this service you have done her—is't not so?"

"Perchance she may be angry that I called you away, sir," he said.

"Have no fear. 'Twas none of thy doing. 'Twas but a whim of mine own—nay, there be other and many reasons for my coming, that need not to be explained to her. What, must I make apology to my own daughter? She is not the guardian of Stratford town? I am no rogue; she is no constable. May not I enter? Nay, nay, have no fear, friend Quiney; when that she comes to understand the heavy errand you undertook for her, she will give you her thanks, or I know nothing of her. Her thanks?—marry, yes!"

He looked at the young man again.

"But let there be no broken heads, good friend, I charge you," said he, as he put his foot in the stirrup. "If the parson have been overzealous, we will set all matters straight, without hurt or harm to any son of Adam."

And now as they rode on together the younger man's face seemed more confident and satisfied; and he was silent for the most part. Of course he would himself be the bearer of the news; it was but natural that he should claim as much. And as Judith's father intended to go first to New Place, Quiney intimated to him that he would rather not ride through the town; in fact, he wanted to get straightway (and unobserved, if possible) to Shottery, to see how matters were there.

When he arrived at the little hamlet, Willie Hart was in the garden, and instantly came down to the gate to meet him. He asked no questions of the boy, but begged of him to hold the bridle of his horse for a few minutes; then he went into the house.

Just within the threshold he met Judith's sister.

"Ah," said he, quickly, and even joyously, "I have brought good news. Where is Judith? May I see her? I want to tell her that her father is come, and will see her presently."

And then something in the scared face that was regarding him struck him with a sudden terror.

"What is it?" he said, with his own face become about as pale as hers.

"Judith is very ill," was the answer.

"Yes, yes," he said, eagerly, "and that she was when I left. But now that her father is come, 'twill be all different—'twill be all set right now. And you will tell her, then, if I may not? Nay, but may not I see her for a moment—but for a moment—to say how her father is come all the way to see her —ay, and hath a store of trinkets for her—and is come to comfort her into assurance that all will go well? Why, will not such a message cheer her?"

"Good Master Quiney," Susan said, with tears welling into her eyes, "if you were to see her, she would not know you; she knows no one; she knows not that she is ill; but speaks of herself as some other—"

"But her father!" he exclaimed, in dismay, "will she not know him? Will she not understand? Nay, surely 'tis not yet too late!"

But here Doctor Hall appeared; and when he was told that Judith's father was come to the town and would shortly be at the cottage, he merely said that perchance his presence might soothe her somewhat, or even lead her delirious wanderings into a gentler channel, but that she would almost certainly be unable to recognize him. Nor was the fever yet at its height, he said, and they could do but little for her. They could but wait and hope. As for Quiney, he did not ask to be admitted to the room. He seemed stunned. He sat down in the kitchen —heeding no one — and vaguely wondering whether any lengthening of the stages of the journey would have brought them in better time. Nay, had he not wasted precious hours in London in vainly seeking to find himself face to face with Jack Orridge?

Prudence chanced to come down-stairs. As she entered the kitchen he forgot to give her any greeting; he only said, quickly:

"Think you she will not understand that her father is come to see her? Surely she must understand so much, Prudence! You will tell her, will you not?—and if she sees him standing before her?"

"I know not—I am afraid," said Prudence, anxiously. "Perchance it may frighten her the more; for ever she says that she sees him; and always with an angry face toward her; and

15

she is for hiding herself away from him, and even talking of the river. Good lack! 'tis pitiful that she should be so struck down, and almost at death's door, and all we can do of so little avail!"

"Prudence," said he, starting to his feet, "there is her father just come; I hear him; now take him to her, and you will see —you will see. I may not go; a strange face might frighten her; but I know she will recognize him, and understand; and he will tell her to have no longer any fear of him—"

Prudence hurried away to meet Judith's father, who was in the doorway, getting such information as was possible from the doctor. And then they all of them (all but Quiney) stole gently upstairs; and they stood at the door in absolute silence, while Judith's father went forward to the bed—so quietly that the girl did not seem to notice his approach.

The grandmother was there, sitting by the bedside, and speaking to her in a low voice.

"Hush thee now, sweeting, hush thee now," she was saying, and she patted her hand. "Nay, I know 'twas ill done; 'tis quite right what thou sayst; they treated her not well—and the poor wench anxious to please them all. But have no fear for her; nay, trouble not thy head with thoughts of her: she be safe at home again, I trust. Hush thee now, sweeting; 'twill go well with her, I doubt not. I swear to thee her father be no longer angry with the wench; 'twill go well with her, and well. Have no fear."

The girl looked at her steadily, and yet with a strange light in her eyes, as if she saw distant things before her, or was seeking to recall them.

"There was Susan, too," she said, in a low voice, "that sang so sweet—oh, in the church it was so sweet to hear her!—but when it was ' *The rose is from my garden gone,*' she would not sing that—though that was ever in her sister's mind after she went away down to the river-side; I can not think why they would not sing it to her—perchance the parson thought 'twas wicked : I know not now. And when she herself would try it with the lute, nothing would come right, all went wrong with her—all went wrong; and her father came angry and terrible to seek her—and 'twas the parson that would drag her forth— the bushes were not thick enough. Good grandam, why should

the bushes in the garden be so thin that the terrible eyes peered
through them, and she tried to hide, and could not?"

"Nay, I tell thee, sweetheart," said the grandmother, whis-
pering to her, "that the poor wench you speak of went home,
and all were well content with her, and her father was right
pleased—indeed, indeed, 'twas so."

"Poor Judith! poor Judith!" the girl murmured to herself,
and then she laughed slightly. "She was ever the stupid one;
naught would go right with her; ay, and evil-tempered she
was, too, for Quiney would ride all the way to London for her,
and she thanked him with never a word or a look—never a word
or a look—and he going all the way to please her. Poor
wench, all went wrong with her somehow; but they might have
let her go, she was so anxious to hide; and then to drag her
forth from under the bushes. Grandam, it was cruelly done of
them, wasn't it?"

"Ay, ay, but hush thee now, dearie," her grandmother said,
as she put a cool cloth on the burning forehead. "'Tis quite
well now with the poor wench you speak of."

Her father drew nearer, and took her hand quietly.

"Judith," said he, "poor lass, I am come to see you."

For an instant there was a startled look of fear in her eyes;
but that passed, and she regarded him at first with a kind of
smiling wonder, and thereafter with a contented satisfaction, as
though his presence was familiar. Nay, she turned her attention altogether toward him now, and addressed him—not in
any heart-broken way, but cheerfully, and as if he had been
listening to her all along. It was clear that she did not in the
least know who he was.

"There, now, lass," said he, "knowest thou that Quiney and
I have ridden all the way from London to see thee?—and thou
must lie still and rest, and get well again, ere we can carry
thee out into the garden."

She was looking at him with those strangely brilliant eyes.

"But not into the garden," she said, in a vacant kind of way.
"That is all gone away now—gone away. 'Twas long ago—
when poor Judith used to go into the garden—and right fair
and beautiful it was—ay, and her father would praise her hair,
and the color of it—until he grew angry, and drove her away
far from him—and then—and then—she wandered down to the

river—and always Susan's song was in her mind—or the other
one, that was near as sad as that, about the western wind—was
it not?   How went it, now?

> ' *Western wind, when will you blow?*'

Nay, I can not recall it—'tis gone out of my head, grandam,
and there is only fire there—and fire—and fire—

> ' *Western wind, when will you blow?*'

it went; and then about the rain next—what was it?

> ' *So weary falls the rain!*'

Ay, ay, that was it, now—I remember Susan singing it:

> ' *Western wind, when will you blow?*
> *So weary falls the rain!*
> *O if my love were in my arms,*
> *Or I in my bed again!*' "

And here she turned away from them and fell a-crying, and
hid from them, as it were, covering her face with both her
hands.

"Grandmother, grandmother," they could hear her say
through her sobbing, "there was but the one rose in my garden, and that is gone now—they have robbed me of that—and
what cared I for aught else?   And Quiney is gone too, without
a word or a look; and ere he be come back—well, I shall be
away by then—he will have no need to quarrel with me and
think ill of me that I chanced to meet the parson.   'Tis all over
now, grandmother, and done with, and you will let me bide
with you for just a little while longer—a little while, grandmother; 'tis no great matter for so little a while, though I can
not help you as I would; but Cicely is a good lass, and 'twill
be for a little while, for last night again I found Hamnet—ay,
ay, he hath all things in readiness now—all in readiness."
And then she uttered a slight cry, or moan rather.   "Grandmother, grandmother, why do you not keep the parson away
from me?—you said that you would."

"Hush, hush, child," the grandmother said, bending over
her and speaking softly and closely.   "You are overconcern-
ed about the poor lass that was treated so ill.   Take heart now;
I tell thee all is going well with her; her father hath taken
her home again; and she is as happy as the day is long.   Nay,

I swear to thee, good wench, if thou lie still and restful, I will take thee to see her some of these days. Hush thee now, dearie; 'tis going right well with the lass now."

The doctor touched the arm of Judith's father; and they both withdrew.

"She knew you not," said he. "And the fewer people around her the better—they set her fancies wandering."

, They went down-stairs to where Quiney was awaiting them; and the sombre look on their faces told its own tale.

"She is in danger!" he said, quickly.

The doctor was busy with his own thoughts, but he glanced at the young man, and saw the burning anxiety of his eyes.

"The fever must run its course," said he, "and Judith hath had a brave constitution these many years that I fear not will make a good fight. 'Twas a sore pity that she was so distressed and stricken down in spirits, as I hear, ere the fever seized her."

Quiney turned to the window.

"Too late—too late!" said he. "And yet I spared not the nag."

"You have done all that man could do," her father said, going to him. "Nay, had I myself guessed that she was in such peril—but 'tis past recall now."

And then he took the young man by the hand, and grasped it firmly.

"Good lad," said he, "this that you did for us was a right noble act of kindness, and I trust in Heaven's mercy that Judith herself may live to thank you. As for me, my thanks to you are all too poor and worthless; I must be content to remain your debtor—and your friend."

CHAPTER XXXIV.

AN AWAKENING.

IT was going ill with her. Late one night, Quiney, who had kept hovering about the house, never able to sit patiently and watch the anxious coming and going within-doors, and never able to tear himself away but for a few hundred yards, wandered out into the clear star-lit darkness. His heart was full. They had told him the crisis was near at hand. And almost it seemed to him that it was already over. Judith was going away from them. And those stars overhead—he knew but little of their names; he understood but little of the vast immensities and deeps that lay between them; they were to him but as grains of light in a darkened floor; and far above that floor rose the wonderful shining city that he had heard of in the Book of Revelation. And already—so wild and unstrung were his fancies—he could see the foursquare walls of jasper, and the gates of pearl, and the wide white steps leading up to these; and who was that who went all alone—giving no backward thought to any she was leaving behind—up those shining steps, with a strange light on her forehead and on her trembling hands? He saw her slowly kneel at the gate; her head meekly bowed, her hands clasped. And when they opened it, and when she rose and made to enter, he could have cried aloud to her for one backward look, one backward thought, toward Stratford town and the friends of her childhood and her youth. Alas! there was no such thing. There was wonder on her face, as she turned to this side and to that, and she went hesitatingly; and when they took her hands to lead her forward, she regarded them, this side and that, pleased, and wondering, and silent; but there was never a thought of Stratford town. Could that be Judith that was going away from them so—she that all of them had known so dearly? And to leave her own friends without one word of farewell! Those others there—she went with them smiling and wondering, and looking in silence from one to the other; but she knew them not. Her friends were here—here—with breaking hearts because she had gone away and forgotten them, and vanished within those far-shining gates.

And then some sudden and sullen thought of the future would overtake him. The injunctions laid on him by Judith's father could not be expected to last forever. And if this were to be so; if the love and desire of his youth were to be stolen away from him; if her bright young life, that was so beautiful a thing to all who knew her, was to be extinguished, and leave instead but a blankness and an aching memory through the long years—then there might arrive a time for a settlement. The parson was still coming about the house, for the women-folk were comforted by his presence; but Judith's father regard-ed him darkly, and had scarce ever a word for him. As for Quiney, he moved away or left the house when the good man came near: it was safer so. But in the future—when one was freer to act—for those injunctions could not be expected to last forever—and what greater joy could then be secured than the one fierce stroke of justice and revenge? He did not reason out the matter much; it was a kind of flame in his heart when-ever he thought of it.

And in truth that catastrophe was nearly occurring now. He had been wandering vaguely along the highways, appealing to the calmness of the night, as it were, and the serenity of the star-lit heavens, for some quieting of his terrible fears; and then in his restlessness he walked back toward the cottage, anxious for further news, and yet scarcely daring to enter and ask. He saw the dull red light in the window, but could hear no sound. And would not his very footfall on the path dis-turb her? They all of them went about the house like ghosts. And were it not better that he should remain here, so that the stillness dwelling around the place should not be broken even by his breathing? So quiet the night was, and so soundless, he could have imagined that the wings of the angel of mercy were brooding over the little cottage, hushing it, as it were, and bringing rest and sleep to the sore-bewildered brain. He would not go near. These were the precious hours. And if peace had at last stolen into the sick-chamber, and closed the troubled eyelids, were it not better to remain away, lest even a whisper should break the charm?

Suddenly he saw the door of the cottage open, and in the dull light a dark figure appeared. He heard footsteps on the garden path. At first his heart felt like stone, and he could not move, for he thought it was some one coming to seek him with evil news; but presently, in the clear starlight, he knew who this was that was now approaching him. He lost his senses. All the black night went red.

"So, good parson," said he (but he clinched his fists together, so that he should not give way), "art thou satisfied with thy handiwork?"

There was more of menace in the tone than in the taunt. At all events, with some such phrase as, "Out of the way, tavern-brawler!" the parson raised his stick as if to defend himself. And then the next instant he was gripped firm, as in a vise; the stick was twisted from his grasp and whirled away far into the dark; and forthwith—for it all happened in a moment—five fingers had him by the back of the neck.

There was one second of indecision—what it meant to this young athlete, who had his eyes afire and his mind afire with thoughts of the ill that had been done to the one he loved the dearest, can well be imagined. But he flung his enemy from him, forward, into the night.

"Take thy dog's life, and welcome—coward and woman-striker!"

He waited; there was no answer. And then—all shaking from the terrible pressure he had put on himself, and still hungering and athirst to go back and settle the matter then and there—he turned and walked along the road, avoiding the cottage, and still with his heart aflame, and wondering whether he had done well to let the hour of vengeance go.

But that did not last long. What cared he for this man that any thought of him should occupy him at such a moment? All his anxieties were elsewhere—in that hushed small chamber, where the lamp of life was flickering low, and all awaiting, with fear and trembling, what the dawn might bring. And if she were to slip away so—escaping from them, as it were—without a word of recognition? It seemed so hard that the solitary figure going up those far, wide steps should have no thought for them she had left behind. As he saw her there, content was on her face, and a mild radiance, and wonder;

and her new companions were pleasant to her. She would go
away with them; she was content to be with them; she would
disappear amongst them, and leave no sign. And Sunday
morning after Sunday morning he would look in vain for
her coming through the church-yard, under the trees; and
there would be a vacant place in the pew; no matter who might
be there, one face would be wanting; and in the afternoon the
wide meadows would be empty. Look where he might, from
the foot-bridge over the river, from Bardon Hill, from the Weir
Brake, there would be no more chance of his descrying Judith
walking with Prudence—the two figures that he could make
out at any distance almost. And what a radiance there used
to be on her face!—not that mild wonder that he saw as she
passed away with her companions within the shining gates,
but a happy, audacious radiance, so that he could see she was
laughing long ere he came near her. That was Judith; that
was the Judith he had known, laughing, radiant, in summer
meadows, as it seemed to him, careless of the young men,
though her eyes would regard them, and always with her chief
secrets and mystifications for her friend Prudence. That was
Judith; not this poor worn sufferer, wandering through darkened ways, the frail lamp of her life going down and down, so
that they dared not speak in the room. And that message that
she had left for him with Prudence—was it a kind of farewell?
They were about the last words she had spoken ere her speech
lost all coherence and meaning—a farewell before she entered
into that dark and unknown realm. And there was a touch
of reproach in them, too: "Tell him he did me wrong to think
I had gone to meet the parson in the church-yard; 'twas but
a chance." The Judith of those former days was far too proud
to make any such explanation; but this poor stricken creature
seemed anxious to appease every one and make friends. And
was he to have no chance of begging her forgiveness for doing
her that wrong, and of telling how little she need regard it, and
how that she might dismiss the parson from her mind altogether, as he had done? The ride to London: she knew nothing of that; she knew nothing of her father having come
all the way to see her. Why, as they came riding along, by
Uxbridge, and Wycombe, and Woodstock, and Enstone, many
a time he looked forward to telling Judith of what he had

done; and he hoped that she would go round to the stable, and have a word for the Galloway nag, and pat the good beast's neck. But all that was over now, and only this terrible darkness and the silence of the roads and the trees; and always the dull, steady, ominous light in the small window. And still more terrible that vision overhead—the far and mystic city, and Judith entering with those new and strange companions, regarding this one and that, and ever with a smile on her face and a mild wonder in her eyes, they leading her away by the hand, and she timid, and looking from one to the other, but pleased to go with them into the strange country. And as for her old friends, no backward look or backward thought for them: for them only the sad and empty town, the voiceless meadows, the vacant space in the pew, to which many an eye would be turned as week by week came round. And there would be a grave somewhere, that Prudence would not leave untended.

But with the first gray light of the dawn there came a sudden trembling joy, that was so easily and eagerly translated into a wild audacious hope. Judith had fallen into a sound sleep—a sleep hushed and profound, and no longer tortured with moanings and dull low cries as if for pity. A slumber profound and beneficent, with calmer breathing and a calmer pulse. If only on the awakening she might show that the crisis was over, and she started on the road—however tedious that might be—toward the winning back of life and health!

It was Prudence who brought him the news. She looked like a ghost in the wan light, as she opened the door and came forth. She knew he would not be far away; indeed, his eyes were more accustomed to this strange light than hers, and ere she had time to look about and search for him he was there. And when she told him this news, he could not speak for a little while; for his mind rushed forward blindly and wildly to a happy consummation; he would have no misgivings; this welcome sleep was a sure sign Judith was won back to them; not yet was she to go away all alone up those wide, sad steps.

"And you, Prudence," said he, or rather he whispered it eagerly, that no sound should disturb the profound quiet of the house, "now you must go and lie down—you are worn out. Why, you are all trembling."

"The morning air is a little cold," said she; but it was not that that caused her trembling.

"You must go and lie down and get some sleep too," said he (but glancing up at the window, as if all his thoughts were there). "What a patient watcher you have been! And now, when there is this chance, do, dear Prudence, go within and lie down for a while—"

"Oh, how could I?—how could I?" she said; and unknown to herself she was wringing her hands—not from grief, but from mere excitement and nervousness. "But for this sleep, now, the doctor was fearing the worst. I know it, though he would not say it. And she is so weak! Even if this sleep calm her brain, or if she come out of it in her right mind, one never knows: she is so worn away, she might waken only to slip away from us."

But he would not hear of that. No, no; this happy slumber was but the beginning of her recovery. Now that she was on the turn, Judith's brave constitution would fight through the rest. He knew it; he was sure of it; had there ever been a healthier or happier wench, or one with such gallant spirits and cheerfulness?

"You have not seen her these last two days," Prudence said, sadly.

"Nay, I fear not now; I know she will fight through," said he, confidently (even with an excess of confidence, so as to cheer this patient and gentle nurse). "And what a spite it is I can do nothing? Did you ask the doctor, Prudence? Is there nothing that I can fetch him from Warwick?—ay, or from London, for that matter? 'Tis well for you that can do so much for your friend; what can I do but wait about the lanes? I would take a message anywhere, for any of you, if you would but tell me; 'tis all that I can do. But when she is getting better, that will be different—that will be all different then; I shall be able to get her many things to please her and amuse her, and—and—think of this, Prudence," said he, his fancies running away with him in his eagerness "Do you not think, now, that when she is well enough to be carried into the garden—do you not think that Pleydell and I could devise some kind of couch—to be put on wheels, see you, and slung on leather bands, so that it would go easily? Why, I

swear it could be made, and might be in readiness for her.
What think you, Prudence? No one could object if we prepared it—ay, and we should get it to go as smooth as velvet,
so that she could be taken along the lanes or through the
meadows."

"I would there were need of it," Prudence said, wistfully.
"You go too fast. Nay, but if she come well out of this deep
sleep, who knows? Pray Heaven there be need for all that
you can do for her!"

The chirping of a small bird close by startled them—it was
the first sound of the coming day.

And then she said, regarding him:

"Would you like to see Judith for a moment? 'Twould
not disturb her."

He stepped back, with a sudden look of dismay on his face.

"What mean you, Prudence?" he said, quickly. "You do
not think—that—there is fear?—that I should look at her now?"

"Nay, not so; I trust not," she said, simply. "But if you
wished, you might slip up the stair—'twould do no harm."

He stooped and took off his shoes and threw them aside;
then she led the way into the house, and they went stealthily
up the short wooden stair. The door was open an inch or two;
Prudence opened it still further, but did not go into the room.
Nor did he; he remained at the threshold; for Judith's mother,
who was sitting by the bedside, and who had noticed the slight
opening of the door, had raised her hand quietly, as if in
warning. And was this Judith, then, that the cold morning
light, entering by the small casement, showed him—worn and
wasted, the natural radiance of her face all fled, and in place
of that a dull hectic tone that in no wise concealed the ravages
the fever had made? But she slept sound. The bent arm,
that she had raised to her head ere she fell asleep, lay absolutely still. No, it was not the Judith he had known—so gay
and radiant and laughing in the summer meadows; but the
wasted form still held a precious life; and he had no mistrust
—he would not doubt; there was there still what would win
back for him the Judith that he had known—ay, if they had
to wait all through the winter for the first silver-white days
of spring.

They stole down-stairs again, and went to the front door.

All the world was awaking now; the light was clear around them; the small birds were twittering in the bushes.

"And will you not go and get some sleep now, Prudence?" said he. "Surely you have earned it; and now there is the chance."

"I could not," she said, simply. "There will be time for sleep by-and-by. But now, if you would do us a service, will you go over to the town and tell Susan that Judith is sleeping peacefully, and that she need not hurry back, for there be plenty of us to watch and wait? And Julius would like to hear the good news—that I know. Then you yourself—do you not need rest?—why—"

"Heed not for me, dear Prudence," said he, quickly, as if it were not worth while wasting time on that topic. "But is there naught else I can do for you? Naught that I can bring for you—against her getting well again?"

"Nay, 'tis all too soon for that," was Prudence's answer. "I would the occasion were here, and sure."

Well, he went away over to the town, and told his tale to those that were astir, leaving a message for those who were not; and then he passed on to his own house, and threw himself on his bed. But he could not rest. It was too far away, while all his thoughts were concentrated on the small cottage over there. So he wandered back thither; and again had assurance that Judith was doing well; and then he went quietly up to the summer-house, and sat down there; and scarcely had he folded his arms on the little table and bent forward his head than he was in a deep sleep—nature claiming her due at last.

The hours passed; he knew nothing of them. He was awakened by Judith's father; and he looked round him strangely, for he saw by the light that it was now afternoon.

"Good lad," said he, "I make no scruple of rousing you. There is better news. She is awake, and quite calm and peaceable, and in her right mind—though sadly weak and listless, poor wench."

"Have you seen her—have you spoken with her?" he said, eagerly.

"Nay, not yet," Judith's father said. "I am doubtful. She is so faint and weak. I would not disturb her."

"I pray you, sir, go and speak with her," Quiney entreated.

"Nay, I know what will give her more peace of mind than anything. And if she begin to recall what happened ere she fell ill— I pray you, sir, of your kindness go and speak with her."

Judith's father went away to the house slowly, and with his head bent in meditation. He spoke to the doctor for a few minutes. But when, after some deliberation, he went upstairs, and into the room, it was his own advice, his own plan, he was acting on.

He went forward to the bedside, and took the chair that the old grandmother had instantly vacated, and sat down just as if nothing had occurred.

"Well, lass, how goes it with thee?" he said, with an air of easy unconcern. "Bravely well, I hear. Thou must haste thee now, for soon we shall be busy with the brewing."

She regarded him in a strange way—perhaps wondering whether this was another vision. And then she said, faintly:

"Why are you come back to Stratford, father?"

"Oh, I have many affairs on hand," said he; "and yet I like not the garden to be so empty. I can not spare thee over here much longer. 'Tis better when thou art in the garden, and little Bess with thee—nay, I swear to thee thou disturbest me not—and so must thou get quickly well and home again."

He took her hand—the thin, worn, white hand—and patted it.

"Why," said he, "I hear they told thee some foolish story about me. Believe them not, lass. Thou and I are old friends, despite thy saucy ways, and thy laughing at the young lads about, and thy lecturing of little Bess Hall—oh, thou hast thy faults, a many of them too; but heed no idle stories, good lass, that come between me and thee. Nay, I will have a sharp word for thee an thou do not as the doctor bids; and thou must rest thee still and quiet, and trouble not thy head, for we want thee back to us at New Place. Why, I tell thee I can not have the garden left so empty: wouldst have me with none to talk with but goodman Matthew? So now farewell for the moment, good wench; get what sleep thou canst, and take what the doctor bids thee; why, knowst thou not of the ribbons and gloves I have brought thee all the way from London?—I warrant me they will please thee."

He patted her hand again, and rose and left—as if it were all a matter of course. For a minute or two after, the girl looked dazed and bewildered, as if she were trying to recall many things; but always she kept looking at the hand that he had held, and there was a pleased light in her sad and tired eyes. She lay still and silent, for so she had been enjoined.

But by-and-by she said, in a way that was like the ghost of Judith's voice of old:

"Grandmother, I can scarce hold up my hand—will you help me? What is this that is on my head?"

"Why, 'tis a pretty lace cap that Susan brought thee," the grandmother said, "and we would have thee smart and neat ere thy father came in."

But she had got her hand to her head now, and then the truth became known to her. She began to cry bitterly.

"Oh, grandmother, grandmother," she said, or sobbed, "they have cut off my hair, and my father will never look with favor on me again. 'Twas all he ever praised."

"Dearie, dearie, thy hair will grow again as fair as ever—ay, and who ever had prettier?" the old grandmother said. "Why, surely; and the roses will come to thy cheeks too, that were ever the brightest of any in the town. Thy father?—heardst thou not what he said a moment ago—that he could not bear to be without thee? Nay, nay, fret not, good lass; there be plenty that will right gladly wait for the growing of thy hair again—ay, ay, there be plenty and to spare that will hold thee in high favor, and think well of thee, and thy father most of all of them—have no fear."

And so the grandmother got her soothed and hushed, and at last she lay still and silent. But she had been thinking.

"Grandmother," said she, regarding her thin wasted hand, "is my face like that?"

"Hush thee, child; thou must not speak more now, or the doctor will be scolding me."

"But tell me, grandmother," she pleaded.

"Why, then," she answered, evasively, "it be none so plump as it were; but all that will mend—ay, ay, good lass, 'twill mend surely."

Again she lay silent for a while; but her mind was busy with its own fears.

"Grandmother," she said, "will you promise me this—to

keep Quiney away? You will not let him come into the room, good grandmother, should he ever come over to the cottage?"

"Ay, and be this thy thanks, then, to him that rode all the way to London town to bring thy father to thee?" said the old dame, with some affectation of reproach. "Were I at thy age, I would have a fairer message for him."

"A message, grandmother?" the girl said, turning her languid eyes to her with some faint eagerness. "Ay, that I would send him willingly. He went to London for me, that I know; Prudence said so. But perchance he would not care to have it, would he, think you?"

The old dame listened, to make sure that the doctor was not within hearing—for this talking was forbidden; but she was anxious to have the girl's mind pleased and at rest; and so she took Judith's hand and whispered to her:

"A message? Ay, I warrant me the lad would think more of it than of aught else in the world. Why, sweetheart, he hath been never away from the house all this time—watching to be of service to any one—night and day it hath been so; and that he be not done to death passes my understanding. Ay, and the riding to London, and the bringing of thy father, and all—is't not worth a word of thanks? Nay, the youth hath won to my favor, I declare to thee; if none else will speak for him, I will; a right good honest youth, I warrant. But there now, sweeting, hush thee; I may not speak more to thee, else the doctor will be for driving me forth."

There was silence for some time; then Judith said, wistfully,

"What flowers are in the garden now, grandmother?"

The old dame went to the window—slowly—it was an excuse for not having too much talking going on.

"The garden be far past its best now," said she; "but there be marigolds, and Michaelmas daisies—"

"Could you get me a bit of rosemary, grandmother?" the girl asked.

"Rosemary!" she cried in affright—for the mention of the plant seemed to strike a funeral note. "Foolish wench, thou knowst I can never get the rosemary bushes through the spring frosts. Rosemary, truly! What wantest thou with rosemary?"

"Or a pansy, then?"

"A pansy, doubtless—ay, ay, that be better, now—we may find thee a pansy somewhere, and plenty of other things, so thou lie still and get well."

"Nay, I want but the one, grandmother," she said, slowly. "You know I can not write a message to him; and yet I would send him some token of thanks for all that he hath done. And would not that do, grandmother?—could you but find me a pansy, if there be one left anywhere, and a small leaf or two; and if 'twere put in a folded paper, and you could give it him from me, and no one knowing? I would rest the happier, grandmother, for I would not have him think me ungrateful—no, no, he must not think me that. And then, good grandmother, you will tell him that I wish him not to see me; only—only, the little flower will show him that I am not ungrateful; for I would not have him think me that."

"Rest you still now, then, sweeting," the old dame said. "I warrant me we will have the message conveyed to him; but rest you still, rest you still, and ere long you will not be ashamed to show him the roses coming again into your cheeks."

CHAPTER XXXV.

TOWARD THE LIGHT.

THIS fresh and clear morning, with a south wind blowing, and a blue sky overhead, made even the back yard of Quiney's premises look cheerful, though the surroundings were mostly empty barrels and boxes. And he was singing, too, as he went on with his task; sometimes,

> "*Play on, minstrèl, play on, minstrèl,*
> *My lady is mine only girl,*"

and sometimes,

> "*I bought thee petticoats of the best,*
> *The cloth so fine as fine might be;*
> *I gave thee jewels for thy chest,*
> *And all this cost I spent on thee,*"

or again, he would practice his part in the new catch:

> "*Merrily sang—the Ely monks—*
> *When rowed thereby—*CANUTE THE KING!"

And yet this that he was so busy about seemed to have nothing to do with his own proper trade. He had chalked up on the wall a space about the size of an ordinary cottage window; at each of the upper corners he had hammered in a nail; and now he was endeavoring to suspend from these supports, so that it should hang parallel with the bottom line, an oblong basket roughly made of wire, and pretty obviously of his own construction. His dinner—of bread and cheese and ale—stood untouched and unheeded on a bench hard by. Sometimes he whistled, sometimes he sang; for the morning air was fresh and pleasant, and the sunlight all about was enlivening.

Presently Judith's father made his appearance, and the twisting and shaping of the wire hooks instantly ceased.

"She is still going on well?" the lad said, with a rapid and anxious glance.

"But slowly — slowly," her father answered. "Nay, we must not demand too much. If she but hold her own now, time is on our side, and the doctor is more than ever hopeful that the fever hath left no serious harm behind it. When that she is a little stronger, they talk of having her carried downstairs—the room is larger, and the window hath a pleasant outlook."

"I heard of that," said Quiney, glancing at the oblong basket of wire.

"I have brought you other news this morning," Judith's father said, taking out a letter and handing it to Quiney. "But I pray you say nothing of it to the wench; her mind is at rest now; we will let the past go."

"Nay, I can do no harm in that way," said the younger man, in something of a hurt tone, "for they will not let me see her."

"No, truly? Why, that is strange, now," her father said, affecting to be surprised, but having a shrewd guess that this was some fancy of the girl's own. "But they would have her kept quiet, I know."

Quiney was now reading the letter. It was from one of Judith's father's companions in London, and the beginning of it was devoted to the imparting of certain information that had apparently been asked from him touching negotiations for the purchase of a house in Blackfriars. Quiney rightly judged that this part had naught to do with him, and scanned it briefly, and as he went on he came to that which had a closer interest for him.

The writer's style was ornate and cumbrous and confused, but his story in plainer terms was this: The matter of the purloined play was now all satisfactorily ascertained and settled, except as regarded Jack Orridge himself, whom a dire mischance had befallen. It appeared that having married a lady possessed of considerable wealth, his first step was to ransom —at what cost the writer knew not—the play that had been sold to the booksellers, not by himself, but by one Francis Lloyd. It was said that this Lloyd had received but a trifle for it, and had, in truth, parted with it in the course of a drunken frolic; but that Gentleman Jack, as they called him, had to disburse a goodly sum ere he could get the manuscript back into his own hands. That forthwith he had come to the theatre, and delivered up the play, with such expressions of penitence and shame that they could not forbear to give him full quittance for his fault. But that this was not all; for, having heard that Francis Lloyd had in many quarters been making a jest of the matter, and telling of Orridge's adventures in Warwickshire, and naming names, the young man had determined to visit him with personal chastisement, but had been defeated in this by Lloyd being thrust into prison for debt. That thereafter Lloyd, being liberated from jail, was sitting in a tavern with certain companions, and there "Gentleman Jack" found him, and dealt him a blow on the face with the back of his hand, with a mind to force the duello upon him. But that here again Orridge had ill fortune, for Lloyd, being in his cups, would fight then and there, and flung himself on him, without a sword or anything, as they thought; but that presently, in a struggle, Orridge uttered a cry, "I am stabbed!" and fell headlong, and they found him with a dagger wound in his side, bleeding so that they thought he would have died ere help came. And that, in truth, he had been nigh within death's door, and was not yet out of the leech's hands; while, as for Lloyd, he had succeeded in making good his escape, and was now in Flanders, as some reported. This was the gist of the story, as far as Quiney was interested; thereafter came chiefly details about the theatre; and the writer concluded with

wishing his correspondent all health and happiness, and bidding him remember "his true loving friend, Henry Condell."

Quiney handed back the letter.

"I wish the dagger had struck the worser villain of the
two," said he.

"'Tis no concern of ours," Judith's father said. "And I
would have the wench hear never a word more of the matter.
Nay, I have already answered her that 'twas all well and settled in London, and no harm done; and the sooner 'tis quite
forgotten the better. The young man hath made what amends
he could; I trust he may soon be well of his wound again.
And married, is he?—perchance his hurt may teach him to be
more of a stay-at-home."

Judith's father put the letter in his pocket, and was for leaving, when Quiney suggested that if he were going to the cottage, he would accompany him, as some business called him
to Bidford. And so they set out together—the younger man
having first of all made a bundle of the wire basket, and the
nails and hooks and what not, so that he could the more easily
carry them.

It was a clear and mild October day; the wide country very
silent; the woods turning to yellow and russet now, and here
and there golden leaves fluttering down from the elms. So
quiet and peaceful it all was in the gracious sunlight; the
steady ploughing going on; groups of people gleaning in the
bean fields; but not a sound of any kind reaching them, save
the cawing of some distant rooks. And when they drew near
to Shottery, Quiney had an eye for the cottage gardens, to see
what flowers or shrubs were still available; for of course the
long wire basket, when it was hung outside Judith's window,
must be filled—ay, and filled freshly at frequent intervals. If
the gardens or the fields or the hedge-rows would furnish sufficient store, there would be no lack of willing hands for the
gathering.

They went first to the front door (the room that Judith was
to be moved into looked to the back); and here, ere they had
crossed the threshold, they beheld a strange thing. The old
grandmother was standing at the foot of the wooden stair, with
a small looking-glass in her hand. She had not heard them
approach; so it was with some amazement they saw her de-

liberately let fall the glass on to the stone passage, where naturally it was smashed into a hundred fragments. And forthwith she began to scold and rate the little Cicely; and that in so loud a voice that her anger must have been heard in the sick-room above.

"Ah, thou mischief, thou imp, thou idle brat, that must needs go break the only looking-glass in the house! A handy wench, truly, that can hold nothing with thy silly fingers, but must break cup, and platter, and pane; and now the looking-glass—'twere well done to box thine ears, thou mischief!"

And with that she patted the little girl on the shoulder, and shrewdly winked, and smiled, and nodded her head; and then she went up the stair, and again loudly bewailing her misfortune.

"What a spite be this, now!" they could hear her say, at the door of Judith's room. "The only looking-glass in the house—and just as thou wouldst have it sent for! That mischievous idle little wench—heard you the crash, sweetheart? Well, well, no matter; I must still have the tiring of thee—against any one coming to see thee; ay, and I would have thee brave and smart, when thou art able to sit up a bit; ay, and thy hair will soon be growing again, sweeting. And then the trinkets that thy father brought, and the lace cuffs that Quiney gave thee—these and all thou must wear. Was ever such a spite, now?—our only looking-glass to be broken so; but thou shalt not want it, sweetheart—nay, nay, thou must rest in my hands. I will have thee smart enough; when any would come to see thee—"

That was all they heard—for now she shut the door; but both of them guessed readily enough why the good dame had thrown down and smashed the solitary mirror of the house.

Then they went within, and heard from Prudence that Judith was going on well, but very slowly; and that her mind was in perfect calm and content, only that at times she seemed anxious that her father should return to London, lest his affairs should be hindered.

"And truly I must go ere long," said he; "but not yet. Not until she is more fairly on the highway."

. They were now in the room that was to be given up to Judith, because of its larger size.

"Prudence," said Quiney, "if the bed were placed so—by
the window—she might be propped up so that when she chose
she could look abroad. Were not that a simple thing, and
cheerful for her? And I have arranged a small matter so
that every morning she may find some fresh blossoms awaiting her, and yet not disturbing her with any one wishing to
enter the room. Methinks one might better fix it now, ere she
be brought down, so that the knocking may not harm her."

"I would she were in a fit state to be brought down," Prudence said, rather sadly. "For never saw I any one so weak
and helpless."

All the same, he went away to see whether the oblong basket
of wire and the fastenings would fit; and although (being a
tall youth) he could easily reach the foot of the window with
his hands, he had to take a chair with him in order to gain
the proper height for the nails. Prudence from within saw
what he was after; and when it was all fixed up, she opened
one of the casements to speak to him, and her face was well
pleased.

"Truly, now, that was kindly thought of," said she. "And
shall I tell her of this that you have contrived for her?"

"Why, 'tis in this way, Prudence," said he, rather shamefacedly: "she need not know whether 'tis this one or that that
puts a few blossoms in the basket; 'twill do for any one—any
one that is passing along the road or through the meadows,
and picks up a pretty thing here or there. 'Twill soon be hard
to get such things, save some red berries or the like; but when
any can stop in passing and add their mite, 'twill be all the
easier, for who that knows her but hath good-will toward her?"

"And her thanks to whom?" said Prudence, smiling.

"Why, to all of them," said he, evasively. "Nay, I would
not have her even know that I nailed up the little basket—
perchance she might think I was too officious."

"And can you undo it?" she asked. "Can you take it down?"

"Surely," he answered; and he lifted the basket off the
hooks to show her.

"For," said she, "if you would bring it round, might we not
put a few flowers in it, and have them carried up to Judith, to
show her what you have designed for her? In truth it would
please her."

"'AND HER THANKS TO WHOM?' SAID PRUDENCE, SMILING."

He was not proof against this temptation. He carried the basket round; and they fell to gathering such blossoms as the garden afforded—marigolds, monthly roses, Michaelmas daisies, and the like—with some scarlet hips from the neighboring hedges, and some broad green leaves to serve as a cushion for all of these. But he did not stay to hear how his present was received. He was on his way to Bidford, and on foot, for he had kept his promise with the Galloway nag. So he bade Prudence farewell, and said he would call in again on his way back in the evening.

The wan, sad face lit up with something like pleasure when Judith saw this little present brought before her; it was not the first by many of similar small attentions that he had paid her—tokens of a continual thoughtfulness and affection—though he was not even permitted to see her, much less to speak with her. How his business managed to thrive during this period they could hardly guess; only that he seemed to find time for everything. Apparently he was content with the most hap-hazard meals, and seemed able to get along with scarcely any sleep at all; and always he was the most hopeful one in the house, and would not admit that Judith's recovery seemed strangely slow, but regarded everything as happening for the best, and tending toward a certain and happy issue. One result of his being continually in or about the cottage was this—that Master Walter Blaise had not looked near them since the night on which the fever reached its crisis. The women-folk surmised that, now there was a fair hope of Judith's recovery, he perchance imagined his ministrations to be no longer necessary, and was considerately keeping out of the way, seeing that he could be of no use. At all events, they did not discuss the subject much; for more than one of them had perceived that, whenever the parson's name was mentioned, Judith's father became reticent and reserved—which was about his only way of showing displeasure—so that they got into the habit of omitting all mention of Master Blaise, for the better preserving and maintaining the serenity of the domestic atmosphere.

And yet Master Blaise came to be talked of—and to Judith herself—this very morning. When Prudence went into the room, carrying Quiney's flowers, the old grandmother said she

would go down and see how dinner was getting forward (she
having more mouths to feed than usual), and Prudence was
left in her place, with strict injunctions to see that Judith took
the small portions of food that had been ordered her at the
proper time.   Prudence sat down by the bedside.   These two
had not had much confidential chatting of late, for Judith had
been forbidden to talk much, and was far too weak and languid
for that, while generally there was some third person about in
attendance.   But now they were alone, and Prudence had
a long tale to tell of Quiney's constant watchfulness and care,
and all of the little things he had thought of and arranged
for her, up to the construction of the wire flower-basket.

"But what he hath done, Judith, to anger Parson Blaise I
can not make out," she continued; "ay, and to anger him
sorely; for yesternight, when I went over to see how my brother did, I met Master Blaise, and he stayed me and talked
with me for a space.   Nay, he spoke too harshly of Quiney, so
that I had to defend him, and say what I had seen of him—
truly, I was coming near to speaking with warmth—and then
he went away from that.   And think you what he came to
next, Judith?"

The pale quiet face of the speaker was overspread with a
blush, and she looked timidly at her friend.

"What, then, sweetheart?"

"Perchance I should not tell you," she said, with some hesitation, and then she said, more frankly: "nay, why should
there be any concealment between us, Judith?   And he laid
no charge of secrecy on me—in truth, I said that I would think
of it, and might even have to ask for counsel and guidance.
He would have me be his wife, Judith."

Judith betrayed no atom of surprise; nay, she almost instantly smiled her approval—it was a kind of friendly congrat-
ulation, as it were—and she would have reached out her hand
only that she was so weak.

"I am glad of that, dear mouse," said she, as pleasantly as
she could.   "There would you be in your proper place—is't
not so?   And what said you?—what said you, sweetheart?
Ah, they all would welcome you, be sure; and a parson's wife
—a parson's wife, Prudence—would not that be your proper
place? would you not be happy so?"

"I know not," the girl said, and she spoke wistfully, and as if she were regarding distant things. "He had nearly persuaded me, good heart, for indeed there is such power and clearness in all he says; and it was almost put before me as a duty, and something incumbent on me, for the pleasing of all of them, and the being useful and serviceable to so many; and then—and then—"

There was another timid glance, and she took Judith's hand, and her eyes were downcast as she made the confession:

"Nay, I will tell thee the truth, sweetheart. Had he spoken to me earlier, I—I might not have said him nay—so good a man and earnest withal, and not fearing to give offense if he can do true service to the Master of us all: Judith, if it be unmaidenly, blame me not, but at one time I had thoughts of him; and sometimes, ashamed, I would not go to your house when that he was there in the afternoon, though Julius wondered, seeing that there was worship and profitable expounding. But now—now 'tis different."

"Why, dear mouse, why?" Judith said, with some astonishment. "You must not flout the good man. 'Tis an honorable offer."

Prudence was looking back on that past time.

"If he had spoken then," said she, absently, "my heart would have rejoiced; and well I knew 'twould have been no harm to you, dear Judith, for who could doubt how you were inclined—ay, through all your quarrels and misunderstandings? And if 'twas you the good parson wished for in those days—"

"Prudence," her friend said, reproachfully, "you do ill to go back over a by-gone story. If you had thoughts of him then, when as yet he had not spoken, why not now, when he would have you be his wife? 'Tis an honorable offer, as I say; and you—were you not meant for a parson's wife, sweetheart?"

Then Prudence regarded her with her honest eyes.

"I should be afraid, Judith. Perchance I have listened overmuch to your grandmother's talking, and to Quincy's; they are both of them angered against him. They say he wrought you ill, and was cruel when he should have been gentle with you, and was overproud of his office. Nay, I marked that your father had scarce ever a word for him when

16

he was coming over to the cottage, but would get away somehow and leave him.   And—and methinks I should be afraid,
Judith; 'tis no longer as it used to be in former days; and
then—without perfect confidence—how should one dare to venture on such a step?   No, no, Judith—I should be afraid."

"In truth I can not advise thee, then, dear heart," her friend
said, looking at her curiously.   "For more than any I know
should you marry one that would be gentle with you, and kind.
And think you that the parson would overlord it?"

"I know not—I know not," she said, in the same absent way.
"But with doubt, with hesitation, without perfect confidence,
how could one take such a step?"

And then she bethought her.

"Why, now, all this talking over my poor affairs!" she
said, more cheerfully.   "A goodly nurse I am proving myself!   'Tis thy affairs are of greater moment; and thou must
push forward, sweetheart, and get well more rapidly, else they
will say we are careless and foolish that can not bring thee
into firmer health."

"But I am well content," said Judith, with a perfectly placid
smile.

"Content?   But you must not be content!" Prudence exclaimed.   "Would you remain within-doors until your hair
be grown?   Vanity is it, then?   Ah, for shame—you that always professed to be so proud, and careless of what they
thought!   Content, truly!   Look at so thin a hand—are you
content to remain so?"

"I am none so ill," Judith said, pleasantly.   "The days pass
well enough; and every one is kind."

"But I say you must not be content," Prudence again remonstrated.   "Did ever any one see such a poor, weak, white
hand as that?   Look at the thin, thin veins!"

"Ah, but you know not, sweetheart," Judith said, and she
herself looked at those thin blue veins in the white hand.
"They seem to me to be running full of music and happiness
ever since I came out of the fever, and found my father talking
to me in the old way."

CHAPTER XXXVI.

"WESTERN WIND, WHEN WILL YOU BLOW?"

THERE was much laughing among the good folk of Stratford town—or rather among those of them allowed to visit
Quiney's back yard—over the nondescript vehicle that he and
his friend Pleydell were constructing there. But that was
chiefly at the first, when the neighbors would call it a coffin
on wheels, or a grown-up cradle; afterward, when it grew into
shape, and began to exhibit traces of decoration (the little canopy at the head, for example, was covered over with blue taffeta, that made a shelter from the sun), they moderated their
ridicule, and at last declared it a most ingenious and useful
contrivance, and one that went as easily on its leather bands
as any king's coach that ever was built. And they said they
hoped it would do good service; for they knew it was meant
for Judith; and she had won the favor and good-will of many
in that town—in so far as an unmarried young woman was
deemed worthy of consideration.

But that was an anxious morning when Quiney set forth
with this strange vehicle for the cottage. Little Willie Hart
was there, and Quiney had flung him inside, saying he would
give him a ride as far as Shottery; but thereafter he did not
speak a word to the boy. For this was the morning on which
he was to see Judith for the first time since the fever had left
her; and not only that, but he had been appointed to carry
her down-stairs to the larger room below. This was by the
direct instructions of the doctor. Judith's father was now in
London again; the doctor was not a very powerful man; the
staircase was overnarrow to let two of the women try it between them: who, therefore, was there but this young athlete
to gather up that precious charge and bear her gently forth?
But when he thought of that first meeting with Judith he trembled, and dismay and apprehension filled his heart lest he
should show himself in the smallest way shocked by her appearance. Careless as she might have been of other things,

she had always put a value on that; she knew that she had good looks, and she liked to look pretty and dainty, and to wear becoming and pretty things. And again and again he schooled himself and argued with himself. He must be prepared to find her changed—nay, had he not already had one glimpse of her, as she lay asleep, in the cold light of the dawn? He must be prepared to find the happy and radiant face no longer that, but all faded and white and worn; the clear-shining eyes no longer laughing, but sunken and sad; and the beautiful sun-brown hair—that was her chiefest pride of all— no longer clustering round her neck. Not that he himself cared: Judith was for him always and ever Judith, whatever she might be like; but his terror was lest he should betray, in the smallest fashion, some pained surprise. He knew how sensitive she was; and as an invalid she would be even more so; and what a fine thing it would be if her eyes were suddenly to fill with tears on witnessing his disappointment? And so he argued and argued, and strove to think of Judith as a ghost—as anything rather than her former self; and when he reached the cottage he asked whether Judith was ready to be brought down in so matter-of-fact a way that he seemed perfectly unconcerned.

Well, she was not ready, for her grandmother had the tiring of her; and the old dame was determined that, if she had her way, her grandchild should look none too like an invalid. If the sun-brown curls were gone, at least the cap that she wore should have pretty blue ribbons where it met under the chin. And she would have her wear the lace cuffs, too, that Quiney had brought her from Warwick: did not she owe it to him to do service for the gift? And when all that was done, she made Judith take a little wine and water—to strengthen her for the being carried down-stairs—and then she sent word that Quiney might come up.

He made his appearance forthwith—a little pale, perhaps, and hesitating and apprehensive as he crossed the threshold. And then he came quickly forward, and there was a sudden wonder of joy and gladness in his eyes.

"Judith!" he exclaimed, quite involuntarily, and forgetting everything, "why, how well you are looking! indeed, indeed you are! Sweetheart, you are not changed at all!"

For this was Judith: not any of the spectral phantoms he had been conjuring up, but Judith herself, regarding him with friendly (if yet timid) eyes; and her face, as he looked at her in this glad way, was no longer pale, but had grown rose-red as the face of a bride. Her anxiety and nervousness had been far greater than she dared to tell any of them; but now his surprise and delight were surely real; and then—for she was very weak, and she had been anxious and full of fear, and this joy of seeing him, of seeing a strange face that belonged to the former happy time, was too much for her. Her lips were tremulous; tears rose to her eyes, and she would have turned away to hide her crying, but that all at once he recalled his scattered senses, and inwardly cursed himself for a fool, and forthwith addressed her in the most cheerful and simple way:

"Why, now, what stories they have been telling me, Judith! I should scarce know you had been ill. You are thinner—oh yes, you are a little thinner; and if you went to the woods to gather nuts, I reckon you would not bring home a heavy bag; but that will all mend in time. In honest truth, dear Judith, I am glad to see you looking none so ill; now I marvel not at your father going away to see after his affairs—so sure he must have been."

"I am glad that he went, I was fretting so," she said (and it was so strange to hear Judith's voice—that always stirred his heart as if with the vibration of Susan's singing); and then she added, timidly regarding him—"And you—I have caused you much trouble also."

He laughed; in truth he was so bewildered with the delight of seeing this real living Judith before him that he scarce knew what he said.

"Trouble!—yes, trouble indeed, that I could do nothing for you, and all the others waiting with you and cheering you. But now, dear Judith, I have something for you—oh, you shall see it presently; and you may laugh, but I warrant me you will find it easy and comfortable when that you are allowed to go forth into the garden. 'Tis a kind of couch, as it were, but on wheels—nay, you may call it your chariot, Judith, if you would be in state; and if you may not go further than the garden at first, why, then you may lie in it, and have some one read to you; and there is a small curtain if you would shut

them all out and go to sleep; ay, and when the time comes for
you to go along the lanes, then you may sit up somewhat, for
there are pillows for your head, and for your back. As for the
drawing of it, why, little Willie Hart can pull me when I am
in it, and surely he can do the same for you, that are scarce
so heavy as I, as I take it. Oh, I warrant you, you will soon
get used to it; and 'twill be so much pleasanter for you than being always within-doors; and the fresher air—the fresher air
will soon bring back your color, Judith."

For now that the first flush of embarrassment was gone, he
could not but see (though still he talked in that cheerful strain)
how pale and worn was her face; and her hands, that lay listlessly on the coverlet, with the pretty lace cuffs going back
from the wrists, were spectral hands, so thin and white were
they.

"Master Quiney," said the old dame, coming to the door,
"it be all ready now below, if you can carry the wench down.
And take time—take time ; there be no hurry."

"You must come and help me, good grandmother," said
he, "to get her well into my arms."

In truth he was trembling with very nervousness as he set
about this task. Should some mischance occur ?—some stum-
ble?—and then he found himself all too strong and uncouth
and clumsy, with her so frail and delicate and weak. But her
grandmother lifted the girl's hand to his shoulder—or rather
to his neck—and bade her hold on so, as well as she might;
and then he got his arms better round her; and with slow and
careful steps made his way down to the room below. There
the bed was near the window, and when he had gently placed
her on it, and propped up her head and shoulders, so that she
was almost sitting, the first thing that she saw before her was
the slung box of flowers and leaves outside the little casement.
She turned to him, and smiled, and looked her thanks with
grateful eyes: he sought for no more than that.

Of course they were all greatly pleased at this new state of
affairs: it seemed a step on the forward way, a hopeful thing.
Moreover, there was a brighter animation in the girl's look—
whether that was owing to the excitement of the change or the
pleasure at seeing the face of an old friend. And as the others
seemed busy among themselves, suggesting small arrangements

and .the like, Quiney judged it was time for him to go: his services were no longer needed.

He went forward to her.

"Judith," said he, "I will bid you good-day now. If you but knew how glad I am to have seen you—ay, and to find you going on so well! I will take away a lighter heart with me."

' She looked up at him, hesitating and timid; and then she gathered courage.

"But why must you go?" said she—with some touch of color in the pale face.

He glanced at the others.

"Perchance they may not wish me to stay; they may fear your being tired with talking."

"But if I wish you to stay—for a little while?" she said, gently. "If your business call you not?"

· "My business!" he said. "My business must shift for itself on such a day as this. Think you 'tis nothing for me to speak with you again, Judith, after so long a time?"

"And my chariot," she said, brightly: "may not I see my chariot?"

· "Why, truly!" he cried. "Willie Hart is in charge of it without. We will bring it along the passage, and you will see it at the door: and you must not laugh, dear Judith—'tis a rude-made thing, I know, but serviceable; you shall have comfort from it, I warrant you."·

They wheeled it along the passage, but could not get it within the apartment; however, through the open door she could see very easily the meaning and construction of it. And when she observed with what care and pretty taste it had been adorned for her, even to the putting ribbons at the front corners of the little canopy (but this was not the work of men's fingers; it was Prudence who had contributed these), she was not in the least inclined to laugh at the efforts of these good friends to be of use to her and to gratify her. She beckoned him to come to her.

"'Tis but a patchwork thing to look at," said he, rather shamefacedly, "but I hope you will find it right comfortable when you use it. I hope soon to hear of you trying it, Judith."

"Give me your hand," said she.

She took his hand and kissed it.

"I can not speak my thanks to you," she said, in a low voice, "for not only this, but for all that you have done for me."

There were tears in her eyes; and he was so bewildered, and his heart so wildly aflame, that he could only touch her shoulder and say:

"Be still now, Judith. Be still and quiet; and perchance they may let me remain with you a little space further."

Well, it was a long and a weary waiting. She seemed too content with her feeble state; there were so many who were kind to her; and her father sending her messages from London; and Quiney coming every morning to put some little things—branches of evergreens, or the like, when flowers were no longer to be had—in the little basket outside the window. He could reach to that easily; and when she happened to hear his footsteps coming near, even when she could not see him, she would tap with her white fingers on the window-panes— that was her thanks to him, and morning greeting.

It was a bitter winter; and ever they were looking forward to the milder weather, to see when they might risk taking her out-of-doors, swathed up in her chariot, as she called it; but the weeks and weeks went by, hard and obdurate, and at last they found themselves in the new year. But she could get about the house a little now, in a quiet way; and so it was that, one morning, she and Quiney were together standing at the front window, looking abroad over the wide white landscape. Snow lay everywhere, thick and silent; the bushes were heavy with it; and far beyond those ghostly meadows— though they could not see it—they knew that the Avon was fixed and hard in its winter sleep, under the hanging banks of the Weir Brake.

"'Western wind, when will you blow?'" she said, and yet not sadly, for there was a placid look in her eyes: she was rather complaining, with a touch of the petulance of the Judith of old.

The arm of her lover was resting lightly on her shoulder—she was strong enough to bear that now, and did not resent the burden. And she had got her soft sunny-brown curls again, though still they were rather short; and her face had got back something of its beautiful curves; and her eyes, if they were not so cruelly audacious as of old, were yet clear-shining and gentle, and with abundance of kind messages for all the world, but with tenderer looks for only one.

"'Western wind,'" she repeated, with that not oversad complaint of injury, "'when will you blow—when will you blow ?'"

"All in good time, sweetheart, all in good time," said he; and his hand lay kindly on her shoulder, as if she were one to whom some measure of gentle tending and cheering words were somehow due. "And guess you now what they mean to do for you when the milder weather comes ?—I mean the lads at the school. Why, then, 'tis a secret league and compact —I doubt not that your cousin Willie may have been at the suggesting of it, but 'twas some of the bigger lads who came to me. And 'tis all arranged now, and all for the sake of you, dear heart. For when the milder weather comes, and the year begins to wake again, why, they are all of them to keep a sharp and an eager eye here and there—in the lanes or in the woods— for the early peeping up of the primroses. And then 'tis to be a grand whole holiday that I am to get for them, as it appears; and all the school is to go forth to search the hedgerows and the woods and the banks—all the country-side is to be searched and searched—and for what, think you ?—why, to bring you a spacious basketful of the very first primroses of the spring! See you, now, what it is to be the general favorite! —nay, I swear to you, dear Judith, you are the sweetheart of all of them; and what a shame it is that I must take you away from them all!"

THE END.

SOME POPULAR NOVELS

Published by HARPER & BROTHERS New York.

The Octavo Paper Novels in this list may be obtained in half-binding [leather backs and pasteboard sides], suitable for Public and Circulating Libraries, at 25 cents per volume, in addition to the prices named below. The 32mo Paper Novels may be obtained in Cloth, at 15 cents per volume in addition to the prices named below.

For a FULL LIST OF NOVELS published by HARPER & BROTHERS, see HARPER'S NEW AND REVISED CATALOGUE, which will be sent by mail, postage prepaid, to any address in the United States, on receipt of Ten cents.

			PRICE
BAKER'S (Rev. W. M.) Carter Quarterman. Illustrated		8vo, Paper $	60
Inside: a Chronicle of Secession. Illustrated		8vo, Paper	75
The New Timothy	12mo, Cloth, $1 50 ;	4to, Paper	25
The Virginians in Texas		8vo, Paper	75
BENEDICT'S (F. L.) John Worthington's Name.		8vo, Paper	75
Miss Dorothy's Charge		8vo, Paper	75
Miss Van Kortland.		8vo, Paper	60
Mr. Vaughan's Heir.		8vo, Paper	75
My Daughter Elinor.		8vo, Paper	80
St. Simon's Niece.		8vo, Paper	60
BLACK'S (W.) A Daughter of Heth.	12mo, Cloth, $1 25 ;	8vo, Paper	35
A Princess of Thule	12mo, Cloth, 1 25 ;	8vo, Paper	50
Green Pastures and Piccadilly.	12mo, Cloth, 1 25 ;	8vo, Paper	50
In Silk Attire.	12mo, Cloth, 1 25 ;	8vo, Paper	35
Kilmeny.	12mo, Cloth, 1 25 ;	8vo, Paper	35
Macleod of Dare. Illustrated.	12mo, Cloth, 1 25 ;	8vo, Paper	60
		4to, Paper	15
Madcap Violet.	12mo, Cloth, 1 25 ;	8vo, Paper	50
Shandon Bells. Illustrated.	12mo, Cloth, 1 25 ;	4to, Paper	20
Sunrise.	12mo, Cloth, 1 25 ;	4to, Paper	15
That Beautiful Wretch. Ill'd.	12mo, Cloth, 1 25 ;	4to, Paper	20
The Maid of Killeena, and Other Stories		8vo, Paper	40
The Monarch of Mincing-Lane. Illustrated		8vo, Paper	50
The Strange Adventures of a Phaeton. 12mo, Cloth, $1 25 ; 8vo, Pa.			50
Three Feathers. Illustrated		12mo, Cloth 1	25
White Wings. Illustrated	12mo, Cloth, $1 25 ;	4to, Paper	20
Yolande. Illustrated	12mo, Cloth, 1 25 ;	4to, Paper	20
BLACKMORE'S (R. D.) Alice Lorraine.		8vo, Paper	50
Christowell.		4to, Paper	20
Clara Vaughan.		4to, Paper	15
Cradock Nowell.		8vo, Paper	60
Cripps, the Carrier. Illustrated		8vo, Paper	50
Erema.		8vo, Paper	50
Lorna Doone.	12mo, Cloth, $1 00 ;	8vo, Paper	25
Mary Anerley.	16mo, Cloth, 1 00 ;	4to, Paper	15
The Maid of Sker.		8vo, Paper	50
Tommy Upmore...16mo, Paper, 35 cts. ; Cloth, 50 cts. ; 4to, Paper			20
BRADDON'S (Miss) An Open Verdict		8vo, Paper	35

PRIOR

BULWER'S Pausanias the Spartan. 12mo, Cloth, 75 cents; 8vo, Paper $ 25
Pelham...8vo, Paper 40
Rienzi...8vo, Paper 40
The Caxtons....................12mo, Cloth, $1 25;   8vo, Paper 50
The Coming Race.................12mo, Cloth, 1 00;   12mo, Paper 50
The Disowned ....8vo, Paper 50
The Last Days of Pompeii.......8vo, Paper, 25 ;   4to, Paper 15
The Last of the Barons.............................8vo, Paper 50
The Parisians. Illustrated.....12mo, Cloth, $1 50;   8vo, Paper 60
The Pilgrims of the Rhine.... ....8vo, Paper 20
What will He do with it ?............................8vo, Paper 75
Zanoni ....8vo, Paper 85
CRAIK'S (Miss G. M.) Dorcas...........................4to, Paper 15
Mildred..8vo, Paper 30
Anne Warwick ....8vo, Paper 25
Fortune's Marriage....................................4to, Paper 20
Hard to Bear......................................8vo, Paper 30
Sydney...4to, Paper 15
Sylvia's Choice.....................................8vo, Paper 30
Two Women..4to, Paper 15
COLLINS'S (Wilkie) Novels. Ill'd Library Edition. 12mo, Cloth, per vol. 1 25
. After Dark, and Other Stores.—Antonina.—Armadale.—Basil.—
Hide-and-Seek.—Man and Wife.—My Miscellanies.—No Name.
—Poor Miss Finch.—The Dead Secret.—The Law and the Lady.
—The Moonstone.—The New Magdalen.—The Queen of Hearts.
—The Two Destinies.—The Woman in White.
Antonina..8vo, Paper 40
Armadale. Illustrated ....8vo, Paper 60
Man and Wife.......................................4to, Paper 20
My Lady's Money....................................32mo, Paper 25
No Name. Illustrated..............................8vo, Paper 60
Percy and the Prophet..............................32mo, Paper 20
Poor Miss Finch. Illustrated......................8vo, Paper 60
The Law and the Lady. Illustrated.................8vo, Paper 50
The Moonstone. Illustrated........................8vo, Paper 60
The New Magdalen...................................8vo, Paper 30
The Two Destinies. Illustrated....................8vo, Paper 35
The Woman in White. Illustrated...................8vo, Paper 60
DICKENS'S (Charles) Works. Household Edition. Illustrated. 8vo.
Set of 16 vols., Cloth, in box............................... 22 00
The same in 8 vols., Cloth............................... 20 00

A Tale of Two Cities.	Paper $ 50	Dombey and Son	Paper 1 00
	Cloth 1 00		Cloth 1 50
Barnaby Rudge	Paper 1 00	Great Expectations	Paper 1 00
	Cloth 1 50		Cloth 1 50
Bleak House	Paper 1 00	Little Dorrit	Paper 1 00
··	Cloth 1 50		Cloth 1 50
Christmas Stories	Paper 1 00	Martin Chuzzlewit	Paper 1 00
	Cloth 1 50		Cloth 1 50
David Copperfield	Paper 1 00	Nicholas Nickleby	Paper 1 00
	Cloth 1 50		Cloth 1 50

PRICE

DICKENS'S (Charles) Works. Household Edition. Illustrated. 8vo.

Oliver Twist ....Paper $ 50	Pickwick Papers ....Paper $1 00	
Cloth 1 00	Cloth 1 50	
Our Mutual Friend...Paper 1 00	The Old Curiosity Shop......... 75	
Cloth 1 50	Cloth 1 25	
Pictures from Italy, Sketch-	Uncommercial Traveller, Hard	
es by Boz, Am. Notes. Pa. 1 00	Times, Edwin Drood...Paper 1 00	
Cloth 1 50	, Cloth 1 50	

Pickwick Papers...4to, Paper	20
The Mudfog Papers, &c...4to, Paper	10
Mystery of Edwin Drood. Illustrated.......................8vo, Paper	25
Hard Times...8vo, Paper	25
Mrs. Lirriper's Legacy ....8vo, Paper	10
DE MILLE'S A Castle in Spain. Ill'd. 8vo, Cloth, $1 00 ; 8vo, Paper	50
Cord and Creese. Illustrated ....8vo, Paper	60
The American Baron. Illustrated ....8vo, Paper	50
The Cryptogram. Illustrated.................... ....8vo, Paper	75
The Dodge Club. Illustrated....8vo, Paper, 60 cents ; 8vo, Cloth 1 10	
The Living Link. Illustrated....8vo, Paper, 60 cents ; 8vo, Cloth 1 10	
DISRAELI'S (Earl of Beaconsfield) Endymion ....4to, Paper	15
The Young Duke ....12mo, Cloth, $1 50; 4to, Paper	15
ELIOT'S (George) Novels. Library Edition. Ill'd. 12mo, Cloth, per vol. 1 25	
Popular Edition. Illustrated..................12mo, Cloth, per vol.	75
Adam Bede.—Daniel Deronda, 2 vols.—Felix Holt, the Radical.—	
Middlemarch, 2 vols.—Romola.—Scenes of Clerical Life, *and*	
Silas Marner.—The Mill on the Floss.	
Amos Barton...32mo, Paper	20
Brother Jacob.—The Lifted Veil...........................32mo, Paper	20
Daniel Deronda...8vo, Paper	50
Felix Holt, the Radical ....8vo, Paper	50
Janet's Repentance ....32mo, Paper	20
Middlemarch ....8vo, Paper	75
Mr. Gilfil's Love Story ....32mo, Paper	20
Romola. Illustrated...8vo, Paper	50
Silas Marner ....12mo, Paper	20
Scenes of Clerical Life ....8vo, Paper	50
The Mill on the Floss.......................................8vo, Paper	50
GASKELL'S (Mrs.) A Dark Night's Work ....8vo, Paper	25
Cousin Phillis...8vo, Paper	20
Cranford..16mo, Cloth 1 25	
Mary Barton....................8vo, Paper, 40 cents ; 4to, Paper	20
Moorland Cottage ....18mo, Cloth	75
My Lady Ludlow...8vo, Paper	20
North and South ....8vo, Paper	40
Right at Last, &c..12mo, Cloth 1 50	
Sylvia's Lovers...8vo, Paper	40
, Wives and Daughters. Illustrated ....8vo, Paper	60
HARRISON'S (Mrs.) Helen Troy...............................16mo, Cloth 1 00	
Golden Rod...32mo, Paper	25
HAY'S (M. C.) A Dark Inheritance...........................32mo, Paper	15
A Shadow on the Threshold.................................32mo, Paper	20

PRICE

LEVER'S (Charles) The Martins of Cro' Martin ....8vo, Paper $ 60
    Tony Butler. ....8vo, Paper 60
McCARTHY'S (Justin) Comet of a Season......................4to, Paper 20
    Donna Quixote...4to, Paper 15
    Maid of Athens ....4to, Paper 20
    My Enemy's Daughter. Illustrated......................8vo, Paper 50
    The Commander's Statue....................................32mo, Paper 15
    The Waterdale Neighbors....................................8vo, Paper 35
MACDONALD'S (George) Alec Forbes.........................8vo, Paper 50
    Annals of a Quiet Neighborhood...........................12mo, Cloth 1 25
    Donal Grant...4to, Paper 20
    Guild Court..8vo, Paper 40
    Warlock o' Glenwarlock.....................................4to, Paper 20
    Weighed and Wanting.......................................4to, Paper 20
MULOCK'S (Miss) A Brave Lady. Ill'd. 12mo, Cl., 90 cents.; 8vo, Paper 60
    A French Country Family. Translated. Illustrated....12mo, Cloth 1 50
    Agatha's Husband. Ill'd.......12mo, Cloth, 90 cents; 8vo, Paper 35
    A Hero, &c... 12mo, Cloth 90
    A Life for a Life.................12mo, Cloth, 90 cents; 8vo, Paper 40
    A Noble Life...12mo, Cloth 90
    Avillion, and Other Tales.....................................8vo, Paper 60
    Christian's Mistake...12mo, Cloth 90
    Hannah. Illustrated............12mo, Cloth, 90 cents; 8vo, Paper 35
    Head of the Family. Ill'd.....12mo, Cloth, 90 cents; 8vo, Paper 50
    His Little Mother ....12mo, Cloth, 90 cents; 4to, Paper 10
    John Halifax, Gentleman. Illustrated...................8vo, Paper 50
                                      12mo, Cloth, 90 cents; 4to, Paper 15
    Mistress and Maid...............12mo, Cloth, 90 cents; 8vo, Paper 30
    Motherless. Translated. Illustrated...............12mo, Cloth 1 50
    My Mother and I. Illustrated..12mo, Cloth, 90 cents; 8vo, Paper 40
    Nothing New..8vo, Paper 30
    Ogilvies. Illustrated...........12mo, Cloth, 90 cents; 8vo, Paper 35
    Olive. Illustrated...............12mo, Cloth, 90 cents; 8vo, Paper 35
    The Laurel Bush. Ill'd.........12mo, Cloth, 90 cents; 8vo, Paper 25
    The Woman's Kingdom. Ill'd. 12mo, Cloth, 90 cents; 8vo, Paper 60
    Two Marriages..12mo, Cloth 90
    Unkind Word, and Other Stories. ....12mo, Cloth 90
    Young Mrs. Jardine.................12mo, Cloth, $1 25; 4to, Paper 10
MURRAY'S (D. C.) A Life's Atonement.........................4to, Paper 20
    A Model Father...4to, Paper 10
    By the Gate of the Sea...........4to, Paper, 15 cents; 12mo, Paper 15
    Hearts..4to, Paper 20
    The Way of the World..4to, Paper 20
    Val Strange ....4to, Paper 20
NORRIS'S (W. E.) Heaps of Money . ...8vo, Paper 15
    Mademoiselle de Mersac ....4to, Paper 20
    No New Thing..4to, Paper 25
    Thirlby Hall. Illustrated ....4to, Paper 25
OLIPHANT'S (Mrs.) Agnes......................................8vo, Paper 50
    A Son of the Soil..8vo, Paper 50
    Athelings ....8vo, Paper 50